CAST THE FIRST STONE

Other titles in the Allison & Busby American Crime series

Five Little Rich Girls by Lawrence Block
The Topless Tulip Caper by Lawrence Block
Pork City by Howard Brown
Finders Weepers by Max Byrd
California Thriller by Max Byrd
Fly Away, Jill by Max Byrd
Juice by Robert Campbell
Always A Bodv to Trade by K.C. Constantine
The Man Whc Liked To Look At Himself by K.C. Constantine
Saratoga Headhunter by Stephen Dobyns
Saratoga Swimmer by Stephen Dobyns
The Autumn Dead by Ed Gorman
The End of A Primitive by Chester Himes
All Shot Up by Chester Himes
The Heat's On by Chester Himes
Run Man Run by Chester Himes
Blind Man With A Pistol by Chester Himes
The Crazy Kill by Chester Himes
Cotton Comes To Harlem by Chester Himes
A Rage In Harlem by Chester Himes
The Real Cool Killers by Chester Himes
The Big Gold Dream by Chester Himes
Florentine Finish by Cornelius Hirschberg
Red Handed by Jon Lewis
Black Money by Ross Macdonald
The Blue Hammer by Ross Macdonald
The Moving Target by Ross Macdonald
The Chill by Ross Macdonald
The Far Side of the Dollar by Ross Macdonald
The Barbarous Coast by Ross Macdonald
Meet Me At The Morgue by Ross Macdonald
The Drowning Pool by Ross Macdonald
Murder by Gaslight by Raymond Paul
The Black Ice Score by Richard Stark
The Jugger by Richard Stark
The Man with the Getaway Face by Richard Stark
Point Blank by Richard Stark
The Green Eagle Score by Richard Stark
The Mourner by Richard Stark
The Outfit by Richard Stark
The Handle by Richard Stark
The Deadly Edge by Richard Stark
The Sacred Monster by Donald Westlake
Trust Me On This by Donald Westlake

CAST THE FIRST STONE

Chester Himes

An Allison & Busby Book
Published in 1990 by
W. H. Allen & Co. Plc
Unit 26, Grand Union Centre,
338 Ladbroke Grove,
London W10 5AH

Originally published in the United States of America by
The New American Library, Inc., in 1972

Printed and bound in Great Britain by
Cox & Wyman Ltd, Reading, Berkshire

ISBN 0 74900 071 6

HE THAT IS WITHOUT SIN AMONG YOU,
LET HIM FIRST CAST A STONE AT HER.

St. John, 8:7

1

IT WAS my first night in the dormitory. It was strange. Everything was strange. After having been choked up for the past ten days I was excited watching them play poker.

During my classification period I had celled up on 5-11 with the other newcomers. Each day after breakfast we had been taken out in small groups for our physical examination by the convict doctors, and interviews by the convict clerks of the deputy warden, chaplain, and transfer officer. We had spent one entire day in the Bertillon office being weighed, measured, fingerprinted and photographed by the convict experts. Many of the convicts who worked in the Bertillon office had been policemen outside and they still had the manner of policemen.

After ten days all information relative to my past and future, my body and soul, had been carefully recorded and filed. It had been done grimly and without sympathy. The convicts who had to do with my classification had been as impersonal as the officials. No one seemed sorry for me. If anything, they seemed happy I'd been caught.

I had been choked up and scared, and had kept thinking of my sentence and my mother and the outside world until I was knocked out with hard dry tears.

We were on the top range of the 10&11 cell block. It was a very old cell block and the cells were small and grimy and very cold. There were two of us in my cell and I had the top bunk. The cold got into my bones and my back ached like chilblains. But I was scared to complain, scared to ask the guard to take me to the hospital. I had slept in all of my clothes except my shoes and with the two thin dusty blankets pulled tightly about me, and I was still cold. One night I had to climb down in the cold to use my bucket. I could hear my teeth chattering like castanets.

The days were slate-colored and once it snowed and left slush. At mealtime there were many lines of lock-stepping convicts crossing the gray prison yard. Coming back from the grim examinations across the dull gray, slushy prison yard to the small, dank, intensely cold cell, I was conscious of my feet being cold, my nose running and my back aching. I was never conscious of much else about those first ten days except that I was scared and very miserable.

I was glad to get out of that cell. Twelve of us had been transferred into the coal-company dormitory directly after supper. As we crossed the barren yard the convict runner, who carried our transfer slips, said the coal company had been made up of Negroes until the previous month. It had been converted into a punishment company for the white convicts, he said. He was a short husky convict, about forty-five, with the sang-froid of a lifer. He might have been trying to scare us. But after ten days on 5-11 I didn't care. I was glad to get there in the light and warmth and sound of human voices.

There were close to two hundred convicts in the coal company. Every one of them looked big and tough in their rat-gray uniforms and hickory-striped shirts. The coal company was located on the bottom floor of a big low flat-topped building that had once been a warehouse. The building had originally been one-storied, but a concrete floor had been laid halfway to the ceiling, converting it into two dormitories. The ceiling was very low. The dining-room company bunked in the dormitory above.

At the front, opening onto the road which came over from the west stockade, were two sliding doors of rusty corrugated steel. Except for an area at the left-front corner, where the zinc-lined washtroughs and open latrine were located, rows of double-decked bunks, spaced three feet apart, extended from wall to wall. There was an office in the corner next to the latrine for the day guards, and a raised guardstand in the middle of the wide center aisle for the night guards. Long wooden tables with attached benches extended down the center aisle, fore and aft of the guard-stand. And overhead were the eternal droplights.

The convicts sat at the tables, in the hard bright light, playing various kinds of games. There wasn't a vacant seat. I went over to the washtrough to wash my hands. But after supper the water was cut off for the night. A convict told me it was against the rules to turn it on.

I went back to the center aisle and watched the games. A blanket had been spread over a section of a table and convicts were playing poker. The cards were new. Old cards stamped with various designs and cut into various patterns were used as chips. One convict was dealing and three others kept an eye on things and sold chips. There were nickel, dime, and quarter chips.

I was all excited and glad to be out of the cells, but I couldn't get used to being in the dormitory right off. It was as if I was in a trance. It was so funny to see the convicts walking about and mingling with each other and gambling, just like people outside. I had never thought prison would be like that. It was warm in the dormitory at night and my back had almost stopped aching. It felt strange to be warm.

In the cells I had been so scared I couldn't think. I was still scared, but now it had thinned out so that it didn't jerk me around and make me wooden, and I couldn't feel it all the time. But I knew it was still there.

"You fish?"

I spun around. A little redheaded guy with freckles was grinning at me. He wore a tight-fitting nylon undershirt, showing his arms and shoulders, and his pants hung low about his hips. His body was smooth and round-muscled. He was the first convict who had spoken to me since I'd been in the dormitory. Everyone had been watching me, but no one had said anything.

"You talking to me, bud?" I asked. I'd picked up the word the year I hung round Bunch Boy's gambling joint; Bunch called everybody "bud."

"Come on, let's walk," he said, jerking his head.

I turned back and looked at the game, without replying. Then I nodded and swung in beside him. There were a lot of fellows walking in the aisle around the tables.

"What you in for?" he asked. He was trying to make friends and I felt superior.

"Robbery."

"Ten to twenty-five?"

"No, twenty. Twenty to twenty-five."

He didn't seem impressed. "That's what I'm in for, too. I stuck up a jewelry store. Who'd you stick up?"

"Just some people."

We made one round and begun another. I was beginning to feel conspicuous. When I was looking at him it was all right, but when I looked away I noticed everybody was watching us.

"Ain't your name Jake?" he asked.

"No, my name's Jim Monroe."

"My name's Henry Hill but they call me Jeep." He grinned. "I drove the jeep for Patton in North Africa."

"Yeah." I didn't believe him.

"Where were you at?"

"At where?"

"In the war."

"I wasn't in the war," I said.

"I've seen you someplace." He snapped his fingers. "Stateline! That's where I saw you. You're out of Stateline, ain't you?"

"No, I'm out of Lake City. Have you ever been to Lake City?"

"No, but it sure seems as if I've seen you somewhere before."

I didn't say anything, and when he didn't say anything for a moment I began to see the things that I had been looking at. There were the bunks, with the dirty duffel bags chunked into fat unshapeliness with the convicts' personal belongings, hanging from the frames; and all kinds of pictures and photographs, framed with inlaid wood and carved wood and cardboard wrapped with different colored strings, stuck about in prominent view. And then I began to see the other convicts that I had not seen before. Some were sitting on their bunks, reading and talking; some were walking around like us; some were playing musical instruments; making rings and cigarette holders and stuff, with their workboxes on the bunks beside them; others were coming in and out from between the bunks with the sliding, sidewise motion of crabs.

And then I began to hear the noises—shoe heels clumping, yells, curses, singing, musical instruments clanking. It all began to seem strange and very far away again.

"Want a cigarette?" Jeep asked.

I jumped. "Huh?"

"Want a cigarette? You smoke, don't you?"

"Sure, thanks. I had a carton but the guys chiseled me out of 'em."

He had a bag of Bull Durham in his hand but he put it back into his pocket. "Come on down to the bunk and I'll get you a ready-made."

"Okay."

His bunk was down in the far corner. It was dark down

there and most of the bunks were curtained. He sat down and I rested my elbows on the bunk frames and stood over him. There was a curtain halfway across the side of his bunk toward the aisle. He drew it closed.

"Sit down," he said, patting the bunk beside him.

"No, I'm going back out and watch the poker game." I was beginning to feel self-conscious.

He pulled a box from underneath his bunk and got a pack of cigarettes. He passed me the pack and I took one and handed it back.

"Keep them," he said, waving.

"No, this will do."

"Aw, go ahead. Take two or three for tonight, anyway."

I took a couple. I didn't want to be obligated. "These will do."

He took the pack reluctantly and held a light for me. When he thumbed the match away he patted the bunk again. "Sit down, you haven't got anywhere to go. Where you got to go? Got to catch a plane or something? Sit down and let's talk."

"No, I got to get a drink of water," I said, turning away. "Thanks for the smokes."

Somebody picked a clear melody on a mandolin. I stopped. A voice crooned: "Carry-ing a torch for you. . . ."

I turned toward the voice. A lad with a babyish face was sitting across on another bunk with the mandolin in his lap. He looked up at me and winked. "Like that one?"

"Yeah, sure," I said embarrassedly and hurried away.

"Come on, come on, cut it, Mike," I heard Jeep saying as I walked away. "I knew him in Stateline. We went to school together."

What the hell? I thought.

A guy was waiting for me when I came out from between the bunks. The first thing I noticed about him was that he was angry. "What was he trying to do?" he asked.

I started to keep on going, then I looked around and didn't see anybody else. I turned back. "Huh? You talking to me?"

"What was he trying to do?" he repeated. "Was he trying to start any funny stuff?"

I started to ask him what the hell business it was of his. Then I started to walk away. Then I remembered I was in prison, and thought I'd broken a rule or something. "No, he just gave me a cigarette," I said. "Aren't we allowed to go to the bunks?"

"Yes, that's all right. I just thought he tried some funny

stuff. These damn punks are after every new kid that comes in here. I just thought I ought to tell you before they get you in trouble."

I felt myself getting red. "Yeah?"

"You don't know him, do you?"

I shook my head, thinking, I don't know you either, as far as that goes. But I didn't say so, I was afraid.

"You don't like him, do you?" he persisted.

"Hell, naw," I said quickly. Then I was afraid maybe I'd said the wrong thing so I hurriedly added, "But I haven't got anything against him." On second thought I asked, "What's the matter with him?"

"He's a fink, Jim," the guy said. "He was the one who ratted on those ten men who were digging out of the woolen mill."

"Yeah?"

"He's a damn degenerate, too. Half of these guys in here are degenerates. Filthy sons of bitches. I don't like that stuff and I don't care who knows it."

I looked at him. He was a tall clean-looking man about twenty-seven, with brown hair parted on the side and a nice-looking face. His pants were pressed and his shoes were shined, and his shirt starched and ironed and bleached almost white, and he wore a tie and a slipover sweater.

"I don't either," I said.

"I knew you wouldn't go for that stuff, Jim. I read about you in the newspapers. You're a college boy. I knew you wouldn't go for that stuff."

"That's strictly for the apes," I said, laughing self-consciously.

He looked so funny I thought, what the hell's the matter with him, and then he laughed too. I started to walk away. He fell in beside me.

"Jesus Christ, man, what did they give you so much time for? Did you shoot somebody?"

"Naw, bud, I didn't shoot a soul." I tried to sound tough. "Wish I had now."

"Hell, they wouldn't have given you no more time for it."

"Hell, naw, not as much. They gave me what they call exemplary justice. How about that, exemplary justice? Can you beat it."

"That's what they do, give you the book. That's supposed to scare the other guys. Ain't that some crap? They wouldn't have given you no more time if you had killed somebody."

"Hell, naw. When they gave me twenty years I thought an atom bomb had hit me." And I wasn't telling any lie, either.

"Boy, that's rotten. That's what's wrong with these people. They get scared and throw the book at every guy that comes along."

The con sitting directly in front of me had raised into three sevens with a pair of aces and he slammed down his hand and turned around and yelled, "Get the hell out from back of me with that stale crap!"

I looked at the guy I was talking to but he didn't say anything, so I said, "Who you talking to?"

"I'm talking to you, gunsel."

"Screw you!" I said.

He started to get up and I got set to hit him when he pulled his leg over the bench, but the dealer put his hand on his shoulder and stopped him. He stopped easy enough.

"Aw, let that kid alone. He's a new kid."

"He's a lippy son of a bitch!"

"You're a son of a bitch yourself!" I said.

"Aw, beat it, gunsel! Shove off! Go get ready for Freddy."

"Who's Freddy?" a con across the table asked.

"I'm Freddy," the first guy said. "Go get ready for me, gunsel."

They all laughed.

"He's liable to already be ready, Freddy," another con said. "I seen him talking to that redheaded punk."

"Boy, that Jeep can turn 'em out."

"How do you know, Mac?" That got another laugh.

"The paper said he was only nineteen."

"And a college boy."

"All he needs is a good turning out."

"Not if he's a college boy, Mac. Them college boys is frantic."

"Aw, let him alone," the dealer said.

"Screw you!" I shouted wildly. "Screw all you dirty sons of bitches!" My face was hot enough to burn and I wanted to fight. I wanted to fight everybody.

But they just grinned. They were just trying to get my goat.

"He's a spunky young bastard," one of them said.

"Yeah, boy, spunk is what gets you kilt."

The guy who had been talking to me took me by the arm and pulled me down the aisle. "Some of these guys are hard losers," he said. "They're superstitious about anyone standing behind them." He grinned to show he wasn't superstitious.

"None of them can gamble," I said.

He looked at me. "You gamble?"

"I can beat all those chumps. None of them can gamble."

"Some of 'em are supposed to be pretty good."

"What the hell did he get puffed up for? I've stood behind guys who were better gamblers on their worst days than he'll ever be; guys who won and lost more money in a single sitting than he ever had."

"They broke me last night and I'm a pretty good gambler myself," he said.

"They must have been lucky, because none of them can gamble."

He didn't want to argue. "My name's Malden Streator," he said. "They call me Mal."

We turned by the door and came on back by the wash-trough and the guard-stand where the guard sat chewing tobacco and reading a magazine; then turned again down at the lower end and came up the other side where the bunks were closer to the aisle. When we passed the game again I looked that con who'd yelled at me dead in the eye. He looked back until I had gone so far I couldn't look at him without turning my head and I didn't want to do that.

"We look enough alike to be cousins," Mal said.

"What are you in for?" I asked, just to say something.

"First degree."

"Who'd you kill, your wife?"

"No, a state trooper. He came across the line to arrest me."

"They can't do that," I said.

"I was in Centralia," he said. "I'd just got in from Chicago. I was running snow from the coast to Detroit and there was a reader out on me. They'd been chasing me and I'd got across the line. I was in the kitchen, eating. They bust down the door and bust in."

"And you let 'em have it?"

"Yeah, yeah, he bust in and I bust his heartstring loose. I bust his heart wide open. I bust that other son of a bitch too, but he lived." His face was flushed and his eyes sparked.

I was impressed. "It's a wonder they didn't give you the chair."

"They did. I was in death row eighteen months and three days and two hours and forty-seven minutes."

"In death row?" I was shocked. "How'd you get out?"

We turned by the front door and came on back out the other side of the aisle. Jeep came out from between the bunks and said, "Want another smoke, Jim?"

"No, I got some left. I still got those two. Thanks, anyway."

Mal waited for me but he wouldn't look at Jeep. Jeep glanced at Mal and said to me, "Come on down to my bunk, Jim. I got something to show you. You know that fellow who was playing on the mandolin when you passed?" He kept looking at Mal. "He's going to play and I'm gonna sing. We're practicing for Sunday service week after next. You know how to sing?"

Mal wheeled around and said harshly, "Hell, naw, he don't know how to sing. He's a man. He don't want to sing with you, anyway."

"I wasn't talking to you," Jeep said.

"Come on, Jim," Mal said.

"He's coming with me," Jeep said, taking hold of my arm.

"Turn loose of me, goddammit!" I snarled, jerking my arm free.

Mal's face had turned brick colored. "Go on, go on, beat it, fink," he said to Jeep. "You dirty punk! Scram! Jim's walking with me."

"You ain't nothing but a goddamn punk yourself," Jeep said. "You're one of those swap-up bitches. One of those secret whores. You go out in the coal shed so can't nobody see you."

Mal turned a sickly white. He started after Jeep. Jeep backed up and put his hand in his pocket. Mal grabbed me by the arm and pulled me down the aisle.

"They're after him already," I heard a voice behind me saying. I felt embarrassed as hell.

"Fighting to start off with," another said. Somebody laughed. My face started to burn.

Mal looked at me to see how I'd taken what Jeep had said. "I ought to go back and hit him in the mouth," he said, getting very fierce.

"You oughta hit 'em when you had 'im," I said. I was getting pissed-off, fed up with the whole thing. It had taken me down again.

He looked at me. "You don't believe that stuff, do you?"

"No, why should I? I don't believe anything."

"I just hate that stuff so I don't even want anybody to believe anything like that about me, even when I know it isn't true."

"I don't blame you," I said.

"Don't get any more cigarettes from him," he said. "If I had some you could smoke mine. But I got broke yesterday. I only got some Bull Durham. I'll show you how to roll your own and you can smoke that until I get some tailor-mades. Everybody in here smokes it, anyway."

We turned at the door and came back down the other side.

"I know how to roll them," I said.

"I'll get you a bag."

"That's all right. I'll have some money by tomorrow. I should have had it already. I told my old man to send me a hundred dollars right away."

He was impressed.

"You can't spend any of it until next week," he said. "I'll get you that bag of Bull Durham and when it's gone I'll get you another one." He stopped and borrowed a bag of weed from one of the gamekeepers. "What did you want so much money for?" he asked, when he'd caught up with me again.

"I want to get a radio but I don't see anybody in here with one. I thought we were allowed to have them."

"We are. They took ours when they moved us down here in this hole. You know, this is a regular nigger's job. Niggers work down here most of the time. We were in school. They shipped us down here for punishment and took our radios."

"Yeah?"

"I had one but when I saw they weren't going to let us have them in here I sold mine."

We had just passed the latrines again and an elderly, serious-looking stiff-backed fellow stepped out from between two bunks and called, "Malden! Malden! Step here a minute."

Mal turned to me. "I'll be back in a minute, Jim. I got to talk to the General. I'll be back in just a minute."

I went over and started watching the game again. I sure wished I had some money. There was a fat fellow across the table, with most of the chips, and he was through playing. He was just sitting there. He'd won his load. He was sitting there tossing in a chip or two on the first card, or maybe looking at the third if the ante wasn't too high. Just trying to catch a big pair and ring the dealer in. Didn't anybody else have any chips worth gambling for. They were trying to ring him in a pot so they could draw out on him. But he was just laying dead.

It was late, close to bedtime. Most of the guys had stopped whatever they were doing and were getting ready for bed. Only a couple of cons were still walking the aisle. The guard had got up and was walking around a little. The seat of his blue serge uniform pants was shiny as glass.

The gamekeeper called it a day and took up his blanket. When the fat guy got ready to cash out a crowd collected. He turned in his chips and said, "I'll come back and get my stuff." All the beggars looked disappointed. He had a few chips left over, thirty or forty cents' worth, and three guys were begging him for them.

While I stood there the lights flashed. The guard rapped his stick on the table top. From all over the prison came the sound of rapping sticks. It was bedtime. And suddenly it was back on top of me—prison and my twenty years. I turned and went slowly to my bunk. I felt numbed.

I had a top bunk next to the outside wall, directly beneath one of the high, barred windows. Hanging at the head was my wooden identification plate with my name and number. I had hung my aluminum coffee pot by a piece of wire to the foot of the bunk frame, and had stuffed my soap, prison-made face towel and tin comb down into it. I had put my Sunday shirt of blue denim and my white string tie underneath the mattress. That, with what I had on, was everything I owned.

Many convicts had wooden boxes. Some were made like trunks and foot lockers with big padlocks. They kept these underneath their bunks at night and on top of their bunks during the day so the floors could be swept and mopped. They were allowed to have these boxes to hold their personal things—tobacco, toilet articles, and such store-bought clothing as we were allowed to have: shoes, underwear, socks and handkerchiefs. But always they were subject to confiscation. The prison supplied a duffel bag but I didn't even have one of those.

I took off my coat, shirt, pants, cap and shoes. I kept on my long cotton drawers to sleep in. My prison number was stenciled in the neckband. I put the rest of my clothes on the foot of my bunk and crawled beneath the ironed sheet and two dull, gray, dusty-smelling blankets.

Most of the convicts slept in their underwear. We changed them once a week when we took a bath. We didn't once take them off the rest of the time, winter or summer. A few of the convicts slept in pajamas, and others, like Jeep, slept in their shirts and shorts.

A moment later the guard began to take count. He started at one corner of the dormitory and went up and down the long aisles, counting the empty bunks. He was an old man, pot-bellied and slump-shouldered, but now he walked rapidly and the convicts scrambled to their bunks to be counted. When the guard finished he rapped his stick on the guardstand. That meant the count was right. If the count had not been right he would have counted again. And then if it had still been wrong, he'd have called in the night captain.

The convicts began moving about again; some to the latrine, others from bunk to bunk borrowing magazines, tobacco, matches. The guard turned off the lights over the bunks. Every third light down the center aisle remained on all night. But there was enough light left to see what went on in any part of the dormitory. There was never complete darkness in any part of the prison. The convicts who bunked near the night lights could read as long as they wished. Several convicts sat on their bunks, taking a last puff on their cigarettes. Smoking in bed was prohibited.

For a time the guard walked up and down the center aisle. When the convicts had become settled for the night he returned to his padded chair on the guard-stand and began reading his magazine again.

I turned over and looked at the ceiling. It was about three feet above my eyes. I felt as if I was someone else. It couldn't be me, Jim Monroe, lying there on an upper bunk in a prison dormitory. It just wasn't so.

"Jim."

I spun over.

Mal was standing by my bunk. "I brought you some matches," he said.

I took them. "Thanks." They felt like splinters and I tried to see them in the dim light.

"They're split," he said.

"Oh."

"I couldn't get back. That guy got to singing the blues and I couldn't get away."

"That was all right."

"Good night."

"Good night."

After Mal left it seemed that something had changed. I looked around and listened. Then I realized it was the silence; it had become silent. Now the whispering started again. A high, falsetto voice piped, "Good night." From another part of the dormitory a similar voice replied, "Good night." Somebody snickered. I slid 'way down beneath the covers and ignored them.

A half-hour later, when I thought everybody had gone to sleep, I climbed down from my bunk and went over to the latrine. Those of us who had upper bunks had wooden stools to step on. I felt very conspicuous going across the floor under the center aisle lights in my large floppy drawers. I hoped everybody was asleep. But as soon as I stepped into the light a great hissing and whistling began. The guard rapped his stick for silence. I gritted my teeth. To hell with 'em! I told myself.

While I was standing at the urinal Jeep came out and joined me. He just stood there. "What'd that guy say about me?" he asked.

"He didn't say any more about you than you said about him," I grunted.

"What you want to do is wait and find out for yourself," he said. He was wearing nylon shorts, which showed his round hairless legs. Practically everybody I'd seen slept in their long drawers. His bare flesh looked obscene.

I felt embarrassed standing so close to him. "Look, let me alone," I said. I went back and climbed into my bunk. I tried to go to sleep but I couldn't. All that stuff that happened in Chicago kept coming back. I could see myself asking that sonofabitching pawnbroker for five hundred dollars for the ring, and him saying just a minute and slipping out in the back room. I'd known he was calling the police. Even if he did have that one ring I had a lot of other stuff. But I couldn't run. I never could run.

I could feel the cops hitting me in the mouth, hanging me by my handcuffed feet upside down over a door, beating my ribs with their gun butts. I could feel the blood running down my legs from where the handcuffs pinched them on the anklebone.

I had stood it as long as I could, I thought, looking at the ceiling. I might have stood it longer if I'd lost consciousness. But there had been too much pain and not enough hurt to lose consciousness. I had confessed.

I had never confessed anything in my life before. Since I was old enough to remember, the beatings I'd gotten from mother and father had taught me one lesson: *Never confess.* No matter what you ever did, always say you didn't do it. Let 'em prove it. But still deny it. That had been the one rigid rule in my code of existence. *Never confess.* Then there would always be a doubt, if not a chance.

But I had confessed. Now it was too new to stand thinking about. I felt like vomiting whenever I thought about it. I felt ruptured and nutted.

I tried to think of my mother. But I'd almost gotten to the place where I couldn't think of her. I tried to think of the boys out at the club. But I'd almost gotten past them, too.

It was thinking of Chicago that I couldn't get past. It came and went and when it went I tried to get some sleep. But it never went far enough so I could get much sleep. I'd sleep a little and then I'd wake up thinking about it. It seemed as if no sooner than I'd gotten to sleep I'd see myself lying huddled on the concrete floor in the Loop detective bureau, confessing.

I turned my head and looked out the window that was just a little above the level of my eyes. I saw the moon in a deep blue sky and a guard-turret with spotlights down the walls. I saw the guard silhouetted against the sky, a rifle cradled in his arm, the intermittent glow of the cigarette in his mouth. I saw the long black sweep of the walls beneath the deep blue distance. When you looked at the walls your vision stopped. Everything stopped at the walls. The walls were about fifty feet from the dormitory building. Just fifty feet away was freedom, I thought. Fifty feet—and twenty years.

2

WHEN THE LIGHTS came on next morning I put on my shoes and socks sitting cross-legged on my bunk, then lay down and stuck my legs in the air and pulled on my pants. I jumped down and got my towel and soap out of the coffee bucket and went over to the trough to wash.

It was very cold in the dormitory in the morning. The

air was cold, the iron bunk frames were cold, the concrete floor was cold, anything you touched was cold. The water that spilled in thin streams from a half-inch sprinkling pipe was icy cold. It was so cold that even the strong lye soap wouldn't lather. I caught some water in my cupped hands and dashed it in my face. Then I wiped at my face with the towel. The homespun cloth felt greasy. Until it had been washed several times it wouldn't absorb any water. I said to hell with it, it was my dirt. I went back to my bunk and put on my hickory-striped shirt, gray vest, gray coat and gray cap. None of the garments fitted. They weren't made to fit. They weren't made up as suits. Over in the commissary, where I'd been outfitted, there were stacks of coats, vests and pants of different sizes, some new and some used. The commissary clerks gave out the used clothes first. They were the uniforms left by the convicts who'd gone out. All of my things were used except my Sunday shirt. My coat was patched at both elbows. It was much too small. My vest was too big and my pants were too short. I had used-shoes also; the heels were run-over and the soles were thin. But I was dressed as well as anybody, better than most.

The breakfast bell rang. The guard knocked his stick. We lined up down the wide center aisle in two lines, two-by-two in each line. The tall men stood at the front, graduating down to the short men at the rear. Two medium-sized men marched at the very front of each line to pace us. I was stationed by the guard, according to height, somewhere about the middle of the line. The guard knocked his stick again and we marched out of the dormitory, down a narrow alleyway between the dining room and a three-storied red-brick building, and turned into a side entrance.

The dining room was a flat, one-storied building with two wings separated by the kitchen. Our company was the first to enter. We marched down the wide center aisle and filed in between the narrow slate-topped counters and stood with our arms folded. Each of us stood behind a stool. There were ten to a counter. We filled twenty-and-a-fraction counters. When everyone had found a place we stood for a moment until the guard was satisfied and knocked his stick. We took off our caps, put them underneath the stools, and sat down. We looked at our breakfast. It was the same breakfast I'd had since arriving.

Aluminum bowls were half-filled with soupy oatmeal. Milk, made by adding water to powdered milk, had been poured over it. But it had been standing for so long that the body of the milk had settled to the bottom in a white scum which covered the oatmeal. The water had come to the top. To one side of the cereal were aluminum plates, holding one link of fried sausage which had cold-welded to the aluminum by congealed grease. It was very cold in the dining room. The food was stone cold. Empty cups were lined against the front ledges of the counters. The knives and forks and spoons were made of some metal that had turned black.

For a moment or so the convicts in our company were silent. We were permitted to talk after we were seated, but no one said anything. I discovered that it was like that every morning when the men sat down to breakfast. Across the aisle another company was coming in, filling the counters. Then the companies began entering from all three doors. Soon the dining room was filled.

The men began to eat. I stirred the oatmeal and the water whitened again. I ate it rapidly. I had noticed before that everyone ate very rapidly. In that way you did not taste the food so much. The oatmeal was slightly sweet.

"Slop," a dull voice said.

The convict waiters stood by the service tables alongside the walls. A convict at my counter called to the waiter: "Get me some bread down here, Mac."

The waiter brought a pan of whole-wheat bread.

"I don't want no goddamn black bread," the convict said. He called to the guard, "Hey, Cap, what about some white bread? I work like a nigger out in that stinking coal pile all day and I want some white bread. It's bad enough to have to eat the rest of this goddamned crap."

"Watch your language," the guard called back.

"Screw my language," the convict muttered.

The guard came up to the end of the counter. "What did you say?"

"I said I want some white bread. I can't eat black bread. I got stomach trouble."

The guard snickered. "Heh-heh, you oughta thought about your stomach 'fore you come in here." He sounded as if he was senile, but I didn't pay him much attention at the time.

"Aw, come on, Cap," the convict wheedled. "You know I can't eat this black bread. I got the piles so bad now I can't hardly lift a wheelbarrow."

"Oh, you can roll a wheelbarrow all right," the guard said. He turned to the waiter, "Give 'em some white bread, first thing you know they'll be saying they don't get enough to eat."

"Ain't got none," the waiter grumbled.

"Go get some," the guard snapped. "My boys are working boys. They work hard in the coal piles. You go get 'em some white bread—and be quick about it."

The waiter went off, muttering to himself.

"Attaboy, Cap," one of the convicts said.

"Tell 'im 'bout it, Cap."

"I'm going to look out for my boys," the guard said.

The waiter returned with the mess sergeant.

"Who sent this boy after white bread?" the mess sergeant asked.

"I did," the guard said. "My boys want white bread. They're working boys, they need white bread."

"You run your goddamned coal company," the mess sergeant said, "and let me run this goddamned dining room."

Our guard walked up to the front of the dining room and looked out of the door. The mess sergeant went back to the kitchen. Finally a convict who hadn't touched his breakfast said, "Who wants to swap some meat for some oatmeal?"

No one paid him any attention.

Twenty minutes after we'd entered, the mess sergeant rang the bell. The companies that had entered last had only been in there about five minutes. But at the ringing of the bell everyone reached for his cap. They held their caps in their right hands, with their arms folded across their chests. Our guard knocked his stick. We stood up and put on our caps and marched out. Our line formed in the center aisle and we went out into the yard. It had begun snowing again. The ground was already covered with dirty black slush. The fresh snow was sprinkling it with white.

Most of the convicts in the company kept straight ahead to the coal piles. A spur of railroad track came up from the powerhouse which was down in back of our dormitory. Piles of soft coal stood waist-high alongside the track. The convicts took their stations. Some went down to the coal shed in the powerhouse building and got wheelbarrows. Others got shovels and lined themselves along the piles. The wheelbarrow gang formed in a long line. As they rolled by the piles, the shovel men dumped coal into their wheelbarrows—one shovelful to a wheelbarrow. When the wheelbarrow reached the end of the pile it was filled to overflowing. The men rolled the coal up on a platform and dumped it into a machine that crushed it into slack coal. Another wheelbarrow line rolled the slack coal over to the coal shed. The wheels of the wheelbarrows had cut deep muddy ruts in the ground. The ruts were filled with black slush. Some of the men tried to straddle the rut as they pushed their wheelbarrows. Others just walked in the slush.

I hadn't been assigned to a job. None of the men who had been transferred into the company had. All of us followed the porters back into the dormitory. After awhile the head guard, Captain Warren, came in to get us. He was the guard I'd noticed in the mess hall. He was a stoop-shouldered old man with gray hair the color of dirty dish-water and a flabby, weather-red face. His washed-out blue eyes peering from behind old-fashioned gold spectacles held an expression of extreme contempt. He was chewing tobacco and spittle drooled from the corners of his mouth. He didn't seem able to control the muscles of his mouth.

He called us into his office down at the front, near the door, and propped his feet on the desk. "It ain't no picnic," he said. "It ain't no picnic. You got to roll coal. They got to have coal to run the powerhouse. Got to have electricity for the electric chair. Oh, it's a tough life. You can't stop just 'cause it rains or snows. You got to roll all the time. You got to roll to keep warm. If you get too hot you get chilled and catch pneumonia. Brrr, it's cold out there this morning." He looked at us as if he thought we were the lowest form of animal life. "I'm going to put you boys to rolling coal. Heh-heh," he laughed at our expressions. "I bet you won't do it no more."

He sent us back to the head porter, B&O, to get some gloves. B&O opened a box and gave each of us a pair of cloth gloves. The gloves were made out of old uniforms. The imprint of a mammoth hand had been cut out of the cloth. Two pieces of the cloth had been sewed together. That was a glove.

I started outside with the others but Captain Warren stopped me. "Go back and report to B&O," he ordered.

"Yes, sir," I said. B&O was an emaciated, big-framed, slovenly man with a disfigured face, unkempt, grayish hair, and a blue cast in one of his watery brown eyes. They called him B&O because he'd been caught on a B&O freight. He had the most evil disposition of any man I've ever met. It was impossible for him to speak a civil word. He was so mad because Captain Warren had assigned me to a porter's job he didn't speak to me for an hour. I reported to him and he walked away. I wandered about the dormitory trying to find something to do. Captain Warren came in and asked me why I wasn't working. I told him B&O hadn't given me anything to do.

"You know what to do, you know what to do," Captain Warren said. "Didn't nobody tell you to rob those folks but you did that. You'll do this, too."

I went to look for a mop. Finally I found one in a pail of water. Another porter came up and said that was his. Then B&O hollered at me from across the dormitory.

"Get that barrel over there and go get some shavings," he ordered.

I found the barrel in a corner. I rolled it out on the floor. "Where do I get the shavings?" I asked.

"At the planing mill. Where the hell you think?"

I didn't know where the planing mill was. But I didn't ask. I picked up the barrel and started outside. Captain Warren saw me when I came around by the coal pile. "Get a wheelbarrow, get a wheelbarrow," he said. I looked around for a wheelbarrow.

"They're down in the shed," a convict volunteered. I went down to the coal shed and got a wheelbarrow and put the barrel in it and started off. I didn't know where I was going. I went around the powerhouse and came out into an expanse of open yard that looked like a ball diamond. I kept on going.

Down at the end of the wooden laundry building a guard stopped me. "Where you going, boy?"

"To the planing mill to get some shavings."

"You're new, aren't you?"

"Yes, sir."

He showed me how to get to the planing mill. I went down some slush-covered alleys between brick buildings. I could hear the steady looms of the woolen mill, and a hundred other sounds of activity I couldn't identify. Finally, after what seemed like a long distance, I came to a tin shed where convicts were cutting and planing lumber.

I went up to the guard and told him I'd come to get some shavings. He pointed to a pile. After filling the barrel I came back the other way, down to the crossroad and over by the sunken gardens next to the dining room, and back of the dining room by the long glass-enclosed greenhouse, back to the dormitory.

It was some prison. There were convicts just walking about everywhere you could see and the waiters hung out the dining-room doors and stared when I passed. They looked me over and asked if I wasn't a new man and if

I didn't want them to get me a better job so I could move into their company. I didn't answer any of them. I was fed up with it because I knew what it was all about.

When I got back with the shavings I put them in the corner and sat out at the table and played gin rummy with another porter until the company came in, about eleven o'clock, to wash up for dinner. After dinner they had an hour to smoke and rest and then went back to the coal pile until four-thirty. Then they came in and washed up again and went to supper. We had soupy beans, tea and bread for supper. By that time it was dark outside. When we returned to the dormitory we were through for the day. Until nine o'clock we could do whatever we pleased, as long as it wasn't against the rules or the guard didn't catch us. We could gamble, read, wrestle, dance, sing, write, study, talk, walk, cry or shout. We could yell as loud as we pleased. Couldn't anybody hear us, anyway, and if anybody did there wasn't anybody to give a damn. The only thing we weren't allowed to do was whistle. I never knew why we weren't allowed to whistle. But if we were caught just whistling softly we'd be sent to the hole.

Right after supper they called out mail. I got a letter from my mother and a note from my father with a hundred-dollar money order inside. The colored runner, Deacon Smith, brought the money order for me to sign. Later I learned that Deacon was the secretary of the Sunday School and assistant to the Protestant chaplain. When the chaplain was away he took charge of the Sunday services.

I wasn't allowed to keep the money but it would be put to my credit in the front office. Deacon had no sooner left than everybody in the dormitory knew I had a hundred bucks to my credit. All of a sudden I had more friends than I knew what to do with. They wanted to walk around with me or give me some Bull Durham. Mostly they wanted to tell me what I could order the next day, which was ordering day.

With all that money I'd seen outside around gambling clubs during the past year, a hundred bucks didn't seem like a lot of money to me. But those convicts in that dormitory were broke and they figured they had a sucker.

Everybody began calling me Jim. All of a sudden they knew all about me; all about my sentence, and my going to the state university and graduating, and being a doctor, one of them said, and another had it a lawyer, and one asked, "Weren't you a fighter pilot?" They had a lot of things to sell me and a lot of things to give me. All I wanted was to gamble. I could have gotten credit in any of the poker games. But I didn't know it.

When Mal came out and asked me to come back to his bunk I went because I didn't have anything else to do. He looked very neat. He had washed and cleaned up after supper, so he must have had some private water because the washtrough was cut off. As he walked ahead of me I noticed that he was taller than I. He must have been about five feet, ten-and-a-half, or eleven. His hips were as wide as his shoulders. That looks odd in a man, especially if the man isn't stout.

He was very pleasant and very friendly. He kept smiling all the time he talked as if he was pleased with something. When he smiled the hardness which his face had in repose was gone and he looked quite boyish.

I liked his bunk. There was an openness about it. Although it was over by the wall there was a light over it that gave it a certain cheerfulness. He didn't have it curtained off as Jeep had his bunk, and there was none of that gloom and secrecy and suggestiveness like the bunks down in the corner where Jeep and Mike were: I liked it because it was open. I didn't have any secrets.

Mal sat down beside me, crossing his legs and leaning his head back against the bunk frame so as to face me. I was sitting with my back to the aisle and my feet on his box, with my arms propped on the bunk.

"Do you draw disability compensation?" he asked. He was just fishing, he knew I hadn't been in the army.

"Naw, state compensation from the industrial commission," I said.

"You mean for an injury?"

"Yeah, I broke my back about three years ago—before I went to college."

"Broke your back! Damn!" he exclaimed. "How do you get about?"

"Oh, it's all healed up now. Just about, that is."

"Damn! Nobody'd ever know it."

"Nobody'd ever know you were in death row, either. Not just by looking at you."

"Naw, guess you're right. How'd you do it?"

"I was working in a steel mill in Gary. I'd just finished high school. I was riding an overhead crane and fell on a stack of plates."

"Jesus Christ! Wonder it didn't kill you."

"It damn near did. I broke my arm, my jaw, and three

vertebrae. I was in the hospital four months." I showed him the scar where the bone had come through my arm.

"Jesus Christ!" he said. "Does it ever hurt?"

"Not often. Mostly when I get cold. Of course I make out like it does to keep drawing compensation."

"How much do you get?"

"Twenty-seven bucks a week. That's for total disability. I can get it for five hundred weeks if I keep stiffing." After a pause I said, "I haven't told anybody but you. I don't know what they might do when they find out I'm in prison. They might cut it off."

"If you'd told the deputy warden you could of got an easy job," he said. "You could of got in the cripple company."

"I don't mind it here," I said. "I don't want to take any chances."

All of a sudden he leaned over and tousled my hair. "I believe you're a slicker, Jim."

I drew back. "What the hell!"

He laughed. "You wouldn't get mad if a girl did that."

I had to laugh, too. "I wonder what a girl looks like," I said.

"Hell, you've only been in here ten days," he said. "Don't tell me you've forgotten so soon."

"It already seems like a million years," I said.

He smiled at me with his eyes half closed. He had two gold teeth in front in the very same places where I had mine.

"We look enough alike to be twins," he said, "only you have dimples and your hair is a little darker than mine and your skin is smoother. Jesus, you've got pretty skin."

"Hell," I said, blushing.

"Mine was smooth, too, but this water and soap in here roughens it." He picked up my cap where I'd laid it on the bunk. "You'd better get a cap like mine. The dye comes out of these things and makes you bald."

"Yeah?"

He showed me his cap. It had a long visor and was lined with black coat-lining material and it was soft.

"What makes it keep its shape?" I asked.

"It's got horsehair inside of the lining."

"Do they let you have them?"

"No, they take 'em if they notice 'em. Some of the guards do. The others don't care."

"I better get me one. How much do they cost?"

"A dollar and fifty cents. But I'll get you one."

"I'll give you the money."

"Oh, that's all right. It won't cost me anything."

"You've got some extra pants, too, haven't you?"

"Yes. They let you have them if you're in some companies, but in some companies they take them."

"Do they give them to you?"

"Oh no, you get them for yourself. They just let you keep them if you're in a company like this, where the work's dirty. We have them made up in the tailor shop."

The runner came around with the papers. "You want to subscribe to the paper?" Mal asked.

"How do you do it?"

"Come on, I'll show you."

We went out into the aisle. "Hey, Mac! Mac!" he called. The short, owl-faced paper boy came over. He was about fifty years old and was doing life. He'd been in twenty-three years. "Jim here wants to subscribe to *The News*."

"How long?"

"Oh, I don't know. About a month. I want a Sunday paper and a morning paper, too."

He wrote the names of the papers on a cashier's slip, filled it out for $2.65, and gave it to me to sign.

I signed my name and number—James Monroe #109-130. "Do I get one now?"

"You got your receipt?" Mac asked.

"What receipt?"

"He means the cashier's receipt for the money order you signed tonight," Mal explained. He turned to Mac. "He hasn't got his receipt yet but he's got the money. He signed a money order for a hundred dollars. I'll vouch for him."

The paper boy looked at Mal. "You can ask the clerk then," Mal said.

"To hell with it!" I said.

Mac jerked out a paper and shoved it at me. I took it and we went back to Mal's bunk. We passed the poker game. It looked good and hot. That poker game sure looked good. But I wouldn't stop to watch it.

"You have to give your history to get a lousy nickel paper," I said.

"So many new men beat them."

"Oh, is that it?" When we were seated again I said, "Man I sure would like to play some stud."

Mal frowned. "I wouldn't if I were you, Jimmy. The night captain comes in sometimes and if he catches them playing he'll take them all to the hole."

"Yeah?" I didn't give a damn.

We read the paper and talked about the news. The sports were still talking about that Rose Bowl game and a little about State's basketball team. There was an editorial about the governor-elect. I discovered that the convicts were very interested in the governors. They read all the news that was printed about all governors.

Some other convicts joined us and borrowed the paper when we had finished. They stood around and joined in the conversation. They talked about the warden and the in-coming governor and the out-going governor and the parole board. Everybody was a son of a bitch. The warden was a pig. The parole board were dirty fink bastards. The governors were all crooked. Everybody who had ever been a governor was crooked. They always had their "goddamn hands stuck out."

They said I was lucky to get a porter's job and asked me if it was true about my plane being shot down over Germany. I said sure it was true. They said I looked pretty young. I said I was twenty-five. They didn't believe it. They asked me how much did I get? I said fifty thousand in cash and eighteen thousand in jewelry. They didn't believe that, either. They wanted to know how I got caught after getting clear to Chicago. I said the dicks spotted me from the readers the Lake City police had sent out. They said that was tough. I said it sure in hell was.

The magazine man came around with a steel rack of magazines slung from his shoulder, and resting against his belly. I bought every kind he had except the comic books. He had more comic books than anything else, but I didn't want any. We thumbed through the magazines and talked some more.

"Every time I see you write your number it sort of shocks me," Mal said.

"Yeah?"

"A hell of a lot of men have come in since I have. A whole city."

"What's your number?"

"99830. . . . Let's see. . . ." He got out a pencil and paper and did some computing. "Nine thousand and three hundred men have come in between you and me and I guess a hundred more have come in since you have. That's a lot of people."

"How long have you been in?"

"A little over five years."

"You're an old-timer," I joked.

"Not yet," he said. "You're not an old-timer until you've eaten out of all the plates."

"Yeah."

"I wonder how many of those nine thousand men went out," he said.

"How many?"

"Hell, I don't know. Let's don't talk about it."

He showed me how to fill out my tobacco order. He had an old form but the regular forms would be passed out the next day. We could order a dollar and seventy-five cents' worth of stuff from the commissary. The order went in on a Friday and the stuff came back Saturday week, eight days later.

"Order me a toothbrush, will you, Jimmy?"

"Sure."

"I'll pay you for it."

"Aw, hell."

I made out a list of what I would order—two toothbrushes, a tube of tooth paste, six boxes of matches and five bags of Bull Durham.

"Get two nickel books of cigarette papers with the rest," he said.

Then he told me about the "outside" order which came back on Thursday. I could order shoes, socks, underwear, and handkerchiefs. I wanted to order a sweater but he said I couldn't have that. He said for me to order some socks and underwear and I said I'd get him some and he said, okay, he'd get me a cap and some pants. I wanted to order some gloves but he said I could buy them cheaper from some of the fellows who got broke in the games.

"Jimmy, you certainly are good-looking," he said. "You are one more good-looking boy."

"Yeah?" I felt a blush coming up.

"Let's say we're cousins," he said.

"I don't care. But everybody will know we're not." I liked him.

"No they won't. They haven't got any way of telling. Let's tell them we're cousins on our mothers' side. Our mothers were sisters."

"It's okay with me."

"Cousin Jimmy. How does that sound?"

"Cousin Mal." I grinned.

He was delighted. "We're cousins. I wish you were my cousin for real. I feel like I'm your cousin for real."

"Aw, hell." But I liked him.

"Everybody has seen us together ever since you came

into the company yesterday," he said. "They'll think I knew you before. I told the General that I knew you before, anyway. I told him that you were my cousin when he called me last night."

"We're just a couple of old cousins in the big house," I said.

He was excited. You could see it in his face and eyes. His eyes were real bright blue and now they were brilliant with excitement. "We ought to cut our arms and mix our blood and then we would be real blood cousins."

"Aw, hell, we don't have to do that."

"Oh, all right."

Then he said, "Your eyes are the same color as mine."

He was good company and very pleasant. That night after the lights had been turned off he brought me a tailor-made cigarette and said, "Good night, cousin." We were buddies.

3

THE NEXT MORNING was gray like the morning before. It had stopped snowing but the ground was covered. The snow had softened and was slushy and the wheelbarrows churned it into heavy muck. Rolling those "Georgia buggies" was a killing job.

It wasn't long before there was some excitement. Old man Warren, who usually sat inside and warmed his chair, had taken the shift outside. Captain Roe, the younger guard, had a sprained ankle and had come inside.

About nine-thirty I saw Captain Warren come running into the dormitory. He went into the office and got Captain Roe and ran back outside with Roe hobbling along behind him. There was a cut over his left eye and his glasses were gone and blood was running down the left side of his face. He had his pistol out and as Roe went outside he drew his also.

All of us porters ran out to see what the excitement was about. Everybody had stopped working and was standing about in groups, talking and gesticulating. Mal saw me and came over. "Johnson knocked old Fuss-face on his can."

"Yeah? What Johnson?"

"You know, that new fellow that was over there on 5-11 with you. He was transferred over here the same day you were. He's got a cut down the side of his face. He said he was a paratrooper."

"Yeah? Yeah? He hit him?" I got excited, too.

"Knocked him on his can."

"What did old man Warren do?"

"He didn't do nothing. He had on his overalls over his uniform and he couldn't get out his pistol. He got up and started unbuttoning his overalls to get out his pistol, and Johnson hit him again. Hit him in the mouth. Hit him up beside the eye the first time and knocked off his glasses. Busted them all to hell. Even if old Fuss-face had got his pistol he couldn't have seen him to shoot at him."

"Yeah? What did he do then?"

Mal smacked his lips like it tasted good. "Johnson ran down by the dining room. I think he's gone to the deputy's office. Somebody told him to beat it over to old Jumpy Stone and he wouldn't let 'em kill him."

"That's when the old man came inside," I said. "I saw him when he came running inside. He took Roe out with him."

"I wish Roe had been here to get knocked on his can too," Mal said.

"Come on, I'll show you where it happened," I followed him down the tracks and saw where Warren had sat down in the snow.

"Knocked him right on his can, didn't he?"

Everybody was talking and laughing and excited, as if they were at a ball game and had seen one of their home team hit a home run. It was fun seeing a guard get smacked. It was something to talk about.

"Man, you oughta seen old Fuss-face scratching for his heat," one of them said, jubilantly.

"That old chump carries two guns, man, and he couldn't get either one of them."

"You oughta seen his face. Looked like a bowl of chow mein."

"Looked like the ass of a bear if you ask me."

"What will they do with Johnson?" I asked Mal.

"They'll probably get him over in the hole and sap up on him."

"Will they shoot him?"

"I don't know, but he'll probably wish they would before they get through with him. If Jumpy Stone's there he'll stop them, though."

"What the hell did it all start about?"

"It was hard rolling and the shovel men put too much on his buggy. He dumped some of it off a couple of times and then old Fuss-face saw him and ran over and told him to get a shovel and put it back on. He kept on going and old Fuss-face ran up and grabbed him and slapped him. And what did he do that for?"

I went back inside. Everybody had quit working and after awhile they all came dribbling in. But they were still excited and kept talking about it and wondering what they'd do to Johnson.

After awhile old man Warren and Roe returned. Warren had the side of his forehead bandaged and painted with iodine. He was all worked up and looking for trouble and he'd strapped his holster on the outside of his coat, where you could see the pearl butt of the pistol sticking out.

"I got another one, too. I got another one, too," he said, when he saw us looking at it.

A convict in the back of the dormitory yelled, "You had 'em out there, too."

Warren turned a splotched red. "Yes, yes, and you'll be the first one I shoot." He had a high, irritating voice and it was harsh and nasty now. "Come on, come on, everybody get outside and go to work." He wanted to abuse them. "You're all laughing, you're all laughing. You should see what I did to him. You should see him before you laugh."

The men were getting sullen. He ran out and shoved a couple of them around and slapped two he found sitting on their bunks. And then he went up by the door, and hit at their legs with the leather strap of his stick as they passed. Roe stood in the background and looked watchful. I got mad just looking.

The guards wore blue uniforms with brass buttons and regulation caps. Old man Warren was something to see, standing there with his shabby blue suit over his flabby old muscles, with gray hair sticking out from underneath his cap and his face red with iodine and a big patch over his eye, abusing the men. Young men. Strong men. Men who could break him in two. There was something filthy about it. Something that outraged the senses.

A couple of sergeants came down and stood around for a time. A big tall one, called Fletcher, and a fat one with red jowls and flat feet. They called the fat one Donald Duck because of his flat feet. When he walked he put down his feet cautiously. He never made a careless step if he could help it.

When we went in to dinner that day Sergeant Cody was in the dining room. They said that Fletcher was treacherous. They said he stood outside a locked cell once and shot a convict to death. His eyes blinked and his whole face jerked and jumped from some kind of nervous disorder. But it was Cody they were scared of. Cody was a quiet man. He hardly ever said anything and he hardly ever hurried. He never repeated an order. And whenever you saw him running, some convict was going to die, they said. He was the most feared man in prison. A big rawboned man with a clay-colored complexion and a rock-hard face, and lips so thin you could hardly see them.

We were subdued in the dining room with Cody standing by the door. He stood relaxed and unmoving. He wore a long black slicker thrown over his shoulders like a cape, and his hands were out of sight. He had his cap pulled low over his tricky eyes. Above him hung one of the signs that were all over the dining room: EAT SLOWLY. CHEW YOUR FOOD. He looked somber and leashed.

It wasn't until that afternoon when we went to the barbershop, two long gray lines of convicts marching through the gray day, underneath the sagging sky, that we learned the actual truth of what had happened to Johnson. The barbershop was upstairs over the hole. It was a long box of a room with the prison-made, straight-backed wooden chairs circling the outer walls. Down the center were the benches where we sat back-to-back, waiting our turns for the two-minute shaves and five-minute haircuts. Before we could get a haircut we had to have a signed slip from the guard. Nobody got a haircut that day.

We had marched down between the dining room and the tin shop and turned west at the front of the dining room and south by the hospital, gabled and antique, and down past the deputy's office and the hole next door. Then we had to stand outside in the cold to wait for a company to leave the barbershop, to make room for us. Our faces got chilled and tight in the cold so that when the hot strong lather was slapped on them the skin cracked open like a scalded tomato.

Kish, the big Greek runner for the hole, came out and told us that Warren and two other guards had broken one of Johnson's arms, cracked his skull, and put him in the hole. Kish said he would be there for a time. He seemed very pleased.

Standing in the cold in the close-packed line, I could see the big new red-brick chapel building across the yard, and part of the west cell house where I had celled on 5-11. I could see the front cell house with its four rows of barred windows, and five-foot strip of polished stone underneath the eaves so the convicts couldn't scale it; and the slanting slate roof. And in the middle the main gates of the prison, where beyond was freedom; and through which more men entered than ever left.

The yard was criss-crossed with brick walks down which the gray men marched through the gray days; to the dining room, to the bathhouse, to the barbershop, to the hole, to the hospital, to the mills, to the Protestant and Catholic and Jewish and Christian Science chapels, to the electric chair. In front of the Protestant chapel was a small, empty pool. They said the band stood there and played marches on clear days, while the convicts marched to their meals. They said alligators were kept in the pool in the summer, but I didn't believe that.

A little beyond where we stood, across the areaway, was a square, gray-stone building which housed the school on the first floor, and the Catholic chapel above. And beyond, a brick walk leading out of sight around the corner, down by the front cell house to the death house.

There was a pile of lumber and iron and wheelbarrows and junk over in front of the west cell house, left over from the building of the new 7&8 cell block.

As we went up the outside stairway into the barbershop I saw one end of the long, flat, one-storied frame building behind the school. It was a dormitory. There were four thousand convicts in that prison which had been built for eighteen hundred.

My whiskers weren't very thick and I'd decided to shave only once a week. But when my turn came I didn't want to say anything to Captain Warren. I went over and got into the chair. The shave left my face raw and burning. When Mal got out of his chair he came over and squeezed in beside me on the bench. He gave me some after-shave lotion, but it burned worse than the shave and smelled like menthol and alcohol.

"What was that barber saying to you?" he asked.

"Oh, he was just kidding."

"What did he say?"

"He said I had baseball whiskers," I said, blushing.

"Nine on each side." It was a stale joke.

When we returned to the dormitory the convicts were sullen and hostile. Old man Warren was pleased. He kept on abusing the men. "You saw what Johnson got. You see what you get for fighting a guard."

He saw two men wrestling playfully. He ran up and jerked them apart and slapped one, and hit the other one across the arm with his stick. The men were very sullen. Warren stopped all the card games. Until he left, after supper, we couldn't do anything but sit around and look sullen.

But that night after the shift had changed, the games were good. The tobacco orders had come in that day at noon and had been delivered to us after we'd signed the yellow bills of sale. I struck a bargain with one of the gamekeepers, a Swede called Ole, and got some matches, two bars of soap, and a carton of cigarettes for a monthly order of the daily *Gazette* and some western-story magazines. I could have gambled with it. There was very little cash in the dormitory and merchandise was taken at the commissary price. But I thought I'd better not, since Mal had warned me against it.

Mal got a checkerboard and we played pool checkers until bedtime. I won fifty-two out of eighty-one games, but I think he was just letting me win. He made some good moves there, once or twice, to lose fifty-two games to me.

The next day was Sunday. We dressed up in our blue denim shirts and our white string ties. My shirt was so large the collar sagged down to my chest. After a breakfast of coffee cake, peanut butter and coffee we lined up for church.

The Catholics and Christian Scientists went first. There were about twenty Catholics and two Christian Scientists in our company. We didn't have any Jews. After they'd gone the Protestants lined up and marched to the Protestant chapel. Everybody who didn't have one of the three other faiths was a Protestant. Church was compulsory.

I didn't have to go. The porters were exempted. But I went to get out of sweeping. In the regular line Mal marched several men ahead of me. But Sunday he fell back in line and marched just ahead, so we could sit together in the chapel.

The yard was filled with long gray lines of convicts. Every walk was filled. All the men were out. It didn't seem possible that the prison could house all those men. Even the honor men came in from the honor dormitory, in their neat blue suits and white shirts, looking like civilians, and filled up the front seats reserved for them. The honor men were big shots. It was something to be an honor man and wear a blue serge suit and a white shirt and look important.

We entered the chapel from the back. It was made like a theater, with the seats graduating up to the roof at the rear. There was a large stage with wings and curtains, as in the legitimate theater. The deputy warden sat in a chair at the extreme left of the stage. His head was bald as an egg, with big dark freckles and he had a flat-nosed pug's face. He was a big man. His body shook from some sort of nervous disorder. They called him Jumpy Stone because on his bad days he was a sight to see. His blue eyes, shaded by tufted brows and enlarged by polished spectacles, looked bright and sharp. He sat there watching us as we entered, with a sardonic expression.

The pulpit was in the center of the stage. Behind it were three heavy oak chairs with black leather upholstering. The chaplain sat on the left. He wore a tailored black suit and his shoes were polished to a brilliant luster. His face was slightly narrow, but well filled-out, and his head was well-shaped. He wore his hair parted on one side. He looked smooth and slick. His name was Preston Douglas Perry.

The guest minister sat in the center. His name was Glisser. There was an anemic, fanatical air about him. Deacon Smith, the colored convict who had delivered my money order, sat at the right.

Behind them, to one side, sat the convict orchestra. They were dressed in their grays but wore white shirts and black bow ties. They looked self-conscious and recently bathed and shaved. To the other side of the stage were two rows of chairs. These were occupied by men and women visiting from Reverend Glisser's church in the city.

Except for the convicts and the chaplain and the deputy, everyone looked very religious. Deacon Smith looked sanctimonious.

Deacon Smith opened the services with a prayer. He had a fine oratorical voice and his enunciation was scholarly. Congregational singing followed. But few of the convicts joined in. Chaplain Perry rose and introduced Reverend Glisser. The convicts knew Reverend Glisser from previous visits. He was greeted by a few scattered boos.

Reverend Glisser had a very bad pulpit manner. He seemed vindictive and slightly hysterical. It seemed as if he hated the convicts. In the course of his sermon he said it was good we were there. I think he meant it was good we were in church, not in prison. But most of the convicts accepted the latter meaning. They began booing so loudly that the deputy finally had to stand up and wave his hands for silence. They respected the deputy and quieted down. The Reverend Glisser went on denouncing sin. To relieve the tension he began telling a joke about "an old darky eating porridge with his fingers." The colored convicts started booing then, and the deputy and nobody else could stop them. They kept booing until Reverend Glisser had to sit down. His face was fiery red. His breath came in gasps and he looked diabolically mean and malevolent.

The chaplain rose and in his confidential voice, looking like a solid con man, prayed for the convicts' souls. He sounded for all the world like a ward heeler at a political meeting. After concluding his prayer he went into the wings and changed into a rubber suit, and came out to baptize some sixteen convicts who had been converted the Sunday before.

The pool was beneath the floor in the center aisle at the front of the stage. When the sections of flooring had been removed the converted convicts lined up and went forward, one by one, and were dipped into the water by the chaplain and an assistant. The chaplain recited in a parrot-like voice, "In the name of the Father, the Son, and the Holy Ghost."

Mal said one of the converts had been brought over from the hole where he was serving out a rap for sex perversion. The deputy seemed amused by the proceedings. Once or twice he laughed out loud. All of us enjoyed it very much. The convicts came out of the water, cold and shivering, their wet overalls clinging to their thin bodies. I wondered how many of them would be in the sick bay the next day.

After it was all over the orchestra began playing jazz. The deputy arose and waved us out. We left laughing and talking. It smelled better outside and I got some of the odor of those smelly convicts out of my nostrils.

For Sunday's dinner we had roast pork, potatoes, gray cooked dried peas, and applesauce. There was a piece of soggy gingerbread at our plates which we could eat there or carry back to the cells for supper. We didn't return to the dining room any more on Sunday. As we marched out we were given two slices of bread and a slab of cheese, from tubs sitting at each side of the doorway. A convict waiter worked at each tub, and the guards stood by and watched to see that no one got more than his share. The cheese sandwich and the gingerbread was our supper.

I sat around and talked to Mal and read the Sunday paper. We played some checkers but he won easily. Then I watched the poker game until I was tired of swallowing bets. I went over to my bunk and took a nap.

When the coffee came Mal woke me. I got my coffee bucket and fell into the line that had formed. Two dining-room waiters had brought over a couple of five-gallon coffee cans of light-colored coffee. As we passed in line they poured our coffee buckets half full. I had forgotten to rinse out my bucket and the coffee tasted like soap. Mal gave me some of his but it didn't taste much better. He said he had put some sugar in it but I couldn't taste it. As a rule he sweetened it with saccharin tablets he bought from the hospital but he had run out, he said. I said that was all right. I didn't like coffee anyway.

"That's right, you're still drinking milk," he said.

I told him about the time I took a quart of milk to a night club. He told me about his wife and showed me her picture. She was a pretty woman. I started telling him about my great affairs. Most of it I made up but some of it was true. But I didn't tell him about Margy or Joan. Those two did not stand telling about.

"You were a hell of a guy, Jimmy," he said, flatteringly.

I liked it. We were down on his bunk eating a couple of roast-pork sandwiches he had gotten from somewhere. He asked me if I'd had any dreams since I'd been in and I said, sure, every night.

He laughed. "*Every* night?"

"Well, maybe I missed a night or two."

"Do you carry on?"

"Carry on?"

"You know, moan or something?"

I laughed. "Hell, naw."

But I felt sort of funny, wondering if I had made any

noise or if anybody had noticed, when it was really happening to me.

We lay there for a long time after we had finished eating, sprawled across the bed, talking about love and life and our experiences, and watching it grow dark outside. We talked mostly about women we had had and what they had said in bed, and whether they had been good or bad, and what we got from them and what we thought they got from us. Mal always brought the conversation back to that whenever we got off of it.

After the first hard knots of food had smoothed out in our bellies and our bellies got warm, we got warm and passionate thinking about the women we'd had. We kept talking about it until every time we'd accidentally touch each other we'd feel a shock. I was startled at the femininity a man's face could assume when you're looking at it warmly and passionately, and off to yourselves in prison where there are all men and there is no comparison.

Mal looked very pretty and his eyes seemed very bright and after a time he said, "You don't believe what Jeep said about me, do you?"

"Hell, naw," I said.

"A lot of guys do that in here but I'm bitterly against it," he said.

We were silent for a time, then he said, "I wonder how it would feel to do something like that."

"I don't know and I don't care."

He was looking at me from underneath his eyelashes. I didn't like the turn the conversation had taken.

"To hell with that stuff!" I said. "Come on, let's play some checkers."

Afterward that whole day seemed like a dream. It didn't seem like it had happened at all.

4

SOMEONE CALLED me out into the aisle that night and while I was gone Mal got into a fight with the General and hit him over the head with a two-by-four. He didn't hurt him much. It was all over when I got back. Some fellows had pulled them apart. They didn't really want to fight, anyway.

The night guard didn't like to take anybody to the hole. When he saw it was all over he went back to the guard-stand without even questioning them.

All the other convicts were laughing about it. Some of them cracked that the fight had been over me. I didn't like that. I asked Mal. But he said it had started about my paper. I had left it on the bunk when I went out into the aisle. The General had picked it up. Then Mal had snatched it out of his hand. One word had led to another. Then the General had jumped up and slapped him. He conked the General with the timber. I didn't like the General anyway so I said, "Swell."

The next day Mal was transferred. It didn't have anything to do with the fight. He had been trying to get a job down at the furnace where the aluminum dishes were molded. When the convict who had it got a pardon he got it. He said you could make money on the job, molding tubes and bowls for cigarette holders and the bodies for cigarette lighters and such. When a con got it he married it. He had been waiting eighteen months to get it.

He was transferred to the 5-5 dormitory. That was in the far end of the wooden dormitory, back of the hole and the Catholic chapel. I helped him to pack and move. He promised to stop and see me every time he came up our way for coke for the furnace.

It was tough seeing him go. He'd been good company. It was in the evenings, when we used to talk, that I missed him most. I didn't know I could miss anyone so much or get so lonely in a big dormitory full of men. I liked old Mal, I sure did like that boy.

Jeep tried to make friends with me, after that. He said he had been in twenty months and had never had a friend —not a real pal, anyway. I said, what the hell did I care? I was sour on him.

Big Ole gave me some credit in his poker game one night but I lost. But the next night another fellow staked me. He said he liked the way I played. I won. But I kept on playing every night and got broke a couple of nights later.

And then I got fired off my job. It had been snowing since the night before and there was so much snow outside that the men couldn't work. We had to sweep and mop with them inside. When we were all through old B&O ordered me to go over to the planing mill and get some shavings.

There were two barrels filled to the top with shavings. The other one was two-thirds full. He wanted me to take that one over and fill it up. I said, to hell with it. He ran up to me as if he wanted to start something. I told him if he opened his goddamned mouth I'd knock out his teeth. He went to the guard.

Captain Warren was off that morning and Roe was in charge. Roe called me into the office and asked why I didn't want to get the shavings. I told him we didn't need any. He said B&O was supposed to be the judge of that. I said it didn't need any judging, we already had more than we could use in a week. He said if I couldn't go get the shavings I could go outside with the coal men the next time they went out. I said, "Yeah," and left it at that.

Old man Warren was there the next day. It had cleared up a little and the men went back to work. When I started into the dormitory with the porters, after breakfast, Roe yelled at me.

"Come on out here and grab a wheelbarrow, Monroe. You've lost your pretty home, my boy." He'd been standing at the head of the tracks waiting for me.

I tightened up inside. "Hell with you, bud," I muttered, but he didn't hear me.

"Come on, come on!" he called, but I kept on inside.

He started after me. One of the porters said, "Man, you better go on out there. You'll get into trouble. They'll bust your head." But I was already in trouble. I was in there with twenty years. I couldn't think of any more trouble than that.

"If there's any hitting done we're both gonna do some of it," I said.

But Roe didn't come inside. He met Warren at the door and said something to him. Warren turned around and looked at me, then he said something to Roe. Roe went back outside to the coal pile and let me alone. It was years afterward that I learned that Warren had given the porter's job to me in the first place because his daughter had asked him to look out for me if he got a chance. I'd gone to college with Helen Warren. I didn't know at the time she was his daughter. But she'd read of my conviction and was looking out for me.

I stayed inside. B&O wouldn't let me work. He said I was fired. Old man Warren didn't say anything to me at all. So every morning while the porters swept and mopped the floors, I sat up on the night-guard's stand and read a magazine. In the afternoons I lay on my bunk and took life easy. I wasn't worried. The other guys did more worrying about it than I did.

One morning old man Warren came to work with his bad habits on. When we went to breakfast he closed the dormitory door and locked it. It was unexpected and I wasn't prepared to work. I had on my brand-new shoes and some silk socks. I didn't have any working gloves. Mal had gotten me a tailor-made cap and some tailor-made pants, with two hip pockets and a watch pocket. I'd gotten to be quite a dude. I felt too dressed up to work. And anyway, I had an injured back, I argued with myself. I was classified as totally disabled. I didn't believe they could force me to work if I didn't want to. When old man Warren told me to get a wheelbarrow and roll some coal I told him I wasn't able.

He told me to stand out there to one side and watch the others roll coal. "I'll stand," I said. "But I won't roll any." I walked over to the corner of the dormitory and stood there. Then I began getting cold. At first it was just on the outside. On my hands and face and in my ears. Then it was in my skin and underneath my skin and down in my chest and around my bones. And then it was in my head. I went over and hammered on the corrugated door. Everybody stopped work to watch me. Roe stood there grinning and cracking at me.

Captain Warren opened the door. When he saw me he

said, "What's the matter, what's the matter? Tired of standing?"

"I'm cold." I was blue in the face.

"Get a shovel, that'll warm you up," he said and slammed the door in my face.

I was ready to fight. I pulled my cap down over my eyes and started to the deputy's office. Roe called to me and asked me where I was going. I didn't answer. He ran into the dormitory to tell old man Warren. I didn't look back.

The deputy warden wasn't in. His clerk asked me what I wanted. I said I just wanted to see the deputy. He asked me what company I was from. I told him the coal company. He told me to go next door and wait for the deputy.

There was a long narrow hallway next door with wooden benches down the wall. It was the waiting room. Newcomers waited there to be assigned to cells. It was the first place they came. Old convicts waited there to be transferred from one company to another. Convicts who had been reported for infractions of the rules waited there to be tried. Convicts who wanted to see any of the inside officials waited there.

At the back of the waiting room was a door leading into the courtroom. Somewhere back of that I knew was the hole.

Kish, the big Greek hole attendant, came out from in back somewhere and tried to start a conversation with me. I didn't feel like talking. He went and stood in the doorway. Then the sergeant they called Donald Duck came in. He asked me what I was waiting for. I told him I wanted to see the deputy. He wanted to know what for. I told him.

"The deputy don't want to see you," he said. "You come on with me." He started back to the coal company with me but before we got there we ran into Warren.

"So you tried to run away?" Warren said.

I didn't answer.

"I found him over to the hole," Donald Duck said. "I'll take him back there and lock him up."

"No, let him stand up some more first," Donald Duck said.

Warren jerked me by the arm. He acted as if he wanted to start something. I let him have his way. Just so long as he didn't hit me. They took me back to the coal pile and left me standing there while they went into the dormitory.

Mal came by and saw me and wanted to know what

was the trouble. When I told him he said, "You ought to go to work, Jimmy. They'll make it tough for you."

"They can't make it any tougher than they're making it."

He looked worried. "I wish you'd go on to work, Jimmy. You can't buck 'em." I didn't answer. "Well, if you won't do it to stay out of trouble, do it for me, then."

"Mal, I like you," I said. "But it's too late now." I was feeling very melodramatic. "I might have gone to work this morning when they first brought me out here if they'd let me put on some working clothes. But it's too late now. I wouldn't go to work now to save my life."

"You'll catch pneumonia."

"I don't give a goddamn what I catch."

"Come on, please, Jimmy."

"It's no use talking, Mal. I'm not going to work."

He looked very worried. Roe saw him and came over and chased him away.

"How you doing, big shot?" Roe said to me. I didn't answer.

When the men quit work that afternoon to wash up for supper Captain Warren took me to the hole. There were two other convicts from another company, charged with refusing to work. One of them looked very young. He must have been about my age. But he acted sort of simple. He kept giggling and whispering something to the other fellow. When Warren told him to shut up he kept on giggling as if he couldn't stop. Warren made him get up and move down to the other end of the bench.

The other convict was very fat and greasy. He was about twenty-five or -six. All the time Warren was in there he kept trying to catch my eye and forming words with his lips behind Warren's back. I couldn't make out what he was trying to say.

"You wait here," Warren said, shoving me toward the opposite bench. I frowned. I was getting good and tired of all that shoving. Warren went next door after the deputy. As soon as he'd left, the fat fellow said, "What say, Jimmy?"

"Hello," I said.

"Don't you remember me? I'm Benny Glass."

"Oh, yeah. Hello. What say, bud?"

"I was in the county jail in Springfield with you last year. I guess it was year before last now."

"Oh yeah, sure." But I couldn't remember him.

"Didn't you get a five-year bench parole for forgery?"

"Yeah."

"What'd ya do, break it?"

"No, I'm doing twenty years for robbery."

His mouth came open. "Je-hesus Christ!"

Captain Warren came in with the deputy and we stopped talking. The deputy stood very erect and walked with short, fast steps. He didn't look at any of us. He walked jerkily and his head bobbed up and down. He kept straight on back to the courtroom.

Kish came in from outside and followed them. There was a grimy old window between the courtroom and the waiting room. I saw the deputy take the middle of the three chairs behind the scarred, flat-topped desk.

Kish stuck his head out of the door and called, "Wilkerson, 102697." The youth got up and went inside. He wasn't giggling now. We kept silent, watching the door, trying to hear what was being said. All we could hear was a jumble of voices. Then the voices stopped. Kish stuck his head out the door.

"Glass, 101253."

When he passed me Glass said, "Jumpy's in his sins today." He didn't come out either. Then Kish called me. I went inside and stood before the desk, leaning forward with the palms of my hands on the desk and my cap stuck in my coat pocket. Kish stood in front of the far door above which was the legend: CORRECTION CELLS.

Warren stood to my right, at the side of the desk. "Take your cap out of your pocket and fold your hands," he said. The deputy was reading the yellow report card before him on the desk. I folded my arms, holding my cap in my left hand. Old man Warren took it out of my hand and said, "See, he's got slick already. He's got a tailor-made cap." The deputy didn't look up. I reached for my cap. Warren said, "Oh, no, I'll keep this." I felt myself getting tight again.

" 'Refusing to work,' " the deputy read from the card. He looked up at me. "You're starting pretty soon, pretty soon, pretty soon, Monroe."

"I gave him every chance," Warren said. "But he won't work. I gave him a porter's job inside, but he quit that. . . ."

"I got fired," I interrupted. "Old B&O wanted me. . . ."

"Shut up! Shut up!" Warren shouted, drawing back as if to slap me. "Don't you interrupt me like that."

I burnt up. I could feel the fire in my eyes and face. My whole body got stiff and wooden.

"I did get fired, goddammit!"

Kish came up behind me and held my arms. Warren slapped me twice in the mouth.

"That'll do, that'll do," the deputy said.

Kish held me for a moment longer to see if I would put up any resistance. I didn't move. I was saying to myself—so he hit me, he hit me. I'm not going to take that. I'm damned if I take that. Then Kish turned me loose. I still didn't move.

After a moment I said dully, "All right, all right. You hit me!" I tasted a little blood on my lips.

The deputy looked at the card again. "What's the matter you can't work, Monroe? What's the matter? What's the matter?" He was very impatient and his eyes were snapping-sharp. I couldn't meet his gaze.

"I'm not able to," I said, looking down at the desk.

"What's the matter? What's the matter?"

"I'm injured!" I shouted. Then I told him about my back.

"There's nothing about it on his hospital card," Warren said.

"I didn't tell the doctor."

"We'll see about it, we'll see about it," the deputy said.

"He's very impertinent, too," Warren said.

"All right, all right, all right, all right," the deputy said, beginning to shake all over. "All right, all right, all right. Refusing to work. Put him in the hole. Put him in the hole." He had a rapid, brittle voice. All the while he talked his head kept bobbing up and down.

"I'm not refusing to work," I argued. "I'll do what I can. I'm just not able."

"We'll see about it in the morning. Take him back, take him back, take him back!" He was very impatient.

I looked around at Warren. "You hit me," I said, biting my lips. I was going back to the hole anyway. I just may as well bust him one, I thought. I kept biting my lips, trying to get up enough nerve to sock him one. But it wouldn't come.

"Watch out, watch out, watch out he doesn't hit you again," the deputy said.

Kish took me by the arm and pushed me through the back door into a small dressing room. There was a bunk against the concrete wall, where he slept. He handed me a pair of overalls and told me to undress. The other two fellows were sitting on the bench waiting for me. They'd already put on their overalls. I stripped naked and put on mine. I could hear Warren still talking to the deputy. But I couldn't make out what he was saying.

"The dirty son of a bitch," I muttered.

"He hit you?" Glass asked. I nodded. "Wipe that blood off your lips," he said. I wiped the back of my hand across my mouth. My lips were swelling. The other fellow giggled. He was a little simple-minded.

Across the room was a heavy barred door. Behind that was a door of solid steel. Kish opened both doors and motioned us to enter. We walked forward into the hole. It was completely black inside. Kish snapped on the lights.

Inside there was a miniature cell block made of solid steel. It sat in the center of the floor. The cells, six on each side, faced outwards toward the thick, windowless walls. It was very cold and damp. My teeth began to chatter immediately. I felt my hands getting numb.

"Put us all together," Glass asked Kish.

"You all want to cell together?" Kish asked.

"I want to cell with him," Wilkerson said, pointing to Glass. I didn't answer.

Kish put the three of us in the last cell, down on the North side. He locked the cell door. There was a steel strait jacket built to the inside of the door. We listened to Kish's footsteps on the concrete floor. Then we heard the outer doors being locked. The lights were turned out. It was so dark we couldn't see one another's eyes.

"What you punks in for?" The voice sounded as if it came from the other side. It had a muffled note. We didn't answer. I could hear myself breathe.

"Who's a punk?" Glass shouted. It came so unexpectedly I jumped.

"Aw, I didn't mean no harm, buddy." It was the laconic, indifferent voice of an old-timer. "You know I didn't mean no harm. Got a cigarette?"

For a time none of us replied. Finally Glass said, "No."

"Got a cigarette paper?"

"No."

"Got a match?"

"No. We haven't got a thing, buddy."

"Go to hell then you goddamn punk. You stinking schmo. You fat gunsel." The voice was still laconic, indifferent, unraised. I felt like laughing.

"Aw, shut up, you screwball," Glass said. "You're stir-simple."

"Your mother's a screwball. Your sister is stir-simple."

This time none of us replied. For a long time it was silent in the hole. "Ain't you even got a butt?"

"Kiss something, rat!" Glass yelled. I wondered why he sounded so vehement.

"Aw, shut up, you fat louse. I bet that's you doing all the talking. I'll catch you out there when I empty my bucket tomorrow morning and kick your ass out your nose."

Glass got agitated. "I'll meet you!" he shouted, jumping around. "I'll fight you! I'm not scared of you!"

He stepped on my foot and I said, "Goddammit, wait and fight him in the morning."

The voice didn't say anything else so he sat down. There was a slab of steel projecting from the back wall for a bed. It was very cold and the cold came quickly up through my overalls. Glass said there were some blankets in the cell. We felt around on the bench and on the floor without finding them. Then we got down on our hands and knees and groped around on the floor. I knocked into something that rattled. I jumped back as if I'd touched a rattlesnake and knocked into Glass.

"What the hell's that?" I asked, shakily.

"That's your bucket," Glass said.

"Bucket? Water bucket?"

Glass laughed. The other fellow giggled. I began smelling the stink. I'd knocked the top off. I fumbled around and found it and put it back on. "We all use the same bucket?" I asked.

"Sure."

"Don't they ever wash it out?"

"Sure, one of us will have to wash it out in the morning."

"I hope it ain't me," I said.

Finally Glass found the blankets stuffed back into a corner. "Here they are," he said.

There were two pieces which must have been one blanket torn in half and another piece, no larger than a face towel. They felt very grimy to touch. We sat on the bench and wrapped up in them as best we could. Glass took the smallest piece. He said he would sit in the middle and we could sit close to him and keep warm.

"Damn right," I laughed. "Hot as you are." After awhile we began to warm each other.

"Twenty years. Jesus Christ. You must have stuck up a bank, Jimmy," Glass commented.

"No, just some people."

"Fat Funky fink!" the voice yelled from the other side. "I bet you got a fat mama."

"Dirty screwball," Glass muttered to himself.

"Aw, let him alone," I said.

We were silent for awhile.

"I'm cold," I said.

Wilkerson hadn't said anything at all.

"I'm hot," Glass said. "I'll put my arm around you and that'll keep you warm."

I had my half-a-blanket wrapped about my shoulders but it wasn't long enough to cover up my front. I held it together at my throat. "Never mind," I said. "I'll get warm in a minute."

Then Wilkerson said, "Put your arm around me, Ben."

After a time the bedbugs began to bite. I didn't know bedbugs could live in that much cold but they certainly worked on me. They bit me all over. I began scratching and moving about. The bench began to hurt the end of my spine. I was cold and itching and thoroughly miserable.

"I want a fire!" the voice yelled from the other side. It sounded hollow and metallic as if the fellow was standing at the back of his cell. "I want something to eat!"

After a time I heard the sticks banging outside. I could just barely hear them. "Damn!" I whispered. It was just bedtime.

I tried to go to sleep. I said to myself if I sit in one position and keep my eyes closed I'll go to sleep. I'm tired, I'll go to sleep. I'm tired, I'll go to sleep. I'm tired, I'll go to sleep. . . . I sat perfectly still. A bedbug bit me. Something crawled over my bare leg. My neck and throat and legs itched intolerably. I itched all over. And then a trickle of pain crept into my body. It began at the base of my spine. It flowed down my legs, up my back. I'll be asleep in a minute, I said. And then it came in a rush. The pain and the itching and the biting and the cold.

"Goddamn, goddamn, goddamn," I sobbed.

"Take it easy, Jimmy," Glass said.

"I'll take it easy," I said.

"We're lucky they didn't put us in strait jackets," he said.

I heard the distant scream of a locomotive whistle. I could imagine the long line of coaches, gliding through the night, with its chain of yellow-lighted windows filled with people, going somewhere, going anywhere.

"Damned if I'm lucky," I said.

That was the longest night I spent in prison. In the

morning the deputy asked me if I was ready to go back to work. I said, "Yes, sir." He sent me back to the coal company. Warren gave me a job sweeping off the wheelbarrow tracks. It was an easy job.

That afternoon I was transferred into the school company to teach school. The chaplain had charge of the school. He sent for me and told me he had heard I was a college student. I told him I'd attended the state university. He asked me how would I like to teach school. I said fine. He had me transferred.

5

THE 5-6 DORMITORY, to which they transferred me, was the coal company dormitory over again, only it was long and narrow. It was housed in the north half of the wooden building which housed the 5-5 dormitory to which Mal had been transferred.

There were the same double-decked bunks and the same center aisle, with the wooden tables with attached benches, and at night there were three poker games instead of one. There was a blackjack game and a Georgia skin game which the colored convicts played. There were also colored convicts in this dormitory.

The outside door was at the end of the dormitory which was the middle of the building, adjoining the door to 5-5. The dormitories were separated by a thin wooden partition. At the back a hole had been cut in the partition through which notes and money and messages were passed from one dormitory to the other. Once or twice each evening Mal sent for me to come to the peephole so he could talk to me. The colored convicts bunked down at the end of the dormitory and the latrine was down there also.

I was assigned to a lower bunk on the center aisle next to the guard-stand. "Right under the gun," Mal said when

I told him. "I'm glad—you won't be able to get into any mischief."

On awakening each morning I had my choice of looking at the convicts dress in their grayed and sweat-stained underwear and sweat-stiffened socks which they wore from week to week and their bagged stinking trousers which they wore from year to year, and their gaunt and patched coats which the officials seemed to think never wore out; or I could look underneath the sagging upper mattresses out of the west windows at the back of the hospital, weather-stained and still asleep, housing tuberculosis and syphilis and cuts and lacerations and contusions and infections and operations and skulls cracked by guards' sticks, and death. With mattresses lying out beside the front entrance, almost every morning, which would be taken away and burned because the convict who had last slept on them would not need them any more; or need anything else any more except a six-foot plot in Potter's Field and the soft, close embrace of mother earth. Or, displeased with that, I could look across the aisle and over the unmade bunks, out of the east windows, at the stretch of dark gray wall against the darker sky, cutting out the smell of burnt gasoline; and a home at night with a mother and a father, and the tinkle of ice in tall glasses, and the unforgettable perfume of a woman's hair.

Or I could lie in bed and pretend I wasn't going that morning, and watch the others spread their sheets and make their bunks and join the ragged soap-and-towel procession down to where the washtroughs were located, by the latrine. No matter how early you arose the colored convicts would have a skin game roaring down by the latrine, as if it had never stopped all night.

At night I could lie and watch the nightly latrine brigade with their open drawers and felt house shoes stolen from the hospital. Or I could read by the eternal droplight overhead; or listen to the steady, planted stride of the night guard making his rounds; or watch the furtive slitherings of those bent on degeneracy and maiming, and sometimes even murder—as was in the case of the colored convict called Sonny who slipped up on another colored convict called Badeye, while he was asleep, and cut his throat from ear to ear.

It was a sort of gurgle that I had heard, for it was late and quiet. When I got down there, peering over the shoulders of the convicts in front of me, I saw Badeye lying there with blood bubbling out of his mouth in large and small and very fine slavering bubbles, like the mouth of a dog gone mad; only the bubbles on Badeye's mouth were bloody, and not quite so frothy, and the blood was running out of his nostrils and down his black greasy skin on the dirty gray sheet, and the blood had spurted out of his throat all over the dusty blanket and his dirty cotton underwear and even on the bottom of the mattress on the bunk above. His arms were half drawn-up and he was flopping very slightly but after awhile even the flopping stopped, and the blood seemed as if it had stopped, and he was lying there in such a pool of blood that you could hardly see him.

Or I could listen to the putrid, vulgar conversations of the convict who bunked above me and who was also a teacher; but I never learned exactly what he was to all those convicts who stopped to whisper every night when the lights were out and when the guard was at the other end.

Or I could talk to the guard whom we all called Captain Charlie. He was a short, sort of cherubic-looking old man. He had taken a liking to me. We talked in whispers about crime and punishment, virtues and vices, history and ambitions. He said it was such a pity that a boy of my age should have to come to prison. We did not talk of politics or of the warden. Although he was very nice he was also very old and couldn't have gotten another job easily. Nor did we talk of convicts. I was determined not to get the reputation of being a rat, or being one. But I enjoyed talking to him. We talked of many other things which were of mutual, but not malicious, interest. Pretty soon he was bringing me candy which his wife, who had once run a candy shop, made especially for me. It was exceedingly good candy except for those pieces they fooled me with which were balls of cotton dipped in chocolate.

If I so desired, in the evenings after supper I could lie on my bunk and watch the evening promenade; up the aisle on one side, down on the other, up and down, up and down, mile after mile, which—put together—would have been a good way out into freedom, but which ended up each night at the bunks where it started. Or I could watch the amateur prize fighters who worked out in the aisle beside my bunk in front of the guard-stand. I could smell them, too, the pungent unwashed bodies.

I could lie on my bunk and close my eyes and say I was back in Lake City at the Lotus Gardens again, or at the Far East restaurant listening to Roy Bugle's *Serenaders* or out to the Hawaiian Gardens, or at Shady Beach, or at the Palace D'Or, or at Hudson Park, or at the baseball park with a double-header playing underneath the hot July sky. Or I could say I was on the road at night doing a cool seventy, with the motor roar spilling out behind me and catching up with me only when I passed through some small town with the heavy-leafed tree limbs hanging low over the road, and the white vine-clustered houses reflecting the sound. I could say I was in White City the night I drove Johnny down to catch the boat; or that I was back at State again boning for my finals; or back at high school playing quarterback on the varsity team. I could say I was in Chicago, too, and had sold that ring and had kept on down to Santa Anita for the winter races, with a pocket full of money. But I couldn't make myself play that game, no matter how hard I tried, or how tightly I closed my eyes or how much I cursed God or Fate or Luck, or whatever you care to call it. Sooner or later, anyway, all my thoughts would come back to Chicago from wherever they had gone, no matter how far, how many miles or how many years, and I'd feel again that sickening, unbearable chagrin as intensely as when the judge had said, *"I sentence you to be taken to the penitentiary where you shall remain incarcerated at hard labor for a period of not less than twenty years and not more than twenty-five years."* And I would wish to God that I had gone to sleep when I had had the chance.

Just by trying hard enough I could keep from thinking about my mother and father and that wild, reckless year I'd lived after their divorce. I could keep from thinking about the guys who hung around the gambling joints and were my friends that year. Although it didn't hurt to think about them because most of that gang were just lucky they weren't in there with me. Only thinking about them made me think about Chicago, and thinking about Chicago made me want to vomit. It made me want them never to know what an utter fool I'd been, what a simple-minded schmo, a square, as to try to pawn that ring in that shop, of all places.

There were many things about that dormitory, things that happened there and things that happened elsewhere while I was bunking there, which afterward I could remember without remembering the dormitory at all. By that I do not mean the dimensional or visual aspect of the dormitory, its breadth and length and height, its bunks and tables and such. That was like a color one will remember long after sight has left the scene. I mean the living, pulsing, vulgar, vicious, treacherous, humorous, piteous, tawdry heart of it; the living men, the living actions, the living speech, the constant sense of power just above, the ever-present breath of sudden death, that kept those two hundred and fifty-three convicts, with their total sentences numbering more years than the history of Christianity, within the confines of that eggshell wood; or, for that matter, kept them within those high stone walls to live on, day after day, under the prescribed routine and harsh discipline and grinding monotony which comes to all after a time.

And there were convicts, too, whom I could remember without remembering the dormitory, as if, telescoping back into retrospect, I could pick them out; where they stood, what they said, how they looked at some given moment—without seeing beyond the circumference of the vision of the telescope, like sighting a buck at three hundred yards.

There was Mal at the peephole, telling everyone who came near enough to hear his voice to tell his cousin, Jimmy Monroe, that he wanted to speak to him; until everyone within both dormitories had heard it said that I was his blood cousin and had remarked that we did look something alike, sure enough.

"Hello, cousin," he would say.

All I could see would be his eye and I would begin to laugh. "All I can see is your eye. It looks funny."

"I can see all of you."

"I saw an ad in the paper," I would say. "Hammon's has a shoe sale on. Florsheims for $15.75. Two pairs for $30. Do you want a pair?"

"You're not kidding, Jimmy?"

"Naw, I'm going to get a pair for myself."

"I need a pair, but I don't know. You won't be straining yourself?"

"Fifteen dollars? What the hell!"

"Fifteen seventy-five."

"Fifteen, if I get two pairs. I'll get you a pair. I don't care what you say."

"I'll make it up to you, Jimmy," he would promise.

And I would say, "Aw, hell."

"I hear you're a big shot now. I hear you're running a poker game," he would say.

"Old Nick the Greek himself, that's me."

By that time we'd have to get away and let some other

cousins talk. He'd send for me again when they got through, or maybe he'd wait an hour or so until the lights went out. If I was busy dealing and couldn't get down for that or some other reason he'd send for me the next day to come over to the window where the furnace was located. I'd stand at the window and talk outside to him while he stood inside of the furnace room, or in the doorway of the sand room where the sand was kept for the molds. That way he was hidden from the tin-shop guard who liked to stand in the window of his second-story office and spy out on the yard, so he could know every time some convict carried a kid to some hiding place so that afterward he could get the kid and have him for himself. He was that kind of a guard. It was also against the rules to talk through the windows of the dormitory.

And there was Lippy Mike the head porter, a big wide-shouldered, athletic-looking, black Irishman, who held his shoulders high and square and walked with a swagger. Everybody seemed to be afraid of him because he had a reputation with a knife, and a scar up over his deep-set insane-looking eyes to prove it. And he also had a knife with a blade six inches long.

He assumed more authority in the dormitory than the guards, one of whom was Captain Bull, big and beer-bloated and slovenly, with tobacco ashes down his vest and a stubble of gray beard, and the heart disease which finally killed him. The other guard was Captain Clem who had a narrow, nasty, greasy face and a sloppy mouth and narrow shoulders and a pot belly and skinny legs, looking young in the face and old in the body, with prematurely gray hair.

Lippy Mike was the most overbearing, arrogant convict I've ever seen. "After this when you're transferred, Monroe, bring your sheet and pillowcase," he had said to me the very first thing with his damned insufferable arrogance. "Thursday's laundry day. Be sure to have your sheet and pillowcase on top of your bunk. And take everything off the floor in the mornings." He had assigned me to my bunk. The guards left the dormitory to him; he ran it.

"Anything else, captain?" I asked.

He had pinned those fanatical blue eyes on me with his shoulders high and square and the butt of the knife sticking out of his left breast pocket. "I'm not your goddamned captain, punk. I'm Mike." And then after a full moment in which he just stared at me he had lifted his gaze to call, "Papa Henry, give this boy a sheet and pillowcase." And with that he had walked down the aisle, high-shouldered and swaggering and when I had said, Go to hell, he had been too far away to hear it.

I never liked that boy.

And there was Hunky Hank who had been in the Lincoln County jail with me when I'd been arrested for forgery. He had helped me run the dice game in the county jail and had helped me fight the time I tried to take on all the colored prisoners on the floor. Here, he and another fellow called Book-me had been running a peewee poker game. He had started me off to gambling in prison because he knew I could. I would spell him on the deal and sell chips the rest of the time. It gave me something to do besides lie on my bunk and brood, which I did a lot of, too. Also I could talk to him, which I couldn't to most of the men.

Hunky was a porter in school at first. Then he got a porter's job in the woolen mill because he thought he could make some money out of it. One of the woolen-mill companies bunked in the dormitory with us across the aisle, and he was just transferred from one side of the dormitory to the other. Then one day he took my Sunday shirt over to the woolen mill to wash and iron it. The guard caught him washing the shirt. It was against the rules. My number was on the shirt tail so they caught me, too. The courtroom guard came around that morning before breakfast and added the two of us to the long line of convicts going to court. We were all sullen because we'd miss our breakfast, even if the deputy found us innocent, and scared because most of us were guilty and were going in the hole. The deputy transferred Hunky to the coal company. He gave me a lecture and sent me back to school. That was how I took over Hunky's half of the poker game to run for him.

There was the school, too. It consisted of eight rooms underneath the Catholic chapel. There were regular schoolroom desks arranged to face blackboards across the front of each room. There were six grades. Two rooms each were given over to the first and second grades. The latrines were in the end rooms on either side.

Each grade was divided into A and B classes. I was assigned to teach 5A. At the time they were studying predicate adjectives. I had not ever learned, or else by then had forgotten, just what a predicate adjective was. I got fired the same day I began. Guerda, the big simple-minded Dutchman whose place I had taken, was reassigned to the job. He was blowing his top over arithmetic. Most convicts have obsessions. That was his. He started right off, as in the past, and for which he had been fired, teaching his version of mathematics. It was indeed a weird and grotesque version. But he was happy. I was "seated," which meant I was demoted to the status of a 5A pupil. And I was happy, too.

A pupil's life was a happy life, if one didn't mind the sitting. We read newspapers and magazines and sneaked smokes, and shot spitballs, and drew funny pictures on the blackboards when the guards were absent. And when the guard was present we baited the teachers. When the superintendent, who was also a guard with a longer title but the same pay, came into the room, we looked intent and occupied. But if he stayed too long we would stump him with some trick question we had thought up for just such an occasion. After that we wouldn't see him again all that day.

In the mornings, for twenty minutes before we went in to wash up for dinner, we marched around the yard for exercise, and again for twenty minutes in the afternoons. But since neither we nor the guards relished walking in the snow and slush and bad weather we compromised on fifteen minutes, or even ten or five, if the deputy was not about.

That was school, more or less, if you include the books which were donated by boards of education throughout the state, and the four other companies besides ours which celled in the 1&2 block, and the programs every Friday where there was speaking and reciting and some singing by the colored convicts.

There were two things about the dormitory which could bring back the whole living, pulsing scene so vividly that I could see it and live all through it again and feel that hurt I felt then, being away from all those things that I liked. I was young and hot-blooded and passionate and liked the living, tangible things. Women and going to bed with them, drinking whiskey and gambling, sports to watch and play, a car to own and drive, the moving picture shows, and nights in a park, and the sunset on the Lake from the pier at Vigo park, and clouds after a rain, and spring—which was always as tangible to me as a woman's kiss. And being conscious of all those endless years that I could not afford to think about and that I tried so hard not to think about that pretty soon I lost all thought of anything that went below the senses of sight and hearing and smelling and feeling. But still I thought of them, those years, even with my eyes and ears and nose and skin. I thought of them with the coldness of being out in the weather with not enough clothes to keep me warm, and with the sight of guards clubbing convicts over the heads with loaded sticks, and with the smell of unwashed bodies and dirty latrines, and with the sounds of sticks banging for bedtime, and the sight of the lights winking.

The first of those two things was Giuseppe playing "In My Solitude" on his electric guitar every morning, just before breakfast, with the loud bell-clear note carrying all over the dormitory.

I never understood why that should have affected me so then that always afterward upon hearing it I could see again that goddamn dormitory and those gray convicts and those gray winter mornings with the fog and the walls and the deserted morning look of the prison yard, and feel again that utter sense of being lost in a gray eternity.

The second was Chump's console radio which Nick one of the deputy's runners who was his old man, they said had bought for him, and which Captain Charlie let him play at nights after the lights were out if the other convicts did not object.

For years I could not hear a radio without remembering Chump, seeing him lying there so proud with his Indian blood darkening his skin, and the important way he felt about owning a console radio; as if the seed of Nick had spawned the radio with him and he had birthed it.

6

THE GUARD who was on duty at the visiting hall looked at my pass and gave it back to me. "Give that back to your mother," he said. "She'll need it to get out."

He took me into the hall at the end of the 1&2 cell

block and he and the hall guard searched me. They made me leave my cap and gloves on the hall guard's table. I was afraid they might take the cap so I kept it turned down so they couldn't see the lining.

When the visiting-room guard ushered me around the corner of the 3&4 block into the long gloomy cavernous visiting hall, with the cagelike cells rearing overhead like the caves of cliff dwellers, and the cell house ceiling so high it was lost, I was still worrying about the cap.

I walked down behind the benches, behind the eating convicts. When I saw my mother I stopped and stood there for a moment, very still, looking at her and seeing her and seeing her look at me, and seeing her love for me, and feeling her eyes on mine and loving her, right then, more than I had ever loved her, or myself, or anyone, in all my life. My love for her overwhelmed me. I was choked with it.

And then I hurried forward and she stood up and we leaned across the table and kissed each other and I lost sight of her. I could feel her hands holding very tightly to my arms and after she had released me and I had sat down I could still feel them very tightly on my arms. Neither of us had spoken.

"I brought you some lunch, James," she said, moving her hands around in the basket of lunch. "I brought you some scalloped oysters. You always liked scalloped oysters."

Her voice sounded very thin and hollow as if it came out of the front part of her mouth instead of her throat. I thought of when the judge had sentenced me and I had tried to say, that's all right, that's all right, only to find that my tongue stuck to the roof of my mouth and my throat was solid and inflexible and that only my lips, in all my face and mouth and throat and chest, would move and they could not make any sound at all.

"Did you, Mother? Let me help you, Mother," I said, but I did not look at her again.

She had been looking at me, now she looked at the basket in which all the while her hands had been moving without accomplishing anything.

"Here is the tablecloth, and here are the napkins, and here are the plates," she recited, taking them out of the basket.

We spread the tablecloth very carefully. She smoothed out the wrinkles and then began to take out the silver and the food. But it did not seem real, neither our actions nor our being there in that prison—in that grimy, gloomy cell house, sitting across from each other—nor our funny, ridiculous efforts to make it real and easy and natural.

There was a dish of scalloped oysters and some potato salad and some bread and butter and a jar of jelly and some cakes. "I didn't bring you anything to drink," she said in that light, weightless voice. "I couldn't find anything to put anything in."

All along, since I first looked at her, I had not looked at her again. I had been watching her hands and looking at the tablecloth and the food and beyond her, through the open bars into a cell where the two bunks to the left of the door had been chained up for the day; at the commode and the shelf where there were pictures and jars and bottles and two combs and one brush and a homemade broom and, hanging on a line of string across the right of the cell, a wine-colored lounging robe—deep-colored against the yellow calcimined walls.

"That's all right, Mother, I don't want anything to drink." My voice sounded muffled and I cursed under my breath. "We get plenty to drink, all we want to drink." I was trying to sound natural and cheerful so that she would think I felt that way, but my voice cracked at the very top.

"You look well, James."

My fork touched an oyster and moved it on my plate. "I feel fine, too, Mother."

She was wearing the old rusty black Persian lamb coat I had bought from a guy who had claimed to be a fence, and it had turned out to be a fake. And underneath she wore a brown woolen dress.

"Do they feed you enough, James?"

Oh, God, she's trying so hard not to cry, I thought.

"They feed us pretty good."

In trying to smile I only succeeded in spreading my lips. It made me feel sick all up in the face, under and around my eyes. The muscles and the skin and all felt sick, as if they were afflicted with leprosy, and my eyes felt sick, as my stomach feels when I want to vomit, and I knew my mother wanted me to look at her but my eyes felt too raw and open and sick for me to look at her, or at anyone. I sat there with my lips spread, toying with the oysters.

"Do . . . do they hurt you any, James?"

"No, Mother. It's not all that bad." I told her about the routine and the schedule. "I was a porter in the coal company at first but now I have a job teaching school."

"I should think that would be nice," she said.

"It's all right," I said, still not looking at her.

"You're not eating anything James," she said.

I stole a glance at her and quickly looked away. "I'm not hungry, Mother. You see, we just finished dinner."

Her eyes were red where she had been crying and all around them the flesh of her eyelids was swollen and her face seemed loose; the skin seemed slack as if some inner support which had held it into shape for all those years had broken loose in her grief. Her hair, showing beneath the brim of the made-over felt hat, seemed grayer but it could have been my imagination, I told myself, but I could not look at her again to tell.

And suddenly I knew that I could not look at her, not only because I did not want her to see the sickness and the guilt and the remorse that I did not want to feel in my own eyes, but because I did not want to see the grief and the sudden age showing in her face. As if not seeing it would keep it from being there or at least keep me from having the knowledge of it by seeing it, although I knew it was there, all along, even before I had seen her. And also I did not want her to see my eyes for her own sake.

"I . . . I thought you liked the oysters that way, James. That's why I fixed them," she said, and I could hear each unshed tear on each word she said, so high and light and damp and filling up. She was trying very hard not to cry.

"I like them, Mother." I moved an oyster, lifted it up toward my mouth, lowered it. If I had put it in my mouth I would have vomited.

"I didn't write because I planned on coming down," she said.

"That's all right."

"What do you think about, James?" she asked.

"Think about?" I was startled. "Nothing. I just keep my mind a blank. It'd be better if I didn't have a mind—if I'd never had a mind."

"You were so smart, James," she said. "You might have become great and famous with your mind." And suddenly she was crying. "Oh, my baby! My little baby! You were so brilliant!"

Oh, my God, and this, I thought, saying, "Don't cry, Mother, please don't cry. I'm all right! I'm all right, Mother!"

"Oh, my little baby! My poor little baby! My poor little baby!"

On top of all the rest. . . . "Don't cry, Mother. Please don't cry. . . ." All these tears, I was thinking. All these tears after all these years, now. All of this love for me, this pure and holy love, this mother's love, and the pity. I don't want the pity. And this son's love for his mother. All this love, now, when it cannot help and does not matter. . . .

"Don't cry, Mother, please don't cry."

She got herself under control. Although I did not look at her I knew she was dabbing at her eyes, and when she took her hands down and held them, restrained and placid, on the table, the red work-coarsened hands with cracked nails, I could not look at them without crying so I looked away.

We were silent for a time.

"Do you still say your prayers, James?"

"Yes, Mother," I lied.

"Things are not so hopeless as they seem, James," she said. "The warden says that if you behave yourself and stay out of trouble you will receive time off."

"Did you see the warden?"

"Yes. I was here before the visiting hour started and he came out of his office and talked to me. He said that you appeared to be a very nice boy."

"He did?"

"He said they liked you very much."

"He did? I haven't seen him yet," I said.

"He said in twelve or thirteen years you will receive a hearing by the parole board and if you behave yourself you will be paroled."

"He said that too, eh?"

"Do try to be a good boy, James," she said.

"I will, Mother, I'll be a model. . . . I'll be a very good boy, Mother," I said. So I won't have to do but thirteen years, as the warden says, instead of twenty, I added under my breath.

She took a Bible from the bottom of the basket and gave it to me. "I want you to have this, James."

"Thanks, Mother," I said, taking it and thumbing the leaves. It was her own Bible. I'd seen it in her room since I could first remember. It was a very old book with a worn, soft-grained leather binding with the words *The Holy Bible* printed in gold leaf on the front, and written in ink on the flyleaf was my mother's maiden name and the date, *June 13th, 1919.*

"I had that before I was married," she said.

"I know." The leaves were very fine and slightly yellowed from age.

"The time is up, madam," the guard said, standing nearby. We had not seen him approach.

Her fingers, folded on the table top, and held so placidly, went rigid. Her whole body went rigid. Down the table I saw the others standing up, kissing, laughing, getting ready to leave.

I stood up quickly and she clambered to her feet and we kissed again. Her lips were trembling against mine and breaking up beneath mine and I thought, please don't let her cry again. I loved her so, not looking at her. I loved her all in my chest and my throat and my head.

As before, I could feel her hands holding very tightly to my arms, and when she let go of me I could still feel them on my arms as before.

"Good-by, James. I'll try to get down next month." She was permitted to visit me once a month. "Be a good boy and pray and read the Bible."

"Yes, Mama," I said, "I will, Mama. Good-by, Mama."

In all that time I had not looked at her again since the first time, when I had loved her so much. I turned away, holding the Bible in my hand, the book which was just so much dead weight since I had lost the God whom it promulgated. And I went down and got my cap and my yellow pigskin gloves. I held the gloves tightly in my other hand and it felt good to be holding them and knowing that they were good gloves and my very own, because they were something both good and tangile and had cost one dollar and fifty cents, and if I wanted to I could cut them up and make them not good, or I could burn them up and scatter the ashes to the wind so that in a little while they would no longer be tangible, only a memory of gloves that I had once owned which would neither give me anything nor take anything away from me, being unimportant.

Just before I stepped through the doorway I looked down the long, dimly lit range with the three cells rising in a sheer steel cliff above and the high concrete ceiling of the cell house, sixty feet overhead, and the dusty, grimy cell-house wall with the barred, grimy windows; and she was standing there, very small in the middle of all that immense masonry of steel and stone to keep in convicts who wanted out, picking up the food which I had not eaten after she had fixed it and brought it down to me, and putting it back into the basket—looking very small and very frail and very old.

7

THE NIGHT BEFORE I had let a hunky called Big John have a dollar's worth of chips in the poker game for a monkey which he had carved from a peach seed, and he broke me. When time came to pay off, Book-me, who was doubling with me, said he was flat and I had to pay him off myself. I didn't have enough and I had to owe him seven dollars and ninety-five cents.

Before breakfast the next morning Hunky Hank sent me word to send him something. They had broke him in the poker game down there in the coal company.

I wrote him a note telling him they had broke me, too. Big John got me with a dollar's worth of chips for a peach-seed monkey, I told him. Book-me was flat and I had to pay off out of my pocket and I'd come up short at that.

On the way to dinner we passed the coal company coming from the barbershop and I flipped Hunky the note. Old man Warren saw it sail through the air and snatched Hunky out of line. The last thing I saw he was frisking Hunky.

We had fried salt pork and potatoes for dinner. I was saving the salt meat to the last because I liked it best. Before I got to it Warren and Donald Duck came into the dining room and called Book-me, Big John and myself from the table.

"What've I done?" asked Book-me.

"Come on, come on, no back talk," Warren rasped.

Warren hadn't made out a report card and either of our company guards, Bull or Clem, could have stopped him from taking us, but they didn't. We went out of the front entrance and turned down in front of the hospital.

"What you taking me to the hole for?" Book-me asked again. "I ain't done nothing."

"Gambling, that's what. You've been running a big poker game every night."

"What the hell you got to do with that?" Book-me said. "You ain't my guard."

Book-me and Big John and I were walking ahead of Warren and Donald Duck. Warren hit him across the back of the head without warning. Book-me fell forward in a sudden arc, caught himself halfway down, turned slightly and staggered off balance. The blow had knocked his hat askew and when he started into Warren it fell on the sidewalk and his hair fell thinly across his forehead. I turned quickly to face Warren and stepped back off the sidewalk.

In looking at Warren I did not see Book-me but I saw Warren draw back again, and when he swung I switched my gaze to Book-me's face and saw his mouth loose and his eyes wide as he came in. I saw the stick hit him across the forehead just above the eye and underneath the flagging hair. A dead white slit appeared on his forehead as if it had been cut open with a knife, and all the sense went out of his eyes. Still in a crouch he went down again, falling into Warren's legs. Warren hit him again and I said, blinking out the nausea, "Goddammit, son of a bitch, don't hit him again! Don't hit him again! Can't you see he's down?"

He had his stick raised and, turning slightly, he struck at me. I caught the blow on my arm and backed up, backing across the ankle-deep slush. He came on and I turned away from him and began walking rapidly toward the hole, pride holding me down to a walk, and fear pulling at my nerves like a million tiny hands until I felt stiff as wood. With every step I kept bracing myself for the blow across the back of the head, and listening for his footsteps behind me, telling myself that if he hit me and didn't knock me out I'd kill him. All the while I kept trying to determine whether the indignity which I had already suffered was worth dying for. I went as far as the hole without looking back, feeling as if I'd fly into a million pieces with the slightest touch.

Big John was standing in the waiting room door. When I came in he said, "They're taking Book-me to the hospital." Looking in the direction I saw two nurses lifting Book-me onto the stretchers.

"They could pick him up and throw him into the hospital," I said. "What they need the stretchers for?" I was just making words.

Big John grunted. Suddenly I was sweating like a horse, all up in my hair and underneath my eyes and back of my neck and in the palms of my hands. I could feel it on my legs, turning icy cold as it seeped from my skin.

We saw Warren and Donald Duck coming toward us. We went to the back and sat down. They brought the deputy and Gout with them. Gout was a short, pot-bellied man with turned-in toes and a swagger, if you can imagine a pigeon-toed, pot-bellied, wrinkled squeezed-in face without teeth, owlish-looking under the pulled-down visor, with a swaggering walk. He had evil, dirty-gray eyes behind gold-rimmed spectacles. The other convicts called him Froggy Hitler. But I always called him Gout. I couldn't improve on that.

His cap bore the legend: *Personnel Officer*. But his duties were those of a transfer clerk. Most of the tranferring of the convicts from one company to another was left to him, although the deputy could overrule his decisions. During the court sessions he acted as prosecutor. Between transfer officer and court prosecutor he had built up the reputation of the dirtiest, meanest, lousiest, lowest, rottenest officer in prison. It was also said that he was a stool pigeon for the warden, who did not get along with the deputy warden, and that he told the warden everything that went on inside the walls. The warden seldom came inside the walls. Before taking that job Gout had been captain of an ore freighter. That had been years before. I never learned why he gave up a good job like that to become a prison guard. But I always wondered. I could never see him as anything but a little old man with a big warped belly.

He gave me one look and reared back, his bloated, froglike body pulling his uniform askew, and put his hands on his hips. "I'll put this one in the soup company," he said, referring to me, "and this one in 1-11." He turned to the deputy. "Give them a taste of the hole first."

"Wait a minute," I began. "I haven't even had a trial."

The deputy ignored us both. He had a sardonic hipped look that morning, aloof and amused and indifferent. I'd heard that what he didn't know about convicts wasn't in the book; that he had a perfect espionage system. He had been deputy warden for seventeen years.

Before he'd come after us Warren had gone over to our dormitory and searched our bunks for cards and chips. He hadn't found any. I kept them at another convict's bunk who had a locked box. But he had found a slice of bread underneath Big John's mattress.

He showed the deputy the note I'd written to Hunky

and the slice of bread he had found. The deputy put Big John in the hole. He told me to sit there. They went outside, the deputy walking straight with short, fast steps and Gout rearing back and trying to swagger, and Warren walking stooped over like an old man, looking out the sides of his eyes at the deputy while he talked, and Donald Duck bringing up the rear, placing his tender feet down on the pavement as cautiously as a man playing chess.

From where I sat I could see across the yard. After a time the companies began emptying from the dining room, the short leaders setting the pace, the tall men tapering off behind them, two by two, stepping out as the line closed up. White men in front, colored men behind. One line and then another until they strung out in four solid lines from the dining room to the four cell houses. And still they came, like an unending story, like the locusts out of the rock. Then suddenly without a trace they were gone. They were gone without a sign that they'd ever been there, without their footprints in the slush. It was startling.

After the guards had eaten, Gout transferred me to the coal company. The first person I saw was Hunky.

"What the hell did you put all those names on that note for?" he greeted me.

"I wasn't thinking."

"Did they hurt Book-me bad?"

"I don't know," I said.

"What'd they do with Big John?"

"Put him in the hole."

Old man Warren came up and chased him away. Warren was happy to have me back with him. "Look at him, men, here he is," he said, stopping the whole job so they could hear him ride me. "Got one fellow's head whipped and another put in the hole. Look at him. A big shot. The chaplain wanted him for a teacher but he couldn't even do that. Running a big syndicated poker game." Some of his rats laughed for him. "Look at him, right back in the coal company."

He looked at me over his glasses. "Which would you prefer to do, *Mister* Monroe? Would you prefer to roll or is rolling beneath your dignity?" That got another laugh out of his rats.

I didn't say anything. I hated his guts. He put me to rolling, without even assigning me to a bunk. But I beat that rap. When old man Warren picked up the afternoon sick call I said I had cramps. That was the one sure thing they'd take you to the hospital for.

In the afternoon the prison doctor was usually absent. His convict assistant held sick call. The regular sick-call line formed at the back of the hospital on Monday, Wednesday and Friday mornings. It was usually a half-mile long. But once each day the company guards took the critical cases over to the hospital lobby.

It was an old gabled building of century-old American architecture. It had a brick base beneath the clapboards and a cupola with a weathercock. There was the main section, extending fore and aft, flanked by wings. Part of the basement was used for a storeroom. A colored cripple company bunked in another part. During the winter the two prison alligators, Ben and Bessie, were housed in a tank of tepid water with the colored cripples.

Warren lined us up in the main hall before the reception desk. There were eight of us. The convict doctor was dressed in a starched white uniform. When it came my turn I told him my back pained me severely and that I was a patient of the industrial commission and drew compensation for total disability and they had me rolling coal which I wasn't able to do. I said it all at once without giving him a chance to interrupt me.

He sent me back into the minor-surgery section to see the convict supervisor, who was a short, curly-headed Italian called Tino. He had gray in his hair and a husky voice, and a way of looking at you as if he didn't believe a word you were saying but that he was on your side, anyway.

After listening to me he went into the chartroom and drew my chart. I told him it wasn't on my chart because I'd been afraid to tell the doctor. He looked up at me, curiously. "It's all on your chart, all right," he said. He put me to bed in C ward. He didn't like old man Warren, anyway, and he would have put me to bed even without the history of my injury being on my chart.

Warren was plenty burnt up about it. But there wasn't anything he could do.

C ward was for new patients and convalescents. The beds were arranged against the wall down each side of the wide center aisle. At the front was the nurses' desk; across from it the bath. It was wonderful to take a bath in a real bathtub again. There were windows opening on the yard. I could see all the activity from my bed. At the back of the ward was a built-on porch containing another row of beds. But those seemed to be reserved for the nurses' afternoon siestas. The windows from the porch opened on the area-way by the wooden dormitory where I had bunked.

Just before supper Mal came around and sent for me to come to the back window. He wanted to know if I needed anything. He couldn't stay but a moment and he kept moving his feet and legs as if he was walking. I said I needed some smoking and my toothbrush and tooth paste. He said I looked funny in the white cotton gown. I told him to go to hell.

The day staff of our ward was two nurses and an orderly. They wore white shirts and tight-fitting white pants. All of them were very bitchy. The little cute one came into the bathroom while I was bathing and said he'd wash my back. I let him. He said his name was Harry. I'd been in too many hospitals to be nurse-shy, and I didn't know then that this was something else.

They served our supper on bed trays. There were two diets, the solid which was No. 1, and the liquid which was No. 2. I had the solid diet. It consisted of milk (or coffee), vegetable soup, bread and butter, steak, fried potatoes and a slice of pie. No wonder everyone tries to get into the hospital, I thought.

That night the paper boy brought me my toothbrush, paste, soap and towel, my bathrobe and some Bull Durham which Hunky had sent me. Later on the magazine man brought a new toothbrush, a new tube of tooth paste, a new bar of soap, a new towel, and another bathrobe which Mal sent me. With my belly full of steak, newspapers and magazines to read, plenty good service, two fine friends, I felt solid good. I could do my time there, I thought. I could lie up there without moving and be satisfied for twenty years.

At six o'clock, when the shift changed, the day nurses donned their uniform coats and took a brisk walk about the yard, grouping off in two and threes. They had yard privileges. That night Book-me slipped over from A ward to visit me. He gave me hell about putting all those names on that kite. I gave him some Bull Durham and tooth paste and loaned him one of the robes. That mellowed him.

Later that night I found out why Tino had put me in the hospital so readily. He was trying to make me. Before the week was out all of them had tried. Even the colored porters. I'd been so mad so long it had begun getting funny by then.

They had a system. They'd take a new convict, if he was young and good-looking, feed him well and keep him there until he was too grateful to refuse. "It's nothing to it," they'd argue. "Everybody does it." There was a song that went: "Slugs do it, bugs do it, even funny looking mugs in jugs do it," or at least that was the way they had it. They had it all worked out. If one couldn't succeed, another would try. Then, after the first one made him, they'd all have him.

The whole hospital setup was a stinking, grafting racket. The doctor came around once a day. If there wasn't anything wrong with a guy whom the nurses wanted to hold they'd chart him with a temperature. The doctor knew about it, but he didn't care.

They charged daily rentals to the big shots and sold the No. 1 diet, drugs and medicines. Every night there was a big poker game in the t.b. ward with hundreds of dollars in it. Sometimes the nurses played high-stake bridge on the porch downstairs. Everyone was either a wolf or a fag. The wolf is the so-called male of the species, a rare and almost obsolete animal. The fag is the female. And there were those who did not want to be associated with the fags, but were not actually wolves, who were loosely classified as wolverines, which was what most of the wolves were when it came to the test.

Everyone who worked in the hospital made money. Each had his own racket. They didn't make any money off me. I fell out with everyone except the supervisor, Tino, who had turned out to be a pretty good egg when he found out he couldn't make me. A lot of guys would have tried to give me a tough way to go. But he didn't ride me. He even insisted that I remain there when, in a huff one morning, I demanded my clothes and said I was getting the hell out of that whorehouse before I knocked out somebody's teeth. He said Gout would put me in the soup company but that if I stayed a couple or three weeks longer I could probably get back in school.

I didn't fall out with the cute little nurse, Harry, either. He was neither a wolf nor a wolverine but just a pleasant bitch who had a crush on me. He made it very pleasant, not sexually of course, seeing that my bed was made with clean linen every day and rubbing me with alcohol and giving me eggnog with whiskey, and now and then the whiskey without the eggnog, and more food—ham and eggs for breakfast, liver and onions for lunch, steak and vegetables and salads for supper—than I could eat. But for all of that I soon got tired of it.

It was a rotten, lousy joint. The hell of it was that they

treated degeneracy as one does normal sex, with no more shame attached to it than one attaches to promiscuousness. I hadn't been in prison long enough to see it from that view.

There were a couple of big-shot bankers up in C ward, smoking their cigars and drinking whiskey and soda and walking about the hospital, in expensive robes, as if they owned it. The doctor greeted them with his horse-toothed smile as if they hired him by the day; which they probably did. That made me understand, more clearly than ever, the difference between robbing a bank from the inside and the outside.

The gangsters got on, too—in fact anyone did who could produce the dough or who was young enough and good-looking enough and willing enough. It was a strictly money-and-sex proposition and if a poor bastard was really sick they patched him up and sent him out before he could embarrass them.

A week of that stuff was enough for me. I felt polluted. I felt as if I had fallen into a cesspool. Every day some poor bastard would die and the doctor would go into another ward and crack about it. The nurses would say to the porters, "Another mattress for the passing show."

To hell with the school company, I thought. To hell with all the companies. I didn't give a damn where they put me, in the soup company or wherever else they damn well pleased. I was getting out. The barber had just gotten through shaving me. He had left my face raw and bleeding. I had called him a fink and he had started at me with the razor. I had picked up the basin of water, of all things. I must have thought I was going to drown him. If Tino hadn't come in and stopped it I don't know where it might have ended, probably with me getting cut.

It was Thursday morning in the middle of March with no break showing in the weather. I was transferred straight from the hospital to the soup company. But I wasn't finished with the hospital.

A week later I caught a cold. I let it get worse, hoping it would get better. In the end I had to go back to the hospital on the Monday-morning sick call, and stand in the line sticking out the back entrance deep into the yard. It was snowing that morning. We were like a line of Monday wash caught in the snow, only we were ragged convicts instead of ragged clothes; underfed and underclothed, standing there in the subfreezing weather to wait our turn at the desk they rigged up for the doctor, in front of minor surgery, to hold sick call. He sat there, flanked by his staff, and dosed out pink tea to everyone who passed. Pink tea was a concentrated solution of Epsom salts with a dash of croton oil. The medicine was saved for the paying patients. He dosed out abuse, too, oral and physical, slapping a convict here, hitting another in the mouth.

There were some with cramps and bloody piles and inflamed appendixes and tumors and cancer and lungs shot to hell; waiting for a shot of this, a bottle of lousy cough sirup, a tin of salve, an emergency operation, a last six months in the t.b. ward, a violent, vulgar, delirious death. Waiting in the goddamn cold.

When I stepped inside the door to wait, with my back pressed against the wall for the line to move up, I saw a burning Bunsen burner. It was all I could do to keep from picking it up and setting myself on fire.

By then, standing in the cold, I'd lost my voice. I couldn't make a sound. All I could do was move my lips. The doctor, the big fleshy Dutch bastard with his flapping white jacket and soiled vest and contempt, thought I was being fresh because he hadn't looked up to see my lips moving, and thought I hadn't answered when he'd asked, "What's the matter with you? What's the matter with you?" He acted as if he was going to get up and slap me. It was said about him that, on losing his third patient on the operating table one morning, he became alarmed and furious and began whining, "What the hell they keep dying for?"

But if he had slapped me that morning there would have been a dead Monroe or a dead doctor. More than likely a dead Monroe. I never saw but two convicts who had killed guards. They were serving life. Both of them had been beaten on the head until they were slap-happy. But they had killed the guards before my time.

It was there, in minor surgery at that same desk, that the syphilitic cases were given arm and hip shots of mercury and Salvarsan. I never knew why they didn't give them penicillin; maybe it cost too much. When they hit some of those poor suckers in the rump or arm they reeled away, vomiting. Their hair would come out and their teeth would fall out. They'd lose their sight and go deaf. A few were cured. The nurses shot them. The nurses were exceptionally rough and impatient on those occasions. It seemed as if they hoped everyone they shot would drop dead so they wouldn't be troubled again.

8

THE SOUP COMPANY, one of Gout's brain children, was created for the sick, they said; for those who had stomach trouble and ulcers and couldn't eat the main-line grub and needed to be on a diet, but weren't sick enough to warrant hospitalization.

It was the 2-10 company on the second tier of 10 cells in the 10&11 cell block, the last of the old, crumbling, dark, damp, dim cell blocks of a past era when prisons were patterned, it seemed, after the dungeons of the medieval ages. It now seemed ready to crumble and fall. There were rotten wooden ranges, that trembled beneath each step, enclosed by waist-high iron railings. The cells had flat latticed bars, so closely interlaced as to make it almost impossible to see inside of them.

"Here we are," the runner said, stopping before cell No. 17. A name plate with the name, Green-100297, hung from the bars at the head of the bottom bunk. The name was flanked by the letters *P* and *T* which designated that Green was a Protestant and that he retained his tobacco privileges. At that time we were given a plug of chewing tobacco on Wednesday, and a twist of dry tobacco that could be used for chewing or smoking, on Saturday. Whenever a convict lost his tobacco privilege the T on his name plate was painted out.

The runner tried the cell door but found it locked. I hung my name plate on the bars at the head of the upper bunk and put my things on the range. The runner went for the guard.

"Ain't your name Monroe?" The voice came from inside the cell, but the lights had been dimmed for the day and I couldn't see the fellow well.

"Yeah, bud. Who're you—Green?"

"Naw, that's just an alias. My name's Starlight."

"Yeah?"

From up the range a voice asked, "Did you get that new fellow, Mac?"

"Naw, Starlight got him in the next cell."

"I got him. All you punks shut up and don't start any signifying."

I still had the two bathrobes and a big brass-bound box. They must have thought I was prosperous.

"You sure are lucky, punk," someone said to Starlight. It was like when a gambler gets a chump in a gambling joint and gets him off to himself in a head-and-head game. He feels good and the other chiselers are envious.

"Do you guys always fight over cell buddies?" I kidded.

"Tell him when they're like him we do," the voice from up the range said.

"What say, Nig?" Starlight said.

"Hiyuh, punk." The new voice was deep and startling.

I looked around. Down below, on the first range, stood the biggest colored man I've ever seen. His shoulders and chest were immense. He was in his shirt sleeves and his black shaved head shone like a billiard ball.

"Hello, good-looking," he said to me. He had a cigar in the corner of his mouth.

I started to ignore him. Then I said, "What say, bud?"

"Don't pay any attention to him," Starlight said. "That's Nig. He's crazy."

"I'll come up there and pop you in your kisser," Nig said.

"Come on," Starlight said. "I'll knock you on your can."

"Come on and get him, Nig," Mac said from the next cell.

"You want to watch that punk—Starlight," Nig said to me. I didn't answer.

"What you saying, Nig?" someone called from down the range.

"Hello, Wop, how you was, kid?"

Another colored convict came out from beneath the range and looked up at me. He was taller than Nig, but thinner, with a long neck and a ball of kinky hair. "He's a burner, ain't he?" he said. Several other smaller colored convicts came out to look at me.

"Ooooowah, man, he's a burner, ain't he?" the skinny convict said again. He had a loud jubilant voice.

"What say, Feet?" Starlight said.

"Don't talk to me, fellow. You tricked me on that prize fight."

"He got you good, didn't he, Feet?" one of the colored convicts said.

"Man, don't say a thing. That fellow beat me out of fifty sacks."

Nig was talking to a fellow down the range. Starlight and Feet were talking. All in a loud voice, ignoring the others. Shortly the runner returned with the guard. He unlocked the cell and let me in. Nobody stopped talking. I carried my things inside and let down my bunk from the wall. Then I looked the cell over. I'd celled in one similar to it when I'd first entered, up on 5-11. But I'd been so frightened at that time I'd never really seen what the cells looked like.

They were narrow and had low, rounded ceilings. The walls and ceilings had been painted with a thick coating of greenish-yellow calcimine which was now beginning to flake. The two bunks hung from the wall by chains. They were made of a framework of steel and wood to which we attached the heavy wire mesh on which the mattress rested. The crevices between the steel and wood were bedbug paradises. Bugs lived and bred in there by the thousands, literally by the millions. Neither fire nor water nor bug juice nor anything except burning the bunks could get them out.

Some of the convicts stole paint and painted their cells in attempts to get rid of them. Others put axle grease about the legs of their bunks, the hinges at the wall, and covered the chains. They even made barricades of grease along the floor at the front of the cell to keep the bugs from entering. Once a year the cells were fumigated. But nothing ever got rid of them. Like the dampness in the old crumbling walls, they were always there.

We used to trap them with mirrors or shiny tin tops placed about the floor. They would crawl up on the ceiling and drop off until the shiny surfaces were black with them. This could keep up all night and the next night and every night. And a year later you could catch as many in a single night as you did at first. On a quiet night you could hear them dripping from the ceiling like drops of water. We'd mash them and trap some more.

I never learned why they crawled up on the ceiling and dropped off on the shiny surfaces. Maybe they were attracted by the light. Most of the time they'd climb up and drop on our faces, and our white pillow cases, and get fat with blood and roll off to the floor, and the next morning we'd find them lying there so full of blood they couldn't move. It didn't do any good to try to smoke them out of the crevices. They would only come out and hide in the bunk. That night you'd be afraid to go to bed. Every time the guard came by you'd have to be sitting on your bucket. I tried it once and set my bunk on fire, and Starlight jumped up and threw the bucket of urine on my pillow case to put it out.

Each of us had a bucket. The 2-11 company on the opposite side of the cell block from us, came around each morning after breakfast and emptied the buckets in a sewer down at the end of the first range. We put our buckets out on the range and they came and collected them and it was somewhat of a disgrace to be put in that company.

But they had a chance to make money and a lot of convicts asked to be put in the bucket company in preference to the soup company. They rented the newer, cleaner, better buckets and kept them disinfected for you. If you couldn't afford to pay them you always got the oldest, most battered buckets, and they were never rinsed or disinfected. It didn't help much if both of the convicts in a cell didn't do it.

On summer days the odor hung in the cells like some vile miasma, thick and putrid, with no relief. There was always an argument and generally a fight when one of the cell mates had to take a physic.

At the end of the range was a long wooden washtrough, similar to those in the dormitories. The water was turned on for five minutes before each meal and half of the company came out at a time and washed. It was then I got my first look at the other fellows in the company. They were a seedy lot with that decayed familiarity of convicts who have lost their pride. There were six cells of colored convicts in the company.

"I thought the men in here were sick," I said to Starlight.

"Hell, naw, ain't nobody in here sick. This is where Gout puts the men he calls 'agitators.' Most of them are gunsels and fags. They got Mother Jones and Snookums in here."

"Who?"

"Oh, they're just a couple of nigger punks. Mother Jones is a tall, bald-headed nigger and Snookums is the little nigger with the straightened hair and red tie."

"Yeah?" I'd seen them go by to wash up.

"They got Chump Charlie, Nick's Indian kid, in here too; and Wop and Blackie."

"Are all of them queer?"

"They're notorious."

"When did they transfer Chump Charlie? I was in the dormitory with him."

"Oh, just last week."

I knew I wouldn't like that company. When we lined up for dinner I was placed between Chump and a bushy-headed Armenian convict, named Mac, who talked so fast his words had no meaning whatsoever. I didn't talk to either of them.

Dinner consisted of soup and bread and coffee. Supper was the same soup, thinned out and warmed over, with tea instead of coffee. Breakfast was some sort of cereal with real milk and sugar—usually it was rice or oatmeal—and coffee. Everyone bellyached about the food, cursed Gout, the warden, and luck. They said they were going to see Jumpy Stone and get out of that company. No one ever did.

After dinner we returned to the cells. The range boy brought me two blankets, a sheet and a pillowcase. One of the blankets was so dusty, dust spilled from it at a touch.

"Why the hell didn't you shake this out before you brought it up here?" I said.

"Not allowed to," he said.

"This is Jimmy Monroe. You want to look out for him," Starlight told the range boy. The range boy went off without replying.

I started to make my bunk. The mattress was old and flat and grimy with a big stain in the center. The other side had dark stains which looked like blood.

"I'll get the range boy to get you a cover," Starlight said.

"Oh, to hell with it!"

A hopelessness overwhelmed me. I felt as if I would never be able to make my twenty years.

There was a stool for the upper bunk and I stood on it and spread the sheet. The working companies came in shortly after we'd eaten. There were three setups in the dining room. The first was for the dining-room workers and ourselves. The second was for the idle companies. The third was called the main line. It was for the working companies. Shortly after they'd come in, the working companies lined up for dinner. There was a banging of steel doors, loud curses, shouts, laughter, and the guards knocking their sticks and calling out their company numbers: "Thoid Ten . . . Third 'Leven . . . Fourth 'Leven . . . Fifth Ten. . . ." I wondered why they didn't call them out in rotation.

After the working companies came back the guards had dinner. Then, after that, all of us left the cell block. The working convicts went back to work and the rest of us to the idle house.

The idle house was a big box of a room on the third floor of an old crumbling mill building. It was filled with hard wooden benches, spaced a foot apart, facing from the ends toward a wide center aisle. There was a guard-stand by the door and one in each corner and two on each side. At the far end of the center aisle was the latrine. As all the latrines in prison, it was unenclosed. And it stank.

Grimy windows let in the light of gray March days. Now put a rickety wooden outside staircase, very steep and wobbly, ascending from the brick walk below, and fill the place to overflowing with cold, stale, smelly convicts jammed side-by-side on the benches and not allowed to read, or talk, or smoke; and only to go to the latrine with a guard's permission.

No convict but a fool would sit there on those hard benches all day and go crazy doing nothing. They read papers, books, magazines; played cards, checkers, and other games, on the benches out of sight of the guards; shot dice on the floor, using a felt-lined cigar box in which to shake the dice; smoked cigarettes, fanning the smoke out of sight to the floor; and mush-faked. Mush-faking was the major industry within the prison. It was the manufacture of gadgets such as cigarette holders and lighters and jewel boxes and rings and pins and similar items from old bones, toothbrush handles, copper coins and gold crowns.

Our company sat on three benches at the north end. There was a small room partitioned off behind us where the prison band practiced. The colored convicts from all of the companies sat together at the other end of the idle house. All day long the band played. It was a very loud and brassy band. It played marches and marches and more marches until you could close your eyes and see the gray convicts marching through the gray days. When the band guard had to leave, for some reason or other, the convicts immediately stopped playing and began a crap game. The convicts from the idle house would crawl down between the benches and slip into the band room to join them.

As soon as we were settled the fellows began getting acquainted with me. "Weren't you the fellow old man Warren caught writing that note?"

"He didn't get it off of me. He got it off of Hunky."

"I saw old Hunky right after that. He said the note

fell into his inside coat pocket and he couldn't find it. Old Fuss Face found it even before he knew where it was himself."

"Yeah? He didn't tell me."

"They sapped up on Book-me, didn't they?"

"Yeah. I hated to see that."

"Say, was that your mother I saw visiting you the other day?" someone called from the end of the bench.

"Yeah." I had to answer them. They didn't have anything else to do.

"Too bad about Big John."

"Damn right," I said. "Put him in the hole over a dried slice of bread."

"I mean about him dying."

"Dying?" I gave a start. "When did he die?"

"He died in the hole. Didn't you hear about it? Caught pneumonia. He told Kish and the guard he was sick but they wouldn't take him to the hospital."

"Damn!" I said. "Damn!"

They asked me about my charge and my sentence and whether I had graduated from college, sure enough, and how old I was and did I expect to get a pardon?

"Hell, you have to be a big shot to get a pardon," somebody said.

"Maybe he's a big shot," another convict answered.

Blackie asked me if I wanted to read his paper. He had moved over to sit next to me. I told him I got a paper.

"You know, it seems to me I've seen you in Toledo."

That was the old approach. I'd gotten used to it by then. "You might have," I said. I'd never been to Toledo but he was a likable-looking little fellow. He was about five feet, three inches tall and weighed about a hundred and twenty. He had long, curly black hair and features that were chiseled so finely they looked fragile. His skin was dead white. When his hair became mussed he looked very girlish.

"When we go in, stop by my cell, I've got something I want to show you," he said. "It's cell No. 13."

"Okay." I didn't stop by his cell. I knew that the best way to keep out of trouble was to keep in your place. But I let him down lightly. I stopped and whispered through the bars as I passed, "The hack's watching me."

That night I asked Starlight about him. "What the hell did a kid like him do to get in here?"

"Who, Blackie? Man, he's every bit of thirty-five years old. He was a machine gunner for the Lucky Lou mob.

Doing double life for machine-gunning two guys in Blackstone Park."

The guard shift changed at six. After supper, when they had locked the men in their cells and taken the count, they relaxed and prepared to leave. For the most part they congregated in the stair well, down at the end of the cell blocks known as the hall, and shot the bull. During that time the convicts did all their extra-cell business. They shouted from cell to cell, from range to range, passed notes, passed objects down the range, someone in each cell moving it along. It was a time of great activity. The range boys who celled in the first cells of each range were still out. They were busy as cats covering up crap, hustling their change—doing whatever anyone wanted done for a price. The convicts passed objects from one range to another by tying them to strings, throwing them over the range and lowering away. When the object reached the desired range another convict would reach out of his cell and draw in the object with a wire hook. Then the sender would shout down directions, and it would be passed on to the next cell to be passed on down to its destination. Every convict had some sort of mirror, if only a broken fragment, and whenever a convict started a note or a package down the range he'd angle his mirror in the bars so he could watch its progress. We could also watch the guards in this way. Although it was against the rules to have such implements, and if caught with them it meant time in the hole, every cell had a hook, a string, a mirror, and many of the convicts had knives, clubs, sections of pipe, homemade blackjacks, and other instruments of aggression and defense.

The cell lights were turned on after supper, to remain on until bedtime. I began to read my morning paper which had been stuck into my cell by the paper boy in my absence. But Starlight wanted to talk. He told me about the time he was a member of The Syndicate, and about the automobiles he had owned and the thousands of dollars he had won in dice games in the army. Every convict had owned at least two Cadillacs and had at least fifty thousand dollars in civilian life.

He was a short, fat, redheaded guy who thought he looked like a prize fighter. Actually he looked like a chubby, good-natured little runt. He was. He told me that they called him the Boston Red Squirrel and that he was in for driving the getaway car during a bank robbery. He said he drew eighty dollars a month disability pension and that he had been General MacArthur's orderly.

The routine of the soup company was: Get up at six, wash, breakfast, idle house, cells and wash, dinner, cells, idle house, cells and wash, supper, cells, bedtime. Saturday afternoons we remained in the cells. Sunday mornings we went to church. We took our buckets to the dining room Sundays at dinnertime and brought back a half-bucket of soup and two slices of bread for our supper. Those of us who had money bought sandwiches and slices of pie from fellows on the other ranges.

On Tuesdays and Thursdays we went to the barbershop and on Fridays to bathe. The bathhouse was across from the idle house. There was a waiting room inside where we stood in line until our numbers were called. Then we stepped to the counter and received our change of clothing from the commissary clerk. Afterward we marched into the showers. In the center, benches surrounded a platform. We sat on the benches, undressed, piled our clothes on the platform. When we were all undressed we stood beneath the showers, often three and four men to each shower. The guard signaled the attendant who turned on the water. Always the water was too cold or too hot. It stayed on for three minutes. We dried and dressed and filed out the doorway, dropping our soiled socks into a basket, under the watchful eyes of the guard. We had to hold up our shirts and underwear, extended so that the guard could see that they had not been cut or torn. This was to keep us from tearing our clothes to get new ones, or holding out so we could get extras. We turned in our towels and got clean ones. That was our weekly bath.

Each morning we were required to sweep our cells. We were not furnished with brooms. We used old newspapers. Afterward the range boy came along and swept the range. If the guard wasn't watching he'd just sweep it off below, where it blew back into the cells and on the ranges beneath. Once a week he would bring around a pail of water and a mop. The water was strong with lysol. Each of us mopped our own cells. He never changed the water. We mopped the twenty-seven cells with the same bucket of water.

"Jim, you ought to give the range boy something," Starlight told me once. "He can do you favors."

"Give him what?"

"Oh, a couple of twists a week will do. Just let him keep

your state-issue tobacco. You never use it, anyway, and they're the pettiest chiselers in the joint."

"What the hell do I want to give him my tobacco for?"

"Oh, he can do you a lot of favors. He can carry messages and pass papers and packages. He can connect with the yard runners and get stuff from all over the joint."

"That's right, too," I agreed. I'd been using the paper boys but I had to give them something each time.

"You have to give everybody a handout," Starlight said. "Everybody in here's got a racket. You have to pay the waiters in order to get something to eat. You have to pay the nurses and the doctors in order to get into the hospital. You have to pay the bucket boy before he'll clean out your bucket."

"Damn right, you have to pay to get your clothes washed if you own any of your own, like handkerchiefs and pajamas and underwear and stuff. If you put them in the laundry you'll never get them back."

"But if you give the commissary clerk a handout he'll furnish you with tailor-made shirts. You pay for everything," he said. "Maybe you don't know it but they charge you for your clothes, your food and all the medicine you get from the hospital. That's why nobody ever has any earnings when they turn 'em loose. You know we're supposed to be getting eighteen cents a day for working in here but some of these poor bastards work for twenty years in here and when they go home all they get is the lousy ten-dollar bill the state gives them."

"Hell, you can get that if you don't do a lick of work," I said.

"Sure. You get more for not working than you do for working. That's why I don't do any work. You don't get nothing but a pain in the ass from working."

"You get the t.b. if you work in the mills," I said. I'd heard that.

"Work in those mills and get the t.b. and die and then they won't even give you nothing but a plain wood box to be buried in." We were just shooting the bull to pass off the time; neither of us really gave a damn about it.

"The only thing you get in here worth a damn for your earnings is some teeth," he said. "They'll give you some gold teeth."

"Yeah? I didn't know that."

"Sure, they'll give you gold teeth. But they ain't worth a damn. They're about ninety-per cent brass and canker in your mouth. They turn green in a week and give you cancer of the stomach. A son of a bitch's got the toothache, so he figures he'll get some gold teeth. Next goddamn thing he's got the cancer and is dead as hell. It don't pay. If you ever have any dentist work done you better pay for it out your pocket."

"Can you do that?"

"Sure. You can buy anything in this joint you want. Whisky, dope. You can pay these guards to take letters out for you. They'll bring in stuff for you, too. I got a buddy in the construction company who it costs a hundred dollars a month, at the very least, just to live in here. Hell, I used to buy three meals a day myself. I used to have a big radio set but it cost me so much to keep it up I had to sell it."

I was getting tired of his crap by then. "Damn right," I said, ending it. "Everything in here's a racket."

"That's the setup," he said. "The only thing you can get plenty of in here, without paying for it in some way or another, is hell."

"And that's free," I said. And that wasn't a lie, I found out. That was the solid truth.

9

THERE WERE many things that happened during that time but all of them that I remember happening, happened to me. They happened to me in sight and in feeling and in smelling and in hearing; emotionally and spiritually. The seasons happened to me. Spring was as heady as a drink of rare old wine, and white clouds in a high blue summer sky happened to me like a choking up of tears. The routine happened to me and the discipline; and being locked up with Starlight to smell his unique stink which he said came from being poisoned by Jap wine in the war; and the sight of the convicts happened to me. Nights happened to me and made me want to see the sky and the stars and smell it out at night.

But nothing lingered, neither the shocks, nor the scares, nor the laughs, nor the hurts. Nothing had a past or a future and when the feeling or the emotion happened, stirring up its definite sensation, that was all. I could not bring it back to conjure up that laugh again, nor could it come back of its own accord to bring those tears.

Each moment was absolute, like a still-life photograph; each happening lived its span and died, unrelated to the ones that came before and afterward. A day was not the seventh part of a week, but in itself infinity.

I thought through seeing and smelling and feeling, and many times I was deeply touched, angered, sickened, amused, frustrated, shocked, but none of these outlived the sensation which spawned them—the simple sound, the simple smell. Everything was an odor, a sound, a picture; hot or cold, blunt or sharp, amusing or irritating.

That was present tense. It was timeless, governed neither by the seasons nor the years, neither by the past nor the future, but in itself complete. It was not automatic because there was thought in it; nor was it meditative because that almost always is retrospective and it was not retrospective. What it was, in fact, as any old-timer could have told me, I was simply doing time.

But although there was thought in it, it was not necessary to think in order to survive. Everything necessary to survival was in a pattern, an old and musty pattern that some poor convict had used before you got there, and which some poor convict would use after you were gone, and which, like the gray stone walls, was eternal. There was no need for retrospection, nor introspection, nor even experience. If you had never lived before, anywhere at all, you still would have no need to know how it was done, as it was all down in the pattern.

The things that happened in the pattern are not the things which stand out most clearly in recollection, but are the things which are completely gone. Only the pattern is remembered, such as dinner, which is not remembered as the midday meal on a Tuesday, February 21st, but as two thousand six hundred and forty-five midday meals strung out like an endless chain of plates of beans and potatoes and cabbage. The things which stand out clearly are those which were done in contradiction or discord with the pattern. So it was with the things that happened to me during my time in the soup company.

The first day of spring happened, but it happened only on the calendar. The day itself was cold and dreary with the bleakness that comes alone to prison—gray, gray top, gray bottom, gray men, gray walls, dull-toned and unrelieved, with the sky so low you could feel the weight of it on your shoulders. At first there was slush underfoot, soggy and soot-blackened, and then the rains came. I learned then what they meant by it never rains in prison. We marched through the rain with our caps pulled low and our collars turned high.

"Take those hands out your pocket! You had 'em out all winter, now you don't want to get them wet."

It was not raining. Fog was the only thing that kept us in our cells.

The warden had us new men over to talk to us. He was the remnants of a large man gone to seed, dressed in an expensive suit made for that man and much too large in the shoulders for the remnant of the man, and too small in the waistline for where he had all gone to. His head was practically bald and his face, seamed and sagging, looked as if it had melted through the years and had run down into his jowls which, in turn, had dripped like flaccid tallow onto his belly. His shoulders had sagged down onto his belly too, so that now his whole skinny frame seemed built to keep his belly off the ground. He had sickly white, vein-laced hands which made one nauseated to look at them. He wore a huge diamond on his second finger.

What he said, boiled down, was simply that he was tough. That any man so completely decayed could wield the power to make himself tough to four thousand human beings so much stronger was a sickening realization.

That night Nig and the night guard had it. Nig was yelling up to some convict on 3-10 and the guard, walking down the second range, heard him. The guard stopped, took the cigar from his mouth, spat on the range, and called below, "Pipe down, down there! What the hell you think this is, a levee camp?" He was standing in front of our cell.

"Come down and make me," Nig called up.

The guard reddened. He was a young, medium-built, dark-haired man with a bluish growth of whiskers. Instead of the regulation uniform he wore a pin-striped, double-breasted blue suit. He kept his coat unbuttoned so we could see the bright butt of the thirty-eight special he wore in the shoulder holster, and after seeing the gun we could smell narcissus perfume, whisky and cheap cigars. That always made me think of whores—the lousy kind. "I'll come down and break your skull, you black nigger bastard!" he snarled.

"Come on."

Someone laughed. He rushed down the range, tugging at his gun. I was excited.

"Come on down, punk," Nig said.

"What'll he do to him?" I asked Starlight.

"Who? You mean what'll Short Britches do to Nig?"

I nodded.

"Nothing. He's not even going down there. Nig's one bad nigger. He's got some old white canvas gloves he puts on and he fights these roaches as fast as they can gang up. Man, he can knock a man down without even drawing back. I've seen him fighting so many of them they hit each other's sticks hitting at him, and every time he hit one of them he'd knock 'im down."

"Yeah?" I didn't believe it. He wasn't my hero. "Why don't they shoot him?"

"Aw, Jumpy Stone thinks he's crazy. He won't let them shoot him."

"Yeah." But he was wrong about the guard not going down there.

Pretty soon I heard the guard down below. "What's the matter with you, Nig?"

"Aw, take it easy, punk. Gimme one of those good smellin' cigars you're smoking."

"You know it's against the rules to talk out of your cell."

"Aw, forget about it, punk. Gimme a cigar."

After a time, after the guard had gone and we couldn't even hear his footsteps, I saw the bluish cigar smoke coming up over the range and smelt the smoking cigar. It looked to me as if Nig was the tough one in that prison.

But the next night I changed my mind in favor of the guard. He took two convicts out of their cells, sapped them with his blackjack, and locked them back again. "Now let that be a lesson."

The block was silent. Then someone yelled from down at the far end, on top somewhere, "Lay down, you bastard."

"I'll come up there and sap you, too."

"You'll come up here and get this." But the convict knew that the guard couldn't locate him.

The night after that two colored convicts down below

got to arguing after the lights had gone out. The guard went down to quiet them in the rough.

"Oh! Oh! Please doan hit me no mo', cap'n. Please doan hit me no mo', cap'n. Ah wasn't doin' nuttin'."

"Short Britches got him another one," Starlight said.

"What the hell's the matter with you black bastards? Every damn night you get into an argument."

"Cap'n, Ah wasn't doin' nuttin. It's him. He walks all night an' keeps me wake."

"What's the matter with you, nigger?"

There was no answer. I had a feeling that the whole cell block was awake and listening.

"Smart nigger, eh? Come on out of there!" I heard the slight suction of the gun being pulled from the oiled holster, the snap of the safety, or perhaps the cocking of the trigger. It was very quiet. "Come out or I'll blow you out."

"Aw, let that poor bastard alone, he's crazy," someone up on our range said.

"Come out, goddammit!"

The Negro came out. His coat was half on, his cap was on backwards. He was coal black and African-looking.

Starlight was standing on the stool so he could get a better view below. "That's Marcus," he whispered. "He's really crazy."

The guard kicked Marcus. After they'd come out on the range I could see them from my upper bunk. Marcus started to run, then stopped suddenly, looking back over his shoulder at the guard, grinning, his eyes white slits in his blank stupid face. He looked crazy as hell. It gave me the creeps. Then he ran out of sight and the guard went out of sight after him. I heard the outer door open and bang shut. I slid back beneath the covers.

"Short Britches is just trying to be like Two-gun Tracy," Starlight said. "We had a young guard in here named Tracy. About my size. He was a real sport. . . ."

I wasn't listening. About fifteen minutes later I heard distant gunshots; one, then two more, then one, then a whole fusillade. Then silence.

"That was inside," Starlight said.

"Say, you hear shooting?" a voice called from above.

"Yeah, sounded like it was inside," came a reply.

"Wonder who it could be?"

"Damned if I know. Did they take that colored fellow out?"

"I don't know."

"Hey, down there! Hey, down there on 1-10. Did they take that fellow out?"

No reply. The colored convicts weren't talking.

"Hey, they just killed Marcus," someone called from the first cell, either on our range or down below on 1-10.

"Where . . . ?" "Who killed him . . . ?" "Was he the colored fellow . . . ?" "The dirty sons of bitches! Who did it . . . ?"

"Short Britches shot him first—"

"He says Short Britches shot him first—"

"Shut up, goddammit, I can hear him!"

"Kish and Short Britches and the night captain were beating him with a piece of pipe, out in front of the hole, and he broke and ran—"

"They wanted him to run."

"Sure, that's why they didn't take him inside where he couldn't run."

"Short Britches shot at him first, then the night captain. He ran around behind the hospital down by the coal company. The wall guard saw them shooting at him and cut loose with his machine gun—"

"Why, the dirty son . . . Why, the dirty . . ." Whoever he was he couldn't find a suitable word.

"A damn dirty shame," Starlight said. "That guy was really nuts."

Well, that wouldn't bring him back, I thought. "How the hell do those guys down there in the first cells know so much about it?"

"Aw, some guard told them. These guards can't keep nothing to themselves."

There was plenty talk, lasting up into the night.

And then Blackie and Wop got into a fight up in the idle house one day. A big good-natured guard, called Big Irish, went down and parted them. It was during the dull hours of the afternoon and Big Irish wanted to get in the remainder of his nap, so he didn't take them to the hole.

Demotte, another guard, gray-haired and squat with a blunt mean face, wasn't satisfied. He went in between the benches to get Blackie to take him to the hole. When Blackie passed Wop, who seemed to be getting off, he hit him on the nose without warning. Blood spurted from Wop's nose and as he staggered up Blackie hit him again. Then Demotte hit Blackie across the back of the head with his stick, and Blackie went down like a sack of cement.

Four convicts jumped up and hit at Demotte at the same time. He ducked one, but the other three hit him. He tried to protect himself but they were on top of him. Someone jerked his stick from his hand and beat him across the head until blood matted in his hair. He fell down between the benches, and the convict with the stick bent over and kept hitting at him.

Before the head guard, who was fat and lazy, sitting on the stand by the door, could get to his feet someone threw a tin cuspidor of sawdust and tobacco spittle in his face. Then a bunch of other convicts grabbed him by the legs and yanked him out of the stand, underneath the railing, down on the floor where they began kicking out his guts. They kept on kicking him until blood started coming out his mouth.

There were three other guards and five hundred convicts. Big Irish stood up and pleaded with the men. A convict snatched the chair out from behind him and hit him across the head. The other two guards tried to run. The last I saw of them they were smothered by convicts. The band guard stuck his head out of the bandroom, took one look and snatched it back. He shut the door and locked it.

Cuspidors were thrown. Windows were smashed. The noise, which began as a confused babble of voices, rose into a shrill, loud, continuous wail, earsplitting and nerve-shattering. Benches were splintered. It seemed as if Demotte and the head guard were being killed. I started to get up and beat it for the door.

Chump Charlie grabbed me by the arm. "Keep your seat. That's the only way to keep out of it."

I heard someone yell, "Let's make a break!"

"Goddammit, let's go!"

"Let's crush through the front gates!"

"Let's go get the pig!"

"Kill the goddamn pig!"

Suddenly I saw that two of them had guns. They must have taken them from the guards. They rushed toward the door. Five hundred wild-eyed, disheveled, freedom-crazed, howling convicts with two guns.

"Let's break down the stockade gates!"

"Down with the stockade gates!"

"Bastard son of a bitch!"

"Shoot the son of a bitch in the guts!"

"Aw, cut his goddamned throat. We want to save the bullets."

At the door they stopped as if they had run into an invisible wall. They backed up, step by step. The two convicts with the guns kept backing into the others until suddenly the others broke for their seats. The hands holding the guns began to tremble. The guns dropped to the floor as if the strength had gone out of the hands that held them.

I don't know what I expected to see. But what I saw shocked me deeply, violently, as I have never been shocked before or since.

One man came through the door. Just one man—Cody.

He wore a dark blue uniform cap, with the gold legend of a sergeant, low over his eyes, and a black slicker buttoned about his throat and wet with rain. He did not rush or hesitate but came steadily through the doorway, his empty hands hanging at his sides, his lips tight and bloodless, his face a burnt-red—raw-edged and hard as baked clay—his eyes a half-hidden tricky gleam beneath the brim of his cap. He came straight ahead across the floor, never hesitating once, and up to the two convicts who had had the guns. He slapped one of them on the side of his head so hard it laid him his full length on the floor. The other one broke to run but he grabbed him by the collar, and holding him at a distance, slapped him until his face was raw and swelling, red and turning blue. Then he said, "Stand over by the door." His thin bloodless lips did not seem to move but his voice came out loud, harsh, uncompromising.

The two convicts scrambled over to the door. Cody picked up the guns, then stood there for a moment looking us over. A convict went crazy from the strain. He jumped up, his arms outstretched to the ceiling as if hollering hallelujah, his fingers stiffened and extended out like prongs, and his hair rising on his skull. He screamed, "Oh, you goddamned dog!"

Before his feet touched the floor Cody shot him five times with one of the guns, so that when he fell he must have already been dead. He fell across the convict in front of him. The convict jumped aside. He fell on the back of the bench, slid slowly off, crumpled to the floor between the benches.

In the silence following the echo of the gun shots I could hear the three buttons of his uniform coat scrape across the back of the bench as he slid to the floor. I could hear, distinctly, the stifled breathing of the convicts and the hard, fast thumping of my own heart. I could hear the moans of the injured guards and, from below, the deliberate, monotonous, mocking, eternal clank of the looms of the woolen mill, beating out their blunt-toned melody. Then from somewhere down below in the yard came the stentorian bellow, "CompaneeeeEEEEEEEE . . . . ! MARCH!"

"Oh, please! Oh, please! Oh, please!" I never knew whether I said it in my mind or aloud.

10

AT THE BEGINNING of summer we shed our coats. We left our collars unbuttoned when the guard wasn't watching. But nothing helped that idle house, sitting up there on a level with the sun, hotter than a Virginia coke oven. "Hot? As a pussy with the pox!" they'd say. On those sultry summer days there was a squad of convicts whose only duty was to revive the men who fell out from the heat.

On Saturday afternoons we had baseball games. Outside teams came in to play our prison grays. We would go and sit out on the grandstand, down beside the walls, getting a tan watching the fellows park home runs over the corner stockade guard tower. It was plenty of fun. Most of the convicts rooted for the visiting team.

There was cash and tobacco and merchandise bet on the games. Afterward there was the necessary fighting to collect the bets. My mother had sent me some undershirts and shorts and I had sold them for cash, and won about forty dollars in the dice game up in the bandroom. When the ball games began I'd stake one of the fellows to a fin and then bet him on the hits. That made it peppier.

Outside visitors always came in with the teams. Sometimes there would be more than a hundred, both men and women. If there were any pretty girls among them we'd always find some excuse to pass their section of the grandstand so we could get our gapper's bit. They'd soon catch on after the parade had started. Some of them would give us a show.

On Decoration Day we had the privilege of the yard. All of the companies except Death Row and the 1-11 company, where the redshirt desperadoes were kept in solitary, were turned out in the yard for a couple of hours before dinner. Immediately dozens of crap games came to life. Several guys got cut, several got caught. Mal looked me up as soon as the rout order was given.

"Give me something, Jimmy," he greeted. "I heard about you breaking everybody."

"Hell, I just gave you four dollars last week. You must be keeping up some kid."

"I don't like that."

"Well maybe you're keeping up some man, then. I heard that the hack up there in the tin shop was sweet on you."

"Aw, go to hell."

"Come on, let's get in this game. I'll stake you."

"I don't want to gamble. Let's talk. Gunner Garson and Red Cork are going to win it all, anyway, and I'll get a chance at them in the dormitory tonight."

"I staked Cocky," I said.

"He argues too much."

"He wins too, sometimes."

"Come on, let's walk." We went down by the dining room, past the powerhouse, toward the ball diamond. There were thirty or forty convicts down there playing ball, with twelve or sixteen men on each team. We went over to the grandstand and sat down.

"There's a game this afternoon, I hear," I said.

"We're playing the Pott's Brewers. They're gonna beat hell out of us."

"Oh, I don't know. We almost beat them before."

"How do you know? You weren't watching the game. Every time I saw you you were passing the visitors' stand."

"Did you see me?"

"Sure I saw you. You thought you were cute with your cap off. I could see you grinning from 'way over where I was."

I laughed. "I was looking at the little blonde in the green dress. Did you see her?"

"Sure, I passed by there myself. I wanted to see what she had to keep you walking all afternoon."

"I sure would like to get that. She didn't have a damn thing on underneath her dress. Every time I passed she'd open up her legs and let me see it."

"She was just teasing you. She just let you see it because you couldn't get it."

"I bet I could if I was out."

"You always want something you can't get."

We were silent after that. Then I said, "I was over to court, Monday."

"I heard. What for?"

"You know that note you wrote on the back of my first cashier's receipt? Something about 'dear cousin, I hope you will always hold me in the high esteem which I hold you—' you know all that slush you wrote."

"That wasn't slush."

"The hell it wasn't."

"I meant it."

"Sure, but it was slush just the same. Anyway, old man Warren was standing by the chapel doorway Sunday and when I went by he pulled me out of line and shook me down. He found the receipt in my pocket and wrote me up."

"What did he pull you out for?"

"Oh, nothing. He's been trying to get something on me ever since I got out of the coal company."

"What did Jumpy say?"

"He asked me were you my cousin."

"What'd you say?"

"I said sure, our mothers were sisters."

"Did he believe it?"

"Hell, naw. He doesn't believe any damn thing. He said that if we were cousins it was a legitimate relationship and one that could not be helped."

"But the other?" he grinned.

"He just implied that," I grinned back.

Some fellows passed and one of them called, "What say, Mal? Is that your cousin?"

"Hello, Joe. Yeah, this is Jimmy."

"He's better-looking than you are."

I found myself blushing. After they'd passed, Mal said, "Bobby Guy is coming to the soup company tomorrow."

"Who's Bobby Guy?"

"Oh, he's just a boy. Doing ten to twenty-five."

"What did you tell me about him for?"

"I just don't want you to fall in love with him."

"No danger."

Nick and Chump Charlie strolled by. "What say, Mal? I see you and Jimmy are catching a little sun," Nick said, smirking.

"Hello, Nick," Mal greeted.

"Hello, Jimmy," Charlie said, smiling around Nick's shoulder. "Are you trying to get a tan?"

"What say, Charlie? What say, Nick?"

Nick hesitated a moment as if he wanted to say something else, then he said, "Take it easy," and went on.

"Don't you know Chump?" I asked Mal.

"We don't speak. I don't like the little bitch."

"Oh!"

"I hear you like him well enough," he said. "You like him well enough for both of us."

"I haven't got anything against him. I don't like him, though."

He looked at me solemnly. "You've changed a lot, Jimmy. When you first came in you wouldn't even talk to anyone you thought was like that."

I became serious for a moment too. "Hell, everybody in the soup company's some kind of freak or other," I said, defensively. "I've got to talk to somebody."

"You don't have to associate with 'em. There are a lot of good fellows in here."

I laughed. "Sure, I know. Just like Sunday School."

"Oh, I don't mean that. I mean who aren't wolves and punks, and aren't always running around trying to find somebody new."

"Where are they? Hidden? Damned if I've seen any of them."

"I know you haven't. They're the last persons you get to know. The fellows who tend to their own business are the ones you never see. There are fellows in here who're taking correspondence courses, and others who write stories and things like that. I'll bet half of the fellows in here don't participate in that degeneracy stuff."

"I don't know."

"I'll bet it's more than that."

"Maybe you're right."

"You know Burns. He's editor of the *Prison Times*."

We had a weekly prison sheet, edited and printed by the convicts in the print shop and distributed throughout the prison every Saturday afternoon.

"Yeah. He came up in the idle house one day and asked me if I wanted to draw some illustrations for the *Times*. He'd heard somewhere that I could draw."

"What did you tell him?"

"I asked him was there anything in it for me."

"What did he say about that?"

"He said he was sorry but all services to the *Times* were gratis, so I said to hell with it."

"They don't get any more than the rest of us. Nobody gets any more than anybody else."

"That's what I'm finding out."

"It would have given you a chance to cell with some fellows who are at least decent. I don't believe you want to know anybody decent."

"To hell with them! The bitches are more interesting."

"Burns has sold thirty-seven stories to magazines."

"Screw Burns." I was tired of it.

"You and Chump."

"That's a lie! He's been after me to, but I haven't got to the place where I can do that yet. But give me time. It's so common around this joint it sounds almost natural. It doesn't even shock me any more to find out someone I like is like that."

"You've been using his radio," he accused.

"Who, Chump's? That's another lie. He had a line run down to my cell and sent down some earphones. I was going to send them back but Starlight kept them. I don't want that bastard to do me any favors. You're just jealous I talk to him and you don't like him."

"You're a damn fool," he said.

The bell rang for us to line up and return to our cells.

"You're another damn fool," I said, standing up.

We started back toward the main yard. "You're going to eat on the main line today. Maybe that'll make you feel better."

"I feel all right. The soup's all right with me. I'm getting along fine on it. I'm gaining weight."

"I don't suppose you're going to give me anything."

For a moment I was tempted to refuse. Then I pulled two dollar bills from my pocket. "Here."

"You shouldn't keep that money loose in your pocket," he said. "Some guard'll shake you down and take it."

"Let 'em take it!" I said.

When we parted in front of the dining room he said again, "You've changed, Jimmy."

My company was lining up in front of the chapel. The band stood about the alligator pool, playing. I could see the four slimy, stinking alligators panting in the shallow pool. Everybody's a whore, I was thinking.

Chump fell in behind me. "Hello, Beautiful." I didn't answer. "I know you got fixed up."

I turned around. "What do you mean?"

"You know what I mean. I know all about Mal."

"The trouble with you is you're a nigger," I said.

He turned red. "That's all right. It'll all come back to

you. When you want me I won't want you. That's the way it'll happen."

"Oh, go to hell!"

Our company guard knocked his stick on the chapel wall and we marched noisily back to our cells. But the holiday spirit still prevailed. The men were running up and down the range, visiting from cell to cell. Mother Jones slipped suddenly into our cell.

"Give me something," he said, patting my pockets. Although he was a tall, slightly bald, rough-looking Negro he had a very pleasant grin.

"That beats me, Mother," I said.

"Aw, you got everything. What we gonna do with him?" Jones addressed Starlight.

"I don't know. Every time I say anything to him he wants to fight."

"How's business, Mother?" I said, realizing with a shock how easily I lapsed into the degraded familiarity of the others.

"Don't talk about it," he said, throwing up his hands.

"What's the matter?"

"They got me locked up here so I can't circulate."

"What's the matter with the boy friends down your way?"

"Them niggahs ain't got nothing. They're poor as me."

"Why don't you give them a break? You never know what they might come up with."

"I'll give them a break with this." He held up his fist. "You the one's got everything. Give me a quarter."

"Price is going down, isn't it?" I asked.

"Up," Starlight said.

Mother Jones grinned. "I wouldn't charge you anything."

I blushed. "Here," I said, giving him the quarter.

"You wait," he said. "Somebody's coming over tomorrow you'll get excited about."

"Bobby Guy?"

He nodded. "Won't he get excited about Bobby, Squirrel?"

"Right up in the air," Starlight said.

"Stuff," I said.

But they didn't tell any lie. I did get excited about Bobby Guy. He was like a doll, small and curly-headed with big brown limpid eyes, a lisp, and a pure peaches and cream complexion. For several days we didn't speak although we looked at each other quite often. We were both waiting for the other to speak first. I knew he had heard as much about me as I had about him. I had built up quite a reputation as a soft touch for a buck, among other things.

Then one afternoon Starlight got called to the hospital. When we came in from the idle house Bobby came into my cell. He moved close to me.

I pushed him away. "What the hell!"

He looked startled then. "Don't you want to?"

Heat came all up in my head and eyes. I could feel my breath getting fast. "I don't know."

Then the guard came up. "What're you doing in here, boy?" he asked Bobby.

"I just stopped to get a cigarette."

"Well, hurry up and get it and get back to your cell. Where do you guys get this stuff?"

When Bobby stepped out onto the range every cell door was cracked, and the whole company was peeping. For three days I avoided him. Then it got next to me like a live wire underneath my skin. I went over to Gout and asked to be put into Bobby's cell. He was by himself at the time and the lower bunk was empty. I told Gout I wanted to be transferred to a lower bunk because it hurt my back to climb up on the upper bunks.

Gout blew up. "You smart punk! You slick city punk!" He came charging toward me, swearing and kicking. I beat it out of his office and hurried away, tight and nervous and unrelieved. I still had that live-wire edge. It was a great relief when they transferred Bobby to the hospital the following week. He was a favorite at the hospital and could get in any time he wanted to.

That was that summer. Heat, and that live-wire edge.

11

IN SEPTEMBER they began to wreck the 10&11 cell block preparatory to building another new cell block like the new 7&8 block. The 10 and 11 companies were broken up and transferred to various parts of the prison. Most of the working companies were transferred to the 3&4 and 1&2 cell blocks. Most of the convicts in the soup company and 1-10 were transferred across the well to the new, four-man cells of the 7&8 block. They were put on 2- and 3-7 and 6-8.

Chump Charlie and I were transferred back to the school company in 5-6 dormitory. Later I learned that Nick had me transferred there to cover for Chump Charlie whom he wanted back in the dormitory.

When I had left 5-6, back in the latter part of February, I had been a bewildered, big-eyed kid, half afraid that every big tough-looking convict might try to rape me, and not having the least idea what the prison was all about. But when I returned I felt that I was solid hipped. I thought I knew the joint and all the types of convicts. I had lost all the intense self-pity of those first few months. But I had gained a pity for the other convicts which was insolent. I felt sorry for everybody. For some I also felt contempt but over and above the contempt I felt sorry for them, too. I pitied them for the long severe sentences they were serving, forgetting mine. I pitied them for their weaknesses, for their degeneration, for their lack of funds. I was a sucker for a beg. I never turned down anyone who had the nerve to beg me. The soup company had set me up; it had given me confidence. Perhaps it was more because the fags recognized me as a man than anything else. Also because the gamblers had claimed me for their own.

There was only one fellow in the whole dormitory whom I hated without pity or contempt. That was Lippy Mike. When Chump and I were transferred that morning it was too late for us to go to school. We waited in the dormitory for the school company to come in. After making my bunk I sat on the bench in the aisle, smoking a cigarette. When the company came in several convicts gathered about me.

"You transferred in here, Jimmy?" I had become a celebrity of a sort.

"Yeah."

"Good."

"What say, Jimmy?"

"Hello, Jimmy."

"I know you're glad to beat that 6-8 rap."

"Damn right."

"They tell me Wop lost five C's in the crap game."

"Sure did."

"I know you got yours."

"You know me."

Most of them I'd either never seen before or couldn't remember. A little hump-backed, sharp-faced fellow sat down beside me. He was vaguely familiar.

"Hello, kid, did you ever make that nine?"

Then I remembered him. He had been in a crap game we staged back of the grandstand during a baseball game one Saturday afternoon.

"What say, Blocker? How you doing, bud?"

"Slow."

"Yeah, man, I made that sucker keep that bet up and made that nine up in the idle house next day."

He grinned. It made him look like a wolf with long yellow fangs. "I knew you were going to clip that chump."

His eyes were almost colorless and he had the longest, slimmest fingers with the longest, cleanest fingernails I've ever seen. His hair fell down over his forehead, his face was narrow and bony with a razor-sharp nose and a long lantern jaw. He looked like a weird story. I liked him immediately.

Lippy Mike was coming down the aisle, swaggering and walking over people. When he saw me he reached down and took the cigarette from my lips. I burnt up. "What the hell's the matter with you, fellow!"

"I was just playing with you, little punk," he grated. "Here, take the damn butt back."

I brushed it away. "I don't want it, goddammit, keep it. Just don't play with me like that."

He threw the cigarette on the floor and stepped on it. "Hey, pappy!" he called.

"Coming, Mike."

"Bring this punk a pack of cigarettes." He turned to me and said, "I'm going to give you a pack of cigarettes, punk, and don't you never speak to me again."

"Frig you," I said.

"What?"

I jumped up. "You heard me."

He dug his hand in his left breast pocket. Blocker jumped up and stepped in between two bunks. Mike took his hand out of his pocket empty and said, "You take it easy, little punk."

"You take it easy your goddamned self," I said.

Mike whirled and walked away. He had a swagger that was so extreme it was almost feminine. Blocker came back and we sat down again. "I went to get Herbie's banjo hanging there," he said. "If that chump had started anything I was going to hang that banjo over his head."

"He's too damn overbearing," I said. I could still feel the blood in my face.

"Take it easy, kid," Blocker said, grinning. "You're still burning." He had a way of making you feel that he was on your side when he grinned like that. I had never liked a convict so well and so quickly.

That first night we began running a poker game together. I didn't know how much money Blocker had. I had almost a hundred dollars in cash. I had won most of it in the crap game where Wop had lost five hundred dollars. Wop's mother had smuggled the money in to him for a pay-off to a guard who had contacts with the governor's office. The guard had promised to get Wop a pardon for the money. But Wop had lost every cent of it in the crap game the same afternoon his mother had visited him.

Blocker was one of those gamblers who have one rigid rule—*never give a sucker a break*. It wasn't just a saying with him. He practiced it. For the first three nights we used brand-new decks of red-backed *Bee's* and got a fast, furious play from all the heavy betters. One convict, called Sailor, who had the reputation of being the institution's hardest better, tied up with me in several pots, the largest of which I took on a pair of deuces. Whenever he stayed he raised the ante to a dollar, bet six dollars on the second card, sixteen-fifty on the third, and on the last he would turn down, or bet forty dollars. You never knew what he had from the way he bet. When I beat him with the deuces I'd caught a flash of his ace in the hole. He started off betting like a man running down a hill and by the time he had bet himself broke, leading it all the way down, chips were piled on the table six inches deep and money was stacked to one side. We had a gallery of onlookers that had dormitory traffic stopped. When I raked in the pot Sailor stuck a fresh cigarette into his holder. He smoked one every deal.

"All I want a man to do is gamble," he said, and got up to go borrow some more money.

I gave these chumps a play. "Come on, Johnnies, let's bet 'em up," I'd say.

Blocker used to spell me on the deal and we'd take turns selling chips. But our game grew so fast we had to hire a couple of assistants. Blocker was a natural poker player. He had poor poker judgment although he had plenty of betting nerve. His best game was dice. He could do more with a deck of cards than a monkey can with a coconut, but he didn't get a chance. The players watched him like a hawk. Even when he was dealing strictly from the top they didn't like him to deal. They all wanted me. They all believed they could beat me, simply because I was young.

Blocker had given one of the guards money to bring us in some cards. The guard brought us a dozen decks of expert-back Bicycle cards. We spent the next two days at school running them up from the fours to the aces. All we had to use was pen and ink. His work was so fine that I couldn't read them rapidly enough. I always dealt very fast; when I had a full game the cards would come off in a blur. The convicts used to gather around just to watch me deal. But by the time I'd take a flash at a player's hole card he'd have it covered by the second. We never played anything but stud poker. For the first couple of days after we'd put down our new paper I shot so many blanks it would have been a dead giveaway to any smart gambler. When you're playing with paper you depend more on knowing what the other fellow has than on your own poker judgment. When you make a mistake it can look pretty obvious.

So we took the cards back to school and painted "horses and mules" on them. And still those players didn't pick it up. I think Sailor did. But I'd deal so fast he couldn't read them. He'd cover his own hole card with his hand, as soon as it was dealt to him, and then lean over and try to read mine. It kept both of us shooting blanks and horsing at each other until we had players crowding in so sometimes I'd have to deal to twelve. From that time on we never used an unmarked deck of cards.

My bunk was the same as I'd had before—a lower on the center aisle by the guard-stand. Captain Charlie was still on as night guard. Chump Charlie was farther down in a corner bunk out of sight, for which I was grateful. Nick had given him a big, flashy, electric guitar. They said Nick had paid four hundred and fifty dollars for it. Chump kept to himself down in his corner and mothered it. For a time he had tried to be friendly. But I had told him, "Off me, sucker."

Mal was still in 5-5. Every night he sent for me to come to the peephole. Blocker asked me once was he really my cousin. I told him no, we'd just made that up. After that Blocker referred to him as my old lady. "Your old lady wants you at the hole, kid."

"Aw, cut it out," I'd say.

"You'd better go down and see what your old lady wants. First thing you know she'll be slipping up on you out on the yard giving you some love licks with a straight-edged razor."

But I kind of liked it though. It gave me something.

Blocker was a queer sort of fellow. I don't think he'd ever liked anyone in all his life but me. He was crazy as hell about me. But not in any funny way. He took great pains to make that obvious. We were straight friends. He understood that I didn't want those convicts to get the idea that I was his kid. He would rather they thought that he was my kid, if there was going to be any misunderstanding. So he always made it very clear that we were only gambling buddies. The quickest way to get him in a fight was for someone to make a crack about me. Most of the fellows thought he was treacherous. He looked like a man who'd slip up behind you and cut your throat. He was really a very good-natured guy. But he didn't talk a lot. Still water runs deep, they said. Quiet men are always dangerous. They did not bother the silent, untalkative men. I don't know why. Most of the quiet sons of bitches were quiet because they didn't have anything to talk about, or else they were simple-minded.

The poker game was very important to us, but it was still out-of-bounds. If the night deputy had caught us he'd have put us in the hole. We still went to school. The routine was the same. I was in the sixth grade in a room on the opposite side of the building from where I had been before. Outside of our window was the brick walk that led to the death house.

One day I got into a minor fight in school. It was about a book of English Synonyms and Antonyms. I had borrowed it from a fellow named Metz to freshen up my vocabulary. That day, when we went to dinner, I left it on the dormitory table. When I looked for it after dinner it was gone. I asked the porters but none of them had seen it. When I spoke to Lippy Mike he didn't reply. That got me salty. I went back to school and asked about it in each room. Then I got really sore and started shaking down the whole school, going through each desk. After ransacking the desks in four rooms I found it in the fifth. The kid, Wilkerson, who had been in the hole with Benny Glass and me, had it in his desk.

"Didn't you hear me asking about this book?" I could feel the blood rushing to my head.

"I was going to give it to you."

I snatched up the book and started to slap him in the face with it. Someone called, "Pst . . . pst . . . Cody."

Sergeant Cody came into the room. I whirled away from Wilkerson, red-faced and jerky. Then Wilkerson whispered, teasingly, "I like you to get mad. You're pretty when you're mad."

Something clamped over my head, hot and tight, blinding me. Turning, I went back and hit him over the ear. He fell half from his seat and clambered to his feet on the other side. I leaned across the desk and hit him twice in the face. When I hit at him the third time my feet slipped and I fell across the desk. While lying there I hit him again in the stomach. He began screaming but he didn't fight back.

"Pst . . . pst . . . Cody," someone kept whispering.

"Damn Cody!" I raved.

Cody took his time about separating us. He took us to the hole. The next morning when we were brought out to face the deputy, Wilkerson said he didn't want to fight. The deputy let him go and kept me a day longer.

Gout was the cause of that. "You back again, Monroe? You're here more often than the deputy." He picked up my report file and looked at it. "You haven't been here but nine months and you've been in court seven times. What's the matter with you?"

"The trouble isn't with me," I said. "Why don't you talk to some of those guys who keep digging at me?"

"We got a place for you guys who can't keep out of trouble," he said. "We'll put you in the red-shirt gang."

When I got out the next day Blocker had a couple of sandwiches for me. "You better let me get you an army, kid," he grinned.

"They need one around here just to keep these chumps in their place," I said.

"Man, you get mad quicker than anybody I've ever seen." We grinned.

"I'm gonna take it easy from now on in," I said.

Then about a week later I had a little trouble about a pair of pants. Captain Bull had given me a pants order and I'd gotten a new pair from the commissary. I sent them up to the tailor shop to have them taken up in the waist, and another hip pocket and two watch pockets put in. The boy who was doing my work then—Hank the Crank—sent them back but they were still too large in the waist. I started to send them back. But Snag, the colored runner for the school, who was a good friend of Blocker's, said, "You better get a tailor-shop slip from Bull. Some of those guys up there might try to clip you for these strides now that you got 'em all fixed up."

So I got the tailor shop tag to give them some protection. And then some sucker stole them. I told Bull and he sent me up to see the tailor-shop guard. The tailor-shop guard wanted me to take some second-hand strides in their place.

"Hell, mine were new," I protested.

"Well, these are all I can give you," he said. "You can take them or leave them."

"I'm going to see the deputy," I said.

When I went over to see the deputy, old Pop Henshaw, the hole guard, asked me what I wanted to see him for. I told him I'd lost my new pants in the tailor shop and I wanted an order for another pair. He looked at the ones I had on and asked me where I'd gotten them. I was wearing my old pair but they were in good shape. I told Pop I got them from Snag, the runner, for relief pants. He told me to keep them.

"Hell, I'm due a new pair," I argued. "I'm charged with them. I got to pay for them out of my earnings. What the hell—I want to see the deputy."

He sent me back to school. I sat there and got to burning, thinking about how I'd been gypped out of my new strides. I was determined to get me another pair, or bust, and I wasn't going to buy them, either. That evening in the dormitory I borrowed a knife and cut the pair I was wearing into shreds.

"You'll get into trouble doing that, kid," Blocker warned me.

"I don't care," I said. "I'm going to get a new pair or die in the attempt."

He grinned. "Well let me fix them for you, then. They'll know these have been cut." He borrowed one of the tin graters the convicts used to grate up scrap soap to make new bars, and raveled off the edges of the slits so they'd look more like tears than cuts. But they still looked like cuts.

The next morning I walked out of school and went over to the courtroom. When Pop Henshaw saw those pants he went straight up into the air. He grabbed me by the arm and rushed me in to the deputy. He told the deputy what I had done. I told the deputy how they'd tricked me out of my new pants up in the tailor shop. The deputy ordered Pops to take me over to the commissary and get me another pair. Pops took me over to the commissary but when the clerk started to give me a new pair he told him to get me a second-hand pair. They were about six inches too short. Pops made me put them on. I was so mad I wanted to knock him down the stairs.

When Blocker saw me he started laughing. "You look like you're coming 'round the mountain, kid," he said.

Later that morning one of the guards hit a convict in school. There was a lot of yelling and gesticulating, and a few blows were passed. A couple of the guards got rubbed up a little. They had to send for the deputy. The deputy was in his sins by then. He was irritable and impatient and twitching like a wino with the shakes.

I waited until he'd gotten the men quieted down a bit and then I grabbed him by the arm and said, "Look at these pants, deputy. These are the pants that Captain Henshaw got for me."

He tried to break away but I held on to him. He was so angry his face turned purple but he didn't do anything to me for fear of stirring up the riot again. Everyone was waiting tensely for him to slap me.

He looked down at my pants. "What's the matter with them, what's the matter with them, what's the matter with them?" he snapped.

"Hell, you can see," I said, holding up one leg. "They're too small and they're too short and, anyway, I'm due a new pair. I'm charged with a new pair."

"Wear those, wear those, wear those," he said, pulling away again.

"I can't wear these, goddammit!" I shouted. "What the hell's the matter with you people?"

The deputy turned clear around and looked at me. He looked as if he was just seeing me for the first time. Several guards rushed up to encircle me.

"Cap Smith," the deputy said to one of them. "Take this lad and get him some new trousers. Tell him about the trouser freak, the trouser freak, the trouser freak we had here. Had to send him to the insane asylum, had to send him to the insane asylum."

On the way to the commissary Captain Smith told me about the fellow who used to bleach his trousers white. As soon as they'd take one pair he'd bleach his new ones white. When they asked him why he did it he said he preferred Palm Beach clothing. They had to send him to the asylum for the criminally insane.

One night Deacon Smith came over to our dormitory and held church. It was during a two-week revival meeting that was going on in the prison and they were looking for converts from every source. All of the colored convicts in the dormitory went down to hear Deacon Smith preach. One of the convicts, called Beau Diddly, got so happy he jumped up and dived head first into a commode. Beau Diddly was a rat and a degenerate and a very ugly, knotty, black Negro. But he must have had a whole lot of religion, or he must have gotten a whole lot on a very short notice.

One night I was sitting on the deal box dealing—all the dealers used boxes to elevate them over the players—when a pistol went off five startling times, outside of the dormitory. It looked as if somebody was shooting directly at me. I had never looked down the barrel of a blasting pistol in the dark. I never knew what it was to be so scared. I jumped straight back off the box and landed in the aisle on the small of my spine. But I didn't even feel any pain. By the time the echoes died away I was underneath a bunk on the other side of the dormitory. Our deal box had fallen open on the floor and merchandise—tobacco, cigarettes, soap, tooth paste, and such—was scattered everywhere. But we didn't lose a single sack of weed. Everyone else was too busy ducking bullets to think of grabbing tobacco.

When it was all over we rushed to the window to see what it was all about. We saw a body twitching convulsively in the circle of light cast by the yard guard's torch.

"One good boy got his final release," somebody said.

One of the bullets had entered through a window and struck the center pillar, less than six inches above Captain Charlie's head. Another had creased a convict's shoulder. Blocker and I gathered up our merchandise and I went back dealing stud. The morning paper said that a convict "Red" Swayzee, had been shot by a guard, Captain Catlin, while trying to escape. It said that the convict had fashioned a ladder of sheets and had wrapped it about his body. He had feigned sickness and had asked to be taken to the hospital. On the way to the hospital he had broken away from the guard and had tried to escape. That was one hell of a poor way to escape, I thought. I supposed he must have been planning on flying up to the top of the wall and then lowering himself down on the other side, with the ladder. But you never knew what a convict thought.

12

AT FIRST it had been summer. We had shed our coats and vests and had gone about in our tailor-made shirts and caps and trousers, our sandals and silk socks. The cells had been stifling during the day, suffocating at night. It was against the rules to sleep naked. At nights we had lain on our sheets and panted.

Summer was the spoiling season. The convicts slipped away from their companies and visited. They held rendezvous in the lumber shed, inside empty boxcars that had been sided with loads of lumber, flour or cement. They wandered aimlessly about the yard, without passes. The boy-girls had a chance to show their shapes. There was a laxity in the routine during summer. Almost every convict liked summer best.

And then it was fall. Blocker and I ran our game. We went to school, to the bath, to the barbershop, to the dining room, to church, to bed. We put on our coats.

And now it was winter again. We added our vests, brought out our gloves, donned our illegal sweaters underneath our shirts, our heavy shoes and two pairs of socks.

The days changed in length. Their color changed from winter gray to spring yellow to summer's blinding white to fall's burnished tints, and again to winter gray. But the pattern was the same. Days in an endless procession, swinging out on the paradeground of days. Days, end to end, stretching back from the beginning of always, out to the end of always. Almost all of the days belonged to the prison. They were steel-laced and unvarying, shaped and molded for eternity. Another day. And then another. What was the difference?

But there were those rare days that belonged to the convicts. Decoration Day. Thanksgiving. And now it was Christmas. We found a clean blue cotton prison sock filled with candy, an apple, an orange, and some nuts beside our plates at dinnertime. We had roast loin of pork, candied sweet potatoes, jellied salad, coffee with milk, and raisin bread for dinner and apple pie for dessert. And afterwards we had a minstrel show sponsored by the warden's wife. The convict cast had been rehearsing since the first of November and now they faltered, cheerfully, through their lines. It was very funny.

"Wuccup, wuccup, wuccup!" said the bear man in the cage.

"Wut he mean by dat?" asked tall, big-mouthed, black, ludicrous Flamdingo, who didn't need any make-up to be an end man.

"Oh, man," the other short black end man interpreted, "he mean by dat he thinks it am a beautiful day and dat he thinks de clouds is awful pretty and dat he thought dat po'k we had fur dinner was mighty fine and dat when he got up dis mawnin' he remember dat it was Christmas and dat he was terrible happy."

"He mean all dat by just dat?"

"Yeah man, he mean every bit of dat by just dat lil bit of dat. What he say in his language mean a whole lot."

"It mean a hell of a lot, you heah me!"

And then the beautiful maiden passes the bear man's cage. The beautiful maiden is played by Renee, the prison's most notorious fag. The bear man begins jumping up and down in his cage and wrestling with the bars. He begins talking excitedly, "Wuccup, wuccup, wuccup, wuccup, wuccup, wuccup, wuccup, wuccup, wuccup. . . ."

And old Flam yelling, "Hey, somebody cum git dis heah bear man, he done talked fo' story books already."

All of Christmas Eve and Christmas day the boxes had been coming. They came all during the night and were delivered as soon as they were received by the guards at the front gates and searched. A crew of honor men brought them around to the dormitories and cells. They had been coming all that week and the week before. But on Christmas day there was a deluge. The lights were kept on all night Christmas Eve. Nobody slept.

Some of the convicts got two boxes, some got three, some got four and five. If you didn't get a box on Christmas you were pitiful, you were the saddest convict I ever saw. My mother sent me a box. I received it first and then, a day later, I received a box from my father. There was a twelve-pound bag of flour in my dad's box. We were allowed to receive sugar and he must have thought it was sugar. I could see him fumbling around in a self-service store picking up a bag of flour, thinking it was sugar, and packing it along with the cheap store cakes and candies and fruits, without looking at it. I didn't know how it got by the guards who were supposed to search the boxes. As far as I knew we were not allowed to receive flour. But perhaps they had let it come on through so I could make some biscuits.

Before Blocker or anyone else had a chance to discover it I wrapped it in some old newspapers and sneaked down and threw it in the wastepaper bag. One of the porters found it the next morning. They wanted to know who got the bag of flour for Christmas. But I never did tell.

Blocker didn't get a box. I shared my mother's box with him and sent my father's box, without the flour, to Mal who didn't get a box either. I bought candy and fruit and meats from all those convicts who would sell them for money or poker chips, and distributed the stuff about to other guys who didn't get boxes. I was very sorry for everyone that Christmas.

We read in the newspapers about two convicts who got Christmas pardons. But they were very remote. Only a few fellows whom I talked to had ever heard of them. I was sorry for all those convicts that Christmas.

There was a beautifully lighted Christmas tree in the yard which had been installed by the electricians from the powerhouse. Its installation had been supervised, as had been all the Christmas activities, by the warden's wife. The convicts called her Ma. They swore by Ma. They loved her and worshiped her. She was the one who always interceded for them. She got them handkerchiefs and permission to wash them. They hated the warden. But they loved Ma.

All the convicts in the dormitory were very excited. Everybody was happy, it seemed. They all wanted to give each other something, or gamble. Everyone had a little money for a time. We gave Dave, who was our newest flunky, some cards and chips and let him run an apple and orange poker game during the season. He took in bushels of them.

Lippy Mike started a game and the guys gave him the play for a time. That was the way with every new game. Blocker and I took it easy for awhile.

It had snowed early that winter and Christmas was cold

and white. It was cold in the dormitory. At night I burrowed down beneath my two new prison blankets and my outside blanket—a warm, fluffy blue and white checked creation of double thickness which had cost me thirty dollars.

My mother had been visiting me as regularly as possible but my father had not been down at all.

But on the whole everything was well under control that winter. I was doing the easiest time I ever did. Everything was hunky-dory. Mal was my old lady, Blocker said. So what? If you didn't have an old lady, you hadn't been out long—you weren't even serving time. But that was long distance. In the dormitory I was little boy blue. I was the dormitory's most eligible swain. All the whores were shooting at me. I was the institution's prize touch. I fattened frogs for snakes. No kid could say that I refused him his beg, whether it was for a fin or a bag of weed. So what? I didn't get anything but what I had always wanted most in life, and that was adulation. I got too much adulation.

They called me the prison's smartest poker dealer. They said what I couldn't do with a deck of cards couldn't be done. They said I'd been a big shot outside, too. They toadied to me. They made up my bunk for me in the morning, shined my shoes, laundered my pajamas, underwear and socks, pressed my uniform. They considered it a privilege to talk to me. It all cost me plenty. Everything cost me plenty. But I didn't have anything else to do with my money.

What a convict has been on the outside means very little in prison, no matter what they tell you. The convicts who were gangsters outside usually turn into finks inside, or they acquire t.b. and die, or they have money to buy their way and then they are still big shots. The toughies who had nothing but their outside reps got their throats cut by hickville punks who had never heard of them. Money talked as loud there as it does anywhere—if not louder.

And the days passed. Square and angular, with hard-beaten surfaces; confining, restricting, congesting. But down in the heart of these precise, square blocks of days there was love and hate; ambition and regret; there was hope, too, shining eternally through the long gray years; and perhaps there was even a little happiness.

Starting off with the morning wash-up: "Git up and knock on de rock . . . Ain' quite day but iss fo' o'clock . . . ! Haw, hawww, hawwwwww! Ah calls yuh, yuh wanna fight. But de white cap'n call yuh dass jes awright . . . !

Hawwwww, hawwwww, hawwwwwwww!" Or maybe it went like this on another morning: "Rich con use his good smellin' soap. An' de slickah do de same. But a po' low-down con use a bar of lye. But he washin' jes de same. . . ."

Ending with the rat-tat-tat of the prison guards' sticks, the flashing of lights, semidarkness and quiet. And in between some died, some left, some entered, but most did the same goddamned thing they had done the day before, and the day before that, and the day before that. But sunsets were no less beautiful than they ever were, if you ever got to see one; nor was the sky any higher, any bluer, any grayer.

In the prison day the one high spot was in the evening after supper when they called out mail. Everyone who had ever received a letter, or ever hoped to receive a letter, ganged about the guard as he stood atop the table and called off the names and numbers on the slit envelopes, stamped with the red emblem of the prison censor. And there were plenty who had never received a letter and did not hope to receive one, who stood there with the others, because, I suppose, the human being is a companionable animal and is not made to live alone. I could get so goddamned filled up just thinking about them I wanted to cry. I could feel so goddamned sorry for them then. The years didn't trouble me then; the twenty years were nothing in my sorrow for all those other convicts. Nothing mattered very much then, not even God; least of all God.

To see a twelve-year robber with a six months' continuance. That was pitiful. That was like looking at a pregnant whore. That was like catching God sloppy drunk. A convict who'd served twelve long, tough, hard years getting a six months' flop by the parole board for "investigation."

"What the hell they been doing all those twelve goddamned years?" he asked, his lips quivering, his hands trembling, his eyes bewildered.

The findings of the parole board were returned with the mail. After a board meeting when word had gotten about that the slips were in the mail everyone who had had a hearing was tense and nervous. They'd gang about the guard when they saw the batch of brown envelopes. As soon as each one got his return he'd rip it open furiously, while others hemmed them all in, to read with avid eyes the cold, irrevocable, unappealable announcement: ". . . *continued until—*"

Seven years! Continued for seven years! "Jesus Christ!"

Some of them would keep their envelopes unopened until the dead of the night when they could look at them in secret. Sometimes they'd never tell what they got.

Some of them got paroled.

Some of them tried to escape.

Some of them did escape.

Blocker stopped by my bunk on his way to wash up that January morning. "All of 1-3 broke out last night." They had moved the redshirt desperadoes from 1-11 to 1-3 when they began tearing down the old 10&11 cell block.

I jumped from my bunk, excited. "Yeah? Last night?"

Another convict came from the washtrough, looking more excited than either of us. "There wasn't but twelve that got out. The rest wouldn't go."

"I wonder how they got out," I said.

"They must have tunneled out," Blocker said.

"Frankie Kane tunneled out two years ago and was almost ready to scram when someone squealed on him," another fellow said.

Suddenly we had a crowd. But we weren't the only crowd. They were bunched together in little knots all over the dormitory. Everyone had forgotten to wash, in their excitement.

"How long's Frankie been in the redshirters?"

"About three years now. You know he was in there when those seven guys crushed through the gate that day."

"He was the leader."

"Yeah, he was the one who knocked old Bringhurst down when he tried to stop them."

"They tell me the warden's daughter came running downstairs with a big forty-five in each hand, trying to stop them."

"Annie get your gun."

We laughed.

"Was Frankie in this bunch?"

"He must have been."

"I bet he was the leader."

"I bet Jiggs was in it too."

"And Earl Linn."

"And Phil Potosi."

"And Tank Tony." They called the role of the desperadoes.

"When'd they miss 'em?"

"I don't know. When the morning guard took his count, I suppose."

"Hell, they count them guys every hour."

"I dont know, then. I guess they must have missed them right away."

"Hey!" someone called from the corner of the dormitory. "Chump's got the flashes on his radio."

We all made a break for Chump's bunk. I snatched up my bathrobe and put it on going down the aisle. So many convicts were jammed up down there I had to climb up on top of an upper bunk in order to see the radio. It was as if I couldn't hear the radio unless I could see it. The others who had radios had them turned on, too, and convicts were grouped about their bunks also. Chump sat there looking as important as if he had planned the break himself.

"*. . . John Sidney Bippus. . . .*" the loud metallic voice of the radio blared. . . . "*John Sidney Bippus . . . Better known as Sid Bip . . . Five feet, five and one half inches . . . Five feet, five and one half inches . . . Weight—one hundred and thirty-two pounds . . . Weight—one hundred and thirty-two pounds . . . Blue eyes . . . Blue eyes . . . Brown hair . . . Brown hair . . . Probably dressed in gray prison uniform . . . Probably dressed in gray prison uniform . . . Serving life for first-degree murder . . . Serving life for first-degree murder . . . Very dangerous if armed . . . Very dangerous if armed . . . CAUTION. . . . Do not attempt to capture this man as he is very dangerous. . . . If seen, notify police . . . If seen, notify police. . . . CAUTION! . . . Do not attempt to capture this man as he is very dangerous . . . If seen, notify police . . . Karl Luther Mueller . . . Karl Luther Mueller . . .*"

"Sid wasn't in 1-3. Sid was in the heart-trouble company," someone said.

"Sid was on 1-4."

"Weren't none of them out of 1-3?" someone else asked.

"Shut up and let us hear."

"Well, listen then!"

"Well, shut up then!"

"Kiss my ass!"

"Kiss your mother's——" There was the usual fight.

We hung about the radio until the breakfast bell rang. Our guards had been listening at another radio and hadn't heard the breakfast bell. They didn't knock for us to line up until one of the sergeants came in to investigate. I had to rush to get dressed. They scrambled pell-mell through the doorway. There was no semblance of order in the line. I was left. I had to run across the yard to catch up.

It was all we talked about at breakfast. The guards were grouped about the walls, talking about it too. The noise of all the talk was a loud, steady hum, like the sound of a powerful dynamo. Excitement was so thick you could feel it.

"Man, if that Sid Bip gets a gun it'll be just too bad."

"You sure ain't told no lie. That Mueller is a desperate sonofabitch too."

"Yeah, but not like Sid. It took the G-men to get Sid in here." Bippus had been convicted of being the trigger man in the murder of Ben Levin, a La Fayette newspaper editor. "They never will forget him around La Fayette."

"You heard what the radio said."

"Damn right."

"Said he was the most dangerous of all five."

"Damn right."

"Wonder what he was doing in 1-4."

"Oh, his ticker went bad."

"You mean he wanted to chisel in on that special diet?"

"Now that's right."

"It'll be just too bad if he gets a gun."

"They never will get him without somebody being killed, if he gets a gun."

"Without a whole lot of 'em being killed."

"They'll never get Sid Bip."

When we left the dining room we saw guards mounting machine guns on tripods in the yard. The convicts marched under the blunt snouts of the machine guns, excited and tense and ready to explode. Another machine gun was mounted on top of the warden's quarters, overlooking the prison yard.

"You better watch out, kid," Blocker said, grinning. "Don't you take a notion to get mad today."

"No worry, with all that artillery about," I said.

By dinnertime we had learned that five convicts from 1-4 had crawled up the ventilator in the 3&4 cell block and lowered themselves from the roof to the front yard with sheets tied together. The night guard had missed them shortly after twelve o'clock.

Sid Bippus was the first to be captured. A housewife on the outskirts of town had seen him slinking through her back yard and had called the sheriff's office. An old, feeble, gray-haired deputy sheriff named Kingman, whom I had cursed out many times when I'd been in the county jail out there, had gone out to this lady's house and had taken Sid out of the barn loft where he had been hiding half-frozen and had brought him back. Sid had been armed with a pistol, the newspapers said, but had put up no resistance.

Mueller was shot and killed a week later in a public park in Indianapolis. Another of the men was arrested and returned from Kansas City, Kansas. By then we had forgotten about them.

And then one day, weeks later, I said to the guy next to me in school, "Say, wake up, Freddy, the sergeant just came in."

He straightened up, rubbing his eyes and grinning sheepishly.

"Damn, you sleep every day," I said. "You must be digging out at night."

"I am," he said, grinning.

He was a good-natured kid of about twenty with a very pleasant smile, and corn-colored hair that flagged across his forehead. He was out of Stateline, they said.

That night about twelve o'clock I was awakened by a shot. I heard several scattered shots and then a sudden fusillade. And then there were some shots which punctured the thin walls of the dormitory and drove the men, rushing and excited, from that entire end. There was some shooting around the corner of the dormitory, and some more shots through the dormitory walls and another fusillade, and some more excitement inside of the dormitory. The excitement inside of the dormitory was more dramatic than the shooting. The shooting was over in about a half hour, although a half hour's shooting was plenty of shooting in prison. It was almost too much shooting without the National Guard being called. But the excitement lasted all night and 'way up into the morning.

In the morning, before breakfast, some of us slipped outside of the dormitory and went around to the other side—the side toward the walls—to examine the bullet holes.

"Hey, look, there's the rope they used."

We looked up and saw a knotted chain of sheets swinging from the bars of the ventilator intake, high up the side of the sheer stone wall of the front cell house. By that time guards were converging on us from every quarter and we beat it back inside of the dormitory. Some of the fellows got caught and taken to the hole.

Later that day we learned that Fred Veeders, the kid I'd spoken to in school the day before, and his brother, Harry, and a crippled convict named Tap Spence had escaped from their cell in 6-1 by digging through the reinforced concrete walls. They had walked down the catwalk between the 1&2 cells, to the end of the cell house where there was an iron ladder leading up to the outside window.

The narrow space between the cells was necessary to install and repair the plumbing and electrical installations. They had then sawed through two of the window bars and lowered the sheet to the catwalk atop the forty-foot section of outside wall connecting the 1&2 cell block with the main west wall, and separating the prison proper from the honor men's dormitory. Although this section of prison wall was the same as the regular outside walls, beyond it was the enclosed dormitory and in order to escape one had to go down it to the west wall. There was a guard tower in the corner where the wall abutted and two power spotlights cast their beams at right angles down the two walls. Just inside, and below this wall, was the death house with its black slanting roof, and beside the death house was a heavy plate steel door opening into the back yard of the honor men's dormitory.

In order to lower themselves from the ventilator intake of the cell house to the catwalk the men were exposed the full route in the blinding glare of the corner spotlight; which would have made them visible even to a casual window-gazer in a passing train a half mile down the railroad tracks which ran outside the walls. After reaching the catwalk they had to walk straight into the glare of light, behind which the wall guard should have been sitting with his machine gun trained on them. But the tower guard was asleep. It seemed impossible for these three convicts to have known he would be asleep on this particular night at this particular hour. They could not see him for all the blinding light which they had to pass through after coming from the black, dark passage between the cells. Nevertheless, he was asleep. They slipped up on him and took his rifle and submachine gun and riot gun and gas gun, and beat him unconscious and tossed him down on the cinders which covered that portion of the prison yard.

After that they evidently waited for the night yard guard to come around the dormitory on his nightly patrol, and then cut loose at him with the rifle and submachine gun. They didn't hit the guard, however. He was the guard who had killed Red Swayzee back of the hospital that night and we were all sorry that he wasn't killed.

But the guard ducked back around the corner of the dormitory and, from its protection, returned the convicts' fire. He was joined by a number of other guards. The three convicts remained in the corner tower shooting at the guards during the whole half hour, without any guards going outside and attacking them from that side. Finally the convict named Tap Spence was shot in the thigh. The Veeders brothers jumped to the ground outside. When Tap made the jump his thigh, which had been shot, split open like a burst watermelon. The Veeders brothers had to leave him there to die while they made their escape. They left the submachine gun with him and two loaded clips. Tap wouldn't let anybody get close to him and finally he was shot by a guard sergeant who mounted the wall by means of a ladder from the inside, and pumped a submachine gun full of bullets down into him from atop the wall. While I still remembered them the Veeders brothers were never caught.

And there were some who were killed by the due process of the law. They were first electrocuted and then the prison doctor ran a long thin needle through their hearts.

There had been quite a lot in the newspapers about Doctor Snodgrass ever since it had been discovered that he was the one who had killed the girl. The papers were full of it all during the trial and after the conviction and they got full of it again, shortly before the date of execution.

He was a well-known surgeon from Springfield, out of a socially prominent family. The girl, whom he had killed by knocking her in the head with a hammer, then severing some important arteries by sticking a knife blade up her ears and reaming them out, was a college student. He had given her Spanish fly during the period of their intimacy in order to teach her various manners of sex degeneracy, and they had smoked marijuana weed together and blown their tops during their sex-maddened tea jags; and he had finally, "in order to obtain complete satisfaction, utterly debased himself before her, receiving the exaltation of his sensation from the stimulation of his utter debasement—" That's what the little pamphlets said, which sold for twenty-five cents, and which were very frank about the matter.

"It don't count on a bop binge, anyway," one of the convicts in school argued.

"Hell, it was young stuff," another confirmed. "She was only nineteen."

We were in school that afternoon, baiting our teacher as usual, when one of the fellows looked out the window and said, "Here comes Doctor Snodgrass."

"Where?"

We jumped up and rushed to the school windows.

"That him?"

"Sure."

"I don't believe it," I said. "I don't believe that's him."

"Sure that's him, the lousy rotten bastard. I'd know him anywhere I see him, as much as I've seen his picture."

"That's him all right."

I still didn't believe it. A tallish, bald-headed man walked beside a stoutish woman clad in a black fur coat with a dark felt hat pulled low over her face, and a handkerchief held up to her eyes as if she was crying. The man had a seamed, ravaged face, as if he had worried a great deal, but at the time he was calmly smoking a cigar. The woman walked close to him on the other side. She was holding his arm. The man was bareheaded and dressed in a blue suit with a white shirt and dark tie. He did not wear an overcoat. They walked slowly. Behind them, about twenty feet, the deputy followed with a guard to whom he was talking. The man and the woman were also talking. There was no one else.

Blocker had come in from the other room and squeezed into the window beside me. "That's him all right, kid."

A convict called Candy yelled from the window, "Take that cigar out your mouth, you rape-fiend murdering bastard!" The convicts didn't like the doctor. There was something about his act of killing the girl, just to keep it from being discovered that he was having an affair with her, that they couldn't take.

The deputy looked up and saw us jammed in the windows and came over and made us go back to our seats. As soon as he turned away we rushed right back to the windows. The school guards didn't object; they were trying to see too. Several other convicts yelled obscenities at the doctor. He didn't give any sign that he heard them. The deputy waved us away from the windows again, but he didn't come over. We didn't move.

The doctor and his wife walked down the brick walk toward the death house and passed out of sight around the corner of our dormitory. The deputy and the guard followed. There was no other excitement on the yard. It was as if they were two visitors to the prison.

I felt vaguely dissatisfied and annoyed. "Damn, don't they have any guards with them when they take them to the chair?"

"They do as a rule," a convict said.

"They ought to have some with that bastard son of a bitch," another convict said.

"It looks funny," I said. It didn't seem right.

"He's a big shot," someone said.

That evening after supper the convicts in the dormitory went straight to the windows that looked obliquely toward the death house. I tried to start a poker game but no one was interested. Blocker said finally, "Come on, kid, let's catch the show."

I got up reluctantly and followed him. The windows were jammed. We tricked a con out of his place by telling him someone was breaking into his lockbox. It was an old gag but he went for it; he didn't think we were the kind of fellows who would kid him.

"That's her," Blocker said.

From where I stood I could see the death house, etched in the twilight glow. I had looked out those windows a hundred times and had it in my sight each time, but I had never seen it before. It was a square, squat house of dull red brick about the size of a two-car garage. It seemed superimposed against the gray stone of the west wall. The guard turret, where Tap Spence and the Veeders brothers staged their midnight shooting spree, was outlined against the darkening sky. There was the end of the brick walk which led from the prison yard, where it was chopped abruptly off by a waist-high iron railing, and looking at it and at the green door to the right, I wondered, fleetingly, how a man would feel after walking the bitter half mile from death row to come to it. Then the twilight suddenly paled and the glare of the prison lights became more obvious. A group of noisy, chattering, well-dressed men came excitedly down the walk and entered through the green door.

"Who're they?" I asked.

"Reporters, mostly," someone replied.

"Did you see the warden?" another convict asked.

"Yeah, I saw the pig," was the reply.

"I saw the doctor," I said.

"Old horse ass."

"They're the witnesses," Blocker said.

Later the purr of a motor sounded. I saw the black sheen of the hearse as it idled across the rough areaway outside the window. It turned, backed up to the green death-house door, and came to a stop. We had become very quiet in the dormitory. After a short time I heard a sullen whine, very faint, come from within the death house.

"Thar she blows!" someone said.

Into the silence I heard someone say, "Murder seems

such a little thing when you're doing it." I looked around and recognized the moralist as Metz. I looked back at the death house.

The green door opened and a hand beckoned. Two men got down from the hearse and went around and opened the back and took out a wicker basket. They took the basket inside and after a moment they brought it out and shoved it back into the hearse. They got in and started the hearse and drove away. That was all there was to it. I could feel a vein throbbing quickly, steadily at my temple. I went back to the poker game and began dealing. "Come on, good gamblers," I called.

Down at the lower end where the colored convicts bunked a voice was singing loudly: "Uncle Bud. . . . Uncle Bud. . . . Uncle Bud got 'backer ain' never been chewed; Uncle Bud got women ain' never been screwed. . . . Uncle Bud, Uncle Bud. . . ."

13

IT WAS in Lippy Mike's poker game that I first noticed Metz. Three of the players had stayed for the last card but when the player, Frenchy Frank, bet two dollars and forty cents the third player turned down. Mike said, "I call it," and Frenchy said, "Put it in the pot," and Mike said, "Goddammit, I'm the dealer, I call it," and Frenchy turned over his cards and threw them into the discard. Mike reached for the pot and Frenchy said, "Let's see what you got," and Mike said, "You don't need to see it, you said I won it." Frenchy said, "The hell I ain't supposed to see it." Mike shuffled in his hand and raked in the pot and said, "I'm taking it and if you don't like it, bastard, you can pat your foot."

Frenchy got up and walked away from the table and Metz said in an angry, intense voice, "Boy, you're lucky, you're lucky, man! You're lucky . . . *lucky!*" shaking his head quickly, violently. "Lucky to be living . . . lucky someone hasn't killed you. . . . Boy, you're lucky . . . LUCKY!"

It was then that I looked at him. He had a narrow, rather handsome, very reckless face with curly black hair cut GI fashion, and the arteries stood out in his large-fingered hands, jerking nervously on the table. There was a ragged scar down the middle of his forehead to the bridge of his nose and now, in his hot red face, it was livid like a jagged line of clotted blood; and as I watched it seemed to twitch as if it was a separate living entity from his face. I had never seen a man who seemed so completely ready either to kill or die.

Mike was looking at him too. "You've said it all," Mike said. He seemed more cautious than afraid.

"What do you mean?" Metz challenged, in his clogged intense voice.

"I mean you've said it all."

Metz looked at him, weighing the words, then passed it. He threw away his chips in the next pot, betting on nothing, then backed away from the table, looking at Mike, undecided, then turned away and went down to his bunk which was at the head of the aisle. Standing, he was tall and flat with the slight stoop that tall men seem to have, but none of the recklessness that was in his face and hands was in his body. There was an indication of rigid control in his body motions, as if his life had been repressed or severely disciplined.

The incident left me with a vague sense of letdown. I had hoped that he would try Mike. He seemed like a man who would be towering in his rages. After a time I quit also and cashed out and went over to see how Blocker was making out in our game. Mike hadn't been open long and most of the play had gone to his game for the time being, making our game slow, so I left Blocker to hold it down and sauntered up to Metz's bunk. He had an upper and he was sitting with his back against the frame, with his feet up on a newspaper spread over the blanket, reading a book.

"Say, your name's Metz, isn't it?" I asked.

He turned his head, then swung around to face me, dropping his feet over the edge of his bunk. "Hello, Monroe," he said. "Yes, it is," he added. "Why?" In repose his skin was whiter and he looked older, perhaps thirty-five.

"I just heard you talking to that starker, Mike," I said. "You certainly told him right. He's a lucky man to be living, as overbearing as he is."

"You know," he said, grinning apologetically, "when I

see that fellow run over someone like that I get so angry I can't see. I'd like to just take something and whip him to death."

"He doesn't do that outside," I said. "He just does it in here because he knows he's got protection."

"You know, he's the sort of fellow I despise." His grin was one-sided and showed several gold crowns.

"He'll get his some day," I said.

"More than likely some little fellow whom he thinks is weak will be the one to kill him."

"That's just about the way it'll happen," I said. While he was rolling a cigarette I picked up the book he'd been reading. It was a textbook on short-story writing. "What you doing, studying short-story writing?"

"Yes, it's rather interesting."

"I was sort of under the impression that you had to be gifted to write short stories."

"Maybe you're right," he said, "although the good doctor here seems to feel, unless I have misunderstood him, that he can teach you the art without your being gifted."

"Maybe he can," I conceded, grinning slowly.

"Oh, I don't ever expect to really write any stories," he said. "I'm a jeweler by profession. I'm just studying this for something to do. You know a fellow has to do something."

"Damn right. I'd like to look it over sometime."

"Sure, come on down and study it with me," he invited. "I'd like to have you. Maybe we could get together and swap some ideas. You know, the most of these fellows are difficult to converse with. They're so damned set in their opinions. It wouldn't be so bad if they weren't so damned ignorant too."

"That's the kind who's the most positive," I said. "I'm going to take you up on that writing course," I said. "I'd like to know something about writing."

"Sure, I'd be glad to have you." That had been shortly after Thanksgiving.

I went down the next night and we ran through a few pages of the text and then we began talking about ourselves. Within a week or so we had developed a close companionship. It came out that he had owned a part interest in a jewelry store in Lake City from which he received a comfortable income, but he had been unfortunate enough in marrying a slut by whom he had a child and whom afterward he had killed. If it had not been for the child he would simply have divorced her.

However, the details of his crime did not come from him, they came from other convicts whom I talked to about him. He seldom spoke of his home life, and never of the woman he had killed. The way it was told to me is that one night he saw his wife riding down Western Parkway in a taxi with another man, kissing him in the taxi, after she had told him that she was going to visit her sisters. He'd gone home and got his pistol and begun searching for her. He was in a taxi also and he had his driver drive up one street and down another, intending to comb the entire city. Finally he had run across his wife and the man, getting into a taxi in front of a restaurant in the shopping center at Western Parkway and Grand Avenue. They were headed in the opposite direction. He had his driver turn around and overtake them down near the Christian Science chapel, not far from the Grand Avenue precinct station. He had leaned from the window of his taxi, aimed the pistol at his wife, and shot her dead. His attorneys had gotten the case down to manslaughter, and he'd been sentenced to seven to twenty years. At that time he'd been in prison three years.

Our companionship was strangely separate from all my other prison activities. Although Blocker and I were still running our poker game and Mal and I were still good cousins, the companionship between Metz and myself did not include either of them, nor the poker game, nor any other phase of prison activity. It was as if we were members of the same club and had discovered a common interest in chess and conversation.

Blocker used to stop by Metz's bunk sometimes and ask, "How're you and the professor doing, kid?"

And Metz would say, "I guess you're cheating everybody's eyeteeth out, Blocker."

"You better come down and let me get some of you, professor," Blocker would say.

Metz would shake his head. "No, you're too slick for me. You know, I never gamble with a man with fingernails as long as yours. You might not be slick, in fact you might even be a square—"

"I am," Blocker would cut him off, winking at me. "You can trim me. I ain't nothing but a square."

"No, sir, any man who has fingernails as long as yours, I let them go."

They were all right with each other. Neither of them ever said anything disparaging of the other that I knew of. But they had nothing in common except gambling and

Metz had just about quit gambling after his flare-up in Lippy Mike's game. On the other hand, Mal didn't seem to care so much for the idea. "Are you still fooling around with that short-story writing?" he would ask.

"Sure, I like it. I think it's interesting."

"That guy can't teach you anything. He doesn't even know as much as you do."

"He's not teaching me anything. I'm just taking a course with him."

"I'll bet before it's done with he'll want you to help pay for it."

"Aw, you're nuts!"

But we kept right on with it all through the winter. It was more the companionship of Metz than the course in short-story writing that interested me. His conversation was a relief from the stale, monotonous babble of the prison. I'd get away from that when we talked. I'd get away from all the sex. I'd get away from all those fags that had leaned on me, surrounded me; and those would-be wolves who had kept shooting at me on the sly, long after they'd concluded that I wouldn't go. Metz was the first really decent fellow whom I had met in prison, although Blocker was my only true friend. After Mal had moved away from the coal company, that first month I was in prison, I had never really liked him. But it was as if he had come to be my responsibility. In some strange way I'd gotten to feel I had to support him, keep him supplied with things he needed, give him money and time. But I liked to talk to Metz.

Almost any subject that came into the conversation was enough for us to argue about. He was so intense in his assertions that many times, knowing I was wrong, I would argue for the sheer delight of trying to outwit him. And because he was a very reasonable fellow I would often convince him of the logic of my viewpoint when I wasn't even convinced of it myself. He was always quick to see the other fellow's point and that made our arguments interesting, without rancor.

Neither of us, it came out, was religious. But Metz claimed to be an atheist. I told him that I didn't believe it possible to be an atheist and he said, why, and I said because I didn't believe any man could live without believing in some force superior to the human being, and he said there wasn't anything superior to the human being, that it was the human being who created the God.

And I said, "I believe that, all right. And I believe, in

addition, that each person who believes in a God has a separate individual God of his own."

"Do you believe in an afterlife?" he asked.

"Not for me," I said, "because I don't believe in it. But I believe if a man did believe sincerely in an afterlife that his belief would create an afterlife. I believe that this life and God and religion and an afterlife, and everything, exists only in the belief that it exists; and if one believes in an afterlife, as he believes that he is living in this life, that for him there will be an afterlife. I believe that the only time anything comes to an end is when belief in its existence comes to an end, and I believe that life and the world will only exist for persons as long as their belief that it exists, exists. I don't know whether I'm very clear," I said.

"Oh, I understand what you mean," he said. "It is your opinion that things only exist in belief."

"Yes, that's it. For us humans, I mean. I don't think it is like that for everything. I think that is why humans are given the power to believe or reject. I believe that afterlife is like flying—as long as people believed they couldn't fly they couldn't fly, but when they believed they could fly they did."

"What about a person flying like a bird without the aid of machinery?" he asked, grinning. "Do you believe that a man with sufficient faith could go up to the top of a building and jump off and begin flying like a bird?"

"I do," I said solemnly. "I believe that if a person could believe he could fly he wouldn't need any building but could fly up from the ground. But I'll never believe that a person can believe that until some person does believe and does fly and I see him and then—" I added, grinning, "I might not even believe it."

"I see what you mean," he said. "But that doesn't give me any argument."

"That's it," I said.

Or we'd argue about sex perversion in prison. He contended that it was unnecessary and spiritually and morally injurious to those who participated in it. He would begin upon the premise that any form of perverted sex was both physically and spiritually degrading, and I'd say, just to make an argument, "They tell me that married people do everything; they say that's part of the sex act itself."

And he'd grin and say, "But these convicts aren't married."

And I'd grin and say, "Don't be too sure about that."

Once I said, "You're right, of course, but I'm not as

positive in my judgment as I was when I came in. I suppose I've changed a little."

"You don't want to change too much," he said, looking at me.

14

I HAD GOTTEN to the place where I left the greater part of the running of our poker game to Blocker. Almost every evening after supper found me perched atop Metz's bunk, feeling him out for a discussion.

We were sitting there that Easter Monday evening, talking about the fatalism of Omar Khayyam. "You know, I like the sound of his work as well, if not better, than the content," he grinned. "Listen to this: 'Then to the Lip of this poor earthen Urn I lean'd, the Secret of my Life to learn: And Lip to Lip it murmur'd—While you live, Drink!—for, once dead, you never shall return.' "

"Look, there's a fire in the 10&11 block!" someone yelled.

We sauntered over to the window. At first there was no great excitement. "Hell, what's to burn over there? They're still working on that block."

"There's all that wooden scaffolding and stuff where they're pouring the concrete."

"Let her burn. There ain't nobody in there."

"And the 7&8 block is fireproof."

"Fireproof and every other kind of proof."

"There ain't nothing to burn in that 7&8 block but the convicts."

From the dormitory window we could see the north end of the 7&8 cell house. As we watched, talking and excited, the smoke thickened, rolled up from the roof, came out of the windows. Behind the smoke the sun set, red and majestic. Fire trucks came in through the stockade. We could hear the clang of the bells, the motor roar. We could see convicts beginning to run across the yard. Negro convicts came running from the coal company in a sudden surge, carrying blankets in their arms. Then white convicts came running from the dining-room company, around the corner of the dining room, cutting across the yard toward the burning cell house. Guards came running. Everyone was running. In all that mob that passed before our view I did not see a single person walking. Excitement ate into us, watching from the window, gutted our control.

"That's bad!" someone said. "That's bad! That's too much smoke!"

Someone else said, "Goddammit, I'm going out! My brother's in 5-8. I'm going out! Everybody else is already out. I'm going out, goddammit, I'm going out!" He broke away from the jam and ran toward the door.

"I'm going out too," I said, breaking after him.

The day guard was standing in front of the door. "Get out of the way, I'm going out!" the convict said.

"We're going out!" I said.

"You can't go out," the guard said.

"The hell I can't!" the convict said. He swung a long arched right and hit the guard just below the eye. The guard drew back his stick and the convict caught it in the air. I hit the guard in the stomach, as hard as I could with my left. I was excited out of my reason. The guard grunted, "Umph!" and doubled over. The convict came up with an uppercut and caught him in the face. I pushed him over to one side. Just as he fell the door opened from the outside and Nick came in, bareheaded and panting.

"Get some blankets, boys," he gasped, in a ravished voice. "Hurry and get some blankets. The boys are burning to death over there. Oh God, the boys are burning to death over there. Oh God, it's terrible, it's awful, they're burning to death in their cells."

I snatched a blanket from a bunk and ran out of the door. Turning, I ran around the back of the hospital and started across the yard. Already the early night had settled over the prison. There was a wind blowing, making the air cool. I was coatless and hatless. I could feel the coolness of the air through my shirt, on my head.

Smoke rolled up from the burning cell house in black, fire-tinged waves. The wind caught it and pushed it down over the prison yard like a thick, gray shroud, so low you could reach up and touch it with your hand. Flames, shooting through the windows and the roof of the cell house, seen through the smoke, looked like red tongues stuck out at the black night. Buildings were shadows in the crazy pattern of yellow light that streaked the black blanket of smoke. It was startling to be out at night. The fire was startling. The night itself was startling—it was like something suddenly discovered—like the night itself had been suddenly discovered and the fire in the night had been discovered.

The front cell house stretching across the front of the prison was a big gray face of solid stone with grilled steel bars checkerboarding the yellow glow of windows. It was like a horizon about the night. The night stopped there.

When I came out into the yard I had the odd feeling that I could hear those convicts a hundred yards away, crying, "Oh, God! Save me! Oh, God! Save me!" over and over again. The words spun a sudden, cold-tight fear through my mind.

I looked up and the whole face of the yard was in my view. It was a mass of churning confusion. Thousands of convicts were loose on the yard. Everyone was running at top speed in a different direction, yelling to one another. Everybody was yelling and nobody was listening. In the background was the burning cell house and beside it the 7&8 cell house. The 7&8 cell house was like a huge, fire-eating monster sucking in the flame and smoke upon the writhing convicts in its belly. And beyond, down past the stockade behind the mills, was the gray stretch of walls, connecting the earth with the sky, closing in a world.

Yellow light shining from the open door of the hospital cut a kaleidoscopic picture into the confusion of the yard; showed flashes of convicts coming into the picture, going out, coming in, going out, everybody running. The confusion swallowed me, made me a part of it, pushing out the memory of Blocker and Metz and Mal, pushing out the memory of the dormitory and the prison. It left me with a compelling urge to run.

I started running across the yard with that high-stepping sense of being too tall to stay on the ground, that marijuana gives you. The harder I ran the less distance I covered. I felt as if I was running up and down in the same spot. I ran harder, lifted my feet higher, until I was churning with motion, going nowhere. And then I stepped into something. I looked down and saw that I had stepped into a burnt-up convict's belly and had pushed out huge globules of vomit through his tightly clenched teeth and over his black-burned face. Suddenly I saw them, prone gray figures on the bare ground, spotting the face of the yard. Still more were coming. Figures of charred and smoke-blackened flesh wrapped snugly in new gray blankets that they had cried for all that winter and couldn't get. I shuddered with sudden cold. "They don't need the blankets," I found myself protesting. "They don't need the blankets. They don't need the blankets, you goddamn fools!"

Suddenly a variegated color pattern formed before my eyes—black, smoke-mantled night, yellow light, red flames, gray death, crisscrossing into maggoty confusion. I plowed through the sense of confusion, down in front of the hospital, feeling that each step I took was on a different color. To my left was the white glare of the hospital lobby; gray bodies on the floor and white-clad nurses bending over them. To my right was the black confusion of the yard with bodies lying in the semi-gloom amid the rushing, cursing convicts. At the fringe of the light where the shadow began, smoke was a thick, gray wall.

I walked forward into the wall of smoke. For a moment I couldn't see. Someone bumped into me hard, knocked me to my knees. The side of my head struck the iron railing about the walk. Out of the sudden hurt a loud voice filled my ears like a roar, "Gangway! Live one! Live one!"

Four men swept by into the stream of the light and ran up the hospital stairs. They carried a writhing body—*a live one!*

I got up and went down and stood on the sidewalk in front of the deputy's office. The blanket which I had started out with was gone and my hands felt light from missing it. I felt in my pocket for a cigarette but didn't have any. A convict rushed by, smoking a Bull Durham, and I said gimme a draw. He took the butt from his mouth and tossed it to me. I caught it and stuck it in my mouth. I stood there puffing on the butt while motion whirled about me as if I was standing in the center of a spinning wheel.

The deputy's office was the hub of the confusion. Everything began there, or ended there, or spun out from there like a ribbon of ticker tape tossed from a skyscraper window. Everything came by me. I saw everything. It was like watching a night barrage of fireworks from the top of a jag. My mind would not acquaint itself with the confusion, the rapid change of action, the finality of every spoken word, of every movement, of every curse, or every yell. I could not meet the shattering necessity of bridging the gap from life to death. The incidents which came quickly and shockingly left. I could not absorb it—the live ones and the dead ones and the strings of greenish vomit down the yellow-lighted walk. I felt only an increasing nausea.

I saw a stream of people entering through the front gates from the outside. Doctors and newspaper reporters and policemen and black-robed priests, and a woman nurse who worked with the strangling stiffs on the yard all night and was never once molested. All mingling shoulder to shoulder with the three thousand and more slavering, running, always-running convicts. They rushed by me, over me; jostled me, cursed me.

Suddenly I was running again, high-stepping and churning. I ran across the yard toward the burning cell block. The acrid fumes were thick over there. I began to cough. I stopped in front of the cell-house. I had forgotten what had prompted me to run.

The scaffolding about the half-constructed 10&11 cell block was burning furiously. Smoke and flames were leaping across the stair well into the 7&8 block where the three top ranges of men were still locked in their cells. I could hear those strangled screams; those choked, unended prayers; those curses and coughs and gasps and moans and wails of those trapped men up there. The wooden joists of the roof had caught fire. I could see the furious flames of the burning roof through the gray smoke which reached down six tiers to the floor.

Outside the cell-house door water covered the ground. Fire hoses were everywhere, like huge writhing snakes in the mud. There were two fire engines by the door. The other trucks were down at the end of the cell house, beyond the chapel. The slickered firemen rushed again and again into the dense smoke-filled block only to retreat coughing, strangling, vomiting. Several lay on the ground unconscious. Insane-looking convicts, naked to their waists, wrestled with the hoses. Water bouncing from the hot stone sprinkled my face.

I started through the door and heard a voice yell from up above, "Get me out of here, get me out of here! You sons of bitches! Oh, you goddamned bastards—" Ending on a choking scream.

I backed out of the doorway. But I could still hear those muffled screams.

"Oh, God! OhhhhhHHHHHHH Godddddddd! Ohhhh

GOOOOOOODDDDDDDDDDD! Get me out of here! Get me out, I say! What the hell you tryna do, kill me? You tryna kill me? I ain't done nothing! I ain't done nothing to nobody! You tryna kill me, you goddamned sons of bitches . . . ? Where in the hell is that goddamned—?"

There was someone up there unlocking the cells, someone said. I didn't believe it. I bent over and peered up through the smoke. All I could see was a vague outline of the block in the gray smoke with a top of flame, dripping water and slime and those horrible choking half-prayers, half-curses.

A big colored convict called Block Buster loomed suddenly in the doorway. He had come out of the gray smoke like a sudden apparition. He had a limp figure draped across his shoulder. The unconscious figure strangled suddenly and vomited down the front of Block Buster's shirt. I looked at the slimy clotted filth, felt my stomach turn over.

"Get a blanket and give me a hand here," I heard a voice say. I could feel my lips twitching as a wave of nausea swept over me.

"No can do," I said in a low, choked whisper and backed away.

A policeman pushed me out of the way to let four men pass with a blanket with a body. I stumbled backward over a fire hose, sat down in the slop. I jumped up and started to run again. I didn't know where I was running—anywhere, so long as it was away.

I didn't know what was the matter with me. I didn't feel scared. I wanted to go up there. My mind wanted to go up there. My mind kept prompting me to turn around and run back and go up there and save some poor bastard's life. But I couldn't. That was all. I couldn't. I couldn't go up there and bring one of them down, for love or money. I just couldn't do it.

I kept running through the confusion with a high-stepping churning gait. My mind was in a gray daze. Blue-coated firemen passed my vision. Their loud megaphoned voices reached my ears. The sights of the policemen were in my eyes. The sights of the living convicts lugging the dead. The sights of the smoke and the flame and the water and the guards. Of convicts who were in for murder and rape and arson, who had shot down policemen in dark alleys, who had snatched pocket books and run, who had stolen automobiles and forged checks, who had mutilated women and carved their torsos into separate arms and legs and heads and packed them into trunks; now working overtime at their jobs of being heroes, moving through the smoke with reckless haste to save some other bastard's life. White faces gleaming with sweat, streaked with soot, white teeth flashing in greasy black faces; working like hell, some shouting, some laughing, some solemn, some hysterical; drunk from their momentary freedom, drunk from being brave for once in a cowardly life. Fun, excitement, something to do . . . something to do . . . something to do . . . something to do. . . .

In the distance, from wherever I ran, I saw the walls.

There was an eternity in which I ran, running and gasping and shoving and running and cursing and striking out blindly with my clenched fists and slipping and running again, in which I seemed to be standing still while the chaos rushed past me, pulling at me, clutching at my sleeves, choking me. I reached the corner of the chapel, forty feet away.

I tried the chapel door. It was unlocked. I walked inside. In the vestibule, just inside the doorway, a convict stood in the darkness, crying. He was repeating over and over again with slow, dull monotony, "Son of a bitch . . . ! Jesus Christ . . . ! Son of a bitch . . . ! Jesus Christ . . . ! Son of a bitch . . . ! Jesus Christ . . . !"

He didn't see me. He didn't seem to see anything.

"Say a prayer for me, dear brother, say a prayer for me." My lips formed the words involuntarily, shocking me.

I went up the steps and into the chapel. Some convicts were shooting craps on the floor down in front of the pulpit. I listened for a moment to the snapping of their fingers, their low intent voices. "Eighter from Decatur. . . . Huhn . . . ! Be eight . . . !" The dice rattled again. One of the players looked up and saw me. "What you shoot, Jimmy?"

I shook my head, feeling my face break crookedly. My mind snapped loose in sudden, grotesque fantasy. God and the devil gambling for the souls of the dying convicts. . . . I bet this nigger murderer. He cut his wife into black bloody hash with a barlow chiv. . . . All right, I'll put up this white rape fiend. Omnipotence touched me. I saw the whole universe standing there before me in its bleached, fleshless skeleton.

Then I heard a slow run on the bass keys of the piano. I heard a sound alien from the confusion outside. I saw the red glare through the frosted panes. I looked toward the stage. Someone had rolled the cover from the grand piano. A slim, curly-headed youth formed a question mark on the stool. He was playing Saul's "Death March," with slow feeling. A pencil-streak of firelight, coming through a broken pane high up on the wall, cut a white stripe down his face. It was like a scar. His cheeks were wet with tears. Then the slow, steady beat of the bass keys hammered on my mind like a hard fist.

"Don't you know people are dying outside, fool?" I asked.

He looked around. After a wire-tight moment he said, without stopping, "I'm playing their parade march to some red hell."

Worms began crawling in my stomach. I backed out of the chapel, into the chaotic night, feeling those worms crawling in my stomach as if I, too, was dead and in the ground and already rotting. Everything was gone, the touch of omnipotence, the skeletoned universe.

Outside the scene had changed as if another act had come onto a revolving stage. A snarling jam of convicts surged in a ragged mass about a circle of policemen who stood about the cell house door with submachine guns.

I heard a voice scream, "The walls are falling."

I saw a policemen's legs begin to tremble. The convicts surged slowly closer. His legs began to shake violently, the knees knocking together visibly. Something strange came out of me and I heard myself laughing. I felt an uncontrollable desire to throw something into that circle of policemen, and set off the fireworks.

"Get out of the way, you bastards!" someone said.

A crippled convict broke from the mass of tightly jammed convicts and ran toward the policemen in a hobbling, one-sided gait like a crayfish. A policeman grabbed him by the collar. The convicts started forward. Then the deputy came into the scene, holding up his hands. "Men! Men!" he pleaded.

I turned and walked away. Suddenly I was running again, arms churning, knees pumping. At the end of the walk I stopped. I stood there, undecided.

Two convicts were talking. One said, "There's Yorky! He won near two hundred up in the idle house yesterday."

The other one looked at him. "What say we clip it?"

"Sure, he don't need it no more."

I turned away and went over into the school. Mal was coming out of the lavatory.

"Where the hell you been?" I asked.

"I was looking for you, then the deputy had me over in the 1&2 block knocking the locks off the doors with a sledge hammer."

"Yeah? What for?"

"Aw, he wanted to let the rest of the guys out and they couldn't find the keys. They can't find the guards. They haven't seen any of the cell-house guards since the fire began."

He was smiling and his face looked very clean and his teeth looked very white, with the two gold crowns shining in the light, and his lips looked very red and he looked very pretty. "They had to knock the locks off the cells in the 3&4 block, too," he said, smiling and looking pretty. "They let everybody out, even the seven guys in death row. They're out, too."

I put my arm about his waist and kissed him. He tried to pull away.

I said, "Goddammit, let me kiss you!" He put his arms around me and we kissed each other.

After a time he broke away and said, "I got to go."

I released him. I didn't feel anything. There was no excitement, no passion, just a lingering feeling of the pressure of his lips.

"I've got to go up in the tin shop," he said, looking at me queerly. "Cap Hardy wants me to go up there and keep a lookout on things the rest of the night."

"Okay," I said, looking at him, watching him turn and go through the schoolroom, watching the motion of his wide hips. After a moment I went outside. I looked around and suddenly I began running again. A convict at the corner of the deputy's office stopped me. "Send a telegram home," he said, thrusting out a handful of Western Union blanks. "Tell the folks you're living."

"Gimme two," I said. He gave them to me. I went back into the schoolroom and made out one each to my mother and father. "I'm living," I wrote. "James Monroe." But I couldn't remember my mother's address. I went out and turned in the blanks to the convict. "I can't remember my mother's address," I said.

"That's all right," he said. "Just put the city on it."

The gray prone bodies got into my eyes. White man, black man, gentile, Jew. The old and the young, the lame and the sound. Some used to be bankers, some politicians, some sneak thieves, some racketeers. Just gray humps on the bare ground now. Whatever they had been, or had ever dreamed of being—whatever their race or their nationality or their background—that foot of greenish vomit hanging from their teeth made them all alike.

Looking at them I didn't get a thing, neither pity nor sorrow now awe nor fear—nothing. I saw Starlight there with the stink gone out of him, lying very still, no longer swaggering about the cell and poking out his fat belly, imagining himself a prize fighter. I saw Mother Jones, long and black and dead. And Blackie, small and delicate and white and dead. And Nig, big and black and tough and dead. I saw them all, scores of them on the bare ground, with their teeth bared and vomit in their lips, and their bodies grotesquely twisted, and their hands scorched and burned and gripping something, and their eyes open and staring at something. Out of the clear blue sky came the quotation with no connection whatsoever in my mind: "While you live, Drink!—for, once dead, you never shall return. . . ."

I walked among the bodies to see if I could recognize any others. Someone began crying loudly at my side. I turned around and saw a lanky black man with a hippo-spread of lips, kneeling on the ground by the body of a little brown-skinned man who was burned all around the mouth. The lanky one was known in the prison as Mississippi Rose. When Rose saw me looking at him he started blubbering louder. "Oh, lawsamussy me!" he cried. "Mah man's dead!"

"You dirty black bastard, robbing a dead man," I said, dispassionately.

"What the hell you got to do with it?" he said.

I swung at his shiny black face. I missed him and went sprawling over a corpse. The soft, mushy form gave beneath me. I jumped up, shook my hands as if I had fallen into a puddle of filth. Then the centipede began crawling about in my head. It was mashed in the middle and it crawled slowly through my brain just underneath the skull, dragging its mashed middle. I could feel its legs all gooey with the slimy green stuff that had been mashed out of it.

And then I was running again. I was running blindly over the stiffs, stepping in their guts, their faces. I could feel the soft squashy give of their bellies, the roll of muscles over bones. I put my face down behind my left hand, bowed my head and plowed forward.

A moment later I found myself standing in front of the entrance to the Catholic chapel. I felt a queer desire to laugh. I went up the stairs, inside, leaned against the doorpost beside the basin of holy water. Candles burned on the white altar, yellow flames cascading upward toward a polished gold crucifix. It was a well of peace amid chaos. I saw the curved backs of several convicts bent over the railing before the images of the saints.

"I believe in God, the Father Almighty, Maker of Heaven and Earth. . . ." The words came unbidden. I didn't know whether I said them aloud or only in my mind. Then they were gone and there was a sneer on top of my teeth. I could feel it underneath my lips, in my eyes. "I believe in the power of the press, maker of laws; in the almighty dollar, political pull, a Colt forty-five. . . ."

I turned and went downstairs, around the school and back toward the dormitory.

"Hey, Jimmy," someone called from the shadows. I looked and saw Hank the Crank. I nodded. "Say, Jimmy, that was Buck who clipped you for those strides," he said. "He sold them to a guy in 5-6."

"It's all right," I said. I went around behind the hole. Two convicts were standing in the shadows, talking.

"Leo clipped the screw and took the keys and went down the range. He's the one unlocked those cells. That's how they got out there."

"Is that so?"

"Sure, that's how they got out there. Leo let 'em out. He just did make it to the end. He brought the kid out with him. That's what I call love."

"That yallar-haired punk they call Aryan Doll?"

The sound of running feet came as a relief. The deputy and a fireman came into view up the darkened areaway between the hole and the dormitory. A voice yelled from the dormitory. "We're burning down the joint!"

A convict stepped into the doorway of the dormitory, holding a gallon can in his hand. I caught the stench of gasoline. I saw the stab of light from the deputy's torch. The convict in the doorway was a suddenly embossed picture on the black night, tall and lanky and starkly outlined. I saw the abrupt stretch of his eyes, saw the sag of him mouth, heard the ejaculation, "What the hell!"

I saw the fireman draw his pistol, jam it into the guy's guts. I heard the guy's grunt, saw him back up from the pressure of the gun, drop the can. I heard the clanking of the can on the wooden steps, heard the guy's loud laugh. Then, for an imperceptible instant, the picture hung. It was like a telescoped picture out of infinity. Then I saw the flash of the gun, heard the roar, heard the laugh choke off.

I watched until the convict fell forward, down the steps on his face.

And then I was running. I ran back to the deputy's office. Several convicts with crocus sacks of Bull Durham smoking tobacco had congregated there. They were giving it away.

"Here, take a bag, kid," a guy said, thrusting it at me. "Take two bags. Take all you want. There's plenty more over to the commissary. We're looting the joint, taking everything." I took a bag and tore it open with my teeth. I rolled a cigarette and stuck it in my mouth and stood there watching them. I didn't have a match. I sucked on the dead cigarette. "They're getting new clothes over to the commissary," the guy said.

I turned and started running. I ran through the bodies on the yard, past the fire trucks bunched at the end of the cell house, through the mud, underneath the ladder of a hook-and-ladder truck, up the commissary stairs. I grabbed a pair of new gray pants and put them on, snatched up a new coat, and ran down the stairs again.

"They're firing the woolen mill!" someone yelled. I turned in that direction, without slowing. I saw convicts inside the mill on the ground floor, sprinkling gasoline about and lighting it. I kept on running. I heard the roar of the fire trucks behind me as they moved down toward the woolen mill. I ran across the ball diamond, looked up and saw the tower guard leveling a machine gun on me, curved back toward the dining room.

The dining room was lighted. Several convicts were sitting inside, eating steaks. To one side several policemen and firemen sat, drinking coffee. A convict looked up from his steak and said, "Go on back in the kitchen and get something to eat, kid. They're giving it away."

"And wash your face," another one said.

I went back into the kitchen and heard a wild, savage yell ring out. I looked up and saw a wide-mouthed colored convict standing on top of the kitchen range. He had a butcher knife swinging from one hand, a cigar in the other.

"Go-on git wut yuh want, white chile," he said to me. "Ef'n airn roach set foot in heah Ah gwina cut his throat." Scars were shiny ridges in his black face. I believed him.

"Old Dangerous Blue," someone said jokingly.

I picked up a piece of cheese, tasted it, put it down. Then I ran out of the kitchen into the yard and kept on up into the tin shop. Mal was sitting in the guard's office behind the desk, reading a magazine.

"What you doing?" I asked.

He looked up. His eyes stretched. "Jesus Christ, what's the matter with you?" he asked.

Weakness came over me in waves. I felt as if I was going to faint. "Nothing."

"Why don't you wash your face? Your face is black. And your eyes look crazy as hell. What's the matter with you, Jimmy?"

I rested the palms of my hands on the desk, leaned my weight on my arms. "Listen—" I began. My tongue felt thick.

He got up and came around the desk and put his arm about my waist. "Come on and sit down and take it easy," he said. "What the hell you been doing? Have you been bringing down those burnt-up guys from the block?"

"Listen—" I said, thickly, pulling away from him. "I want you for my woman."

I felt his arm go rigid. "I don't understand what you mean."

I wet my lips, swallowed hard. The words were difficult to get out and I felt very weak and lightheaded. My eyes felt hot and dry and sticky. "Listen, don't give me that stuff. You know what I mean."

"You don't know what you're saying, Jimmy," he said. "Come on and sit down." He tried to pull me around the desk. "Come on and sit down and take it easy. You've gotten too excited."

"I know what I'm saying," I said. "I want you for my woman—my old lady. I want you right now. I don't want no more of this goddamned cousin stuff. I'm through fattening frogs for snakes."

He released me and stepped away. He was looking at me queerly. "You don't want that really, Jimmy?"

I looked at him but I couldn't see him well. I wondered if he asked the question straight or in rebuke. He was smiling in a funny sort of way. He looked strangely inhuman, like neither man nor woman. His eyes looked sick. I rubbed my hand hard down my face, bowed my head, then looked up steadily at him.

Suddenly I felt repulsed. "You can go to hell," I said. "Once and forever."

I went back down the stairs and kept on back of the hospital. Blocker was standing there with a convict called Pete. Pete was sitting on the ground, wrapped in three blankets, leaning back against Blocker's legs. "Old Blocker saved my life," Pete greeted me. "If it hadn't been for old Blocker I'd be a dead son of a bitch. I'd be buzzard's meat.

Old Blocker saved my life. Yes, sir, this old son of a bitch saved my life."

"Looks like you been fighting smoke, kid," Blocker said, grinning his yellow-fanged grin.

"I'm tired," I said. "Goddamn, I'm tired!"

"Sit down and take it easy, kid," he said. "Here, wait a minute." He pulled Pete back against the hospital wall and took one of the blankets and made a place for me beside him. "Here, sit down with this redheaded bastard and take it easy."

I sat down. Blocker sat down on the other side. The three of us sat there talking intermittently. "Boy, I thought I was a goner," Pete would say. About three minutes later Blocker would say, "Out of all those fine young kids up there I had to get a horny son of a bitch like you." After some more minutes had passed I would laugh. Sometime later Pete would say, "Old Blocker. Man, why don't you learn to cook?" And after another interval Blocker would say, "I said to myself, goddamn, there's Pete; if I let him croak then all the chumps'll be dead."

We felt very friendly, sitting there in the darkness back of the hospital.

"I wish I could go to sleep," I said.

Blocker said, "Give it time, kid. You know what I told you—never rush your luck."

15

SITTING THERE between Blocker and Pete, beside the hospital, through the slowly passing night, trying to fight off nausea, memories kept going through my mind like the fire itself. I tried to shake them off. I tried to unhook the whole damn thing, my mind and the memories. I tried frantically, as one tries to get off clothes that are burning. I finally got it unfastened from within my skull but I couldn't get it through my skull. The memories just kept on going around loosely in my head. But, finally, when they came to the pawnshop in Chicago I got rid of them. I didn't get rid of the pawnshop and how I stood there and let them come and arrest me. But I got rid of all the rest of them. That was the last time I remembered them.

In the early morning sunrise there was an eerie quietness over the prison. Most of the convicts had gone somewhere to sleep. Those few who still wandered about were like the early vultures about a carcass.

"Let's look her over," Blocker said, stretching.

"Okay," Pete said, getting up.

I followed. I felt dirty and disheveled, weary and stiff. My joints felt a thousand years old and the inside of my head felt hollow and queer. I kept feeling an impulse to laugh; I wanted to cackle. But I repressed it. I knew it would sound weird.

Rounding the corner of the hospital we came into a line of police reserves that reached from wall to wall, like a human blue-coated fence, separating the cell houses from the industrial buildings. They stood erect and silent and somber in the early light.

"Jesus, all the police in the world must be here," Pete said.

Blocker gave his sly chuckle. "Better watch yourself, kid," he said to me. "There's the law."

"I bet they'd cook and eat those dead convicts," I said.

Blocker jerked about and looked at me. "Take it easy, kid," he said.

"Hey, where you boys going?" one of the policemen asked.

"None of your goddamned business," Pete said. The cop reddened. We walked past, slowly, indifferently, secure. We knew that the policemen weren't looking for trouble that morning. "You hear that rotten bastard?" Pete said in his high, breaking voice. "Asking me where I was going after I damn near burnt to death last night."

"I know you don't want that stuff," Blocker said.

"I ought to go back and hit him in the mouth," Pete said.

"That's original," I said.

They both looked at me. Blocker said again, "Take it easy, kid."

"Say, looka there, look what they're doing," Pete said.

As we came into the yard we could see the dead They looked very dead in the sunlight. There was a truck backed up to the middle walk and a group of convicts were bringing the bodies over and stacking them neatly into the truck, one on top of another.

"Just like they were logs of wood," Pete said.

"They don't care," Blocker said.

The deputy stood to one side, directing the work. As we passed we heard him say, "Hurry up, hurry up, hurry up, boys, get them away before they begin to spoil, get them away before they begin to spoil."

There was a forlorn and forsaken look about the yard. It reminded me of a fairgrounds after the circus had left. The bodies were like the litter that has been left behind, like the scraps of paper and rags and crushed boxes and faded wet posters and piles of trash.

We kept on over to the 7&8 cell block and went up and looked at the cells. All that remained was the smoke-blackened walls and charred remains of the wooden rafters of the cell-house roof, and the half-burnt mattresses and the Sunday shirts half burned away; the remains of a coat, a blanket, a pair of pants, a wooden box, a pair of shoes shrunken into curled knots, a bathrobe burnt down the middle of the back. In one cell we saw a blanket draped over something over the commode, and when we pulled it away we saw a convict bent over the commode with his head rammed down in the water.

"My God!" Pete said and turned abruptly away and vomited all over the floor.

I stood there for awhile and looked at the body. The hair was partly floating in the dirty water and there were red-blistered burns on the back of the neck and ears, and a big hole was burned in the back of the shirt. His hands were tightly gripping the edges of the commode as if he had been trying to ram his head clear down the sewer.

"Come on, kid, let's get out of here," Blocker said.

I spat on the floor and turned to go. A colored convict came into the cell and looked about. He glanced indifferently at the body. "You know him?" I shook my head. He saw a half-burnt radio at the head of the bunk and took it. "He don't need this," he said, grinning at me. His teeth were decayed and tobacco-stained. He looked like a small scavenger animal.

"He don't need that," I said, going out on the range after Blocker and Pete.

As we went along we found the cells were full of them, white and colored convicts rummaging in the ruins, like maggots in a piece of rotting meat. They took everything they found that was even remotely valuable or had ever been of any value. They took those things that would not do them any good, but which they had always wanted, and now had a chance to take from the soot-blackened cells.

"Damned dirty buzzards!" Pete said.

"They're not hurting anybody," I said.

"They're not going to find any money, anyway," Blocker said. "Most of the guys who had any layers had it on 'em and they've already been clipped."

"I just hate to see it," Pete said.

"We'll get our share of it just as soon as they start gambling, won't we kid?" Blocker said.

"Let's go eat," I said.

We went back across the yard to the dining room. Breakfast was being cooked but it wasn't ready. They told us to wait awhile and they'd have breakfast for everyone. We went over to the 5&6 dormitories and past the front gates to the 3&4 cell block and then to the 1&2 cell block and finally back to our dormitory. Most of the convicts were sleeping. They were sprawled across the bunks in two's and three's with their clothes wrinkled and twisted about their bodies. I noticed that most slept with their mouths open and drooling saliva. I stretched out on my bunk. I was very sleepy but I couldn't sleep.

After a time the breakfast bell rang and we went over to the dining room and had breakfast of bacon and eggs. There were no lines or companies. They came over in groups and filled up the empty seats. The policemen stepped aside to let them pass and stood about and watched us eat. There was very little talk. Everyone seemed sleepy and exhausted. They ate doggedly. When we left the dining room we saw the last truck load of bodies starting away. "Go wash up and get something to eat," the deputy told the men who had just finished loading it.

"They got bacon and eggs for breakfast," someone said.

"Hell, come on," another convict said. "We can wash up in the kitchen. I'm hungry."

Blocker and Pete and I went over and sat on the front steps of the hospital and watched the activity on the yard. From where we sat the prison looked about the same, now that the bodies had been moved. We saw only three regular prison guards and they had hangdog expressions and stood about grinning at every convict who passed. The stone and steel and concrete, solid, immovable, eternal, rooted prison was much the same. The birds sat on the wires and cheeped. The new grass was as green as it had been two days before, and freedom was as distant as freedom always is. Only the convicts were different. They were too weary and stunned to be violent. But they were quietly determined to obey no more rules, to work no more in the shops and mills. Mostly they wanted to sleep. They returned to their cells and dormitories, doubling up with the convicts who had come out of the 7&8 cell block alive. They lay on their bunks or sat about the tables talking listlessly or lackadaisically playing cards, as if with their last remaining ounce of energy they had to show that they would be defiant.

For the most part they were very orderly. Word had gone around that two companies of soldiers were patrolling the walls outside. Just before dinner the police lined up and marched out through the front gate. National Guardsmen and naval reserves, little apple-cheeked boys with tight fitting blue sailor pants, came in to take their place. Martial law prevailed, although no one seemed to know just what it meant. That first day after the fire no effort was made to restore the routine of the prison. No orders were issued. The convicts and the guardsmen and the sailors wandered aimlessly about the yard.

Shortly after noon the two largest national broadcasting systems installed mikes on the main walk down near the front gates. News analysts interviewed some of the convicts who had gathered around. Most of the convicts who showed any manner of heroism during the fire were asleep at the time. Those who got a chance to talk over the air were the loud-mouthed phonies. I noticed that they all shouted into the mikes. They ignored the questions of the interviewers and shouted loudly about their great heroism. One began proclaiming that he was innocent of the crime for which he'd been convicted. They had to pull him away from the mike. Most of them just told how many convicts' lives they had saved.

A colored convict called Hard-Walking Shorty because he was a small, gnarled man with a game leg, began by clutching the mike as if it was an all-day sucker and shouting, "This is Hard-Walking Shorty. Hello, world! I'm a man of a few words but a lot of action. I brought down thirty men from 6-8. I doan know how I did it. I was stumblin' through the smoke and flame with two men on each shoulder. . . ." Before he got through he had saved over four hundred and ninety-nine men by actual count.

In fact, the dozen or so convicts who went on the air, by their accounts, had saved more lives than there were convicts in the prison. The news analysts didn't seem to realize that the convicts were simply talking for a pardon. Finally the men began blaming the warden for the fire. The warden sent a couple of honor men down into the front yard to cut the broadcasting lines. But by then many of the convicts who hadn't gotten any closer to the burning cell block than I had had become national celebrities.

That night it was rumored that during the confusion of the fire one convict had changed into civilian clothes, picked a pass from a reporter's pocket, and walked calmly through the front gate. But he was the only one who escaped. Even the condemned men who were out on the yard did not try to escape. The convict whom the fireman shot in front of the dormitory and another who was shot by a guard—shot in the guts with a shotgun loaded with bird shot—were the only ones who had been killed. Their bodies had been hidden under some tarpaulin in the hole and the next morning loaded on one of the trucks with the burnt convicts, without word of the killings getting about. We learned afterward that the bodies had been taken to the fairgrounds and laid out in rows on the tables until identified and claimed. Those that were not claimed by relatives or friends were buried in Potter's Field.

During the night the guardsmen were organized into patrol groups. Machine guns were mounted at strategic points about the yard, on top of buildings, and along the walls. When they saw the machine guns next morning some of the convicts permitted the guards to line them up and march them back to work. But most of the convicts still maintained their defiance.

That morning a Committee of Nine was organized by the convicts, in defiance of the warden. Dunlap, the instigator, called a mass meeting of the convicts on the yard that afternoon. The committeemen circulated among the convicts, passing along the word. They wore badges which said *"Committee"* and assumed the authority of guards.

Most of the convicts attended the meeting that afternoon. The yard was jammed with milling, noisy convicts. The patrol units of guardsmen and sailors were spaced along the outer walks. They carried rifles, riot guns and gas grenades. A platform had been erected by the alligator pool, and the p.a. system borrowed from the chapel. Dunlap mounted the platform and called for silence. He was a short, powerfully built man with a forceful personality. He said it was the idea of the committee to direct a campaign of passive resistance against the warden.

"We just want to get rid of that bastard. We don't want

to riot. We don't want to destroy any property. We don't want to harm any of the guards or officials. Just ignore them if they say anything to you. Now this is the idea We won't have any more companies, no more routine, and no more work until the welfare department has completed an investigation and appointed a new warden and a new order of guards." Everybody screamed and whistled and hurrahed. "The only person we want to keep is the deputy," Dunlap said. "The deputy is all right. We're going to ask the governor to appoint him warden." The convicts shouted their approval.

The deputy was standing at the edge of the mass of convicts, bobbing his head. We felt that he condoned the proceedings and in time the rumor grew that he had instigated them. Before the fire he had never been actively disliked as had Gout, the warden, and others, but he had never been very popular. But following that meeting the convicts began to worship him. He couldn't do anything wrong. He was the only official whom the convicts would obey. For a time the other officials and guards would not set foot within the yard. They congregated in the front offices and remained there all day.

Passive resistance was the order of the day. In conversation it took the place of the fire. All you could hear was "down with the pig." The committee ran all activities within the walls. The deputy worked with them. The laundry, dining room, and powerhouse were kept in operation. All other activities were suspended. The convicts ate, slept, and gambled. They had that punk they'd always wanted, stayed up all night, ran wild in droves like hungry wolves, stole from each other and robbed each other with knives at throats in the darkness, raped each other. But no one escaped.

It was bitchery and abomination, Sodom and Gomorrah in the flower of its vulgarity, stark and putrid and obscene, grotesque and nauseating. I moved through the sickening, stinking, sordid, sloppy, sensuous sights and scenes hollow-eyed and stunned, as if I was walking in my sleep. All that time I couldn't sleep. I lost weight rapidly and became very thin. Nothing I saw made any impression on me. I could no longer see any connection between the convicts and humanity. I didn't even think of humanity at all.

Tables were carried outdoors and the convicts gambled on the yard. Blocker and I ran our game on a desk we dragged from the school. At night we dragged it back inside the school. We took turns to eat because our game ran continuously, day and night. We had to hire three extra dealers to work shifts, and six tough convicts to protect the game from being robbed.

Bunks had been moved into the school to house convicts from the 7&8 cell block and, for a time, the school became the center of gambling and perversion. One night some convicts got hold of a package of marijuana weed. A dozen or so convicts stripped naked and had a "circus" in one of the schoolrooms. Convicts came from all over the prison to watch.

Occasionally Blocker and I would leave the game and wander about the prison to see what was going on in other places. We always took along two bodyguards. I saw a colored convict in the coal company who had twelve radios stacked about his bunk. Most of them were burnt and damaged beyond repair. None of them would play. But they were now his and he sat in the middle of them, looking very proud.

The fags paid fabulous sums to have articles of feminine apparel and make-up smuggled inside. It was said one cop made enough money from this business to buy a new car. In the 3&4 cell block the fags paraded about in their silk panties and nylon stockings and bright colored kimonos and diaphanous negligees. They wore heavily padded pink and black satin loincloths and their legs and arms and armpits were shaved. Their bodies were powdered and their faces rouged and their mouths heavy with lipstick. During the day they switched about the yard, rouged and powdered, but wearing their uniform trousers and silk blouses. They solicited around the gambling tables and at night they returned to their cells and did business.

Mississippi Rose, the liver-lipped colored convict whom I had seen robbing the dead Negro on the yard the night of the fire, had opened a red-light dive on 5-3. He had curtained off the front of the cell and covered the inside light with red tissue paper. Chick, a small blond fellow, had his hair marcelled. He had a cell on 5-4 where four or five fags worked in turns. The most popular girl-boy of all was a small, girlish sailor who was very animated and cute and had quick little movements and a bright little smile. It was rumored that he was charging twenty-five dollars and getting it.

A canteen had been set up in front of the chapel where ice cream, cake and cigarettes could be bought. All day long it was crowded with convicts spoiling with their kids.

The following Sunday services were held in commemoration of ". . . our dear dead comrades," as Deacon Smith defined them. I attended the services in the Protestant chapel. The chaplain said a prayer for the departed souls. That was the first time I had seen him since the previous Sunday. I hadn't even thought of him. Afterward Deacon Smith said a prayer and several visiting ministers prayed. I thought that the souls were getting a great send-off. Then a fat-faced fag sang "My Buddy." Tears poured down his cheeks like showers of rain. Many of the convicts began crying. I began crying also. I wondered what the hell I was crying about. But I couldn't help it. The chaplain said another prayer for the living convicts and we got up and sauntered out. As we crossed the yard we saw little black Doorbelly chasing big black Gravy down the main walk. Doorbelly had a brick in each hand and Gravy was highballing. The guardsmen were laughing. Doorbelly cut loose with one of the bricks and smashed a dining-room window. One of the committeemen ran over and stopped him.

There was plenty of money. I heard a National Guardsman who was watching a crap game say, "By golly, there's more money in here than I ever seen before." There probably was.

That was passive resistance—that mad surging degeneration of human beings.

And finally, as it had to be, there was a riot. None of the convicts who witnessed it thought that it was very much of a riot. But the papers carried headlines three inches tall. I wasn't there. The night before I had gone to the hospital for an opiate. I couldn't sleep. They had given me a shot of morphine. I just collapsed, they said.

What was known as the front gate was a series of heavily barred, interlocking anterooms, extending from the front offices through the front cell house to the prison yard. These rooms were at different levels and separated by heavily barred doors, electrically operated. The last of these rooms, just before entering the yard, was called the guards' room. It was here that the guards were checked in and out when the shifts changed and here they left their coats and parcels which they were not permitted to take inside. A guard remained on duty in this room at all hours to operate the gate that opened into the yard. The guard whose duty it was to operate the gate leading to the next room sat on the other side of the second gate. The last three gates were operated from the warden's office, out front.

The guards' room was flanked by the stair wells of the

3&4 cell block and the 5&6 dormitories. There were bars in between. The convicts could see through the bars into the guards' room.

The riot was started by an argument between a convict in the 3&4 stair well and a guard sergeant in the guards' room. Some convict on 2-3, hearing the argument, shouted down to the convict, "Aw, hit him in the mouth." The convict couldn't possibly hit the guard who was standing some distance on the other side of the bars, so the suggestion was rhetorical. But it made the sergeant mad. He snatched out his pistol and fired several shots in the direction of 2-3, wounding an innocent convict in the arm. The shooting brought the whole surging mass of convicts out of their cells. They charged down the stairs and pushed against the bars, screaming epithets at the guards.

A number of guardsmen rushed in from the yard and forced the convicts back up on the ranges at bayonet point. Machine guns were mounted in the stair well and at the head of each range. Finally the convicts were forced into the cells and warned that if they came out on the range they would be shot. That was the riot. But it gave the warden a chance to say that the convicts were disorderly and he blew it up.

That night the guardsmen constructed a wire-enclosed stockade on the ball diamond and set up two rows of pup tents. They strung lights around the wire enclosure and placed machine guns in each corner. The next morning the major and his staff deployed the guardsmen in battle formation about the yard, and all the way to the stockade. The convicts were then taken from the 3-4 cell block and marched down to the stockade. The other convicts stood about in vantage points, keeping their distance from the soldiers, and watched. It was done very quietly.

That afternoon I awakened and was released from the hospital. I noticed immediately that the convicts had become subdued.

That night the convicts in the stockade set fire to their tents. The guardsmen let the tents burn down. They didn't replace them. After that the convicts in the stockade had to sleep in the open on the ground.

Slowly the routine was re-established. The major ordered a nine-o'clock curfew. Notices were posted that anyone seen on the yard after nine o'clock at night would be shot on sight. No one was shot, but it was risky business running that blockade at night. Once Blocker and I dropped a bag of merchandise, running from one dormitory to another, but were afraid to go back after it.

Two days after the riot the convicts in the stockade were put on short rations. The guardsmen began corralling the remainder of the convicts. The convicts were gathered from a dormitory or cell block and lined up on the yard. They were required to give their names and numbers and were then assigned to companies. The guards returned to take over the companies. Many of the convicts hid out in the industrial buildings and the burnt cell house to keep from being put back into the companies. But most of them were caught trying to slip into the dining room.

When Blocker and I were caught I told of being a patient of the industrial commission. Blocker was humpbacked. We were put over in 1-6 dormitory with the cripples. The convicts in the dormitories upstairs kept me very nervous by throwing buckets of water and bottles down at the soldiers on the first floor. Although the guardsmen were youngsters their officers weren't. The top sergeant, in charge of the soldiers in the dormitory, was very tough. He told the convicts that the first time one of his boys was hit he was going to smoke them out. Sure enough, when one youngster got hit on the head with a pop bottle the sergeant took his squad up there and brought those convicts out like rats. He kicked them down the stairs so fast they piled up three-high on the landing. After that it was very quiet in the domitories.

I was getting very tired of all the death and violence. It was a relief when they split up the dormitory and moved the real cripples down to the tag-warehouse basement. Blocker and I were moved with the others. All we had to do was stay inside the thick brick walls and keep out of everybody's way. I was grateful. It was the dormitory where the coal company had bunked before the fire.

Before then I had always had a physical aversion toward people who had lost their legs or arms or eyes. I had always been slightly repulsed by the sight of anything deformed. But down there in the cripple company I got over it. I learned to take those twisted, one-legged, one-armed, peg-legged, crutch-walking, evil, cranky, crippled convicts as I did any others.

I jumped up in our poker game once and shouted at a fellow, "I'll take something and knock your goddamned brains out. Don't think I'm going to be light on you because you only got one arm." Before I knew what was happening he had taken his one arm and slapped me off the bench. He had his knife out and was over me and if it hadn't been for several fellows grabbing him he might have cut my throat. I found out that those cranky devils didn't expect anyone to be light on them. One of the cripples could snatch off his peg leg quicker than a man could draw a knife, and brain you while standing on one leg. They said that the deputy used to lock his peg leg up for a week when he became too unmanageable.

Suddenly the prison got tough. The convicts in the stockade were labeled agitators and returned to the 3&4 block where they were kept locked, day and night, in their cells. Their food was brought over twice a day from the dining room and kicked beneath their door.

The Committee of Nine were rounded up and put in the hole. Most of us had forgotten the committee by the end of that year, but even then, those who had not died were still in the hole. They said that Dunlap hung himself. One went blind. Three died of tuberculosis. The convicts who had cheered them when they had been in power said later they were fools to try to fight the warden.

The committee and the convicts in the 3&4 cell block took the fall. They took the fall for everything that had happened or would happen or had ever happened. They took the fall for all the humiliation which the warden had suffered from the roastings he received from the newspapers. They took the fall for the rout of discipline, for the starting of the fire, for the convicts who were burnt to death. They took the fall and the warden weathered the storm.

The guard personnel was changed. A few of the old guards returned, and under the protection of the soldiers, they became insufferable. But most of the new guards who were hired were young, athletic fellows—ham prize fighters, second-rate wrestlers, neighborhood bullies, clip-joint bouncers, psychopathic vets and big beefy red-faced ex-coppers who had been kicked out of various police departments for cruelty. The ex-coppers were hired as guard lieutenants. Twelve yard lieutenants took the place of the sergeants. Cody was made the head lieutenant. Cody had not been seen within the prison since the day before the fire. But when he returned he was the same Cody. Another lieutenant was called Pick Handle Slim. He was an ex-railroad dick. He got his name from beating frozen hobos to death with a hickory pick handle he carried with him. He was a tall, flat-chested, maniacal Texan. There was a lieutenant called Dog Back. He was from Arkansas. There was a lieutenant called the Hangman. He was a sadistic little gray-haired kill-crazy man. All of them were as tough as a man can be when he's got the law on his side, and the only gun, and orders to whip a convict's head as long as his head will last.

"Talking in line!" one would say, jerking the convict out.

"But, lieutenant, I ain't said—" And before he could finish he'd have his skull split open and be stretched his length on the ground.

There was a bull-necked, ax-faced yard captain with the title of director. He had a gas-tank belly and a mile of shoulders and a Mussolini complex. His uniform was always immaculate; his Sam Browne belt polished, his mustache waxed, his brass buttons shined. He strutted about the yard, with Gout trotting at his heels like a yellow dog.

All of those convicts who had stayed out in the freedom of the yard and kidded Blocker and me because we let them get us in the cripple company now broke for the protection of our company like rats from a sinking ship. But there was only room for a few. Most got caught in the awful grind.

The yard became physically dangerous. A convict ran the risk of being killed by marching across the yard silently in line, obeying every order that was given him. Those young, crazy hacks, given authority for the first time in their lives, were unpredictable. They had been taken from the streets and suddenly given power of life and death over companies of convicts. They got to be so tough they would go in the hospital and discharge dangerously sick patients on their own authority. They'd put convicts in the hole without anyone's permission or knowledge.

One Sunday afternoon nine young guards went up on 2-3 because some unidentified convict had cursed at a guard whom he could not see and did not recognize. They started at the first cell and took the convicts out on the range, one at a time, and beat them all into semiconsciousness and locked them back in their cells. When the night crew came on at six o'clock they found fourteen delirious, bloody-headed convicts in the cells along with the others who were injured less severely. The night captain came over and inspected them and decided they had been fighting among themselves. He took the fourteen delirious men over and locked them in the hole. Two died before morning. Six went crazy, they said. We were very fortunate that only the lieutenants were permitted to carry pistols. A great number of convicts owed their lives to this fact.

A riot squad had been created. They consisted of twelve armed guards and a lieutenant in charge. During the day, when the convicts marched across the yard, they stood at attention in front of the Protestant chapel. Each wore a ring-handled forty-five in a side holster. The two at each end carried knapsacks of tear-gas bombs. Those next to them held submachine guns propped at their thighs, while the four in the center held riot guns at rabbit-shooting angles. At the least sign of a commotion in the lines they'd dash across the yard and level down on the entire company. God help a convict who got out of place. It was power on parade, and an ever-present reminder that the wages of rioting was death. Rioting was a term which covered a multitude of minor infractions, the wages of most of which were death.

"Look at the toys," the convicts would whisper as they marched down the other side of the yard. "All they need is a tree over them and you'd think it was Christmas."

"All they need is dirt over them and I'd know damn well it was Christmas."

"Hell, take one man with one gun—"

"Step out of line, Burke!" the guard would order. "I saw you talking." Burke would step out of line. Four men from the riot squad would dash across the yard. Too bad Burke didn't have that one gun.

The deputy's wings had been clipped. He had been shorn of all authority for condoning the actions of the Committee of Nine. He was the deputy warden only in name. And only that because he had powerful friends in the welfare department and the warden couldn't fire him. Now the director held court. Gout, looking like a bloated frog in dog harness, had been demoted to transfer clerk and the director's boy.

It was now the warden's prison. He owned it. "I hold the destiny for you four thousand convicts in the palm of my hand," he said. He did not lie. They said he was afraid to come into the yard. A hundred different convicts had sworn separately that the moment he stepped into the yard they'd hang a knife in his ribs. One day when the lines were marching from the dining room he came into the yard and stood to one side of the main walk, talking casually to two visitors. Three thousand convicts marched past his turned back within touching distance. He never stopped talking nor did he once look around. They were his convicts.

16

Ever since the first of the year there had been talk of the laws being changed. It had begun as soon as the new governor had taken office. The newspapers were mostly for the change. There were enough amateur penologists around to fill the prison, but most of them were loose. In the late summer after the bills had been drawn up by the legislative committee the *Prison Times* had been filled with it each week. So when it actually happened we were pretty much prepared for it. But still, the night when word came in that the state legislature had passed the first of the three bills you could hear us yelling all the way to town.

At the time we were celling in 2-2. During the prison reorganization we'd been moved three times, first to the 1-6 dormitory and then upstairs to 3-6 dorm, and finally over to the four-man cells on 2-2. We cripples had been a great problem during that get-tough period. We couldn't work; they couldn't whip our heads. They didn't know what to do with us. Finally they hid us over on 2-2 where they didn't have to watch us goldbricking, and labeled us "agitators."

It was about ten o'clock at night when we got word that the bill had passed. The yelling began in the front dormitories, where the news came first, and in five minutes the whole prison had it. We jumped from our bunks and clung to the bars and cut loose. We scraped our buckets on the bars, banked our stools against the doors. The morning papers said that all available police had been rushed in riot cars to the prison, and the army camp had been alerted.

It had all grown out of the fire. There had been a great deal of agitation about the congested condition of the prison due to the severe, harsh laws. Public sentiment had turned in favor of shorter sentences. Three bills were introduced that went through the legislature like a landslide.

Those two hundred and seventy-seven convicts really did us a great service, even if they did have to die to do it.

The first of the bills set a statutory minimum and maximum for all criminal felonies. It was retroactive. As a consequence the sentences of all convicts then serving time which exceeded the statutory minimum, reverted to the statutory minimum. The statutory minimum for robbery was ten years, the maximum twenty-five years. At the judge's prerogative I had been sentenced to a twenty-year minimum. At the passage of the bill it reverted to ten years.

The next bill, called the "good-time law," provided for a graduated scale of time off for good behavior. This brought my ten years down to six years and five months. By these two bills thirteen years and seven months had been sliced from my minimum.

The third bill instituted a new parole board of four members to take the place of the old parole board of three members. We were glad to see that old board go.

The three bills were to take effect within sixty days. The *Prison Times* issued a special edition explaining the laws. The statutes were quoted in full and explained, item by item. A good-time scale had been drawn up for sentences of from one to twenty years minimum.

By October the parole and record clerks had computed the amount of time each convict would be required to serve. Slips were put in the mail informing us when we would be eligible for parole. I got my slip among the first. Our company guard brought them around with the evening's mail. Briant, my cell mate, was doing second-degree life and he didn't get any. They had to wait on a ruling by the attorney general. There were only the two of us in the cell at that time. We'd had others but they'd gone.

I opened the envelope and read the single line that I would be eligible for a hearing by the parole board in May, 1952. I was so happy and excited I could hardly breathe. I was exultant. I had to talk to keep from leaping in the air. But, being a convict, I couldn't say anything good about the legal processes. I had to beef or else not talk at all.

"What the hell," I said. "I'm supposed to be eligible in April. Those sons of bitches are trying to beat me out of a month."

Briant came over, plumping the stump of his arm in the palm of his hand. "Let's see."

I handed him the slip. "When did you come in?" he asked, with that quizzical expression he wore when he was getting ready to contradict you.

"December."

"Did you come in the last or first of December?"

"What the hell's that got to do with it? You talk like a damned prosecutor."

"Unless you come in before the fifth of the month they don't count it."

"They don't need to count it," I said. "Look here." I got down the issue of the *Prison Times* that contained the good-time scale. "Figuring it out by this scale here, I'm supposed to serve six years, four months and eleven days. That would throw me up in April."

"They count the eleven days for a month," he said. He had on that patient grin he wore when he was getting set for a long enjoyable argument. "That's your month of April."

"That's what I'm arguing about," I said. "They count it for a month when it's in their favor, but when it's in our favor they won't even count twenty-five days for a month."

"You've got a good argument," he said, "but you're wasting it on me."

Suddenly I was furious, boiling with all that hot rebellion I'd been feeling of late against the least thing that appeared to jeopardize my rights. I had become very conscious of my rights. I was also furious with Briant for not agreeing with me. I had been realizing for some time that I was losing my control. I would become raving mad at the slightest thing. I found it hard to take a direct order from a guard. And it burnt me up for anyone to find fault with me or disagree with anything I said. But I liked Briant. I didn't want to be angry with him. "Goddammit, they figure every convict's a fool," I said. Briant took on that sanctimonious, exasperating, abiding look he wore when he realized that I was mad. He just looked at me and wouldn't say anything else.

I could hear the convicts' excited voices as the guards passed out the slips on the other ranges.

"Hey, Harry, when you make it for?"

"I don't know, I ain't got my slip yet."

"Ain't you guys getting your slips?"

"The guard ain't got down here yet."

"Say, hey, fellow, say, hey, cap, this ain't mine."

"I got 'em now, I got 'em now, I got 'em now, boy, I got 'em now—Look out there, Broadway, here I come!"

"January next year, man; I'm on the turn. . . ."

The whole cell house had come alive with voices. "Hey, Joe . . . ! Hey, Charley . . . ! Hey, Soldier . . . ! Hey,

Ray . . . !" All asking the same question: "When you make it for?"

The voices were all excited and loud, merging into a high, steady din.

"Everybody's happy," I said, trying to sound cynical.

"I bet you're as happy as anybody," Briant said. "You lost thirteen and a half years in that shuffle."

"Watch out there, deacon," I kidded. "You sound like a card slicker talking about shuffle."

He grinned. "I'll bet I could beat plenty of you young jerks playing cards, who think you're so slick," he said. "When I used to gamble before I got religion—" He was a former West Virginia coal miner, full of God, Lewis, and the Bible.

"Save it, pops," I cut in. "That sounds like the beginning of one of those endless stories." I was beginning to show my excitement in spite of myself. My voice had taken a higher note and I was talking silly.

"You're happy all right," Briant said, complacently. "You can't tell me you're not happy over losing thirteen and a half years."

"Hell, I never thought I'd have to make my twenty years, anyway," I said.

"Well you won't now unless you lose an awful lot of time."

"Now we got to be bothered with that, too," I said.

But I was plenty happy all right. Those four years seemed very short. Looking at them, after having stared so long into the gray opaqueness of those solid twenty years, it seemed as if I could look right through them and see the end; see freedom in all its glory, standing there. It was a new and different kind of freedom than any I had seen before. It was a cool, merciful, present freedom, like God, that was always there at the end of a long straight road. It was like the promised land which you look forward to knowing that it is not here now, but yet it is not too far away, and with care and caution and faith it can be reached in time. In Johnny Time. Johnny Time was a little boy now. It was like driving down that long parkway, knowing that you will reach the city some sunny day if the tires hold out and the motor doesn't conk out or the law doesn't get you, or you don't get into a wreck or get caught in any of the thousand and one things which can happen to you but which you never think about happening as you sail down that long white road.

It was so unlike the first freedom, the completely lost,

completely remote, merciless, indifferent, impossible freedom at the end of twenty years—always at the end of twenty years—never coming closer; which left you feeling that you were walking on a treadmill, trudging doggedly, persistently, continuously, deliberately onward but never coming closer.

And although at that time freedom was in its embryo form, being more or less the feeling that it was the city at the end of the road, still it was not to be taken too seriously. You could never take freedom too seriously, for then it would kill you. It was just something at the end of time which made the days shorter and bearable and pointed and containing meaning and ambition and aim and end—mostly end.

The next morning when we marched around the yard for exercise I fell back with Blocker and he said he would go up that May.

"There'll be many a man going out of here the first of next year," I said. "I hear there's fifteen hundred eligible for parole immediately."

"They won't let them all go at once," he said. "You can bet a man they won't do that."

"No, I guess not. But even at that they'll have to let a hell of a lot of them go. Maybe they'll let some out each week. But even at that, there'll be more and more coming up for a hearing each month."

"I don't know what they're going to do," he said. "But you can bet a big fat man they ain't going to dump no whole lot of convicts out of here at one time."

And he didn't tell any lie. When the newspapers found out the number of convicts eligible for immediate parole they fell out for dead. All those wonderful editorials calling for a change in the laws began to read like, who's responsible for this awful crime wave?

"Let these men out," one newspaper said, "and our women and children won't dare walk the streets without a police guard."

"These newspapers are a son of a bitch," I said to Briant one night. "One day they're all for the convicts and the next day a convict is lower than whale turd."

Briant didn't answer, so I started needling him. "When the hell you second-degree lifers going to get your slips?"

"Some of them already have theirs," he said. "I suppose I'll get mine soon."

"If I hadn't got mine when they first came out I'd be

going nuts by now," I said. "I'd be over to the deputy's office every day pitching me a bitch."

"I thought you said you didn't care whether you got your slip or not," he said. "You said you knew you wouldn't have to serve twenty years, anyway."

"That's not what I said. I said I never thought I'd have to do my twenty years. That's a little different. And I didn't say I didn't care whether I got my slip or not, because I care like hell. If they're going to cut one single convict's time they're supposed to cut mine, too. I got the same rights as any other convict."

"You haven't got any more rights after you come in here," he said. "You see that sign over the door when you came in?"

"Over what door?"

"Over the door to the prison—the outside door?"

"No, what did it say?"

"It said, *Ye who enter here leave all hope behind.*"

"I don't believe it," I said. "I don't believe they'd put a sign like that over a prison gate. Why some newspaper reporter would have had it all over the papers a long time ago."

"I don't care whether you believe it or not, it's over there." He turned and yelled over to the next cell. "Hey, Boone, ain't there a sign over the gate which says 'Ye who enter here leave all hope behind'?"

"Sure is," Boone called back. "Why?"

"Monroe don't believe it."

"He will believe it."

"Hell, all the one-armed people stick together," I said. "I don't believe either one of you."

"You will believe us," they both said, in unison.

"You're too pessimistic," I said.

Briant held up his nub arm and said, "Hey, boy, what you mean I'm one-armed? I got two good arms, I only got one hand."

"You only got one arm too," I said. "That other thing's a wing. It ain't no good."

"I got more strength in it than you got in either of yours," he said, flapping it about.

"Say, quit flopping that thing around me," I said. "First thing you know you'll have it off at the shoulder."

He rubbed the soft, pulpy stump across my head. "How's it feel?"

"Hey, don't do that, goddammit," I said.

"It won't hurt you."

"I bet I'll hurt it."

"You can't hurt this stump," he said. "That's a good job. Dr. Castle, the bone specialist who comes in here sometimes, said that's the best job he ever saw."

"Aw, don't go into that brag again," I said. "You got a good stump. The doctor did a good job. He made a swell cushion. Now forget about it."

He climbed back on his bunk without replying. He was hurt.

"Aw, hell, can't you take a joke?" I said. "I was only kidding." But he wouldn't say anything else. Those cripples were a sensitive lot about the surgical jobs on their stumps.

17

WITH ONLY four more years to do I thought of learning some trade or profession I could practice when I got out. The warden had given the convicts permission to take correspondence courses and many of them had enrolled in one thing or another. The newspaper and magazine boys sold the courses, for which they got a fat commission.

I stopped Okay Collins, the magazine man, one night and asked what courses he was peddling. He said he could enroll me in courses in agriculture, chicken farming, mechanical and civil engineering, architecture, writing, air-conditioning, economics, political history, ancient literature, and law. That law course caught my fancy. Maybe it was because I was pretty excited about law at that time, especially the law that had cut my minimum down thirteen years and seven months.

I asked him how much the law course cost. He said I'd have to make a down payment of fifty dollars and sign a promissory note to pay twenty dollars monthly until the full five hundred and eight dollars was paid. Then, if I passed the examinations, I would receive a degree in law and all I'd have to do after that was pass the bar examinations and I could practice. That is, of course, if I ever got back my citizenship.

"What the hell kind of a lousy school is this where you can get a degree in law for five hundred and eight bucks?" I asked.

"Hell, you call that hay?"

"Naw, but it ain't Harvard, either."

"Why, fellow, this is the same school the welfare director studied his law from," he said.

"From is right," I said.

"He majored in medicine at the university," Okay said. "And then later, while practicing medicine, he took this course, and when he had completed it he was able to pass the bar examination the first time he took it."

"Was that a great achievement?" I asked.

"Well, no, but it just goes to show that this course will give you a complete knowledge of the subject," he said with his tongue in his cheek. "And then, too, even if you don't intend to practice law, it's a good thing to know. It is indispensable in any kind of business; in fact as a prisoner you will find it invaluable. They give you a copy of the constitution of the United States with your first lessons and when you have completed the course you will receive a revised edition of this state's criminal code."

"All that for five hundred and eight bucks? And a degree too," I said.

"Not only that but—"

"That's enough," I said. "I'll take it."

I signed a cashier's slip for fifty dollars and, about two weeks later, I received a set of yellow, paper-backed pamphlets in the mail. Some of the titles were: *History of Law; Legal Reasoning; Case Law; Statutory Law; English Common Law; Civil Law; Criminal Procedure* . . . and such. There was an outline and schedule for study, a list of reference books, and sets of questions to be answered and mailed in each week. The headquarters of the school was in Chicago.

I found the *Preface* the most illuminating part of the entire course. It explained all about the "legal mind." To succeed in the profession a lawyer needed most of all a legal mind, that is the ability to be reasonable and logical and to think concisely and quickly and sharply in the clinches. I felt certain that I would make the ideal lawyer as I felt there was probably no one in all the world more reasonable and logical than I; no one who could think more concisely, quickly, and sharply in the extremities. I became slightly obsessed with the cold clear reasonableness of my thoughts and if anyone disagreed with their reasonableness I was ready to fight.

For a time I studied diligently and sent in my lessons on time. I received high grades and a personal letter of commendation from the school president. What I found most interesting was the history of the law. I developed a profound respect for those ancient boys, Moses and Justinian and Napoleon, who had drawn up all these rules in the first place. I was also fascinated by case law. The courts' opinions in many outstanding American civil and criminal cases were reproduced in full and, although it was tedious reading, I was completely intrigued by those old boys' structural logic. They built up to their findings like a contractor building a house, starting at the foundation and building to the roof. Some of them, however, seemed to get off the foundation at times and once off they could get a long way off. In the course of time I came to see the necessity of exemplary justice, such as had been meted out to me. It was as necessary to take steps to prohibit crime as to punish it, I concluded. This did not make me feel any better toward the judge who had sentenced me, but I derived a certain satisfaction from learning of his mental processes.

I read so much about the legal mind and legal reasoning that I developed an interest in psychology. My mother had sent me a set of textbooks on the subject the year before, and I began studying them along with the law. I felt that I should know more about the anatomy of criminal impulses in order to understand, more thoroughly, the psychology of jurisprudence. As it had been throughout all my life, I believed most of what I read in books. I found it difficult to reconcile the human compulsions expounded by psychology to the social restraints impounded by law, but I did not let this throw me. When I had finished applying my "legal mind" to the "psychological equations of humanity" I arrived at what I thought was the understanding of what I referred to, for lack of a better term, as the human factor. I thought a great deal about the laws governing homosexuality and concluded that they were outmoded. Although biologically there were only two sexes, psychologically there had always been three, I concluded, with great originality. I was becoming very educated, I thought. There was no telling how educated I might have become in time if we had stayed on 2-2.

But the week before Christmas we were transferred to

the 2-6 dormitory and the prison activity took hold of me again. We had a nice Christmas and a fine New Year's Day with lots to eat. By that time the warden had worked his spite out on the convicts for "passive resistance." In addition, it had become stylish to be humane. Everybody was humane to the convicts along through there. Everybody sympathized with them, pitied them. "Rehabilitate the convicts"—that was the hue and cry. The only drawback was that the convicts, who were the parties of the first part, didn't know just what the hell it meant. I imagined that some of the humanitarians must have found it very trying indeed, in their efforts to rehabilitate those convicts who couldn't understand what they were trying to do and were suspicious of them for doing it.

"Man, there's a catch in it somewhere, you hear me. It just ain't right for a convict to be treated so good."

"You ain't told no lie."

"Damn right. I ain't been able to sleep worth nothing since they passed those laws. I'm losing weight, my appetite's left me, I'm nervous all the time, and when I do get to sleep what do I have but nightmares? I dreamt last night I had lost all my good-time, and had to do them ten full years, and I woke up sweating wet. That good-time's all right, it's fine, but it's a hell of a lot of worry. It's got me scared to breathe for fear I might lose some of it."

That was the way with it that Christmas. The convicts had the good-time like the man had the bear. They were very good convicts that Christmas. But it worried them. Every moment they looked for something to happen which would make them lose their good-time. They lost all their joy and happiness in suspicion, and when the parole board didn't release those fifteen hundred convicts who were eligible the first of the year they showed their relief.

"I knew it. Mac, I knew it all along. I knew there was a catch in it, somewhere. You can't fool me. Mac, I been out too long. I'm hip to all that stuff. Rehabilitate the convicts —you get that, Mac? The old slide game, the old short con—conning us convicts right out this American country. . . ."

But the good citizens of the state and their official lawmakers—the legislature—and their unofficial lawmakers, the press—were not to be outdone. They were going to rehabilitate those convicts if it killed them. So next, the welfare department established a "Classification Bureau." It consisted of three specialists—a psychiatrist, a psychologist, and a sociologist—and their staffs. They outlined a great and far-reaching program. They were going to inaugurate a system of classification within the prison. After systematic examinations each convict would be classified according to his desire to lead a straight and normal life. The repeaters and degenerates would be separated from the first offenders and the reformed. The old men would be separated from the young, the industrious from the slothful, the wolves from the fags. But first they were assigned the task of interviewing convicts who were eligible for a hearing by the parole board. As there were fifteen hundred convicts then eligible, and hundreds more coming up each month, that was as far as the bureau ever got.

Anyway, as soon as the sharp edge of their zeal and enthusiasm and high fervor of humanitarianism, inspired in part no doubt by the regularity of their pay checks, wore down and was blunted on the stolid, unyielding unresponsiveness of those convicts, the members of both the classification bureau and the parole board reverted to type. They became callous and indifferent and cynical as does everyone else, sooner or later, when dealing with convicts.

Many of the convicts refused to report to the classification bureau when they were called. They were given their choice to be examined or put in the hole. They went in the hole.

"They'll never get me over there and trick me," Pink Panties said. "I know I'm one and that's all there is to it."

Old man Lajole said, "I went over there like a fool, and do you know what that fellow asked me? He asked me had I ever had relations with a man. I told him I was a gentleman, by God, and I picked up my hat and went over to the deputy and I told the deputy, by God, I don't mind answering some decent questions even if I don't see any sense in 'em, but by God, when a fellow starts asking me that stuff that's the limit. I'm not a degenerate, I told the deputy, and I won't have anyone saying I am. The deputy said I didn't have to go over there any more, by God."

"Did you see that little fellow with the bald head and the hunched shoulders, with his glasses sitting up on the top of his nose?"

"Yeah, that's the psy-psy—"

"Psychiatrist," someone supplied.

"Yeah, that's him. The—what'd you call him, Mac?"

"Psychiatrist."

"Yeah, that's him all right. Batty a-looking beauty as I ever saw. He gave me some sugar to taste then he ast me whether it was sweet or sour. I said, 'Say, what's the matter with you, fellow, who's crazy around here, you or me? This is sugar, when the hell did sugar ever get to be sour?' And he said, 'Oh, it's just a matter of routine,' and I said, 'Some hell of a routine, if you ast me, why any goddamn body knows that sugar's sweet,' and he said, 'Never mind, just answer my questions and let me do all the knowing that's to be done,' and I said, 'All right, bud, it's your party.' So he gave me some vinegar to taste and then he ast me, 'Sweet or sour?' and I licked my lips and looked solemn as an owl and said, 'Sweet as sugar.' Then he looked up at me and said, 'Does it have the same taste as the substance which you tasted before?' And I said, 'Yeah, only it tastes a little wetter.' He looked at me and then he looked at his papers he had there and then he wrote down something. Then he stuck me with a needle and ast, 'Blunt or sharp?' and I said, 'Blunt.' He began looking suspicious then. Then he stuck me again a hell of a lot harder and I said, 'It's still blunt, bud.' He turned red as a beet and said, 'You go on back to your company,' and I said, 'Suits me, bud.' "

"Haw-haw-haw, he thought he was giving you the needle and you were giving him the needle."

Pretty soon the classification bureau was just a joke. After it was rumored around that a convict who had refused to be interviewed by them had been granted a parole, it was through. They could have packed up their five-hundred-dollar solid-mahogany desks and cut on out, right then, and saved the state a hell of a lot of money.

That was the way it was that year. The prison was all different. It was easier. It had never been so easy. But the dormitory was the same. It had never been tough, so in still being easy we missed the feeling of the change which touched the others in the mills and shops and on the yard. We convicts in the cripple company seldom felt the heavy, merciless, brutal weight of prison as the others in the mills and shops did. We went along smoothly, serenely, easily, spoiling away the years. There were, of course, our petty arguments and troubles and vexations, and now and then the officials, noticing that we were having it so easy, clamped down a bit and gave us a taste of discipline, but never the excessive discipline that eternally lay over the working men. It seemed as if we were more on the edge of prison than actually inside, but yet could look over into the prison and see all the teaming, driven, brutal life; the savage flareups and merciless quellings; all the constant hell that everyone was catching but us. We slept and read and lied and talked and gambled our days away and called it tough. As one colored convict said, we ate our good-doin' bread and called it punk, slept on our good-doin' bed and called it bunk.

"Man, what is you talkin' 'bout! You doin' better heah than you ever done before. You get yo' three meals a day—"

"Man, what you mean? Ah always had three meals every day—"

"Yasss, but dese is regular. You has a man to wake you up in de mawnin'. You has a man to car'y you to breakfus. You has a man to watch over you an' protect you. You has a man to shave you an' a hospital for you when you sick. What mo' you want? You couldn't git all dat in de Majestic Hotel."

That was the way it was in the dormitory that year. They moved quite a few other convicts in with us; convicts who had been in working companies and undergone operations and were put in with us to convalesce; or who had been injured in some way or other and were allowed to remain idle for a certain number of days. We always felt condescending toward them as if they didn't really belong with us in our dormitory. By then we had developed a class system. The upper-class cripples were those who had been in the company ever since the fire. It was as if our ancestors had come over on the Mayflower. The others were lower-class climbers. We treated them very coldly until they finally muscled into our class and in turn treated other climbers with the same coldness. It was different with the fresh fish from outside. We were always glad to get a new one from the street. Especially if he was young and good-looking or had any money.

Blocker and I had begun our game immediately. By then it was an obligation. Everyone wanted us to run a game. If we hadn't there probably wouldn't have been any to amount to anything. Many of the poker players wouldn't play with any other gamekeepers. We still used marked cards. I think by then everybody knew it. But they would rather play with us with our marked cards than with anybody else. One thing, we always gave them a play. Nobody could say he didn't get his gamble in our game.

The game held little interest for me, then. I got Candy to help Blocker run it. Now and then I'd go down and play a little in the field. I was still interested in my law course and my psychology books and I devoted most of my time to them. There was a convict called Signifying Johnson who muscled in on the job of selling chips. When the poker game got dull Blocker started a dice game. He had a kid named George to help him. He left the poker game to Candy and Signifier.

George was a good-natured little kid with long black hair that fell down over his forehead and we used to tease him a lot.

"This is my kid," Blocker would say. "Don't you bother this kid."

"That's all right," I'd say. "I'm going to take him away from you." Then I'd lean over and whisper to George, "I'm coming down and see you tonight."

George was a straight little kid and it would just slide off of him. He didn't have to holler because he was never hit. One night on the way to the latrine I got the idea to stop and tease him, so I slipped down the back aisle and sneaked up beside his bunk—he had a top bunk—and then jumped up and grabbed him by the shoulders and said, "Kiss me, you sweet little punk," leaning over him as if I was really going to kiss him.

The only thing about it was I had the wrong fellow. I had sneaked up to the wrong bunk. A little fat, old, bald-headed man called Pappy Yokum jumped up in bed and gave one look at me and his eyes got big as saucers. "Hey, what tha— Help! Leggo!" I had already let him go. I backed away frantically and beat it down the aisle in one direction, and he jumped out of his bunk and started highballing it in the opposite direction. Several guys seeing the rumpus congregated about him and asked him what was the trouble and he told them I'd just tried to rape him. I went down and told him that I had made a mistake and apologized. By then the guard had come down to see what it was all about. I told him we were just trying to catch a rat I saw trying to climb up in his bunk. It wasn't until afterward I realized how funny that was. After he'd gone back to his bunk I told Blocker and George and Candy and Signifier the whole story and we had a good laugh.

"Can you imagine that old man figuring somebody would want to rape him?" Candy said.

"That ain't the trouble with him," Signifier said. "He's just hoping."

Along near the end of February the industrial commission doctors came over to examine me again. They wanted to know if I'd been in a cast and I told them no, I hadn't, and they wanted to know why, and I told them I didn't know why. They gave the doctor hell. The doctor told them I had refused a cast. So they called me back to give me hell. They told me if I didn't think I needed a cast I didn't need any compensation, so I told them I'd go in a cast whenever they wanted me to. So the first of March the bone specialist, Dr. Castle, came in and X-rayed me. The next week when he visited the prison again he called me over and wrapped me in a cast. That was one quick job.

"When did you have a bath last?" he asked.

"Four days ago," I said.

"Well, you won't have any now for six weeks," he said. "That's how long this cast stays on. So four days won't make a hell of a lot of difference, will it, now?"

That made me angry in the first place. He stood me naked in the center of the floor, straightened my spine by sight, padded my body with cotton, then dipped the plaster of Paris gauze into water and wrapped me up from my hips to my chest. That was all he had to do except send in his bill to the Industrial Commission. I stood there for an hour waiting for the stuff to set, then the nurse took me into C ward and put me in a cot. The springs sank down in the middle and the cast cut me across the thighs.

"This cot gives too much," I told the nurse.

"What do you want me to do?" he asked.

"I want you to stop it from giving, goddammit!" I said "That's what you're here for, that's what you get special grub and special privileges for."

"To hell with you," he said.

I tried to get out of the cot but couldn't get my legs up far enough, so I wiggled over to the side and tried to drop down to the floor. The nurse came over and shoved me back into the center of the cot and I hit at him. "Get your goddamn hands off of me, you bastard!" I said. He drew back and started to hit me but the guard walked in and he stopped.

"What's the trouble here?" the guard asked.

"This goddamn bed gives and this bastard won't fix it," I said.

"You want to watch out how you talk to people around here, boy," the guard said.

"They want to watch out how they talk to me, too," I said.

"This punk's too fresh," the nurse said.

"What's the matter with this cot?" the guard asked.

"There isn't anything the matter with it," the nurse said

"You're a damned liar," I said. "It gives in the middle

and makes my cast cut me. You can see for yourself," I said, throwing back the covers.

"The cast is too long," the guard said, looking at it.

The nurse didn't say anything.

"Isn't there some way to cut off some of this cast?" the guard asked.

"I don't know," the nurse said. "I'll get the supervisor."

Jake Ingalls was the supervisor then. He was a swell convict. "Hello, Jimmy," he said, coming in.

"What say, Jake?"

"What's the trouble, kid?"

"This bed gives," I said. "It makes the cast cut into my thighs." The covers were still at the foot of the cot where I had thrown them, and I pointed to where the edge of the cast dug into my legs.

"Get Monroe's chart," Jake said to the nurse. When the nurse came back with the chart Jake looked at it and said, "The doctor ordered slats for this bed. Why didn't you put some slats under the springs?"

"I didn't notice it," the nurse said.

Jake looked at him. "Put some slats under it," he said Then he turned to me. "That'll fix you up, Jimmy How are you getting along otherwise?"

"Fine."

"Getting plenty to eat?"

"Yeah."

"Okay, I'll see you, Jimmy."

"Okay, and thanks, Jake."

"You'll be all right now, Monroe," the guard said, taking a different attitude now.

"I hope so," I said.

But the next week an influenza epidemic hit the prison and the hospital became overcrowded overnight. All of us who were not on the danger list were moved downstairs into the basement, underneath the north wing, to make room for the flu cases which were coming in at the rate of two dozen a day. There were no hospital cots in the basement, only the double-decked bunks that had been used when it was a cripple-company dormitory years before. It was damp and dirty and stinking. The epidemic had struck so suddenly there had been no time to prepare for it. They assigned us guards but the nurses were too busy upstairs with the flu cases to give us any attention. The only time we saw a nurse was when they brought down our meals, if the orderlies were all busy.

I was assigned to a bottom bunk. It sagged in the middle

and no one had the time nor inclination to stiffen it with slats. My cast cut into my thighs until they ached and it was very difficult for me to get up to use the bathroom. Each time the nurses came around with our meals I called it to their attention but none of them did anything about it. I sent word to the doctor and to the convict doctor and to Jake Ingalls, but received no reply. I stood it for three days.

There was a vacant room off from the dormitory that had once been used for a storeroom. On the way to the latrine I'd noticed it contained a few old barrels and a couple of tables and benches. I managed to hobble over there in search of some boards to use as slats but I didn't find anything I could use. All I found was an old rusty tenpenny nail. I took it back to my bunk and began cutting off my cast with it. It was very tedious work, with the point of a dull nail, and it took all that night. But by morning I had scraped a hole from the top to the bottom of the cast deep enough so I could tear the cast apart. I tore it off and threw it into the wastepaper container. That was the fourth day we had been down there.

That morning, just before dinner, the doctor and the convict doctor and the supervisor and two nurses came through on a tour of inspection. All the bunks were occupied by that time, for as soon as a patient upstairs passed the danger point he was hustled downstairs to make room for the next case. The doctor stopped briefly and asked everyone how they felt. When he stopped at my bunk I told him that I was feeling fine. I was lying down with the covers pulled over me and he couldn't tell that I didn't still have my cast.

"Having any trouble with your cast?" he asked.

"I was but I'm not any more," I said.

"Fine," he said and started away, grinning his big horse-toothed grin and appearing very amused about something. But after he'd gone a few steps he stopped and turned around, frowning. He came back and said, "Let's see your cast," and reached down to draw back the covers.

"I took it off," I said.

For a moment he hung there with his hand still extended toward the bed and his mouth half open with unspoken words. Then he turned a dull, splotched red. "Took it off?" He sounded incredulous.

"That's right," I said. "Took it off."

He straightened up slowly, controlling himself with great

difficulty. "What did you do with it?" he managed to ask, squeezing out the words.

"I threw it in the trash can," I said.

And then he blew. He went off like a V-Two Rocket. His hands flew up in a wild frustrated gesture and his body swerved in my direction as if he was going to jump into the bunk and strangle me. Then he caught himself and kept turning until he had made a complete circle, and his hands jerked at his hair. "What in the hell did you do that for?" he screamed in a high, shrill, completely uncontrolled voice.

"It was hurting me—" I began, but he rushed away without listening. He walked furiously, straight ahead into the empty storeroom, then he turned around and came storming back.

"Now what will I tell Dr. Castle? What will I tell the industrial commission? What will I do, what will I do?" He tore at his hair. "You—you dolt! You feather-brained idiot! You—you—" He wheeled away and stormed out of the door, roughing over the half dozen patients collected there to request various prescriptions. I felt half scared and half rebellious and tight with nervousness. Goddammit, they ought to have come down and fixed my bunk in the first place, I kept telling myself, trying to justify my action and keep from feeling scared.

Right after dinner the doctor sent the hospital runner downstairs after me. I got dressed and followed him upstairs. I was wooden with scare and nervousness and rebellion. The doctor and Dr. Castle and the deputy and the director were waiting for me in the doctor's office.

"Why did you take your cast off, Monroe?" the director asked.

"It was hurting me," I began. "I sent word up to the doctor and he wouldn't—"

"My God, you were just down there three days!" the doctor exploded.

"Three days is a long time when you're in pain," I said.

"My God, you're not the only patient in this hospital," the doctor raved. "You act as if you were the only patient in the whole damn prison. This hospital is filled with men with temperatures of over a hundred. Who do you think you—?"

"Let's hear what the boy has to say," Dr. Castle cut in. The doctor controlled himself. Dr. Castle was one of several very famous specialists who gave their services to the institution free of charge. It provided a source of study and research and practical experience for various internes studying under them.

"The bunk sagged in the middle," I said. "It's one of the regulation dormitory bunks with the springs at the ends and when I lay down it gave in the middle and the cast cut me across the thighs. I sent word up to the doctor and the nurses and everybody, telling them about it, but no one came down to do anything."

"So you tore it off?"

"Yes, sir."

"Do you know that cast cost the industrial commission one hundred and seventy-five dollars?"

"Yes, sir."

"Here we're fortunate enough to have a specialist come in here and do the job for half price as a favor to you and you rip it off without a moment's thought, without—" the doctor began but Dr. Castle cut him off. "Couldn't you have waited for a few days, boy? You realized, of course, how busy the doctor must have been."

"No sir, I didn't realize it," I said.

Dr. Castle began getting red. "But you could have waited a day or two longer, couldn't you? It wouldn't have killed you to have waited just a couple of days longer, would it?"

I didn't answer. I stood there, straight and stubborn, cloaked in a mute rebellion. They're all against me, I thought. They don't want to hear my side. They want me to admit that I was wrong. To hell with them, I thought. To hell with them, sitting there like fat pompous gods caring less than a damn about a convict's personal feelings. Screw 'em!

"I don't know what the officials think about this, but I feel that you should be punished," Dr. Castle said, red and angry. He stood up and put on his hat and walked out.

The deputy didn't say anything. The director looked at the doctor. The doctor waited a moment for them to upbraid me and when they didn't he said, "Have you a backbrace?" He wouldn't say my name.

"Yes." It was just a wide belt I wore sometimes.

He waited for me to go on. I didn't elaborate.

"Where is it?" he asked.

"Over in the dormitory."

"I'll send Tim over to get it." The hospital runner was named Tim. "You'll have to wear it. You can't have another cast."

"I'll go over and get it myself," I said. "He doesn't know where to find it."

"Well, go over and get it!" the doctor shouted. "Go over and stay over! Go to hell! Get out of my sight!"

I turned and started outside.

"Wait a minute," the director called. "I'll send Tim with you." The deputy hadn't said anything.

It had begun to rain, so we ran across the yard. I was out of breath when I got to the dormitory. Chump Charlie saw me first and asked, "What you doing out the hospital so soon? I thought you were going to be in for six weeks."

"Got to get my brace!" I gasped. I went over to my bunk and began fishing in my bag for the belt. Chump rushed down to the game and told them I was in trouble. Blocker and Candy and Signifier came running up the aisle.

"What's the trouble, kid?" Blocker asked. He looked at Tim.

"Nothing much," I said. "They gave me a raw deal over there and I cut off my cast."

"What did you do with it?"

"I threw it in the trash can."

Candy said, "I bet that big pot-bellied bastard over there pitched one for sure."

"It was his fault," I said. "The son of a bitch had me put down in the basement."

"Come on, we got to get back," Tim said

"Take it easy," Signifier said. "You ain't in the hospital now."

"They're not thinking about putting you in the hole, are they?" Blocker asked.

"I don't think so," I said.

"Well, take it easy, kid," he said.

"Let us know if we can do anything for you," Candy said.

"I'm all right," I said. "I don't need anything."

Tim and I ran back to the hospital. I still had on my house shoes and my feet got wet in the cold March rain. The doctor said the belt was too small to do any good. He sent me back to the basement. I undressed and went back to bed. They didn't say what they wanted me to do and I didn't ask them. That afternoon two new nurses were assigned to the basement. Neither of them had ever worked in the hospital before. One was from the barbershop and the other from the woolen mill. One had been convalescing from the flu himself. They didn't say anything to me and I didn't say anything to them. I was apprehensive until suppertime. I thought they would try to take me off of the hospital diet and put me back on the main-line grub. Only a few of us in the basement got the special diet. The others who were convalescing from the flu got the same as the convicts got in the dining room. But when the food came around I still got the hospital diet. After that I settled down to stay there for the remainder of my time, if necessary. If they can stand me I can stand them, I told myself. I sent back to the dormitory for my pajamas and bathrobe and some playing cards and magazines and my books.

But I caught the flu and a couple of nights later I ran a high temperature and my throat became sore. I supposed it was from getting my feet wet. The doctor had begun visiting us every morning and when he came through the next morning I went out in the aisle and tried to stop him. "My throat's sore, doctor, and I've been running a temperature all night." He hadn't spoken to me or even looked in my direction since the powwow in his office and I thought if I got directly in his path he'd have to answer me.

But he brushed me aside and passed without replying. His stooge, the convict doctor, also passed me without speaking. I stopped Jake Ingalls and said, "What's the matter with them?" nodding toward the doctor and his stooge.

"Anything wrong, kid?" Jake asked, pleasantly.

"I've got a sore throat and a hell of a head," I said.

He looked at my throat and took my temperature. When the doctor turned and came back he looked at Jake, but Jake kept on examining me without noticing. "You've got a touch of the flu, kid," he said, making out a prescription. "I'll get this filled and send it down to you. Take a dose of salts and lie down and take it easy." He called to one of the nurses, "Hey, Elmer, give Monroe a dose of salts and put him to bed."

When I returned to the dormitory after five more weeks, things seemed duller and stranger than ever. I couldn't work up even a passing interest in gambling any more. It seemed like a senseless pastime and I couldn't see for the life of me how I had spent so much time and thought on it before. For a time I lay on my bunk and read novels and magazine stories, when I wasn't studying. The only interesting things that happened any more were the things which happened in the stories I read. The life in them seemed to me the only real and true life which existed. The prison life came to be something of an unreality which surrounded me and in which I existed but did not live. It seemed as if it was all make-believe, like a scenario that had been written long years before, and we were only acting out our short parts on a stage, going through the actions which the script called for and uttering the written dialogue, and that in time the play would end for all of us and afterward, if we ever chanced to look back on it, it wouldn't mean a thing.

And by then I was getting tired of it, not all at once but just a slow build-up of weariness, an unseen growth of distaste, a softly simmering exhaustion from doing time, an imperceptible accumulation of aversion for the prison and the prison life; for what it consisted of and existed for, and for the sight of it and the smells and the sounds and the repetitious, monotonous, theatrical voice of it; and for the deliberate, mocking, patently different, but everlastingly the same, continuity of actions which strung the years together like a haphazard sequence of situations written into a long, dull, rambling, dry, undramatic play. It came at first as a loss of interest in all the things that had formerly so intrigued me, as a sort of staleness that I thought was in the prison but which was really in me; in my mind and thoughts and reactions toward prison and prison life. The outside world was gradually building up in my thoughts. It was not the world in which I had lived for nineteen years, but one in which I had never lived and which had never existed anywhere but in my mind. My mind was building a world out of the stories I read and the thoughts I had in the silence of the night. It was an utterly fantastic and unreal and impossible-to-exist world. It was a Utopian creation which I was dreaming into existence.

Somewhere near the end of May I got a typewriter and began teaching myself touch typing from the instructions which had come with the typewriter. I was progressing rapidly when one day, while wrestling with little George, I sprained my back. It was the first time I had really hurt my back since I had been in prison and I was frightened.

At first I refused to be taken to the hospital. They weren't going to get me over there and kill me, I told myself. I wore my back-brace every day and even slept in it, hoping that it would correct the ache, but instead it got worse. It got so bad I couldn't keep up in line and had to leave the dormitory some time before the company in order to get to the dining room with them. I knew that, sooner of later, the deputy or director would notice it and they'd have me in the hospital, whether I liked it or not. Hobbling across the yard one day I passed the doctor and it seemed as if he got a look of gloating in his eyes.

My mother was with her people in South Carolina at the time. I wired her a hundred dollars to come and see me immediately. She arrived three days later. I told her all my troubles; about the cast and my back and my fear of being killed if I went back to the hospital. I knew that no matter how much in the wrong I had been, or how much I deserved it, she wouldn't want me to be hurt. And no matter what I might have thought before about her, or might think about her afterwards, that was the truth. I knew I could depend on that.

She went to the warden and told him the story. At first the warden scoffed at the suggestion that my life would be endangered in the hospital. He refused to intercede. But my mother begged and pleaded for me. Finally he promised her that no harm would come to me while I was in the hospital. He sent one of his clerks inside to take me over to the hospital. When the doctor saw me coming in, with the warden's clerk, he wouldn't speak to me. But Jake Ingalls saw that I was taken care of. I stayed flat on my back for two weeks. Then, as suddenly as it had come, the ache left. My back felt as well as it had ever felt. I returned to my company.

My mother had remained in the city during the time I was in the hospital. I wanted her to stay there near to me for a longer time, so I gave her the power of attorney to draw my compensation. It would not be enough for her to live on, I knew, but it would help. The papers were drawn up for one year and I signed them. I felt much safer with her living in the city.

18

DURING the last week in July we were transferred back to 2-2. I was put into a cell with Chump Charlie, Big Loony, and a tall, skinny, dried-up Mississippi red neck called Pappy Calhoun. It wasn't as tough in the cells as it had been before because in some miraculous manner, during our stay in 2-6, we had changed from "agitators" into legitimate cripples. How this had come about, since we were the same convicts with the same afflictions and attitudes, I didn't know. But it was so, like the world when God got through making it.

There were also cripple companies on 1-2 and 1- and 2-1, part of whom were also from the dormitory. During the afternoons, when the weather permitted, we were taken out behind the wooden dormitory in the area facing down from the death house along the outside wall. It was a recreation period for all four cripple companies. We pitched horseshoes and played softball, visited with each other or just strolled about in the bright sunshine. Later we were given permission to use the old baseball diamond as our playground. It had not been in use since the year before the fire. Weeds had overgrown the diamond and the wooden grandstand had rotted. But it was still good enough to hold those who wished to sit idly in the sun, and we pulled up a few weeds so we could see the base lines and played softball on the old diamond, with our raggedy balls made out of rocks wrapped in cotton socks and wrapped with hospital tape. Someone got hold of a set of rings and pitching quoits became popular also. It was very pleasant to get outside in the sun each day.

In the mornings when we remained indoors the cells were unlocked and we had range privilege. We could visit from cell to cell and Blocker and I ran our poker game the same as we always had. After supper we were locked up again but the four of us in our cell used to play seven-up or gin rummy or canasta until bedtime. Chump always insisted on being my partner. It was very hot in the cells. Each evening after supper Nick would bring Chump a bucket of warm water so he could take his "bird bath." Chump had a safety razor and all kinds of lotions and powders. He shaved every day and twice a week he shaved the hairs from his legs and underneath his arms. After he bathed he rubbed his skin with lotions, and powdered himself all over, and dabbled perfume underneath his arms and between his legs and back of his ears until the cell smelled like a whore house. It was impossible for the guards not to have noticed it because the convicts in the cells on either side, and above and below and even halfway down the range, could smell him when a breeze was blowing through.

"I hear you, Chump," someone would yell at him.

"Do you hear me?"

"We hear you over this way too, Chump?"

"How do I sound?" he would ask, winking at me and looking very pleased with himself.

"Sound like a mel-o-dee. Sweet-lee and loving-lee. . . ."

He'd get a great kick out of them. Later on while we were playing cards, he'd wear nylon undershirts and silk pajama trousers. His smooth, powdered and lotioned arms would be exposed, his freshly shaved and powdered face sticky with complacency, and his hair parted and falling down on each side like a careless bob; and smelling as bitchy as a doll on the make. If you could blame Nick for going for him you could do more than I could do, sitting there with my nostrils clogged with perfume and my eyes filled with the sight of his smooth, round hairless arms; or lying on my upper bunk across from his while he winked at me and made kissing sounds with his lips, his eyes as raw and open as those of a depraved woman watching a stallion in heat.

"Come on over when they go to sleep, daddy, I'll be nice to you," he'd say, forming the words soundlessly with his lips.

And there I was, choking on the perfume, looking into his heated eyes, watching his begging lips as he lay there in the semigloom of his upper bunk with the aisle light just missing him as it shone into our darkened cell, making his arms and legs—accentuated by the pink satin loincloth—look like an old oil painting. Myself as cocked as a hair-trigger forty-five, thinking of all the whores I should have had to carry me through all those years. Thinking, I'm a convict doing time and what in the hell have I got to lose? Thinking, after all, as simple as it is, what am I going through all this thinking for? And then, at the last moment, reneging, losing all desire and wanting to hit him in the mouth; cursing him, calling him everything but a child of God, while he lay there shivering with each curse as if I was whipping him with a switch and ecstatic currents of pain were passing through his body, going finally into a convulsion; while I lay there all night with an excruciating ache, until finally, just before dawn, I went to sleep.

The next morning Chump said, "Hello, Jimmy," in a tenor lilt as if we had really had a session the night before. But the session had been all his.

"Good morning, Big Loony," I said.

"What do you say this fine morning, Pappy?"

I turned to Chump and said coldly, " 'Lo." But Chump

didn't let it bother him; he was as smug as if he had had it all his way.

Chump kept after me, getting something, it seemed, from my abuse. It was the fact he thought he was going to win me that made me begin to hate him because I was afraid that he was going to do it. He thought he was so very clever and smart and wise, on top of being pretty, that sooner or later he would make me fall for him. And I was afraid that this was true.

On candy-ordering day I would buy two boxes of candy and give them away and then help him eat his box and the extra one Nick would bring him. On nights when Nick sent him hot sandwiches from the kitchen, when he could get the night guard to bring them up, I'd always eat the choicest sandwich and let Chump eat the one I left. And when my underclothes and socks got dirty I'd have Chump wash them in the cell although he always sent his own out by Nick, to have them laundered. When we went out on the yard I made a point of obviously avoiding him and if he so much as spoke to me directly I'd turn him off with the most brusque reply I could think of. And still I couldn't stop him.

Once he said, "God, Jimmy, you treat me so rough when I love you so much. You're asking me to take a hell of a lot, Jimmy, a hell of a lot."

"You can always quit, honey, when you get tired," I said.

I derived the greatest pleasure, however, when I could hurt him enough to make him cry. Then I would say, "I can stand you when you're hot and bothered because that's the way you are, and I can put up with the things you say because a bitch like you might say anything, but you're just contemptible when you try to impose your tears on me because you know I don't want to feel sorry for you and I'm not going to."

"What do you want with me, anyway, Jimmy?" he asked. "Don't you even love me a little?"

"To tell you the truth, I never think of you in quite that way," I said. "When I think of you at all, I think of you loving me and not ever as me loving you."

"I'd kill you for that if I didn't love you so much," he said.

"You've got a hell of a lot better reasons than that if you were going to," I said.

His eyes got hot and feverish. "You certainly do ask me to take a lot," he said.

"So it's like that now, is it?" I said, feeling all the contempt for him that it was necessary for me to feel to keep from despising myself. But I despised myself, anyway. I couldn't keep from despising myself.

I was getting very tired of the prison and disgusted with myself. Everything was like stale, flat beer sitting warm and pallid in the sun; like a flaccid, bloated corpse just before it begins to rot. Tired of the prison and disgusted with myself. But the prison was indifferent. The days did not give a damn and the nights were no less long. Sunsets came and sunsets went and the walls were rooted just as deeply into the everlasting earth. Stone and steel, and time coming and going but never staying, and ever the eternal same. And I was getting tired of it. Tired of hearing and seeing and feeling and learning of the perfidy and degradation of convicts and of myself. Tired of murder and rape and jobs and punks and hacks and monstrosities.

And then a simple-minded convict had to write another simple-minded bastard to tell him to keep his mouth shut and Tommy Tucker, to whom he had given the kite to be delivered, had to take it to the director and the director had to have the convicts over and get the truth out of them with a three-hour clubbing; and the two damn fools had to break down and confess that they were the ones who had set the prison afire and burned up two hundred and seventy-seven other convicts. And I had thought, my God, what the hell did they do that for? they'll only burn them now and that will make two hundred and seventy-nine. What the hell did any of them do any of it for? What did Tommy have to rat for? And why couldn't the officials, for once, have let it pass and no one but themselves would ever have been the wiser nor have thought about it nor have given a damn, one way or the other, how the prison fire had started? Since it had and since the two hundred and seventy-seven bastards had died and since, now that they were dead, there wasn't anything anyone could do to bring them back to life; neither clubbing two incidental convicts into unconsciousness nor burning them to death in the electric chair nor giving Tommy Tucker an honor job, which was the customary reward for such services beyond the call of duty; which by then you knew so well you could close your eyes and see, and be tired of—be so completely tired of.

But that wasn't the way it turned out, which only made the difference you didn't allow for so much the same as all the other differences in the past which you had not allowed for which were the same old differences. The way it turned out was that one of the fellows hanged himself in the hole one night and the other got life and waited for a year to hang himself, and Tommy Tucker was transferred out to the prison farm and his natural life commuted to take effect within ninety days. But after sixty days he couldn't stand the farm any longer, after having stood the prison for nine years, so he ran away. He was away a week and was caught and brought back and his pardon revoked, so he hanged himself too, making it a grand slam. And then none of them held any malice or animosity against one another, nor did anything they had ever done any longer matter for the grass rooting in their rotten hearts was certainly no less greener, as Omar might have said, than grass rooting in the hearts of saints.

We were transferred back into the 2-6 dormitory late that year.

One night Chump said, "Kiss me, Jimmy."

I said, "My mother's coming over to see me next week, Chump, and I don't want to kiss you until after she comes because I want to kiss her, you see, and it'll take a full week to get my mouth clean now from kissing you before."

He went for his knife and I thought for a moment it was going to be on. But he put the knife away and went down to the front end of the dormitory and walked back and forth for hours and that night when he came back to bed he said, "I'm through, Jimmy. I still love you but you ask me to take too much."

After that he let his beard grow long and his uniform get dirty and baggy and he gave away all his nylon underwear and silk pajamas and began wearing the state-issue drawers again and sleeping in them and looking like hell. And still I didn't get anything out of it.

It was about then that they installed an improved motion-picture machine in the chapel, and that Christmas most of us saw the first decent movie we had seen in years. After that we saw a picture each Saturday. The idle companies went in the morning and the working companies in the afternoon. The honor men went at night.

Another year was gone. The things they brought they took away. The things they left I didn't want, such as the shame and the self-contempt and the feeling of being a convict at last. They left a great weariness also. I was getting very tired and disgusted.

19

AROUND the first of the year we got a number of newcomers who were drawing disability compensation from the Veterans Administration. We already had quite a few old-timers drawing pensions of one kind or another from the first world war. We even had a couple of grandpappys drawing pensions from the Spanish American War. And there were a number of crippled vets in our company who'd been in prison several years and didn't know before then that they could draw disability compensation for injuries sustained in civilian life. When they found out from the newcomers they, too, could get on the government gravy train they rushed over to the deputy's office and sent in applications. It wasn't long before we had more than fifty vets in our company drawing pensions of from twenty to one hundred and fifty dollars monthly.

It was comical how some of those vets got fleeced out of their money. Wives who hadn't visited them since their imprisonment began coming around regularly on visiting days. Those who didn't have wives were tricked into long-distance affairs with other convict's sisters or mothers or aunts or cousins or sweethearts—and even in some cases with other convict's wives. A convict would tell the vet about the woman—his sister or mother or friend—and then help the vet smuggle a letter out to her. The next thing you knew the woman had a pass from the welfare department to visit the vet, and before you knew what was happening the vet was sending her his monthly check. In some instances the vets never even saw the women and just knew them through secret correspondence. But that didn't stop them from giving those women their money.

One of the convict nurses in the hospital had a rather pretty sister who used to come over to the chapel on Sundays with the outside visitors. He'd point her out to the vets on his sucker list and the next Sunday he'd have her smile at them. That was all that was needed. He promoted seven vets at the same time. Then one Sunday she didn't show up and the following week all seven suckers got letters from her stating that she had become ill suddenly and had to have an expensive operation and didn't know where she was going to get the money to pay for it. She got more than two thousand dollars from those guys. Shortly afterward the nurse got a pardon.

The officials did all they could to stop this racket but the vets went over to the deputy's office and swore out affidavits that these women were their wives, in many instances women they'd never seen. You couldn't blame them much. They'd been going along for years, forgotten, woman-starved, and friendless. Month after month the money piled up in the front office. They couldn't spend it. They were lonely and frustrated. Suddenly they found themselves with five hundred or a thousand dollars to their credit. They were ripe for plucking by the first woman to say, "I love you," or for that matter by anyone—man, woman, or child—who wrote in from the outside on some scented stationery with an enclosed picture of a pretty girl. It didn't make any difference whether the picture had been bought from some cheap studio or whether the woman ever existed. They believed that these women, whose pictures were enclosed in these perfumed letters, were interested in them because that was what they wanted to believe. One guy had a picture of a well-known movie actress inscribed, "For my darling Ronnie, with all my love, Yvonne." It hung at the head of his bunk and he sent Yvonne eighty-five bucks every month. Several guys tried to tell him who the dame was but he didn't believe them. We got a great laugh out of it.

The colored boys really preened themselves. They went in for purple lounging robes and sky-blue silk pajamas and yellow socks and long, tan, pointed shoes; buying not one pair, but two and three. One colored boy named Sanders bought eight pairs of shoes, five tan and three black, for which he paid about twenty dollars a pair. The warden called him out to his office and asked him what he wanted with so many pairs of shoes.

"I wants a pair for each day in the week and two for Sunday," he grinned. The warden told him that he didn't have that many pairs of shoes himself. "That's all right," Sanders said. "Don't you worry. I'll buy you a pair next ordering-day."

But I could understand what he meant. Outside they say clothes make the man, but in prison it's shoes that make the convict.

Another colored boy called Fofo, who was drawing a hundred and twenty dollars monthly, discovered he had over three thousand dollars to his credit. He'd been in about four years then and hadn't had a visit in all that time. All of a sudden he sent to Alabama for his wife, whom he hadn't seen since he went into the army at the beginning of the war, and had her set up housekeeping in the city. Then he got the ugliest, blackest fag in prison and set up housekeeping for himself inside. The officials did all they could to save some of his money for him. They stopped him from ordering anything from the outside and cut down his commissary order to fifty cents a week. But they didn't think to stop him from ordering newspapers and magazines because they all knew old Fofo couldn't read. So he'd get the paper and magazine men to give him cash for money orders, four dollars in cash for a five-dollar slip. One day it was discovered that he had sent in cashier's slips for over four hundred dollars worth of papers and magazines. In three months they had him. He was stone-broke. The warden froze his compensation so he couldn't touch it. His fag hit him over the head with a hockey stick. They transferred the fag to the girl-boy company on 5-4. The last he heard of his wife she was living with another man. But he was a good-natured old boy and he didn't let it worry him a bit.

The honor men who clerked in the cashier's office did a booming business selling cash for money transfers. The standard rate was four for five. Some of those convicts got pads of cashier's slips and wrote out money transfers like bank checks. That money out in the front office didn't seem real. A convict would write out a fifty-dollar money-transfer slip without batting an eye, and then turn around and squawk like hell about having to part with a dollar greenback for something he really needed.

Our day guard, Captain Tom, got his. I had to give him credit. He had those convicts buying him shoes and gloves and underwear and bathrobes and blankets, anything which he could use that they were allowed to order. He must have gotten more than a dozen pairs of shoes. I never knew how he got all that loot out through the front gates, but he managed somehow.

During the Christmas week we had been issued safety razors, and for a time we received one blade each week.

Then some guy decided to cut his wrists and they stopped issuing the blades. We had the razors without the blades. That gave Captain Tom the idea of starting a retail-drug-store business in the dormitory. He began bringing in all sorts of toilet articles which he sold for fantastic prices—lotions and creams and shaving creams and razor blades, tooth paste and soap and talcum powder and shaving brushes, cold creams and vaseline and rouge and mascara. The items which were more strictly prohibited, of course, were the highest-priced. Polack Paul handled the stuff for him. In a short time Polack Paul had four lockboxes of cosmetics and junk, and was doing a rushing business all over the institution.

There was so much money in the dormitory everybody wanted to run a game. They weren't satisfied any more with just Blocker and me running the only game. There were a lot of disputes and arguments and agitation. It got to the place where the gamekeepers had to get up in the morning, before the lights came on, and spread their blankets on the tables to reserve their space. The tables were covered from end to end of the dormitory with guys running games. Some guys made a racket of putting down their blankets and then selling the space later in the day. There were a number of fights and if someone moved somebody else's blanket it always resulted in a fight. It got to be such a problem that Tom called me down to his desk one day.

"Jim, these fellows who can't get to run a game keep writing out to the warden and over to the deputy, telling them about the gambling that's going on up here," he said. "I don't want to stop the gambling but they're going to take me off this company and put me somewhere else if it keeps on like this." He laughed deprecatingly. "You know, I don't want to get on one of those working companies, Jim. It'd kill me doing all that marching and climbing, up and down those stairs, with my heart." Tom spoke in that confidential whisper one usually associates with the ward politician.

"We'll take up our game for awhile if you say so," I offered.

"Naw, I don't want you to do that," he said. "I just don't want this thing to get out of hand and get the brass-ass down on me." I could understand what he meant. All he had to do all day was sit up there in his padded chair and snooze and take us to the dining room and back. "I'll tell you what we'll do," he said. "You get the best fellows down there, the ones who can bank a game and pay off, and we'll give them each a day to run a game. We'll just let chances go around, then nobody'll have a beef. Now I'll tell you how we'll work it. We'll let them have four games a day and no more; two games for the white fellows, and two for the colored." About a third of the convicts in the dormitories at that time were colored. "The white fellows can have one poker game and one blackjack game, or whatever else they want to play except dice; I don't want any dice games. And the colored fellows can have one poker game and one skin game."

"Okay, Tom, I'll see what I can do," I said.

"And listen, Jim, tell them that it will cost them a buck a day for each game, and you collect it for me." He winked.

"Okay, Tom," I said grinning, and started away.

"Wait a minute, Jim," he said. "I've been thinking about taking a day for myself. I'll tell you what we'll do. You pick me out four good fellows, two white and two colored, and I'll take Wednesdays and bank all the games and split fifty-fifty with the dealers. Pick me out some good boys who know their stuff. I'll tell you, you run the poker game for me, Jim, and get Blocker to run a blackjack game for me. Then you and Blocker take a day for yourself. You get a couple of good colored boys to run the colored games for me, and a couple to run the colored games for you; some good boys who know how to keep their mouths shut and make a buck for themselves. That'll give you a day and me a day and they can split up the days that are left."

"That ought to do it, Tom," I said. "I'll straighten it out."

And that was the way we ran it. It made me a sort of boss of the gambling racket for I had to give out the days and collect the tribute. Blocker and I took Sundays, which were the best gambling days since we were locked in from dinner on. We picked out fellows who had money and gave them Saturdays, Fridays and Thursdays, which were the next best days, respectively. We only allowed one game to each banker or each combine. Tom had Wednesdays. We gave the rats Mondays and Tuesdays, which were the dullest days, to keep them quiet.

There must have been four or five thousand dollars in cash in the dormitory at that time. It couldn't have been any secret from the officials, with all the rats we had in the dormitory, but they didn't bother us. Perhaps they thought it was all for the best. Those convicts had too much good old government money right through there to sit on it and not gamble, and by having the gambling controlled we kept the fights and disputes down to a minimum.

It worked perfectly. The only thing about it, if you got reckless in your game and took a heavy loss you'd have to wait a week, until you put down your game again, to get it back. Captain Tom was the only real winner. The rest of us would play back our winnings in the other games during the week. But Tom went to stashersville with his; when he got that green in his pocket it was long-gone from that joint.

On top of which he sold all the tobacco and merchandise he took out of the games. None of the gamekeepers paid the winners in cash if they could help it; everyone wanted to hang on to his cash. So they would go to Tom and get as much merchandise as they needed and give him the cash to hold for them until they could redeem it with more merchandise, which few ever did. At one time Tom had so much tobacco and merchandise he had to store it in the lockbox where the porters usually kept their mops and buckets and soap and stuff. This was no shoe box, either. It was four feet wide and eight feet long and five feet deep, big enough to bury a half-dozen convicts in. Tom had it filled with Bull Durham tobacco, tooth paste, soap, and such. He lost half of the tobacco because that on the bottom got wet once, and molded.

The deputy warden got his, too. Every time a convict came to court, the deputy would plank some kind of subscription list in his face. The convict would sign for a dollar, or five, without even knowing what it was for, or without caring, for that matter. It was better to toss away a few dollars than go to the hole.

And we got ours, too. Blocker and Candy and Signifier and myself. But we'd chump it off like all the others. It was catching. There was so much no one thought of saving any of it—not until Captain Tom began draining the dormitory, anyway. One day Blocker and I did some calculating on Tom and we figured that he was taking about a hundred dollars weekly out of the dormitory.

Blocker went up for a hearing by the parole board that May and was granted a parole to take effect on the first of June. That was the quickest parole I'd ever heard of. He had looked for a flop because of his reformatory record. That was what first called my attention to the fact that a convict's record didn't mean a damn thing when he went before that board. The second- and third-timers made parole just as quick, if not actually quicker, than the first-timers. There must have been a reason for this, but I never discovered what it was.

I certainly hated to see Blocker go. I was glad, though. But I knew how much I was going to miss him. All down the line he had been solid with me, on the high spots and in the dumps, in trouble and smooth sailing. We had been flush together, broke together. He had always been on my side, right or wrong, and not once since I had first met him in September, almost four years ago, had a harsh word passed between us. In all that time we had never been separated. What had been his had been mine and what had been mine had been his. He had never given me a word of advice other than, "take it easy," nor a word of censure; and the times he had made suggestions had been all for my own good. I certainly did hate to see him go.

We hadn't expected him to make parole so we hadn't saved for it. We had made good money but we had frittered it away. When the time came for him to leave we had about one hundred and twenty dollars in cash and I had thirty-five dollars to my credit in the front office. He had six dollars in earnings and the ten dollars they'd give him on leaving. That made a total of one hundred and seventy-one dollars. I told him to take it all and signed the thirty-five dollars over to him. He could use it better than me. He had a whole bag of such clothing as underwear, pajamas, bathrobes and shoes which we had taken in from our games.

"Well, kid, I certainly wish you were going out with me," he said that morning before they called him.

"I wish so, myself," I said.

"Is there anything you want me to do for you, kid?"

"Nope, I'm okay. Just keep out of trouble."

"I'll write to you," he said, "and if I get lucky I'll send you some dough."

"You needn't bother," I said. "There's plenty here."

"I'll write you, anyway, kid," he said.

"I won't look for it," I said. "So if you don't, I won't be disappointed."

They called him then. "Well, don't shoot no blanks, kid," he said.

"I'll try not to."

We shook hands.

"When you get out look me up around Akron or Detroit. Just ask someone where's the biggest crap game and I'll be there."

"I will," I said. "I hope you're in the money."

"Never give a sucker a break, kid," he said with that crooked, wolfish grin. "Never give a sucker a break."

I grinned back at him. He went down the aisle. At the stairs he turned. I threw up my hand and he went out. I certainly did miss him. He was one swell fellow.

After he had gone our games went to pot. I began losing, while dealing. That had never happened to me before. Candy couldn't win, either. And Signifier couldn't gamble; he liked to signify too much.

They had said I couldn't gamble without Blocker. They had said he was holding me up and without him I would blow like a burst balloon. It was true. After he left I couldn't win. I tried hard enough. But luck had turned its back on me. Or maybe it was just that I had lost confidence. I lost steadily from that time on and if I hadn't had the take from all four games I would have been stony in a week. Maybe I was trying too hard. I'd sit in those games and chew up cigarette holders as if they were matchsticks. I chewed a ten-inch holder down to a nub in a single day. And not once did I leave a game winner. It troubled me. For a time I wanted to win so badly it became an obsession. After that I quit studying. I dropped my law course. I stored away my books on psychology. All I wanted was to just once win a pile in one of those lousy games. It was slowly killing me.

The movies which we saw on Saturdays helped. According to the statement which the warden gave to the press, the motion-picture projector had been purchased from our amusement fund, whatever that was, and had cost ten thousand dollars, with an additional seventeen hundred dollars for the screen. But the way we figured it was that the warden had some money on hand at the time which couldn't be explained, and he was being investigated again. Anyway, we were glad to have them, and whether eleven thousand, seven hundred dollars for the projector and screen was cheap or expensive, we never settled. But we conceded that the business was worth it, no matter what it had cost, so long as it had cost someone else.

Visibility in the chapel was very good as the seats were steeply graduated, like an indoor arena. However we were a little cramped for knee space. But we put up with that. We didn't even kick about it very much; just enough to appear normal. If we hadn't kicked about some feature of the pictures the officials would have sworn we were cooking up a riot or a break or something. And we liked the pictures too much to kick about them. We really went for the pictures.

For a time the company that sold them the projector sent in an operator each week to run it, but soon a couple of smart convicts had learned how to operate it and the civilian wasn't needed any longer. Those convicts could learn anything and everything but how to stay out of prison. As the *Prison Times* put it, in a slightly different way: "A convict will pay a million dollars for freedom if he has it, and then turn around and gamble his million-dollar freedom against fifteen dollars in a drugstore cash register."

Anyway, we went for those pictures. They were some good pictures, too. Some solid good pictures. All of them were good. There never was a bad picture shown in that prison until the novelty of seeing them had worn off. If we had been the movie-going public that year every last picture would have been a box-office hit. A lot of the convicts used to stay in their cells in preference to going to the baseball games. The blind convicts never went. But for the pictures the blind convicts sat down front. The only convicts who stayed away from the pictures were dead convicts.

We liked everything about the pictures, the stories and the scenery and the action and the dialogue and all. But it was women's voices that got the closest to us. Those and the songs. We were song-starved and we were always woman-hungry. When a woman began to speak on the screen you could see us leaning forward in a solid wave.

It was about then that I began to pity myself, and next to looking out a window at the women in the street, pitying yourself will kill you quicker than arguing with a gun if you're a convict. I lived a part in every single picture and when they'd end I'd be brimming full of self-pity. My God, how I could pity myself. I often cried at sentimental scenes; all of us tough, lousy, low convicts cried at sentimental scenes. We sat up there and blubbered like a bunch of kids. But it was good for us, it gave us a chance to cry out all those tears we had been saving for so long, trying to be so awful goddamned tough and take it like a man. "He can take it," they would say, as if the son of a bitch had won the Congressional medal or a Rhodes Scholarship. What the hell of it? Who the hell ever gave a damn if a convict could take it or not? And if he could take it, what the hell could he get out of taking it besides a bloody head or death? And for what? "He can take it!" Goddamned right, he can take it all right, I used to think. It was good to see the movies and get a chance to cry.

We lived in those pictures. My God, how we lived in those pictures. And what did we get from them? Plenty, I supposed. Plenty of tears and self-pity, anyway.

They helped us, though. They helped us a lot. They made us softer, more human. They gave us a certain perspective that many of us had lost. Oh, they did a lot for us, morally, spiritually, emotionally. But they hurt us too. You had to leave all that beautiful make-believe and come back to the cells and dormitories, back to the rooted, immovable, eternal prison of stone and steel. You had to come back to the gutless, stale, callous convicts. Worst of all you had to come back to yourself.

20

OH, BUT THOSE officials were good to us that year. We had baked ham and candied yams and lemonade on the Fourth of July. We swilled our lemonade and called for more. By then the new industrial building had been completed and most of the mills had moved into it. The new 10&11 cell block had also been completed and filled. Built onto the end of this block and isolated by a wall of tool-proof steel, was the new 12 block which housed death row and the redshirt desperadoes.

The prison school was reopened and a young redheaded graduate student from the state university came in and took charge of it. There were eight grades in the school this time and special courses in "business and commerce" and "shorthand." It was an excellent school and the young university student who had charge of it was an excellent young man. Everything was excellent that summer.

A boxing tournament called the Stonewall-Gloves Bouts was scheduled for Labor Day and all the convicts who thought they could box signed up for the elimination series.

A gym was rigged up in the basement of the Protestant chapel and a big ex-pub called Bull Doggie was appointed the head trainer and referee. Bull Doggie was serving life, and was also wanted in New York for murder, but he knew the fighting game. He had for his assistant Frankie Kane, a reformed redshirter. For two months they worked with the stonewall glovers, classifying them according to weight divisions, eliminating the duds, and grading them according to ability. Those who made the grade went into training. They were given special grub and excused from all other duties. A temporary ring was built down in a corner of the ball diamond and a couple of homemade punching bags were hung underneath the grandstand. The glovers did their road work around the diamond in the morning and punched the bags or worked out in the ring during the afternoons.

For the rest of us a recreational program was instituted. The program was arranged so that every company went down to the ball diamond two afternoons each week. We took calisthenics and afterward played softball. Two young physical-education students from the state university directed the program. It was a big thing. The school companies had Mondays and Thursdays, the idle companies Tuesdays and Fridays, and the working companies Wednesdays and Saturdays. Our movie hour was changed from Saturday mornings to Saturday afternoons. The diamond had been cleared and the two softball diamonds had been laid out. The outfield grass was cut and the infields remade with new earth brought in from the outside.

At one o'clock the band would assemble on the yard and we'd come out of the cells and dormitories and line up behind them. Then the band would break into a march and lead the procession down toward the diamond, followed by company after company, the convicts swinging their shoulders and keeping time. There's a rhythm in a lockstepping line similar to that of a chorus line, and when the convicts wanted to they could march in matchless unison; hands, arms, shoulders, legs and feet swinging in rhythmic precision. It was a parade. Hep. . . . Hep . . . kick out your right foot, kick 'im in the belly if he don't keep step. . . . Hep. . . . They came up with that old pappy jive.

We passed the new brick industrial building, looming to our left, huge and bulldogging. We passed the powerhouse to our right, with its tall brick chimney and finger of gray smoke against the white-clouded sky. We smelt the stink of burning garbage; over the band's brassy blare heard the screaming whistle of a train passing outside. If we had looked we could have seen the walls, rooted and immovable, enclosing the scene, chill and ancient and unthawed by the sun's warm rays. But we didn't look at the walls as we went down to the diamond to play softball. We made as if we didn't know that they were there. We weren't convicts doing twenty-eight thousand goddamned years; we were cadets marching around the stadium before an Army-Navy game, we were Shriners parading down Hollywood Boulevard.

"AwwwwwwwWWWWWWWWW, it don't mean a thing if you ain't got that swing. . . ." That's the way we chirped it.

Oh, we had a time. The ball game fever swept the prison like natural elevens, and although we convicts in 2-6 were supposed to be crippled, we were in the thick of it. We went into it heart, body and soul. We talked softball, dreamed softball, ate softball, slept softball. It was in our blood like the red corpuscles.

When word had first come out that we would have softball that summer Captain Tom brought in a half-dozen softballs and took us back of the old wooden dormitory, down by the death house, so we could practice. We cleared away some of the rocks and made a make-shift diamond. Tom wanted us to have a team that would make a showing, at least, so we really practiced in earnest. Since I was the boss of the gambling racket in the dormitory I inherited managership of the team. That was the way our minds worked. They made me the catcher, too, but that was because we couldn't find anyone else to do it. Second base was my love.

We had three colored convicts on the team, Johnny Brothers at first, Baldy at short, and a boy called Snakehips in left field. Candy was at third and Chink and Jerry in the field and everybody at second, it seemed, because we never could find a good second-baseman. In short field we had a slim Okie cutie called Cotton Top. He was about the most perfect player I ever saw, although he wasn't very well-liked. He was like a ballet dancer on the field. We had two pitchers, a little crippled kid called Beauty who was pretty wild, and a big, crabby black boy called Mose, who could really throw them in. He used to pitch them by so many batters that every team we played had the umpire go out and watch his delivery to see if it was legal. But he was so surly that you could never tell what he was going to do. Even Johnny Brothers couldn't get along with him. "Evilest nigger God ever made," Brothers used to say. I was the only one who could do anything with him at all, and I had to beg him and plead with him and damn near get down on my knees and pray to him to keep him pitching. But Captain Tom and I always had our chips down and were playing it for blood. We had to keep Mose pitching in order to win.

At first we were scheduled with other half-cripple companies. But they were pushovers for us. After that they gave tougher opponents. We got a great bang out of beating those teams that thought they were tough. But it was one hell of a job managing all those cranky convicts.

Tom would say, "Whew, these fellows have the damndest dispositions of any people I ever saw."

And I'd say, "You haven't seen them perform yet."

We'd have to pay them and beg them, and every now and then blow up and curse them out. But Tom stuck right with them. He argued with them and begged them and bribed them and pleaded with them, and every now and then he'd get so mad he'd put one of them in the hole on a trumped-up charge, for making an error. That fellow, Tom, went softball crazy. Candy and I wanted to win, too; we had our dough up, too. But Tom would bet fifty or sixty dollars on each game and we had to win for him—we had to win for his peace of mind as well as his money. Between games he would take us out all day long to practice. The lieutenants reprimanded him for keeping us out so long and finally, they ordered him to stop taking us out at all. He didn't stop but he wouldn't keep us out so long. Instead, he had the tables moved in the dormitory and stacked down at one end in order to give his pitchers space to practice. He had Mose warming up so long one morning before a game that Mose's arm got so tired when he got out on the diamond he couldn't get the ball up to the plate. Tom swore that he had sold out to the other team and would have put him in the hole if it hadn't been for Johnny Brothers and me.

The staff of the *Prison Times* drew up the schedules and sent scorers down to the games. At first the university students umpired. Tom would try to bribe them to make decisions in our favor but they never went for it. He'd go over to the print shop and find out who we were scheduled to play next and then he'd go over to the company and try to bribe the best players to throw the game. And, my God, don't let one of our own players drop a ball, or strike out with the bases loaded. Tom would swear they were throwing the game. He had Jerry transferred down into the mills because he caught him talking to the coal-company guard the day we were to play the coal company.

But many of the other guards were just as bad as Captain Tom. All of them had spies in each other's companies and they'd all try to bribe the players to throw off. None of them ever tried me because they all knew that I was Tom's righthand man. But they tried Brothers and Candy and Mose. Mose would take their money and then go out and beat their team. He was certainly one evil colored man.

The rivalry between the teams was terrific. The officials condoned gambling on the games. It was nothing to see a company bring a half-dozen pillowcases full of tobacco and merchandise down to the diamond to bet on their team. They said the guard on 3-3 lost his home betting on his team. But none of them had it quite as bad as Tom.

You should have seen Tom walking up and down the firstbase line, with his big belly sweating in the sun and his white shirt sticking to his body, and his face red as paint, his cap cocked on the back of his head with a lock of hair down in his eyes; talking a mile a minute in a disjointed babble of sighs and prayers and curses and cheers. At the end of each game he would be utterly weary, with sagging shoulders, and his eyes registering the beginning of a heart attack. His unlighted cigar, which he had lighted a hundred times, would still be unsmoked but now chewed to a frazzle with slimy strings of tobacco hanging from his slack mouth. The first thing after we got back to the dormitory, even before we sainted players got our rubdowns, someone would get out a bucket of warm water for him to soak his feet, and someone else would have to apply hot towels to his arms and cold towels to his head and work on him until it was time for him to go off duty, so he would be able to get away on his own power. He played each game harder than all twenty players combined.

And then the very first thing the next morning, as if he had lain awake all night and thought about it, he'd be out scouting some newcomer who had just entered the institution the day before, trying to find out if he could play softball. He'd slip over in the 10 block and up to the 5th range, where the newcomers were celled, and interview every one of them. If one just so much as said he had played softball at any time in his life Tom would tell him, talking through the side of his mouth in that ward-heeler's whisper and acting as confidential as a race-track tout about to give you a tip on a horse that ain't won a race since Count Fleet was a colt, "You act crippled now, and I'll get you over in the cripple company. I'll get you over there before they have a chance to ship you down into the mills."

"Do what, sir?" the confused convict would ask.

"Hey!" Tim would whisper, his face up against the bars. "Pst, come closer," talking even lower than a whisper. When the convict would get close enough for him to kiss he'd ask in his low stage whisper, "Got any smoking?"

"Why, er, no, sir—"

He'll pull out a dime and give it to the convict. "Take this and buy some," he'd whisper in a way that'd make you think he'd slipped a guy a thousand-dollar bill. "And don't forget there's plenty more where that came from. We have everything over in the cripple company. Best company in the joint." He could make the cripple company sound better than freedom itself. And then he'd look up and down the range, knowing damn well that the company guard was over in another cell block with a hospital pickup list. "Now don't forget now, just act crippled. Fall back in line. Act like you can't keep up. Let the line get 'way ahead and just keep on hobbling across the yard. Don't let any of the lieutenants bluff you. Just tell them you're crippled and can't keep up. I'll get you."

"Yes, sir."

"Get it?" he'd ask, stretching his eyes, interrogatingly.

"Yes, sir, fall back, act like I can't keep up, don't let the lieutenants bluff you, just tell them you're crippled and I'll let the line get 'way ahead and then I'll get you, er, I mean you'll get him, er—" By then the convict would be so confused by all of Tom's confidential jive he wouldn't know what he was saying.

"Yeah, that's—er, what did you say?" Tom would ask, his eyes stretching in earnest this time. "Er, say that again," he'd shout, not so sure now if the convict had sense enough even to act crippled much less play softball, and getting a vague idea that he had lost another dime. "Er, never mind. What position did you say you played?"

"Second base."

"Yeah, well here's another dime, get yourself some more smoking. And be sure to act crippled, now."

Then he would come back and tell us he had scouted Joe Blow for second base. "Hey, Jim, call Johnny Brothers, tell him to come down here a minute, tell him I got a kid coming in soon that can really play that second base."

Tom wanted a second-baseman as bad as we wanted freedom. More than likely he'd get the kid into the company and the kid would get out on the diamond and couldn't catch pennies in a wash tub if they were raining from heaven in a cloudburst, and would act as if he'd never seen second base before or a softball game either, for that matter. Tom would get so excited the director would have to come over and put him completely off the diamond, clear over behind the wire fence that enclosed the players' field, and he'd walk up and down out there chewing his unlighted cigar to a frazzle and thinking up ways and means of getting the kid transferred to Siberia.

When we played 3-4, which was supposed to be a breather between the coal company and the band, they beat us and Tom fell out with a heart attack and had to be rushed to the hospital on stretchers. We were leading by a score of one-to-nothing, going into the seventh and last inning, when Mose blew up and walked the first two batters to face him. He steadied down and struck out the next two but I let one get through me and the two men on base advanced. The next batter swung blind at one of Mose's high fast ones and hit it on the nose. It sailed far out in left-center field. Snakehips and Cotton Top started for it at the same time and when it became apparent that they were going to collide, you could hear Tom yelling a country mile, "Let it alone, you black son of a bitch! Keep away from it! Oh, you black African bastard!" When they bumped, Tom keeled over as if dead.

Snakehips was sore for days after that and I had to go around and placate him. I had to tell him that Tom didn't mean any harm, that he was so excited he didn't know what he was saying. When that didn't soothe him I had to take him down to Tom and have Tom apologize.

"Aw, Snakehips, old boy, you know how a man says things when he gets excited," Tom said. "Don't take it to heart, old boy. Here, take this dime and go down and win yourself something." After Snakehips had gone he turned to me and said, "It's a hell of a racket, ain't it, kid? You have to kiss the black bastard's behind and then pay for the privilege." But Tom was crazy about Johnny Brothers. Brothers was the best first-baseman in the joint. He could get anything Tom had—up to a dime, that is.

Candy and I bet heavily on our games but we had to split our winnings with the rest of the players for fear they might throw a game. Tom had told us not to use anyone who wouldn't bet on himself, but if we had done that we wouldn't have had any team. Most of the guys thought it was smart to bet against themselves, then when they lost we'd have to give them part of ours. Tom wouldn't give them anything himself. He'd let them have their way in the dormitory, however. He was really strong with that. All you had to do was play softball for him and you could do whatever you wanted to in that dormitory with impunity.

When we really got to going, like the time we knocked over the colored convicts in the coal company, who were supposed to be so hot, we took over. On rainy days we'd not only move the tables so we could practice inside but we'd move the bunks, too. The rest of the convicts got to resenting Tom so that practically everyone who wasn't on the team had written out to the warden, ratting on him. One day the warden called him out and showed him the notes, a whole stack of them. He told Tom if he couldn't do better he'd find himself up on 6-11 with a mill company. Tom had us lie low for awhile and then he pinned hell on those rats. He shut down all the games, enforced the silence rules and even stopped the colored convicts from having church services during the day.

Toward the middle of the season Tom was so filled up with softball the other guards began avoiding him. And later, when the guards began umpiring the games, all of them went nuts. It was all the deputy and director could do to keep peace between the guards. If Tom couldn't bribe the guard who was umpiring he wouldn't let us play unless the director was on the field. The time we played 1-4 the guard who was umpiring kept sending word back to us to wait out the pitcher. 1-4 had a hell of a fine pitcher and he wasn't throwing anything but strikes. He was striking out so many of us that the umpire called time, and came over to our bench to get a drink of water. While he held the cup to his lips he turned his back to the players on the field and whispered to those of us who could hear him, "Listen, you fellows, quit striking at those balls. I've got forty dollars bet on you."

"What balls?" Brothers asked. "That chump ain't pitching nothing but strikes."

"They'll be balls when I get through calling them," he said.

The dining-room and hospital teams played on Sunday afternoons. Each week the best team from one of the other groups was selected to go out and play one or the other of them. The hospital and dining room would play and then the winner would play the team chosen for that week. The men in the company were permitted to go along with the team and it gave them all a Sunday afternoon outside, while everyone else in the whole joint was locked in. It was a very special occasion and there was great rivalry among the teams to be selected. The dining room was supposed to be the best team in the prison and besides beating the hospital regularly they beat all the other teams sent out to play them.

Tom wanted us to play them. He would rather have had us play them than have had strawberry shortcake for dinner the rest of his life. And Tom truly loved strawberry shortcake. Just a little strawberry shortcake was enough to give him gas pains and slow up his ticker, but he'd eat it until his stomach bulged. He'd eat three or four helpings, knowing that it was a gamble whether he'd be alive the next day. But he would have given up his shortcake for an entire week if he could have gotten us a game with the dining room.

He kept after the warden to let us play the dining room until he almost got fired. They told a story around the prison about the last time Tom asked the warden to let us play the dining room. The warden was attending a big political banquet in a downtown hotel. The governor and the welfare director and a United States senator and a lot of other big shots were present. Tom happened to stop by the bar and learned that the banquet was in progress and the warden was present. He called a bellhop and sent word to the warden that he'd like to see him for a minute. The warden sent word back that he couldn't leave right then, but for Tom to stop by his office the next day.

"You go back and tell him this is important," Tom instructed the bellhop, tipping him a whole buck.

The warden reluctantly came down to the bar to see what Tom wanted. "What's happening that's so important it won't wait, Tom?" he asked. "Don't tell me it's a break they're cooking. I would have heard myself."

"Listen, Tris," Tom said. "You've been putting us off all summer. My boys are going along great now. We've beat the coal company and we've beat the band. It looks to me as if anybody's entitled to a shot at the dining room it ought to be us now."

They said that the warden fired Tom on the spot. But Tom came in the next morning and begged himself back. The warden warned him that if he ever mentioned softball to him again he'd fire him and make it stick. But we got to play the dining room one Sunday after all. The *Prison Times* scheduled it. The whole company came along. It was like a picnic. Everyone took along their Sunday-afternoon snack, and ate down on the diamond. We all had a swell time. At least everybody but Tom. We lost. Everybody said we won a moral victory but the score was five-to-three. If Johnny Brothers and myself, who were supposed to be the best players on the team, hadn't made two errors each we might have beaten them. We won our bets, anyway, because we'd gotten four runs from everybody. Tom had even gotten six runs, so it wasn't that he lost any money. He just hated to see us lose the game. He wanted to get us another game with them and spent all the rest of the week trying to persuade the editor of the *Prison Times* to schedule another game. But it was too late in the season.

All-star teams were picked from the school, idle, and working companies. The morning of Labor Day we had a play-off for the intra-wall championship. Johnny Brothers, Mose, Candy and I, were picked to play on the idle companies' all-stars. We lost to the working companies' all-stars and they lost to the school all-stars. Then the dining room played the school all-stars and beat them, winding up the season without a loss.

We had a fine dinner of roast chicken and watermelon, and that afternoon we went back to the diamond for the boxing bouts. A ring had been built in the center of the diamond and we stood back of a wooden railing and watched the stonewall glovers do their stuff. They were very lousy fights. A colored heavyweight was the best of the lot. He was fighting another colored convict with a fancy-Dan style and he caught up with him in the second round and knocked him clear out of the ring. It was a very hot day and the heat had beaten most of the fighters before they entered the ring. We wished they had given us a picture show instead. But it was nice to be out all day.

All in all it was a big, wonderful summer. We had lemonade three or four times every week and on those especially hot nights they brought us ice cream that a big firm out in the city had donated. The big provision concerns were always giving us something that summer—lettuce and lemons and watermelons and tomatoes and hams and milk. There was a fellow named Angelo Lonardo who used to send us in whole boxcars of overripe bananas, until some of the people connected with the United States Treasury Department sent him down to Atlanta for not paying taxes on the income from his numbers' racket, and then he needed somebody to send him some bananas.

Oh, it was an excellent summer. You should have seen all those desperate gunmen and murderers playing softball and slopping ice cream that summer. Sid Bippus and Smiling Joe Raskowski and Nigger Newman. It was some summer.

But it got over.

21

THE DAY got off to a lousy start in the first place. It was a gray October day with a cold, fine drizzle. We were clad in our coats and vests, with our caps pulled down over our eyes. The grass was gone and the walks were wet. It was winter again.

We had oatmeal and chalk for breakfast. We hadn't had that in a long time. I had been expecting doughnuts and ham gravy. I was disappointed. It was a little thing but in the stuffy, stinky dormitory with the wet gray drizzle looking in from the outside, it grew.

Switz came over and said, "Let me look at your paper, Monroe."

I nodded. He picked it up and read the headlines. " 'Killed a sheriff,' " he said. "I bet that son of a bitch needed killing." He felt he had to say something because I had let him read the paper. I walked away without replying.

Johnny Brothers and Black Boy and another colored convict were trying to get a fourth player for a game of cards. "Sit down and pick up the cards, Jimmy," Brothers said, dipping his head and grinning as was his habit. Every time he did that I remembered I had heard that he had cut another colored man thirty-six times and I always wondered if he had dipped his head and grinned before he started chiving on him.

"Whatcha playing?" I asked, sitting down.

"Pinochle."

"Okay, Black Boy, you and I got 'em," I said.

We played until dinnertime. After dinner I sat around

and looked out the dingy windows at the gray day and waited for my mother's visit. But she didn't come. I felt a dead letdown and began slowly filling with a vague, general annoyance at everything and everybody. Supper was also sad. I forced down some of it because I knew that I ought to eat something. On the way back the day seemed colder and the rain wetter. The prison seemed bleaker and uglier. Freedom had never seemed so far away. When the mail was called I received a letter from my mother.

Dear Son:

Your letter came Wednesday. I had written to you before receiving it but if I had known that you were going to write I would have waited to write to you, but I thought perhaps you were going to write to your father.

I planned coming down there today, as I told you, but it was raining this morning and I didn't want to risk it. [I looked at the postmark and saw that it had been mailed that morning.]

I think I told you that I am not very steady on my feet any more and can't get around so well. My arthritis troubles me when I go out in wet weather and I try to avoid it as much as possible. Your mother is getting to be an old woman. I will be sixty-one years old next month. [I could feel the muscles knotting and pulling down my face.] My arms get so weak at times I can't raise them. I had to go to a specialist. He told me I am overworking myself and that I just need a rest.

Now, James, I know that prison must be a very trying place and that you are getting tired of being there—[Oh, goddamn, why did I have to say anything about that? I thought with a groan.]—but you must remember that you brought it all on yourself. I am doing all I can to get you out, but there are some things that you must do for yourself. You have not been a very good boy and the warden told me that you have given the officials considerable trouble since you have been there.

Your father might be able to help you get out of there. But the thing for you to understand is that he *isn't* trying, and neither are any of all those people with whom you associated and on whom you spent time and money when you were free. You cannot control the rest of the world, but you *can* and *must* control yourself. Remember that. If you are a good boy you will come up for parole in two more years. All you need to do is behave yourself. And you will not need to ask the help of anyone. It is all left with you. [Who in the hell's help was I ever asking? I thought. I had the impulse to ball up the letter and throw it away. But I read on from a sense of duty.]

I want you to understand, James, that I *am* trying to help you, but I am only one person. You make things hard for yourself. You are so hardheaded that you will never listen to me, you think I don't know anything.

I am almost down and out. Same days I can make it, and some days I can't. Some days my legs will not carry me up to the store. Pretty soon, I hope, it will all be over and I can rest. . . .

I folded the letter across several times and tore it into very small pieces and took the pieces out into the aisle and carefully dropped them into a cuspidor. I wonder what I said to start all this, I thought. And then, suddenly, and very queerly, I wanted to do something for my mother to make her happy. Right then I would have died for her, lied, killed, stolen; anything for her. I stood there for a moment, blind with desperation, wanting to make the greatest sacrifice that anyone has ever made for the love they hold their mother. I wanted to die a thousand, tortured deaths for her in my momentary ardor of self-immolation.

I went down to the poker game and took out ten dollars' worth of chips. I lost that and bought another ten dollars' worth. In an hour they had me. I looked at the table and then looked at Candy. He had been losing, too, and only had a few chips left. He split them and shoved one half my way. But they weren't worth the trouble. I shook my head. . . . Losing, losing, losing, I thought. Losing all the time. That thing is really on me, I thought; solid on me.

Signifier had three nickle chips left. He said, "You can have half of these if the dealer will lend me his knife to divide them." I didn't look at him. . . . Every single time I lose, I thought. My eyes slid across the table. . . . All that goddamn stuff about me begging her for help. When in the hell did I ever beg her for help? I just said I was tired. Well goddamit I am tired, I thought. Tired!

I let smoke dribble from my mouth and nostrils, trying to control myself; watched it eddy upward toward the cardboard sign that hung from the light by a string—SPITTING

ON THE FLOOR AND WALL FORBIDDEN. I didn't see but one word: FORBIDDEN, and my gaze felt bruised against it.

The deal began again and stopped at me, tentatively. Starrett said, "Going or gonna get left?"

I picked up the card which he had dealt to me and sailed it down the aisle. I didn't feel any anger. It was just an answer to his question.

And then suddenly, the accumulation of all my feelings and sensations and emotions and thoughts; all my hates and fears and humiliations and irritations and stagnations, all the rotten filth, not only of that day but of all those years, began to boil up inside of me. It spewed up from those years of being half scared of everything and trying not to show it; half scared of someone thinking I was a girl-boy, half scared of someone running over me or taking advantage of me, half scared that I might feel remorseful for my crime, or sorry for my mother, or sorry for anything I had ever done—so that I wasted all my sorrow on those indifferent convicts. And those years of being so damned scared to think about the past or the future, and all the while all the actual brutalities and cruelties and hardness and abomination of the living, rotten, degenerate prison touching me; and all the while never letting on that it had, or that anything had ever touched me, or could touch me —as if it was a game of life and death being played within me in which I would be the horrible loser if I ever let on. All those goddamned years trying to make out I wasn't ever scared. Those years of trying to be tough and trying to be smart and trying to prove I wasn't weak, as if there was a dreadful penalty on tears; and trying to know so damned much more than a nineteen-year-old boy has any business knowing. Those years of trying so awful goddamn hard to make them recognize me as a convict, as if it was a special honor, like a doctor's degree, when all the while I was even afraid to admit to myself how utterly different was everything inside of me when I let it be; trying all the while to push whatever there was in me that was good down the drain, and forget it, and become someone else whom I never really was until I tried to make myself so.

And all those people rising like a row of slimy spectres to leer at me; those convicts on whom I had leaned so heavily in my need for companionship—a need which I had never known I had until after Blocker left, having convinced myself all along that they leaned on me—Mal and all the chiselers and punks and sycophants in between. Whispering to me, in their soundless voices, that I had never been anything by myself, that I had always needed the feeling of having a mob of followers in order to make it at all.

And now it was oozing up and out of me, through my mouth and eyes and ears and nose; coming out of the days filled with dullness and sameness and violence and death—the brooding days with the slow change of shadows, the slow change of seasons, with the everlasting scene, eternal and the same; the mocking days and the deliberate days and the indifferent days with their pieces of sunset wedged between two buildings, with their distances horizoned by a wall, with their bar-checked square of stars and their three-foot parade of moons from the window casement to window casement. Coming from the sickening fear of violence, the scare of being scared, and the scare of being humiliated and of feeling cheap; of telling myself that all I had left was my feelings and I didn't want them hurt.

Now I was tired of it. Tired of pretending I wasn't scared when I was, tired of pretending I was tough when I wasn't, tired of having to pretend. Tired of everything about the prison that made it necessary.

I put my hands, palms downward, on the gray blanket and stood up, straddling the bench. I spit the butt from my lips. It broke up and scattered tobacco shreds over the back of the playing cards. Candy, Johnson, Starrett, Polack Paul, Coky Joe, Tony, and Dutch all looked up at me. I swung out from the bench and walked down the aisle. I felt a sticky heat in my eyes, blood in my face. My lips felt thin and stiff as paper, my muscles jerked. I noticed that the convicts walking up and down the aisles for exercise got out of my way.

At the front, the night guard, Captain Charlie, threw up his hand. " 'Lo, Monroe." I wheeled and strode back down the aisle, without replying. My shirt felt moldy and my pants chafed me. And then, the dormitory began seeping into my consciousness; a steady hum of noise, air thick with the odor of tobacco fumes and unwashed bodies, the drift of faces stamped with the full stupidity common to convicts, rows of bunks in ugly pattern, steel bars cutting across the raining night. Five years! I had lived in it for almost five sonofabitching years!

God Almighty Knows stopped me, touching my arm. "Wanna buy some cracklin', Jimmy? Great big brown 'uns ri' frum de frigid zone." Cracklings were pork scraps from which the lard has been rendered. Barrels of them were shipped into the prison to be made into soap. The convicts cooked them into mulligan stews. They tasted fine.

I looked at him. "Huh?"

"Wanna buy some brown 'uns, hot outen de oven?"

I didn't want any but I said, "Where are they?" without thought.

"Ah'll get 'em tomorrow. Uh boy over to de soap house gonna bring me some in."

"You haven't got them?" Insensate fury shocked me like a current. "What the hell you stop me for? What's the matter with you, are you crazy?" He backed away from me. I wanted to hit him so bad I could feel it all up in my eyes. A swift chop to his jaw with my left, cross a right to his neck, watch his eyes pop out. I leaned forward on the balls of my feet, tensed my body. He scuttled down the aisle. I watched him for a moment and then turned in the other direction.

I knew that I was looking for trouble. Trouble-trouble. The niggers had a song for it. "Trouble-trouble, had it all my days. Trouble-trouble, gonna carry it to my grave."

My searching gaze lit on Captain Charlie. Captain Charlie's my friend, I thought. He used to give me candy. I ought to go up and bust him one, I thought. Sitting there, chewing his plug with unruffled indifference, while all us convicts doing more than a thousand years walk around him and obey him. My old gray-haired friend, my old friend, old Captain Charlie.

My feet carried me in his direction. I couldn't see anyone but him. I wondered what he'd say if I just walked up and hit him in the mouth. My old friend, a lousy hack. A lousy hack for my one friend. There never was a hack a friend of mine, I thought. I'm a convict. There never was a convict who had a friend. I wondered what they would do with me if I hit him. I'd lose some time. They'd put me in the hole for thirty days. Damn the hole! I thought. Damn him! Damn everybody!

I walked faster. I wondered if I had the nerve. I stopped in front of Captain Charlie's desk. He looked up from his paper.

"How're you getting along, Jim?"

My paper-thin lips cracked into a smile. I licked my lips. "Fine, cap, how're you getting along?"

"Oh, I'm doing pretty good for an old man. My wife was asking about you."

I licked my lips again. "Tell her I'm doing fine. I hope she's doing fine, too."

"She's getting along nicely, thank you." I turned away.
"Well, keep out of trouble, Jim," he called.

I rocked down the aisle. That was it, I thought. You're a convict and you can't hit a guard. A guard can hit you but you're scared to hit a guard. And then the one time you get up enough nerve to hit a guard you can't do it because he's your friend. Because he said his wife asked about you. But I ought to have hit him, anyway, I thought. It wouldn't make me any more of a rotten bastard than I already was. I felt the muscles jerking in my face. Suddenly I wanted to scream.

Turning, I bumped into the corner of a bunk and everything crystallized into definite objects with shapes and names. I saw the dormitory again with all that wide-eyed horror with which I had first seen a prison dormitory four years, eight months, six days and seventeen hour ago.

The two rows of double-decked bunks, tables down the center of the concrete floor, backless benches, eternal droplights, white walls grayed with dust in the background, dirty windows with black bars against the sightless night, iron joists holding up the low concrete floor of the dormitory overhead.

Dirty duffel bags hanging from the bunk frames—coats, shoes, towels, mirrors, hanging from hooks on the bunk frames—pictures of loved ones in fatuous poses stuck about in prominent view—countless cutouts of half-naked women taken from calendars and magazines.

The convicts, a variety of men doing a variety of things; reading, studying, drawing, playing cards, playing musical instruments, making beaded bags, making inlaid jewel boxes, typewriting, talking, laughing, cursing, coming in and out from between the bunks with the sliding sidewise motion of crabs. A prize fighter prancing down by the latrine, showing off his muscles. A deaf convict studying a law course similar to the one I had once studied. A one-armed convict rolling a cigarette. A sleeping nigger brushing at a fly crawling over his face. A timetable sticking from a lifer's pocket. A slim, bald-headed man called Stick, wearing purple shorts, stamping a crease in his pants stretched out on the floor.

All those years with those maimed, crippled, half-witted mentally-deficient, scum-of-the-earth convicts who had lost their sense of morality, who didn't know right from wrong; convicts whose minds had gone and who had never had any to start with, one-armed black greasy niggers and one-legged pock-marked hunkies; convicts from the dirty gutters of cheap cities—maimed and witless and one-eyed, degenerate and crazy.

Heat rolled up from the base of my brain. I wanted to lose my reason, my perspective, my sight and all my senses; everything that had ever held me to the semblance of a human being, a convict human being. I wanted to become a blankness, unrestrained, unemotional, so I could do a blindly dangerous act. I wanted to kill someone. I wanted to shoot some bastard in the guts, watch him bend over and hold his guts in his hand, watch him topple over and die.

Sweat trickled down into my eyes, stinging them. The warm salt taste of blood came up in my mouth. I must have bitten my tongue, I thought. I decided to go down toward the latrine, over on the other side where the colored convicts bunked. Down into Black Bottom. See what the hell they were doing, see what old Johnny Brothers and Black Boy and Coots and Cryin' Shine and Badeye Lewis and Smokey Joe were doing.

They were skinning; a group of vari-colored faces ringed about the table, cards spinning face-upward from the box, soft intense curses rising like thick smoke. Some stood, others sat. Black shiny niggers with bluish scars, brown niggers with seal-smooth skin, spotted yellow niggers, and pimply white niggers. Black Boy was dealing. He had a shaved head and a scarred face. I stopped to watch.

"Wanna pike, Jimmy?" someone asked. I shook my head.

Black Boy looked up, looked down, wearing his white, perpetual grin. He was serving life for killing a white cop; as bad a nigger as ever grew to be a man. A card fell. A tall white nigger in a pressed shirt, shiny tan shoes and creased pants turned over the card he was playing. He had greased hair and dull eyes. Hands reached for the stacks of chips about him. He picked out the trey of spades and said, "Throw back, all you niggahs who caught me."

Black Boy brought him a tall stack of chips. Others carried their bets to him. He paid the bets. Black Boy spun the cards. The eight spot fell.

"Mah hatred," someone said.

The tall white nigger called St. Louis Slick picked up a stack of chips.

Black Boy said, "Ah ain' got no hatred, lesson it be de man. Wanna bet some mo', Slick?"

"Throw down."

They pressed their bet. Black Boy turned a card. "Some mo'?" . . . "Throw down." . . . He turned another card. "Some mo'?" . . . "Throw down." Chips were stacked high. Black Boy drew a card half out the box, knocked it back. "Hotdammit, betcha some mo'!" . . . "Throw down."

Johnny Brothers stood up and called over his shoulder, "Hey, Cue Ball Red, come look at this one. Chips stacked knee-deep." Black Boy spun the card. The trey of clubs flashed in the spill of light and fell on its face.

"Dead men falls on their face," someone said.

Black Boy raked in the stack of chips. Slick turned ashy. "You shot me, din yer?" he stated in a flat, accusing voice. "You shot me!"

"Who, meeee? Me shot you. Whataya mean, Slick?" Black Boy looked as innocent as a new-born babe.

Slick snatched up the card box and flung the cards through the air. "Now ast me tuh pay for 'em, you black son of a bitch."

Black Boy never lost his grin. "Sho, Slick, pay for 'em," he said. His voice was flatter but untroubled. Slick walked away. Some convicts began picking up the cards. Off to one side another colored convict strummed a uke. Feet patted time. A slurred baritone recited: "Dat's whut Harlem means tuh me." Another convict cut a step, shoulders swaggering. Hands clapped in rhythmic beat.

The days passed and they didn't know it, I thought. I went up front, feeling out of place down there. On the way I passed two colored convicts sitting side-by-side on a lower bunk, with a Bible opened between them, rocking from side-to-side and singing a repetitious chant, "Oh, de li'l black train's a'comin'. . . . Oh, de li'l black train's a'comin'. . . . Oh, de li'l black train, she's a'comin' down de track. . . ."

One was a shiny black man with a chunky body and kinky, cotton-white hair. The other was a lean, dull black man with jutting knotty eyebrows and a cast in one eye. Probably in for rape, both of them, I thought. Singing a black man's song to a white man's God. They didn't know what the hell it was all about, I thought. They didn't want to know. It was just an emotional outlet, a substitute for sex. Just getting off, I thought.

I walked on. My feet felt heavy and my mouth tasted sour. I took a squashed cigarette from my side pants pocket and lit it. I noticed that my hands were trembling. The cigarette tasted like hell. The dormitory began getting into my eyes again. I stopped stock-still and closed them tight. But I could still see the dormitory through my closed eyelids; I could see it from memory. I could see all those rotten years strung out, like putrid stinking corpses rising from their graves. I walked quickly over to a window and looked out into the night. Searchlights illumined the yard in a sketchy brilliance. Buildings loomed dark and ghostly. A guard turned the corner of the chapel, trudging his weary rounds, coat collar turned up against the rain.

And then a queer, rushing kaleidoscope of faces and places and things came out of the past as to a drowning man. . . . The girl and I were sitting on the stairs of the darkened apartment, making love. I was kissing her. I wondered why she wouldn't, when I knew she wanted to so badly. A dim light on the landing above made her face a white blur beneath black hair. . . . I was saying, "Stick 'em up!" and the man's face was turning suddenly, desperately white. . . . I caught the high skyey punt running back, turned in a wide sweep, whirled away from the first tackler, stiff-armed the second; the stands were yelling frenziedly for a touchdown, the din was a tangible quality about me, inspiring me with a wild desire to push on. . . . The girl across the bed from me hesitated before stripping off her panties and I slowly turned my gaze from her. . . .

I came out of it feeling stifled. A wet towel steamed on the radiator beside me. The vapor caught in my nostrils. I couldn't breathe. I opened the window. The cold, wet air blew against my hot face. I breathed deeply. I stared into the night. My mind sped up as if a foot had been jammed on the accelerator of my thought-impulses, began whirling like a runaway disk. My thoughts began to fuse together like white-hot melting glass. . . .

Is there no pity? I thought. Is there no pity in this god-damned world? I didn't want to beg for it to whoever I was begging. But I couldn't help it. I wanted pity. Goddammit, somebody please pity me, I begged inside.

A convict on a near-by bunk called to another convict, "Aw, go to hell, you convict bastard!" That's me, I thought.

I squeezed back to the center aisle and went back down to the latrine. I felt brimming full, another drop of anything would overflow me. I leaned against the washtroughs, took out my last squashed cigarette and tossed away the package. A crowd was collected near by in a noisy discussion. "That ain't the last you'll hear of that guy, you mark my words. . . ." I looked at the speaker. He was a very young boy, as young as I had been five years ago.

Another convict took the subject away from him. "Hell, he'll get caught in a week and that'll be the last you'll ever hear of him." His voice got on my nerves.

Then a colored convict took it up, "Ah'll bet mah life 'gainst a copper cent that wen they ketch that guy—"

"Make it even money," I said.

All of them stopped talking to look at me. I knew most of them by name. I looked at them and spat on the floor. Then I moved over to the other side of the trough so my back was to them. I lit the cigarette and took three rapid drags without exhaling. I could feel the smoke down to the bottom of my lungs. My skin felt tight on my face. But I felt a vague, sour satisfaction. I had killed the conversation. I had killed something, anyway.

For a time it was comparatively quiet. I heard the convicts walking away, as the crowd broke up. Then sounds crept into my mind. A broken commode leaked with a monotonous gurgle. It was the monotony I heard. I felt suddenly that something was wrong with me. It was as if I wasn't working right any more, as if something had come loose inside of me.

I started back to my bunk. I felt if I could just get back to my bunk and lie down I'd be all right. It was as if I had hurt myself in some kind of way and was trying to get home. If I could just get home I'd be all right. But it seemed like miles back to my bunk. I seemed to be walking all right but I didn't feel as if I was moving. I began getting scared I wouldn't be able to make it to my bunk. Off to my right a wail arose: *"AllllllLLLLLLLL night loooooo-OOOOOOONNNNNGGG Ah set in ma cellllllLLLLL an' moooooaaaaaaaAAAAAAAANNNNNNN. . . ."*

I could feel the muscles tightening all over my body. I could feel my right eye jumping in my head. I tried to steady my vision, but everything was flashing in a mad, weird dance. Vision lost all sense of perspective. Steel bars closed in upon me from all ungodly angles. I got to get home, I thought, or I'm going to vomit on the floor. I tried to move but I didn't seem to be able to move. It was as if I was standing still, through the relentless march of time. I'm being left behind, I thought. Don't leave me behind, please don't leave me behind, I was begging in my mind. I bent forward and tensed myself for a running start. But when I tried to run I felt as if I couldn't move. I gave up. I'll never make it now, I thought. If I could run I might make it. But I can't make it, dragging along as I am now. It's too goddamned far.

It was then I came upon the idea of killing myself. It was more as if I had come up on it than thought it out. It was as if I had known for a long time that I would meet it somewhere on the road and had tried to keep from taking that road, but even then I had known that it would be on any road I took and that sooner or later I was going to meet it. It was more as if I had just recognized it when I came up on it finally.

And when I recognized it I just stood there and let it come up to me rather than trying to run from it, or running forward to meet it. I just let it come and take me. I couldn't make it home, anyway, and so it was the next best thing. It was all right, too, because it wouldn't even hurt anybody. It would be the best thing for everybody. My mother wouldn't have to keep on worrying about whether I was a good boy or not and nobody else would even give a damn. And it would be the best thing for me. I would do it and then I would be through with it and I wouldn't have to be afraid of meeting it on any other road. I wouldn't have to worry any more about whether what I did was good or bad. I would do it and then I would be completely through with all the doubts and fears and all this misery.

But even after I'd made up my mind to kill myself I didn't know how to do it. I stood at the end of the aisle, weakly bracing myself against the table. There was something wrong with my breathing and I felt myself gasping slightly. I felt a little nauseated, too. My mind quickly turned over a number of ways I could kill myself. I could borrow a knife and cut my throat, but the picture of the colored convict who had gotten his throat cut years ago in the 5-6 dormitory came to my mind and I discarded it. I couldn't bear the thought of all that blood slavering from my mouth and nostrils. I thought of cutting my wrists with a safety-razor blade but I was afraid somebody would see me and try to save me before I died and I didn't want anybody trying to stop me. That would be intolerable, I thought. Hanging would be the best, I thought. I could tie the rope to one of the overhead stanchions and jump over the wire enclosure and the fall would break my neck immediately. But I couldn't think of where I could get enough rope unless I waited until the next day and I had to kill myself right then. There was no need of fooling around waiting any longer. I had waited too long as it was.

Finally I decided to climb up on the wire and jump off to the first floor. It was only about a ten-foot drop, but if I dove headfirst I could probably burst my skull, anyway. I decided to do that. I felt very confident that it would kill me because it was my time and any way I tried I knew would work. I pushed away from the table and started over toward the side of the dormitory. I was very weak and had to cling to the bunk frames for support. I got to the wire and began to climb up one of the supporting posts. I noticed a couple of convicts sitting near by on their bunks, watching me curiously, but I didn't even care about them seeing me. They wouldn't know what I was doing until it was too late to stop me.

The wire was about chest-high, but I was pretty weak and before I got to the top of it the lights flashed for bed-time. I thought, "Goddammit, that would happen. I can't even kill myself because I've got to go to bed." I stepped back off the wire and went back into the aisle. I didn't have any difficulty at all getting back to my bunk. But I felt such a stifling hatred for the routine I could hardly breathe. A convict can't even kill his damned self, I thought. Nothing about it struck me as being even vaguely funny or ridiculous. It seemed only natural to be stopped from doing something I wanted to do. I didn't even think of defying the signal and going ahead and killing myself, anyway, as I might have a half-hour earlier. I felt only an intense frustration. I felt smothered by the routine. They'll be sorry they flashed those goddamned lights, I thought.

I undressed automatically and climbed into my bunk. I was very tired and I went to sleep immediately. But I kept dreaming that I was falling. Each time, just before I landed, I woke up. But as soon as I got back to sleep I began dreaming again that I was falling. I'd wake up again and try to stay awake, but I'd doze off and begin falling over again. I don't know how many times I fell before daylight.

The next day I remembered every detail of trying to kill myself. But I wasn't shocked by it. I felt a vague sense of regret, of postponement. It was as if something had failed to happen that should have happened. I didn't feel so much as if I'd gotten by it, as that it was just postponed. It had just gone on up the road a little way and after a time I'd come up on it again. I felt as if there were two of me and one of me was death. It didn't make me rebellious or in-different. But it made me desperate for freedom. I didn't want to meet my death again inside the walls. I wanted to get outside to die. I didn't even think to figure out the difference but I became very conscious of the outside world.

For the first few nights afterward I couldn't sleep. I lay awake and tried to make up pictures of the outside world. I called to mind various undertaking establishments I had seen and then I would try to rid myself of the picture of my body lying in a casket in one of them. At times I thought of how old I was getting. I was twenty-four. I had never voted, I thought, once. It started me off to crying in my pillow, even though I knew had I been outside all the time I probably wouldn't have voted, anyway. But it seemed as if something very vital had been taken away from me.

I thought of all the chances I'd thrown away and of all the people I'd hurt and disappointed. I thought of Margie, whom I'd got pregnant, stepping from my car and being run down and killed. I had kept that one buried for a long time. My head would grow so tight with my thoughts that my stomach would get a hollow, sick feeling and I'd find myself gagging slightly, as if I wanted to vomit. I'd feel I couldn't bear my thoughts another single minute without dying. But they stayed with me for hours, days on end.

I wrote to my mother and asked her to go see the governor herself and plead for my release. "Just sit in his office until he talks to you," I wrote. "Tell him how badly you need me. Tell him you are old and can't support yourself. Play on his sympathy. He must have some kind of feelings. Get Reverend Bentley and all the other influential people you know to write him in my behalf. Please, Mother. I can't stand this any more."

Then I sat down and wrote the governor a long letter myself. I had to get the warden's permission first. He let me have the letter form because I'd been in five years. I told the governor about my studying law and short-story writing and touch-typing, in an effort to improve myself. I told him I had become converted to religion.

> At all times I may not have appeared the model prisoner, but I swear, Honorable Sir, that at all times my intentions were the best and the discrepancies in my record are the result of honest misunderstandings. I have never tried to hide my wrongdoings from the officials, for the simple reason that I have at no time realized they were wrongdoings until it was too late to amend them, for they all grew out of intentions that were right. I will admit, Honorable Sir, that I have never become oriented to the life of prison, and many of the measures which are necessary for the preservation of discipline I have never truly understood.
>
> As perhaps you know, Honorable Sir, a perfect record is not always indicative of good purposes; nor does it always prove that a convict is ready for free-

> dom; but oft-times it is merely the manifestation of what we term "stir wisdom," or in other words, the result of knowing how to serve time, and that, I must confess, I do not know and perhaps never shall. But I contend that I do know how to be a good citizen, and that is my highest ambition.

Then followed the weeks of waiting, of suspense and anxiety and half-scared hopes. And all the time I was tight inside and sick and going crazy. I kept to my bunk mostly, reading, studying a little, sullen and uncommunicative and tense. I practiced typing and now and then I played a game of cards, but my heart was never in it. I was too empty, I thought, too drained of all emotion. I was like a spring gone dry. There were days I felt light enough to fly.

22

WRINKLEHEAD, Dutch Henry, Signifier and I were playing Canasta, with Dew Baby kibitzing, that Saturday morning when Nick, the deputy's runner, brought in a new convict. We stopped playing to stare at him. A banjo ukulele, swung from plaited shoestrings was looped about his neck and he carried a small grimy pillowcase of belongings. At each step his knees buckled and knocked together as if the strength had suddenly gone out of them, and his feet flew out at grotesque angles. He seemed to catch himself at the brink of collapse at each step, so as to make mere walking seem extremely hazardous. It reminded me of the wobbly motions of a splay-legged colt learning how to walk. I felt a strong impulse to laugh.

"Who's the kid?" Signifier asked Nick when he came back up the aisle.

"Duke Dido."

"Not the brother of the Princess?" I said, recalling my year of Virgil.

"What's the matter with him?" Dutch asked. "Walks like a hobbled horse."

"Don't no one seem to know," Nick said. "The doctor thinks he stiffing to dodge work."

"Does he throw his knee out of joint himself?" Dew Baby asked.

Nick grinned. "He's got it bad, ain't he?"

"He's about to fall out with it," Signifier said.

"He'd be a bitch of a panhandler," Dew Baby said.

Wrinklehead began dealing again.

"Don't forget what I told you," Dutch said to Nick.

"About that—"

"Yeah, about that little business," Dutch cut him off.

We all laughed. I pushed my cards away. "Want to play my hand, Dew?"

"I don't care," Dew Baby said, blinking his lids. "You're going to quit?"

Nick walked away and Wrinklehead asked, "What's the matter, Jimmy?"

"Oh, I'm just tired of Signifier trying to cheat all the time," I said.

"I'm glad you're quitting," Signifier said, getting up himself.

"What you going to do, you going to quit too?" Dew Baby asked him.

"I'm going down and get some water," Signifier smirked.

"You're going down to talk to the kid?" Dew Baby asked.

"I'm thirsty," Signifier said.

"What you going to do, you going to sound him out?" Dew Baby persisted, blinking his lids and getting excited.

"I'm going to sound out the drinking fountain if that's what you mean."

"I'm coming with you. You're not going to get away from me," Dew Baby said, taking hold of his arm.

Signifier shook him off. "Naw, he'll think we're trying to gang up on him if you go down there blinking your eyes. He'll think you're a psychopathic killer and get scared."

"Aw, Signore," Dew Baby said, falling all over Signifier. "Aw, Siggy."

"You fellows rush a kid too fast," Dutch said. "You don't do nothing but queer everything. You make a kid freeze up."

Signifier started away. "You're too slow," he called back to Dutch. "You can have him when I get through with him."

"Aw, let me go with you, Siggy, you know two are better than one," Dew Baby said.

"Let him go on and rank it," Dutch said. "He ain't going to do nothing but signify, anyway."

I got up and went over to my bunk. I felt disgusted. Once I would have been up with that pitch, I thought. I don't know, I thought; a man grows up. My bunk was an upper on the aisle and I climbed up on it and opened a magazine. But instead of reading I watched Signifier approach Dido, out of the corners of my eyes. Signifier stopped at the foot of Dido's bunk and said something. I saw Dido stop and turn around and look at him and make some kind of answer. There was belligerence in his every gesture. After a moment Signifier turned away and came up the aisle. He looked so chagrined I laughed out loud.

Still wearing the uke strung about his neck, Dido had followed him, wobbling along in his grotesque walk. He must have thought I was laughing at him. He jerked his head around and the strike of his eyes caught me in the middle of the laugh, chopping it off as with an ax. His chin lifted, tilting his head to the side as if steering it, and the most contemptuous sneer I had ever seen grew across his wide, mobile lips. He looked as if he wanted to spit on me. Then he raked a slashing discord across his ukulele, dismissing me, and wobbled on, chin high, head tilted, lips sneering, not looking at any of us.

Dew Baby, Dutch and Wrinklehead sat at the table and silently watched him pass. All of the fun was taken out of all of us. He doesn't mind letting us know what he thinks of us, I thought. I knew that it took either a lot of nerve or a real and genuine indifference for a new convict in a dormitory to make enemies as recklessly as that. It reminded me a little of myself when I first entered the old coal-company dormitory.

I watched him go down the aisle. Strangely, I felt a lot of admiration for him. His shoulders were rather wide but stooped, and in walking his body slouched and all of his movements were awkward and jerky and grotesque. Every step seemed a precarious action, bordering on actual disaster. Long black hair was a tangled mass above his head, growing thick down the back of his neck and over his ears as if it had neither been combed nor cut in months, and his clothes, all of which were state-issue, were in a sad state. His brogues were battered and run-over and half-laced, and his trousers were so bagged they looked like elbows in a chimney pipe. Every now and then when he raised his arms to strike a careless chord on the uke, his elbows stuck through holes in both shirt and coat sleeves. He did not wear a vest and the top two buttons of his shirt were open. His neck was slender and collumnar, and his throat was as lovely as a woman's. Halfway down the aisle he stopped to watch a poker game and I noticed that he had an attractive profile with a longish jaw and fullish lips.

"What did he tell you, Johnson?" I called to Signifier.

He and Dew Baby came over to my bunk. "He didn't say anything. He just said he didn't need any help."

"Help? What kind of help?"

"Siggy asked him if he could help him make his bunk."

I could picture that. I grinned. "Wonder if he gambles," I said, thinking ahead.

"Sure that punk gambles," Signifier said. "Ever see a punk who didn't gamble?"

"Why don't you try him out, Jimmy?" Dew Baby leered. "Give him a couple of bucks and put him on the track. All the kids fall for that."

"Hell, I don't know anything about him," I said. "He might be straight for all I know."

"Aw, he's a fag if ever I saw one," Signifier said. "I can look at 'em and tell. He'll go. If somebody don't turn him out before this week is over I'll walk up and hit old Tom Craig in the mouth."

"Aw, Siggy, you wouldn't do that," Dew Baby said, falling all over Signifier.

Wrinklehead came up and said, importantly, in his tongue-tied voice, with his eyelids fluttering and the whites of his eyes showing, "What you mugs talking about? You talking about that fag?"

"How do you fellows get so sure about the man?" I said.

"You can't fool me," Wrinklehead said.

"That's what Belle used to say about you," I told him.

"Aw, that—" he couldn't get the words together.

"Go on and sound him out, Jimmy," Dew Baby urged.

"Not me," I said. "I'm trying to get out of this joint. I don't want to get into any jam now."

Dew Baby looked suddenly envious. "Trying to get a pardon, Jimmy?" I nodded. He wanted to ask more but I didn't give him any opening, so he said lamely, "I hope you get it, Jimmy, old Jimmy, I hope you get it."

Signifier lost interest and turned away. All of them left. Dew Baby was hanging on to Signifier, saying, "Old Siggy, old Siggy." Wrinklehead was still trying to get out what he wanted to say about Belle.

I looked down the aisle for Dido but didn't see him. Then I looked over to see how the poker game was going and saw him playing. Well, if he's gambling already he must either be good or a sucker for it, I thought. And if he's a sucker for it somebody's sure to get next to him because he can't have enough dough to keep himself going or he wouldn't look as he does. That night after supper I stood around the games to see him play but he didn't play any more that day. He passed a couple of times and once he stopped beside me to watch the others playing. When he left I returned to my bunk to finish reading a story. Later that night I saw him down in Black Bottom, strumming his uke for the colored convicts' breakdown.

All of the Sunday games belonged to me although it had been quite some time since I had helped in running them. But that Sunday morning I told Candy I would deal for awhile. If he plays at all he'll have to play in one of my games, I thought. But by church time he hadn't shown up and we had to knock off until after dinner. On the way to dinner I noticed him in line, about six men ahead of me. He seemed to walk better in line than when alone, although he looked deliberately trampy in his ragged uniform and beat-up cap.

After dinner I told Candy to take over for awhile. "If Dido starts to playing send for me," I said. "I want to look him over and see what he knows."

"Who's Dido?" Candy asked.

"He's the kid who moved in yesterday."

"Oh!" Candy looked at me.

"That slouchy bitch was playing with me yesterday afternoon," Starrett said. He had been standing behind us. He had the Saturday poker game. I had seen Dido playing with him but I didn't like the idea of him eavesdropping on my conversation.

"You've got a nasty mouth, bud," I said.

Both he and Candy looked at me. "Can he play?" Candy asked Starrett.

"Naw, that bitch can't play," Starrett said, emphasizing *bitch.*

Dido walked past us at that moment. He looked at Starrett curiously, as he would at a worm.

"Give me some chips here, boy, let's get to gambling," Starrett blustered in a loud voice.

I hope he knocks your goddamn eyes out, I thought, but Dido went on down the aisle. When he came back he stopped for a moment to look on. I thought he was going to play and took over the deal. He watched me deal for awhile and once I looked up and caught his eyes. I nodded. His expression didn't change. He looked at me for a moment, then went back to watching the play. After awhile he wobbled off, strumming a slow melody.

It was late that evening, long after the coffee had come around, before he came back and took out five dollars' worth of chips. I shot him some aces and kings, and for a time he was lucky enough to hit them. But I could see right away that he was an absolute chump in a poker game. He tried to play every hand and he had no judgment whatsoever. If he was in a pot and someone raised, he seemed to take it as a personal challenge and would call, no matter what he had. His playing was all emotional. He ran his chips up to ten dollars and then everybody began horsing at him on the sly. Starrett began betting at him openly and pretty soon he caught on to it and began calling everything Starrett bet. I kept shooting him aces because I didn't want Starrett to beat him. A couple of times when Starrett had him beat on the fourth card, I topped the deck with dead hands to hit his ace in the hole. Then he began plunging, feverishly. His eyes glittered and his face became flushed. He was all wrapped up in it.

He's got it bad, I thought. It was a passion with him. He thought he could gamble but he couldn't. But I knew he'd lose his soul trying. I'd seen a thousand like him.

I kept shooting him pairs to hold him up. I didn't think he could take losing very well. Then Polack Paul got caught in a hand and said, "I bar that deal, Monroe," and I had to pay him the whole seven dollars and sixty-five cents he had lost since he had sat down. Then the others who didn't know what had happened got suspicious. On the next deal Starrett was backed up with kings and I hit aces on the third card. Dido stayed with a pair of jacks, and Starrett kept raising him into me. Starrett figured I had aces but he was willing to lose seven or eight dollars to get Dido broke. I kept saying I had aces and flipping the top ace in the gambler's signal for him to pass. But as long as Starrett bet he called. Then finally Starrett got out. I made a token bet on the last card and said to Dido, "Well, I guess these two big red aces take it, eh, kid?"

He looked up at me and said slowly, "That's what they got to do," his voice low and husky; and set in his stack.

Starrett burst out laughing and I got hot under the collar. "Take your chips out, kid, I've got you beat," I said.

Dido's chin came up and his head tilted and his whole face twisted into that contemptuous sneer. His eyes were wild and feverish and his face was flushed. "Where I come from, when you win, you put your money in the pot, turn over your hand, and show what you got," he said, his head bobbing up and down and the sneer sounding in his voice also.

I looked at him solidly for a moment. He had a longish, reckless face with high cheekbones and too much thinness down the cheeks and a high, smooth forehead topped by that mat of black hair. His face was sweaty and greasy and his sloe eyes, slanting slightly upward at the edges, gave a slightly Mongolian cast to his features. Now his eyes were black and glittering, like the eyes of a cornered snake. He's got a tree-top jag on excitement, I thought. I turned my ace out of the hole.

"See, I wasn't kidding, I've got aces," I said. "Take your money out, I'm not trying to beat you."

He turned sheet-white and emotions dropped across his mobile features like a picture slide. "Call it and win," he said hoarsely, licking his lips and lifting his chin still higher. "That's what you've been sitting there on that hard seat for all day, isn't it?" His mouth was ugly with the sneer.

I burnt up. "Call it," I said, tossing in a chip.

"Pay it off," he demanded.

"I'm the dealer," I said.

"Aw, come on, goddammit, and take the pot and let's get to gambling," Starrett snarled, counting his chips. "I'm fourteen bucks loser here."

Dido turned and looked down his nose at him, but before he could say anything I wheeled on Starrett and shouted, "Shut up, goddammit, I'm running this game." I took a long time to put in the chips. Starrett sat there fuming, getting ready to blow up. I was set to knock out his teeth. When I finished counting out the chips Dido turned his cards down and said, "You win." He stood up, completely disdainful of everyone. All of us were compelled, against our wills, to look at him. He stood there for a time, aloof and contemptuous, with his foot on the bench, and looked back at us, strumming a soft slow melody on his uke. Starrett glared at him but he seemed oblivious of it. Dutch came up beside him and said in a loud voice intended for all of us to hear, "Want to play some more, Gypsy Kid?"

I frowned with quick jealousy, wondering how Dutch

had got to know him so well. Dido turned and looked down his nose at him. He had a fine chiseled nose. "I see I made a mistake," he said, and turned his back to Dutch and wobbled down the aisle.

I watched Dutch's eyes get small with rage. I chuckled. "You can take it over now, Candy," I said.

I got up and went over to my bunk and changed into my flannel pajamas and got into bed. There was a novelette in a magazine that I wanted to finish. But I couldn't keep my mind on it. I was still reading the same paragraph when Signifier and Dido turned in beside my bunk. I was startled to realize that I wasn't surprised; I had expected him.

"Duke said he wanted to meet you," Signifier said, winking.

"You're the Jimmy Monroe who writes," he said. "I've read a lot of your stories." All the excitement had gone out of him and he was cool and pleasant. He spoke in a low, liquid voice, chime-clear.

I knew I was being jived lightly but I was flattered anyway. "What stories did you read?"

"Oh, I read, er, several of them."

"How did you like them?"

"I thought they were very good," he said. "I wish I could write. I've tried but I've never had anything accepted."

"Did you read the one about the gambler who ran a pool on his electrocution hour?"

"I thought that one was excellent," he said.

"The ending was a surprise, wasn't it?"

Signifier was looking from one of us to the other. He didn't know what we were talking about.

"Maybe for some people, but I guessed it," Dido said.

"You're a kind of cute little guesser, anyway," I said. "Now what made you guess I'm trying to write stories?" I had never even thought about writing stories since before the fire.

"All right, you win," he said, giving in. "I saw the typewriter."

Signifier had been getting impatient. He felt left out. He started to make some crack or other, but he changed his mind and turned away. "Wish you luck, Jimmy," he said.

After he had gone both of us became strangely shy. "What are you reading?" Dido asked, making conversation.

I turned up the cover of the magazine. "Do you read it?"

"When I can get it," he said. And then all of a sudden he said, "Signifier didn't tell you my full name. It's Duke Dido. They call me Gypsy Kid sometimes but I don't like it. And I'm sorry I put you in the middle out there in the game. I was so excited I didn't know until afterward that you were trying to help me." The words bubbled out in a quick, live rush, drawing my stare to his mouth. He had full, deep-red lips, colored like a rose, and his skin was smooth and slightly olive-tinged. When he talked his red lips were a smear of mobile motion across his face, shadowed by the line of fuzzy down on his upper lip. "You'll forgive me, won't you?" His eyes were serious and intense, like those of a little child, and he looked very young, perhaps nineteen, and enchantingly naïve.

"Oh hell, that was all right," I said grandly. "I figured you were a little out of practice."

He became suddenly rueful. The abrupt change was startling. "You mean you saw I couldn't gamble and took pity on me," he said. Now the life was gone out of his voice. "I know I can't gamble but I don't like to be shown up."

"I wasn't trying to show you up," I said. "I wanted you to win."

"Did you?" His eyes lit up and sparkled. "Why?"

I was flustered. "Oh, I don't know. I guess it's because I admire you in a way."

He was thoughtful for a moment. "I wonder why," he said. "I don't always admire myself."

"But you do sometimes?"

"Oh yes, lots, but why would you?"

"Oh, the way you treated Signifier and all of us yesterday. It's always so much easier to compromise."

"You don't like a person who compromises?"

"*Like* isn't the right word. I might like them, but I won't admire them."

Completely and abruptly he went through another change and laughter bubbled from his lips, giving a disturbing girlishness to his face. "In other words," he slurred, in a laughter-filled voice, "you admire me but you don't like me."

I had never seen anyone with such mobile features. I was completely fascinated. They seemed to ripple with a thousand continuously changing expressions, as the play of light and shadows in a movie musical.

"I admire you," I grinned, "but I don't know as yet whether I like you or not. Is it important?"

"Which way, whether you like me or don't?" He was very close to me, without moving.

"Either way."

He sighed, going away from me. "The question is unfair." And then he was completely gone. "When you know me better—" he paused, then added, "if you ever do, you might not even admire me. I'm the old, original compromiser." He sounded cynical and a little bitter. "Do you know where I got that fin today?" I nodded. "You heard him," he said, remote and brooding. "You know why he let me have it, too, don't you?" I nodded again. "Do you know why I accepted it?" he asked.

I looked him straight in the eye and said, matter-of-factly, "Of course. Because you're going to pay him back."

At first he looked startled. And then he blossomed like a morning-glory and smiled, showing white, even teeth. Smiling, he was beautiful. It was as if his face contained an inner life which changed its expression with each passing emotion. It looked so delicately alive I felt a strong impulse to touch it with my fingertips. His eyes would grow bright, dim, serious, earnest, mischievous, bitter, sparkling, and then suddenly cold; so that you knew instantly, as if touching piano keys, which note you had sounded. I had never seen anyone so sensitive to moods.

"You're rather swell," he said and turned away.

All the next morning he seemed to avoid me. I started toward him several times, but each time he suddenly had business somewhere else. Not long after dinner I saw him come down the aisle with Dutch. I watched them, frowning, but when they passed my bunk I looked away. Later I saw him playing cards with Signifier, Dew Baby and Wrinklehead. Shortly before supper I walked down by his bunk to look for him. But he was over on a lower bunk in Black Bottom, flanked by two colored convicts, one with a guitar and the other with a banjo, and they were beating it out. There was a crowd about them. He saw me and waved for me to come over. But I shook my head and after getting a drink of water returned to my bunk.

After supper I took my typewriter up to the front of the table near the guard-stand and began composing another letter to the governor, concerning my request for a commutation of sentence. But when mail was called I received a reply from the first letter I had written. It read:

Mr. James Monroe,
Serial No. 109130,
State Prison.

Dear Sir:
The Governor directs me to acknowledge receipt of your letter of recent date making application for a commutation of sentence. He asks me to advise you that your communication will be given careful attention.

Yours very truly,
Frank J. Allison
Executive Secretary
to the Governor.

I read it over again. It sounded like the real thing. I tried to restrain my jubilance; it would make it all the harder if I was disappointed. But all my wild, urgent desire for freedom flooded back. The convicts and the prison became detestable again. I discovered that all along in the back of my mind I had been thinking about Dido. I took myself sharply to hand. This is my chance, I told myself. If I don't get out this time I might never get out. I didn't want to get into a jam or get involved in one of those sordid prison affairs. It was too easy to lose your sense of judgment.

Dido came up and sat down across from me. "Hello, Jimmy," he said, smiling eagerly. He noticed the letter lying open beside the typewriter. "Good news?" he asked.

"Oh, hello," I said, coolly. I folded the letter and stuck it into my pocket and got up and walked away before he could say anything else. I left the typewriter open on the table. I knew no one would bother it. I had started to my own bunk but changed my mind and kept on down to Candy's instead. "How did we do yesterday?" I asked Candy. He collected from all the games and gave me half of the net take.

"We made thirty-nine forty altogether," he said. "Johnny Brothers and Black Boy are swinging out."

Dido passed us on the way to his bunk. He held his head high and looked straight ahead. He was sneering.

"Oh, hell, let 'em swing out with a few bucks," I said. I felt like a heel on account of Dido. "Let 'em keep the whole damn take. Who am I to have a gambling syndicate?" I had started to say, who am I to pass judgments?

"I'll look after them if you don't want to," Candy said.

He nodded down toward Dido's bunk. "What's the matter with you and him?"

I tried to look surprised. "Why, nothing."

"He just passed and didn't say anything and you and him were acting like long-lost brothers last night."

"I didn't see him," I said, then added, "Oh, he's all right. He's a pretty intelligent kid. He's straight, too."

"Well, he'd better keep away from Dutch Henry if he wants to keep that way," Candy said.

I went back front where I had left my typewriter, and began running through some finger exercises. My mind kept going back to Dido and I felt ashamed of the way I had spoken to him. I wanted to go down and apologize but I couldn't bring myself to do it. For a time I banged away savagely on the typewriter keys.

The guard shift changed while I was still there and Tom threw up his hand. "G'night, Jim." I waved. Captain Charlie stopped for a moment before he made his rounds, to ask how I was progressing on my plea for a commutation of sentence.

"I got a letter tonight from Allison." I showed him the letter. "It's just a form letter," I said. He read it and handed it back. "Anyway, it means they're keeping me in mind," I said.

"Well, if there is anything I can do for you let me know," he said. "You're one boy who deserves to be released. I don't believe you'd ever get into any more trouble."

"I want to get you to write a letter for me later on," I said.

"Any time you say, Jim."

When he had gone I locked up my typewriter, went back to my bunk and changed into my pajamas and went to bed. I tried to read my story. After a time Dido stopped by. He was tremulous, undecided. His face was loose and quivering and his lower lip trembled slightly.

"Howdy," he said tentatively.

"You caught me again," I grinned a welcome, holding up the magazine.

"Same story?"

"Same paragraph," I admitted, rolling over on my side to face him.

He came closer, without moving. "Was it I, again this afternoon?" he asked.

"No, it was me this time."

He looked at me speculatively. "Why?"

"Oh, I don't know. I'm trying to get a pardon and I want to stay clear."

For a moment he was blank. And then he was instantly, completely angry. "You're taking a lot for granted, aren't you?" he choked, trying for control. "You couldn't be wrong, could you? Just this once?" The sneer was back in his voice.

"The hell with it," I said. "I apologize."

He thawed slowly, as if half-afraid he was wrong in doing so.

I lit a cigarette and extended him the pack. "Smoke?" He took one and lit it and held it in his mouth.

"Are you disappointed in me?" he asked, his head tilted, talking around the cigarette and squinting one eye against the smoke.

"I'm not decided," I replied.

Our gazes met and we got charged from each other, full and violently. Our faces were less than a foot apart before he broke his eyes away.

"Remember the pardon," he said, sounding gaspy.

I felt choked myself. "Damn the pardon."

"You wouldn't mean that in the morning."

"I know I wouldn't."

"Don't ever do anything you wouldn't mean the next morning. It's never worth it."

"I don't know, it depends—"

"Anyway, I don't go up for five years yet, so it would be better if it never came to that. I'd be here so long after you left."

"Maybe I'd make it worth it."

His eyes struck up. "That's a hell of a lot of loneliness. Is anything worth it?"

"Want a couple of bucks?"

Everything went then. "Now you've gone and done it," he said, going dopey-faced. "I had so hoped you wouldn't."

I took a deep breath. "I'm a gambler," I said.

"Just to think," he said, "a moment ago you were rather grand. It would be better if I hated you, better for both of us."

"That's better than your being indifferent, anyway," I said. "My old grandpa used to say, son, if you can't make 'em love you—"

"I could hate you very easily," he said, leaving me.

That was Monday.

23

TUESDAY was bath day and the first section was called right after breakfast. Our company was too large for all of us to bathe at once so it was divided into two sections. Those with the oldest numbers went first. I was in the first section. The second section was waiting outside the bathhouse when we came out. I located Dido and called, "Catch!" I threw him my bar of soap. He smiled delightedly.

There was a light kidding waiting for me back in the dormitory but I denied everything. "You guys got me wrong," I said. "I'm not making any play. I'm going to get a pardon and I'd be a fool to get involved in something like that."

"That ain't nothing," Signifier said. "That ain't no more than you've always been."

I didn't like that. After a bath I always massaged and brushed my hair to keep it from coming out. Just as I had finished Dido came up. His hair was meticulously combed and brushed and his skin looked scrubbed. He didn't have his uke hanging from his neck and he looked almost civilized.

"Why, you look nice and shiny, like something new," I said.

"I washed behind the ears and when we go to the barbershop I'm going to get a haircut. And guess why?" His eyes were radiant.

"I give up. Why?"

"So I can look good to you. Aren't I brazen?"

"I should say so," I said.

"Thanks for the soap," he said. "You're thoughtful. I can't repay you until the first of next month. My mother only sends me two dollars a month and I've spent it."

"Smoke?" I offered him the pack. He took one. "Where is your mother?"

"In Los Angeles." His voice was different when he talked of her.

I began getting down my typewriter. Although I had long since ceased mailing the exercises in my law course, I still worked on them occasionally. I had come to the place in case law where we were required to write an opinion in a hypothetical case involving water rights and I was anxious to tackle it. I gathered up some typing paper, carbon paper and copy sheets.

"You type well," Dido remarked. "Did you learn it here?"

"When did you see me typing?"

"Oh, I see everything you do," he said.

"Yes, I taught myself. Do you type?"

"A little, but not as well as you."

"You can practice on it sometimes when I'm not using it," I offered.

"Oh, can I? Thanks, darling."

My head jerked up. *"Darling?"*

He was suddenly flustered and blushing. "That slipped out. It's a habit of my mother's I took from her."

"Listen," I said, putting the typewriter back on my bunk. "You haven't been in here long, have you?"

"About a year. Are you going to lecture?"

"Yes."

"Must I listen?"

"That's up to you."

"I'll listen. Who's the first heel you're going to tell me about?"

"Me," I said. "I've been in here five years and I'm rather lousy. It won't do you any good to be seen with me. I've got a kind of a bad reputation that I don't really deserve. They'll swear you're a fag and keep after you until it breaks you down. If they can't do that they'll team up on you and give you a really tough way to go. If you've been here a year, you know how it is. You'll have the name without the game." I paused.

"Is that all?" he asked. I couldn't tell what he was thinking.

"That isn't all I'd like to say, but that's all I'm going to say. And I just said that because you remind me a little of myself when I came in."

"Aren't you going to say anything about Dutch Henry?" he asked. "Dutch told me never to smoke behind you or get too close to you while you were talking. He said you had t.b. and syphilis. He said you caught syphilis from a habit you have of wetting pencils in your mouth."

We both began laughing at the same time. "Dutch is all right," I said. "That kind of a knock is a boost." Then I became serious again. "But I mean what I said."

"It's a new approach to me," he said.

"Now it's you who's taking a lot for granted," I said. I ran my hand in my pocket and skinned off a ten-dollar bill. I held it palmed and said, "We're friendly strangers. Let's shake on it."

"So I'm not being given a say," he protested. His shoulder's sagged a little more than usual and his smile was forced, I thought. But he put out his hand.

I pressed the bill into his palm, squeezed his hand and took my hand away. "It's only ten dollars," I said. "It won't break me. Consider it as a gift from me to myself. I've always wanted to be as big as a ten-dollar bill. Remember, we're strangers."

Turning away quickly, before he could reply, I carried my typewriter down front and planked it on the table. Signifier came up and sat down beside me. "How're you and the kid making out?" he asked.

"He won't go," I said. "I'm cutting out."

"I wouldn't argue with you," Signifier said.

Dutch and Dew Baby came up and sat down across the table from me. "You got the best go, James," Dutch said. Dew Baby looked on, blinking his lids.

"You've got the wrong fellow," I said.

Dido came up and sat down on the other side of me. "It's all right to talk to you out here, isn't it?" he asked.

"Sure, as long as I'm out here it's all right." I turned to the others and said, "I just told Dido it wouldn't be advisable for him to talk too much to me because someone might get the idea that he was my kid."

"What did he tell you about me?" Dutch asked Dido.

"He didn't tell me anything about you," Dido said, lifting his head in the beginning of a sneer.

"Now, take you, for instance, Dew Baby," I went on. "You and Dutch. If you saw Dido hanging around my bunk all the time and talking to me, the first thing you'd say was that he was mine, wouldn't you? Of course you would," I went on before Dew Baby could deny it. "But if you never saw him talking to me you couldn't say it, could you?" They didn't answer. "Could you?" I insisted.

"Aw, Jimmy," Dew Baby said. "Old Jimmy."

Dutch stood up, red and angry. "You're not so slick," he said. I knew I had made an enemy.

"Wait a minute," Dido stopped him as he was turning away. "Here's the fin I owe you and another fin for interest. Thanks." He tossed the ten-dollar bill onto the table. His lips were curled.

Dutch picked up the ten and tossed it back. "Keep it and buy yourself some panties," he said. He was in an ugly mood.

Dido went red. He snatched up the ten and hurled it at Dutch's face. Dutch turned sheet-white and started over the table and Dido scrambled to his feet. Signifier jumped up to stop Dutch and I grabbed Dido by the arm and pulled him away. When Signifier noticed that Dutch had a knife he jumped out of the way. Dido snatched a wooden name plate from a bunk frame. I stepped in between them, weak from that sickening fear of knives I've always had. Captain Tom came up and jerked Dutch away.

"We don't want any fighting in here," Tom puffed, then he saw the knife and said, "You know better than that, Dutch. Give me that knife." Dutch gave him the knife. "Now cut that out," Tom said, looking at me. He wanted me to finger the fall guy but I was no rat.

"Just a mistake, Tom," I said.

Turning away he glanced at Dido. He turned back and looked at him squarely and then we all turned to look at him. He appeared wild and reckless and sneering and disdainful but what struck me was that he did not look in the least afraid.

"We don't want any of that in here," Tom said to him, then turned and looked at me, enquiringly.

"He's a ball player, Tom," I said, grinning. "Got five more years, too."

Signifier laughed and the tension went out of us. Tom ducked his head and returned to his seat. A crowd had collected by then and Signifier said, "Who got my ten?"

I closed up my typewriter and went down to the poker game where Candy was playing.

"What was the matter with Dutch?" he asked.

"Aw, that fellow's crazy," I said. "He wants to jump on every kid he can't make."

After dinner the hall guard took the company to the barbershop. Tom stayed in the dormitory with those who didn't go. I had a safety razor and only went on haircut days. While the dormitory was quiet I got down my typewriter and started working on the opinion in *Jones vs. McClellan.*

McClellan had dammed a stream known as Apache Creek which had supplied both his and Jones' ranch with water. McClellan had diverted the water into another channel to power a flour mill. Cut off from his supply of water, Jones had brought suit to enjoin McClellan to restore the stream to its original channel. I had all of the testimony recorded in the text. I had to write the opinion, referring to all statutes and judicial precedents which would serve to determine the legality of my action. It was quite challenging and required a lot of concentration. I had just written the heading when Tom came over.

"Can that fellow Dido really play ball?" he wanted to know. It was the week of Thanksgiving but he was already thinking of next year's team.

"Sure, he's good," I said. "He's from California. You know, everyone plays softball out there." I didn't know anything about it but it sounded good.

"What position does he play?"

"Field."

"We need a good fielder," he said. That's what I know, I thought. "Can he hit?" he asked.

"A slugger," I said.

When the rest of the company came back from the barbershop I stopped Dido. "Can you play—" I broke off when I noticed his haircut and said, "Say, how did you ever get in here? You look fifteen."

"They took me for my big brother," he grinned.

He looked better with his hair cut but he had lost something, also. I was trying to figure out what it was when he said, "What was it you were going to ask me whether I played?"

"Oh yes, can you play softball?"

"No, but I can play tennis."

"Damn the tennis. Where the hell are you going to play tennis? Have you ever played any at all? Softball, I mean."

"Maybe a little, but I can't play."

"Well, from now on you can. You can field like Joe D. and swat like Ted Williams, in case anyone asks you."

"But I can't, though," he said.

"Who can? But I just told Tom that you could, and if you want to stay in this dormitory and get along you had better say you can, too."

"But they'll find out—" he began.

"They won't find out until next year and by that time maybe everything will be different."

"Say, I want to talk to you," he said, abruptly.

"Well, I'm busy now," I said.

Watching him walk away I was repulsed by the grotesqueness of his carriage. He'd look so much better if he carried his shoulders erect, I thought. But it didn't mean anything to me, I told myself.

He went over on clothes-order and got a complete new outfit from shoes to cap. Right after supper he stopped by my bunk. He looked almost like a different person.

"Look what just a casual gift from you has done to me," he said brightly.

"Life is a funny thing," I said. For an instant his eyes dulled, then brightened again, but now they were all on the surface like afternoon sunshine on water.

"Do tell, Grandpa," he lilted. There were a few beads of sweat on his upper lip.

"I've given away a lot of dough since I've been in here," I went on doggedly, "but every penny of it had strings, some kind of strings. It either did something for me or I looked for something in return. I got something out of it for myself. And the one time I wanted to give away something as small as a sawbuck with no strings at all, the strings come back from the ten."

"Didn't you want anything?" His eyes were wide and mocking.

"No."

"Really?" He went remote and distant and if his knees hadn't buckled he would have swirled away, but they did and the effect was grotesque. I was again repulsed.

I'm a complete damn fool, I told myself. I'm trying to get out of here and I'm letting it get close to me.

Tom called out the mail and I received letters from both my father and mother. Signifier came over while I was reading them and said, "Jimmy, you wouldn't fool me, would you?"

"It seems as if I'm only fooling myself," I said, and before I could elaborate Dido came up.

Signifier had a big broad grin on his face. I knew what he was thinking.

"I just got a letter from my mother," I said. "She says she talked to Allison, the governor's executive secretary, and that he told her the governor is planning to pardon quite a few deserving inmates during the Christmas holidays and that I was in line for consideration. I think I'm going to make it." I was all filled up with it.

"That's swell," Dido said. "May I read it?"

"Sure." I handed him the letter.

"She writes a nice letter, Jimmy," he said when he had finished. "I hope you get your pardon." He handed me the letter. "That would mean so much to you." That was a funny way to put it, I thought. Then he said, "I received a letter from my mother, too. Would you like to read it?"

"Sure we would," Signifier said, having been left out of the conversation long enough. "Bring it on down."

But Dido kept looking at me until I nodded, then he hurried down to his bunk. I watched him walk away, feeling that slight aversion.

"He seems like a good kid," Signifier began fishing. "Full of life."

"He's too damn flighty," I said.

I picked up the mirror so I could watch him approach without his knowing I was watching. I didn't want him to know we were talking about him.

Signifier said, "Here he comes." When he got there I was examining my teeth in the mirror.

He handed me the letter and I read it. "She writes a swell letter," I said, surprised.

"Why are you surprised?" he asked.

"Oh, I, er—" I was embarrassed. "I didn't expect her to be so intelligent," I said, making it worse. "I mean she is so sympathetic and knows just what to write. She must love you an awful lot."

"She does," he said. His voice was reverent. "She was so young when I was born. We grew up like lovers; like brother and sister. She was only fifteen when I was born."

"Does she look like you?" I asked.

"Want to see her picture?"

"Sure," Signifier said.

He had brought the snapshot with him. The corners had been clipped off, as if it had once been framed, and on the back was written, "To my darling son." She was clad in slacks and a sweater, with her hands in her sweater pockets. She was shockingly beautiful.

"She's good-looking," Signifier said. "How old is she?"

"That's personal, you damn fool!" I exclaimed. Then I said to Dido, "She's a very fine-looking woman." I knew I sounded stilted, and wanted to say something spontaneous but the strange sense of shock had confused me.

Dido began laughing. "You're too precious for words,"

he said to me. "I wish I had a better picture. She's really better-looking than that."

"Say, is she married?" Signifier asked.

Dido laughed. "You're a rat, Signifier."

"Yeah, that's me. I'm a rat, and everything."

"You're a darling," Dido said.

"Have you got the rickets in your legs or have they been broken?" Signifier asked.

"The kneecaps have been broken," Dido said. "Unless I exercise a lot they slip out of place."

"Oh, I thought you were throwing your knees out of joint," Signifier said. "I thought you were a contortionist."

"When I was up in the mill I didn't get enough exercise—"

"Don't pay any attention to this guy," I cut in. "He's just signifying."

"He's a good kid," Dido said, winking at me.

"What mill were you in, the woolen mill?" I asked.

"Cotton mill. On 5-10."

"What was the matter, couldn't you keep up in line?"

"It wasn't that," he said. "I got into a fight with my cell buddy." My gaze went involuntarily to Signifier and I caught his smirking look. I looked away. Dido didn't notice. "He thought he was a prize fighter," he went on. "I got tired of him trying to run the cell." I could picture that part of it, all right, and the sneering manner in which he would have challenged him. But I couldn't picture him doing much fighting. He reminded me more of the kind of convict we called spunky, with the kind of contempt we called a guy a fool. I didn't like to think of anyone knocking him down. It made me slightly sick. He seemed so completely incapable of fending for himself.

"You mean you really hit him," Signifier said.

"This guy is just trying to get your goat," I said.

Signifier started laughing. "You wouldn't hit your cousin, would you?"

Dido didn't understand. "My cousin?"

"I thought maybe you and him were cousins, like you and Jimmy are."

"Nix up, Johnson," I said.

But Dido had picked it up. "Oh, is this some of Jimmy's past? Tell me about it, Signifier."

I jumped down on the other side of the bunk and started to walk away but Dido ran around to head me off. "Are you getting angry?" he teased.

Signifier was laughing.

"Go to hell!" I said.

Looking at his suddenly hurt eyes I turned quickly away and went out to the poker game. He came out after a minute and sat across the table from me. He had a dollar he'd gotten from somewhere.

"Hello," he gushed as if he hadn't seen me in ages.

I didn't reply. I was suspicious about the dollar. Dutch was dealing. He gave him a very sour look.

But Dido seemed oblivious of both our attitudes. "Let's save, Jimmy." He sounded very complacent.

"Oh, all right," I consented, ungraciously.

He kept me extremely nervous. He talked to people as if they were dogs, sneering and looking contemptuous, until any moment I looked for someone to jump up and pop him. It was more a cat fight with him than a poker game. It was a relief when he got broke. And then, like a damn fool I said, "You can play some of my chips," pushing half my stack toward him.

But he was feverish by then and had lost all his sense of reason. "You're already out on the limb for a sawbuck," he sneered. "You don't want to go any deeper, do you? You're not getting any dividends, you know."

I was furious. "That tells me just what you are," I said, drawing back my chips.

"Give me a dollar's worth of chips," he said to Dutch.

"Where's your money?" Dutch said.

Dido started from his seat, a dull, blotched red. "Do you want me to break up this game?" he shrilled in a high, breaking voice.

I felt sick, knowing he would try.

"Ain't nobody going to break up this game," Dutch said. "Put up your money when you want chips."

"He's got money," I said. "Give him the chips."

Dido snatched a handful of chips from the chip seller, then turned on me, "I don't need any of your recommendations."

"You've got to live in here, boy," I said. "You can't run over these people like that. The rule of the game is that you pay for your chips when you get them. You can't tell a man how to run his own game."

Dutch was just waiting. Dido looked at him and returned the chips. "Give me an ante," he asked Dutch.

Dutch gave him three nickel chips.

Dido turned back to me. "I'll take those you wanted to give me now, darling," he said, looking penitent.

Well, that lets me in for it, I thought. I'll have the name

without the game. "How would you like to take a flying frig at yourself?" I said.

He lost the three chips in the first pot, without looking at me again, then he got up and left. After a moment I heard him strumming his uke, loud and defiantly, down at the far end of the dormitory. What I can't understand is why I feel I must protect him all the time, I thought. Then I began losing and lost fifteen dollars, sitting there worrying about him. I was hot and sweaty and disgusted.

When the lights went out I marched down to his bunk and said, "Listen, how'd you like for me to hit you in the mouth!"

He was lying on his side with his face near the edge of the bunk, looking at me intently. "I don't know," he admitted solemnly. "I won't know until you do it. I might like it." In the half-shadow his face was smooth with a dull even sheen like old ivory. All of his features were a blurred soft outline, giving him an exotic appearance, and his sloe eyes were wide and deep and filled with little lights.

I gritted my teeth. "Let me tell you something—"

"You're so masculine," he interrupted in a low voice.

"Damn, you're exasperating!" I said. "You keep me scared for you all the time. Why do you treat people so lousy all the time?"

"Maybe now I won't need to any more."

"You're a pretty nice boy when you want to be," I said.

"I want to be for you," he said.

That was Tuesday. The next morning he asked, "Do you still mean it this morning, Jimmy?"

"Yes," I said.

"As much as you did last night?"

"Yes," I lied.

"I wonder," he said.

All that day he hung around me while I worked out the roughdraft of the opinion I was writing. When I had finished, I let him read it.

"It's simply great, Jimmy," he said. "Honestly, this is great."

I was surprised at his reaction. I knew it stank. But I was flattered, too. "What makes you think it's good?" I asked.

"Why, it is," he said. I looked to see if he was kidding me. He seemed sincere. I put the piece aside. I'll have to write it over, I thought. He thinks it's good and I can't let him down.

"Come on, you can practice typing some," I said, moving over so he could sit before the typewriter. Everyone was watching us together, but I didn't mind it now and he seemed impervious to it.

He was stiff and awkward on the typewriter. "I feel self-conscious," he said.

"Do you want me to go away?" I asked.

"Oh no, I'd be worse if you left me."

But after a time he grew tired of it. "Come on down to my bunk and let me play for you," he said.

"Okay." I put away the typewriter and followed him down to his bunk. He got down his uke and said, "Let's sit on the lower bunk."

"That's old man Foley's bunk," I said. "He's awfully cranky."

"Oh, he and I are good friends," he said.

"Yeah?"

"All old folks are friends of mine," he said. "They like me."

"Everyone would like you if you gave them half a chance," I said. "You're a rather likable person when you're not putting on your act."

"Is it necessary for people to like me?"

"Not particularly so. But there's no sense in going around with a chip on your shoulder and antagonizing people needlessly."

"I'll be nice to everyone, Jimmy," he said. "I'll make everyone like me. Because you want me to, Jimmy."

"That isn't a good reason and I don't particularly want you to. And then you might become so nice that everyone would want to take you away from me," I grinned. "Then where would I be? No, you'd better keep on being your same old sneering self."

"You'd always have the pardon to look forward to."

"Sure."

But the fun had gone out of the moment. He began picking out melodies in individual notes on his ukulele. He was an excellent musician with a true sense of rhythm but he had a love for melody. It was very pleasant and soothing and the melody was very clear. I began to realize how much I had missed music since I had been in there. He played "Summertime" and "Make Believe" and "Stardust" and other old tunes that I liked.

I had never owned a radio although there were dozens in the dormitory; I had always been afraid of getting too close to the outside world. But they had to keep them tuned down, and there was something in live music you couldn't get over the air.

It wasn't long before we had an audience. The other convicts had heard him playing and seeing me with him had gathered about.

The two colored convicts with the guitar and banjo came over and he invited them to join in. I started to get up but he said, "No, keep your seat, I like to have you where I can touch you." We had a musical. Everyone liked it. Captain Charlie stopped by for awhile and listened. Music hour was between seven and eight but Captain Charlie let them keep on playing.

"Don't play so loud though," he cautioned.

It wasn't until the lights winked that the gang began to break up.

"It's better now?" he asked. I didn't reply. "Don't you think it's better?" he insisted.

"Sure."

"You don't sound very enthusiastic, Jimmy. You do think it's better, don't you?"

"Of course I think it's better," I said.

"You're not ashamed of me?"

"Of course not."

"I was very nice to everyone, wasn't I?"

"You were swell," I said.

"I noticed you didn't feel embarrassed. You won't ever feel embarrassed or ashamed of me, Jimmy?"

"No."

"Honestly?"

"Honestly."

"I'm glad, I couldn't bear it."

"I've got to go down for count now," I said.

"You're coming back and tell me good night, aren't you?"

I knew the convicts within hearing range were listening to us and I was a little self-conscious, but I said I would.

The next day was Thanksgiving. We had a nice dinner of roast turkey with oyster dressing and cranberry sauce, and that afternoon I began rewriting my great legal opinion. Dido came down and sat beside me, strumming an aimless note every now and then until I felt like screaming.

"Are you always so industrious, Jimmy?" he asked.

"No, I'm setting an example for you," I said. It was true.

"I'm awfully lazy, aren't I?"

"I don't mean in that way."

He was puzzled.

"I'm trying to show you how to relax," I explained. "How to occupy yourself with something worth-while."

"You're a darling to take so much trouble for me," he said.

"But it would make me feel a whole lot better, too, if I knew you could occupy yourself with something worthwhile, or anything," I said, somewhat lamely. "You seem at loose ends all the time. I don't know just how to say it. You're the same when you're gambling. Haywire, that's it. You're so haywire, so radical."

"And I was just going to ask you to let me gamble some," he said, looking disappointed. "I've been a very good boy the last two days, haven't I?"

"I haven't got any money," I lied. "I got broke the other night."

"Oh well, it's not important."

I tried to concentrate on the piece I was writing but he made me nervous and distracted me, sitting there.

"Goddammit, quit picking that uke!" I shouted finally.

"Am I disturbing you?"

"No," I lied. "Only when you pick the uke." Then after a moment I said, "Haven't you got anything to do? You want to read some magazines?"

"I'll go away and let you work," he said. He stood up, then he said, "Do you want to read something I wrote?"

"Oh, I don't care," I sighed.

"Go ahead and do your work," he said. "I'm not going to disturb you any more."

He looked so hurt that I said, "But I do want to see it."

He hurried off down the aisle, and when he returned with it he said, "It's not very much. I'm writing a song, too. I love music."

I picked up the single-typed sheet with a forced resignation, thinking, maybe after this he'll find something to do. But after the first line I was caught, startled:

> Shadows, they are all about me. In the stench-laden corners of my dungeon they are black sentinels at the black gates of death, forbidding me sanctuary. On the slime-encrusted floor they lie motionless, writhing in the eyes of my fear. They hover alive in the space about me, vampires of thought, drinking the life of my soul. Shadows, flung into space by sharp corners, breaking off at unknown angles, falling on concrete floors, climbing black walls. Shadows, receding before light, racing rapidly off to hide behind bars, making blackness. Shadows of bars swinging out into space to fall with soul-bruising heaviness on

shadows of men. Shadows of shadows, no longer men, victims of the night eternal, victims of the shadows. . . .

"Did you write this?" I asked.

He nodded. "Do you like it?"

"I think it is exceptional," I said. It gave me a funny feeling, though. A creepy sort of feeling. I was sick with being afraid for him.

"It came to me one night in the cell," he said.

I could picture him lying on his bunk in his darkened cell, haunted with terrible fears. "Come on, I'm going to get you some money and let you play some poker," I said.

He started to take the piece but I said, "No, leave it there, I want to read it over."

"I'm going to win today," he said. "All for you."

I read his piece over. I always thought of it as "Shadows" after that. For some strange reason it provided a compelling incentive for what I was trying to do. My memory became sharp, my thoughts began assembling into a logical pattern. Everything within me seemed to struggle for a sanity. The cold, pure clarity of legal reasoning had never been so welcome. I wrote on my opinion rapidly and with assurance. The right terminology came without search. When I had finished it I felt confident of its merit. I was jubilant.

When I was closing up my typewriter Signifier came up and told me that Dido was winning. I felt excited and glad. I went down and stood behind him with my foot on the bench. He looked up and smiled and then divided his chips.

"Want to play, Jimmy?"

I shook my head. "Too crowded."

There were already ten in the game and a dozen more waiting for a seat. Everyone wanted a chance to horse at Dido. He had a large stack of chips and was bulldozing the game. He was getting an immense kick out of it. After a time he said, "You can play my hand, Jimmy, if you want to."

I noticed several of the players about to protest but I grinned and said, "No, you keep on, you're doing fine." They were all relieved; they figured they might catch him in a pot and get even and they knew I wouldn't give them a chance to get their money back. But after awhile he lost interest and quit, anyway.

"I want to be with you," he said.

He was so happy and excited over winning that his eyes shone and he could hardly talk. "I waited until I got a pair before I'd call and they thought I didn't have anything and bet into me and I—"

"You turned them wrong-side out," I supplied.

"When I got a big stack of chips I ran them with nothing. I just took their money."

"I finished the thing I was working on, too," I said.

"Oh, let me read it," he said.

I got it and let him read it.

"This is genius," he said. "I didn't know it could be that much better. You are a genius, Jimmy. Are you as happy and excited as I am?"

"Yes," I said.

24

DIDO AND I were talking one day—what about I could never afterwards recall—but in the course of the conversation he said, "Sure, but a convict is human, too," and that started us off on something new that I never forgot.

"We know it, but who else can you sell it to?" I said.

"It is enough to sell it to yourself," he said, surprising me.

"You're full of little philosophies," I said.

"That's what prison does to you," he said. "You come in as a neophyte and go out as a sage."

"Of course I can't blame people much for not thinking of us as being human, too," I said. "People have just so much sympathy inside of them and they don't care to spend it on convicts."

"I can't blame anybody for anything," he said. "What deacon may have rung a bell with larceny in his heart, or what angel carried heaven's tidings to hell?"

"That sounds like Omar," I said. "Where do you get so much fatalism?"

"It's not mine," he said. "It's life's. The other person in everybody's bed is death."

"What big teeth you have," I said, sarcastically.

But he was serious. "I'm twenty-four," he said.

"Now isn't that a lot of living?" I said. "You'd better tie your long whiskers off the floor."

And deeply serious, brooding, remote, he said, "It might not be so much but it was plenty for me until I met you."

I jerked around and looked at him. He meant it. "That's a funny thing to say."

"Everybody needs a purpose," he said. It didn't sound right.

"You have a mother," I argued.

"I'm such a disappointment to her," he confessed.

"Sure, I'm a disappointment to my mother, too," I said. "She had her heart set on me. But if I needed a feeling to pull me through the twenty years I started with, I could have gotten it from her."

"You don't know my story," he said. "I've gotten all of that already. You see, I was in the reformatory and my mother sent me three-hundred dollars to come home on."

"And you got broke and got into trouble and came back to prison," I supplied. "I understand. But mothers are funny things, little boy. They wouldn't sell you out for that, no matter how much of that stuff called mother love you destroy and abuse. They still have just as much left. It's like a spring that never runs dry. Your mother wouldn't ever fail you, little boy."

"She wouldn't," he said. "It's me. I was out twelve days. I didn't even get out of the state. You were so right when you called me haywire—" He broke off and asked, "Have you ever been scared?"

I was slow in replying. "Of life? Of what it can do to you? Of the nights? Of being alone? Scared of thoughts and feelings and memories?" I took a deep breath. "Sure, I've been scared," I confessed. I had never confessed that before to anyone. "I've been scared a lot of times. I'm still scared a lot of times."

"You're so much like me, and yet so different."

He was silent for a moment and I said, "But I don't think about it. If you don't think about it, it can't hurt you."

But he didn't hear me. "That's some of it, but not all," he said slowly. "Have you ever been afraid of people not understanding you, and grown up feeling that no one ever understood you, not even your mother; and when you had given everyone a chance to understand you, and no one ever had, telling yourself that you didn't give a damn if they never did—that you simply did not care? And then being wild and reckless and uncaring and saying, Take me or leave me and to hell with everybody, and not really meaning it? All the time so scared and lonely and away from everybody in a shadowed world and wanting so badly for someone to tell you that you are right; or if not that, for someone to tell you that you are all right, anyway?" When he stopped he was crying.

I wanted to hold him in my arms as I would have a little baby and comfort and reassure him; I felt so tender toward him. "You're all right," I said. "You're all right, kid."

A spark of worship flickered in his eyes. "Sometimes you're wonderful," he choked.

"It's only that you brood too much," I said. "It's only in your mind that no one understands you."

Suddenly he was laughing. "But of course you don't understand; how could you? You don't have to be afraid of yourself. You don't have to be afraid ever—" and now he was deeply bitter, "of doing something so sickening that you want to hang yourself a moment afterward, and still not being able to help it."

"I don't know, I've done a lot of things that I'm not proud of," I said.

"But they'd still stand telling," he said.

"Let's don't talk about it," I said. For the instant I hated him for everything he had implied; all the moments and all the men.

Now it was his turn to reassure me. "You're wrong, Jimmy," he said. "It never came to that."

I felt better. "The trouble with you is that you have a fatalism, but it isn't a true fatalism," I said. "You don't actually believe it or it wouldn't desert you when you need it most."

"Now you're getting fleas in *your* beard," he said. We laughed.

Sometimes in the evenings we'd stand beside his bunk with a magazine opened on the blanket and real aloud to each other just because we liked to hear each other's voices. At other times we'd stand in the window and watch the sun setting beyond the bathhouse. "God, I wonder what's beyond that horizon," I'd say, and he'd say, "You can take it from me, Jimmy, it's not what you think."

"I'd be willing to chance it, anyway."

"I hope you will and I'll pray to God that you'll never be as disappointed as I was."

"You sound like you've been a lot of places."

"I have, but that horizon was always there, between me and the other side." And looking at me, he'd say, "And then I met you and something is happening to me. I don't know myself just what it is, only that the horizon doesn't matter any more because the other side is all inside of me now."

"You don't have to worry any more," I'd say, and he'd give me one of those scintillating smiles.

On Tuesdays and Fridays he was taken to the hospital for treatments and I asked him why. "I have sinus trouble," he said.

"You don't show any of the symptoms," I said.

"But I have it very bad at times," he said. "It's all up here." He tapped his forehead just above the bridge of the nose. "Sometimes it's so bad it almost drives me crazy. My mother has it too."

"I never thought it was very serious," I said.

"It is, though," he said. "It is very serious and I hope you never have it. Ninety per cent of all the people who have it go crazy, or maybe it's ninety per cent of all the people who go crazy have it. Anyway, it's—"

"Ninety per cent," I said. "Like corn whiskey."

"—very serious, James Buchanan Monroe, and it will drive you crazy, and I hope you never have it."

"If it drives you crazy you'd better go over and have something done for it because you're crazy enough as it is."

"I'm much better now, aren't I?" he asked.

"You're splendid," I said.

The next time he went to the hospital he signed up for an operation and about the middle of December they took him over to the hospital to operate on him. I got Captain Tom to take me over to see him and I brought him the soap and toilet articles he would need. The next day when they operated on him, I got Tom to take me back on sick call and I was there when they wheeled him out of the operating room. I walked beside the stretchers and touched his hand and told him to take it easy, but he didn't need me then because the anesthetic was still with him. When the anesthetic left him was when he needed me, but I wasn't there.

The long letters I sent over daily by the paper boy helped him a lot, he said in his replies. And those few lines he wrote to me helped me a great deal, too. It was dreadful in the dormitory with him away. I didn't know it could get so dreadful in a dormitory filled with convicts.

Signifier elected himself to cheer me. "You look terrible," he said. "You look heartbroken. Cheer up, he'll be back in a month or two. You better get hold of yourself, you'll come down with t.b."

I paid the colored porter and the head nurse in A-ward a dollar a day each to look after him. But I didn't tell him because I thought he wouldn't have wanted me to.

They let him out the day before Christmas. It was just like going home when he came back.. They wanted to keep him in a week longer, he said, but he told them he had to get out in time for Christmas.

"I told them it was a matter of life and death. I told them I just had to get out," he said. "I just had to be with you this Christmas, Jimmy, there might never be another one."

There was no answer to that.

I asked him how they had treated him and he said everyone had been swell. They all knew he was my friend and they were fine, he said.

"They've got a swell bunch of fellows over there anyway," I said, and he said, "They are, really, but I had expected them to be sort of snotty."

"They've just got a bad rep," I said. The chiseling sons of bitches, I said under my breath. "But they're all right," I said.

His mother had sent him two dollars, his monthly allowance, in a letter, but during the Christmas excitement it had been overlooked by the mail censor, and he received the two one-dollar bills with the letter. He had bought a bottle of sodium-amytal capsules with it. They were given to the t.b. patients as opiates, but taken two or three at one time with coffee, they gave a wonderful jag. The capsules were blue so we called them blue boys. After we got jagged we figured no one would know what we were talking about when we said blue boys. But everybody called them blue boys.

About eight o'clock that night they brought me a box from my mother and he got one from his mother about an hour afterward. The boxes had been coming in all that day and they let the lights stay on until twelve o'clock to deliver them. We had a very fine jag from blue boys and were filled with good eats from home. We sang Christmas carols loudly while he played the accompaniment on his uke and at midnight we were so excited we couldn't sleep and sat up and talked all night about all the Christmases we remembered.

Christmas morning we took some more blue boys with our breakfast coffee and were wonderfully jagged when we went over to the show. Everything was very funny and delightful and we laughed all during the show.

We took some more blue boys with our dinner coffee and that afternoon we played poker and lost and it was all so funny and nice. Everything was so funny and wonderful, just like a dream. We laughed at the prison and laughed at losing pots. We had completely forgotten the other convicts in the game until one of them exploded with pent-up laughter and then they were all laughing. We thought we would die from embarrassment. We had to quit and go away. But it was all like that. We didn't know there was anyone else in the dormitory. Christmas seemed to belong to us alone.

Everyone began talking about us, even Captain Tom and Captain Charlie. But we thought they were very stupid and funny people and we made little jokes about them and laughed behind their backs. Signifier and Candy came down the day after Christmas and helped us eat what was left of our boxes. We were very witty and hospitable hosts and pressed chicken and cake on them until they were stuffed. We teased them and made little quips about them which we thought, in our state of entrancement, they didn't understand. Then we gave them some blue boys. Candy took all of his the first thing the next morning and went down in the colored convicts' skin game and bamma-ed an eight spot through. When you play a blind card, after you have fallen and lost, they say you have bamma-ed it, because the boys from Alabama who think they are tough play that way. Sometimes another piker picks your card and plays it without knowing you are playing it too, and if you can shuffle your card into the dead at the end of the deal before it is noticed, all anybody can do is just grumble.

But Candy wasn't smart enough to get away with it and he got everybody's money terribly mixed up. It took half of the convicts in the dormitory, including Dido and myself—especially Dido and myself—to get it straightened out and Candy wanted to fight all of us with the little home-made knife he carried, with the blade so short you could hardly see it. It took Tom and the hall guard and Polack Paul and a half-dozen other convicts to keep the colored convicts from biting off his ears. Tom called Dido and me aside and told us to get rid of that dope and not to give Candy any more of it. But we were so jagged we could hardly wait to get away before we were laughing again.

Later in the week Dido received a typewriter his mother had sent him for a Christmas present. I had never seen him so happy and excited. "Oh, isn't she swell?" he gushed.

"She's perfect," I said.

It wasn't a very good typewriter but we never let on that it wasn't the very best. That night he took it apart while I sat by and watched, with varying degrees of apprehension.

"Maybe you ought not to do it," I said. "Maybe she wouldn't like it."

"She'll love it," he said. "You'd love her, Jimmy. She was so young when I was born, only fifteen, and she didn't know how to raise me. I'm her love child. People used to think she was my older sister." He worked while he talked. "When I was old enough so we could talk she taught me a swell way to live. Whatever we thought was right, honestly and sincerely, we took for right and acted on it and lived by it. And all my life I've felt that way." He stopped and looked up at me. "Don't you think that's a swell way to live?"

"Yes," I lied.

"It is, Jimmy," he said earnestly, like a little child. "Everything would be wrong if you couldn't feel that it was right. In the middle of the night when you're awake and can't sleep, when you think about it you have to feel it's right."

We took the last of our blue boys New Year's morning. The whole week had been like a wonderful dream. The next day we had headaches and a nasty taste in our mouths. But we didn't have any regrets.

"You don't know how swell it is not to have any regrets," he said.

Later on I discovered that I was one hundred and thirty-five dollars in debt. My typewriter was in pawn and his was all apart. We had jumped on a fellow and broken up his game and the only thing that had kept us out of the hole was Tom and Captain Charlie looking out for me.

"You had a ball," Signifier said enviously.

"When did you take your blue boys?" I asked him.

"I'm a chump," he said. "I took mine that same night and didn't do anything but sleep through breakfast."

We laughed. When he left Dido said, dreamily, "It was like a sweet delirium."

The second week in January I received a letter from my mother telling me to be brave and cheerful and not to become despondent because I hadn't received a Christmas pardon. The legislature hadn't adjourned until Christmas week, she wrote, and the governor had been so busy with the budget he hadn't had time to consider my case. "Reverend Bentley talked to Mr. Allison again and he seems to think you will get some action this coming summer," she wrote.

"Are you sorry?" Dido asked.

"Yes," I said, "but I had forgotten it until now."

"Then I'm sorry," he said. "But I'm not sorry for our Christmas. I couldn't be sorry for that."

"I'm not, either," I said.

When we wrote home that Sunday he said, "I told my mother about you last time, Jimmy. Do you want to say something to her?"

"Tell her that I think she is very swell people and that I think of her as my very own mother and that I love her very much."

"I'll tell her. She'll like that."

"I'm going to tell my mother about you," I said.

He looked up, as startled as a deer. "I hope she doesn't dislike me."

"Oh, she'll love you," I said. I had my doubts.

He looked very queer when I said that but I didn't think anything about it at the time.

"You never speak of your father," I said.

"You don't speak of yours, either."

"Mine's in Terre Haute," I said.

"Mine's in San Francisco."

We looked at each other.

During the weeks following we became very literary and read O. Henry together. Once I said, "You're a sweet child."

His reaction was abrupt. "Oh, how lovely!" he exclaimed, his eyes turning smoky with wistfulness. "Call me that always."

And then we ran across the name "Puggy Wuggy" and he said, "What a darling name and it just fits you."

"Me!" I said. "What the hell?"

"You have a Puggy-Wuggy nose that quirks when you're about to laugh—" he said, his husky voice teasing and his eyes alight with mischief.

"That's no compliment," I said.

"—and I love it and I'm going to call you Puggy Wuggy—"

"The hell you are!"

"—and you're going to call me Sweet Child. Won't that be nice?"

"No," I said.

We loved O. Henry. "He knew a lot about people," I said.

"Prison was his school," he said. "He did his bit in Ohio, working in the hospital—"

"Selling blue boys no doubt, if they have 'em over there."

We laughed.

When my mother came over that month she asked me about Dido and I told her he was the most intelligent convict I had met in prison. He's about my age and his mother lives in California and he's a swell friend, I said. It was all about Dido. But she wasn't sold.

But his mother was entirely sold on me. Her next letter was addressed to her "two sons," and she said as soon as she got the money she was coming to visit us both; she wanted to see us very much.

"If you get out this summer I want you to go and live with her," he said.

"Is she as nice as you?" I asked.

"Oh, she's much nicer."

"Maybe I'll fall in love with her," I said. "She seems very young and I go for the Dido family."

He was very enthusiastic. "You will, Jimmy. I'll write her and tell her you're coming. You will love her—" he broke off. His face settled so abruptly it was ugly in the change. "You said you'd fall in love with her. What did you mean?" he asked. His voice was flat as mud.

I could have told him that I didn't mean a thing because I didn't. But some perverse impulse made me say, "After all, I'm a man. I've been in here five years. What else could I mean?"

"She's not like that," he said. "She's just as good as your mother. She's better than anyone's mother. She's deeply religious."

"But she's a woman just the same," I said, impelled by some imp of cruelty. "And she's beautiful."

He stood up, dull-eyed, dopey-faced, remote. His shoulders sagged, his head drooped forward, his hands hung lifeless at his sides. I noticed that they were large hands.

"There were some swell moments, Jimmy," he said. "I'll remember those." There was a grinding nonchalance to his voice that jarred me. His lips twitched as if he was trying to smile, and then they stopped as if he had given up and his eyes filled with hurt. He was very ugly. He turned away as the hurt came into his eyes, and walked down the aisle with his knees buckling again.

For a moment I stood there, watching him. Then I thought, well, that's Dido. I sat on the bench and leaned back against the table and lit a cigarette. And then it hit me, a wave of hurt. My stomach became hollow and sick and I filled with a cold, draining fear. I realized suddenly that I was trying to get up and go after him. But the thousand emotions which were rushing through me had assumed weight and the weight anchored me to my seat. I was stunned. After a time I began trembling violently. I had to get up and walk about to stop it. I passed him in the aisle but he looked away without speaking. I winced.

In twenty minutes everybody in the dormitory knew that we had fallen out. I went over to my bunk and stretched out, fully dressed. Signifier came over and asked me what was the trouble. I shook my head. I couldn't talk. Then Candy and Dew Baby and Wrinklehead came over. "No beef," I said. "We just cut out, that's all." They started planning how they would gang up on him and run him out of the dormitory. But I shook my head again. "Let him alone," I said.

Later that night he got into trouble in the poker game. A fight started between him and Starrett and Starrett went after a knife. Dutch gave Dido a knife. Signifier came over and told me that Dido was about to get into a knife fight. It made me sick enough to vomit. It was like hearing of your sister in a knife fight. I pulled myself up and went out and tried to talk to Dido. He was standing in the aisle waiting for Starrett. His face was a dead dopey white, his lips a bluish bruise, his eyes lidded. There was that drugged remoteness in his face. He had the knife in his hand and when I saw the naked blade a drawing coldness moved from the front of my body through to my back, contracting my lungs and heart. Goose flesh rippled down the back of my legs.

"Don't do it, kid," I said.

He turned and looked at me. "Frig you and everybody else," he said.

Bleakly pitying, we looked at each other. "Honestly, I didn't mean it," I said.

A flicker of life brushed across his face. "But *you,* Jimmy, I put *you* in the *stars.*" His voice was accusing.

I went down to Starrett's bunk as he was getting his gang together. I pushed one of the fellows to one side and leaned over and touched Starrett on the shoulder. He had his big dirk out and was wrapping his left arm with half of a prison blanket. He went into a crouch.

"If there's a fight here tonight you're going to die," I said. Then, before he could reply, I backed away and returned to my bunk. I stood there wondering what I would have to do. I could feel my lips trembling. I couldn't keep them from trembling. There are some things which I just don't understand, I thought. Who'd have ever thought a person like Dido would take what I said like that?

Everyone in the dormitory had seen me talk to Starrett and they all knew what it meant. But Candy was the only one who came down to see if he could help me. He had a couple of knives he had borrowed and a piece of loaded pipe. I didn't even see anything funny about so many weapons. I took them and laid them on my bunk and said, "Thanks, Candy, but you stay out of this."

"I'll be around," he said. He went out and sat at the table.

Starrett came out into the aisle and looked over at me and stood for a moment, indecisive. Someone had gone for Captain Charlie and he came down the aisle. Starrett went back to his bunk. Dutch came out from between two bunks and said something to Dido and Dido walked down towards the latrine with Dutch. I put the two knives and the piece of pipe underneath my pillow.

Captain Charlie stopped at my bunk and said, "You don't want to get into this kind of fight, Jim. You behave yourself. I want to see you get out of here."

"It's all over now," I said. "It was just a little rumble."

"Let the others fight," he said. "You've got more sense than that." He was very angry with me. "What kind of fellow is that Dido, anyway?"

"He's all right," I said. "You just got to get to know him."

He pursed his lips and walked away without replying.

A few minutes later the lights winked. When I tried to unbutton my shirt my fingers seemed numb. Finally I got undressed and got into bed. I turned over on my stomach and lay watching the dormitory. Every time someone got up to go down to the latrine I tightened up. I lay there all night, wide-awake. That was the most miserable night I had ever spent. I was so damned scared.

All the next day I was scared. I saw Dido again at breakfast time but he didn't look at me. I was scared to death for him. He never had a friend but me, I thought. And then I had let him down. But he must have really thought that we were right, I thought. I was just beginning to believe it because I never had.

He was with Dutch all that day. He was very reckless and sneering and don't-caring and treating everyone like dogs. I hated seeing him with Dutch. But I knew Dutch would protect him for a time and I wasn't quite as scared.

Late that night, long after the lights were out, Dido came down to my bunk. "Could it ever be the same again, Jimmy?" he asked.

"It ought to be better," I said. "I've learned so much."

"You'll probably never learn that all life is give and take, Jimmy," he said, "but I can't blame you, for that's mostly a tough lesson."

"The trouble with me is I've been in prison too long," I said.

He was brooding. "I hate myself for doing this," he said, "but I can't help it."

"Take me out of the stars," I said. "It's just a dream—it isn't true."

"All dreams are true, Jimmy. They're true as long as you dream them."

"Let's not be so deep, boy," I said. "We'll get our beards entangled." Suddenly we were laughing. It was very good to laugh again.

But we knew what it would be like if we ever broke up. We had only felt the breath of the loneliness—the scared cold nights and empty days—and we knew what the full measure would be. It stained our friendship with a hopeless, futile desperation, as if it was only borrowed and would have to be returned.

25

THEY PUT some more bunks in the dormitory and shifted us about so that Dido wound up in the corner where he could look out into the street. We'd stand with our feet on the bottom-bunk frame and lean across his bunk, side-by-side, and look out the window at the gray winter days and talk. He liked to talk about Los Angeles and the people there. He told me so much about Hollywood Boulevard and the time he drove somebody's car at ninety miles an hour and got arrested when he was twelve, that I felt I had been there too. He liked to tell me about the people. He loved the people there.

"They're the most natural people in the world," he said. "They do the things they want to do, and aren't afraid to live."

"Everyone else seems to think a lot of them are rather queer."

"Queer? That's a funny word."

"I mean sexually."

He looked at me strangely. "There's really nothing lost when a physical change is made unless you feel that it's wrong. It's the feeling that it's wrong that makes it queer."

"How did you feel?" I couldn't help but ask.

"It never came to that," he said again. I didn't know why I needed to be reassured so often.

"Do you think queerness in prison is right?" I pressed.

"That's an odd question—" he began.

"Why is it odd?"

"Do you?" he countered.

"Not particularly so," I said.

"You can be rather brutal, Jimmy," he said, hurt.

We talked of feelings and reactions. He told me how he abhorred fat people and how his mother's best friend had wanted him to love her when he was twelve and how distasteful the suggestion had been. I asked him about women and he said he had had many women, perhaps more than the average person, but while he satisfied them they had always left him with a vague incompleteness.

"Emotionally I was never satisfied," he said. "I needed to swoon. I couldn't surrender; I needed to be conquered."

I was shocked and repulsed but entirely fascinated.

"By a woman?" I asked. I really wanted to know.

"By love," he said. "It's like when you keep crying after you've been whipped, until finally you love the one who whipped you. I needed to be exhausted." He broke off and looked at me. "Have you ever been exhausted by love?"

"I reckon not," I said.

"Does it sound low?"

"Not particularly so," I lied. "I just don't like to hear about it."

"You don't have to worry, Jimmy," he said. "You give me everything just as you are."

We talked of our past lives too, and I told him of my dreams when I was a little boy. "I read a lot," I said, "and I guess I must have built up a dreamworld about me. I came to feel that the things I did and the things which happened to me, such as eating and studying and sleeping, were things which really didn't count; the real things were the things I dreamed, the castles and the soldiers and me being a general and a hero and all."

"Tell me more," he said. "It explains so many things."

I told him about my growing up on a farm, and living in my dreams, and how tense I'd become when my parents moved to the city. "I felt that I was different from other boys," I said. "I didn't want to be different. It was then I came to feel that I had to prove something. At first I hadn't cared much for doing it. It was like fighting. I hated to fight. But when someone hurt you, you fought them. That was the way it had been in books. And if you won they stopped. That was the way it had been about proving something. It was something I had to do to prove I wasn't scared or different. I was always looking for something that wasn't there."

"Oh, God, Jimmy, do I give you anything?" he asked.

"You give me everything," I said.

"I want to—I want to give you everything."

We were silent, and he said, "Tell me about the girls."

"There weren't any girls. Not then," I said. "I was pretty much alone."

"Were you ever in love?"

"Once, I guess." I told him about a girl I had known for one day when I was thirteen. "I guess she's the only one I ever really loved. I never felt quite that same way about any of the others."

We were silent for a long time while twilight deepened into dusk, and then I told him about high school and getting hurt. "I'd planned on enlisting in the army but I got hurt before I was old enough. I guess that scared me more than anything. I had always been sort of athletic and after I broke my back I felt that I was no more good for anything. I tried to go to college but I couldn't stand it. I felt I was the only Jodie there. There was something about being a Jodie at that time that killed me—now I wouldn't even give a damn."

"What were the women like?"

I smiled at him. "All kinds. When I quit school I bought a car." I told him about Margie killing herself. "I really liked her but I felt I was too young to get married. I couldn't bear the thought of being tied down. I told her I'd pay for an abortion." I took a breath and let it out. "But she didn't want it that way." He let the silence run. After awhile I said, "I guess that was the end of me. My parents were divorced soon afterward, but that was anti-climax." We watched the car lights pass on Spruce Street. "You know the story," I said. "It's very trite. It's been told a hundred-thousand times and it's always the same. Who gives a goddamn, anyway?"

"I like the way you tell it," he said.

"How else could I tell it?"

"You know how you could tell it. Like all the others do. With that touch of gaudy glamor."

"But I'm talking to you," I said, and that explained it.

After a time he began telling me of himself. He said that when he was born his father left his mother, and she went to work as a nurse for an old invalid woman who was a member of a very wealthy family in Pasadena. He grew up with the three small grandchildren. And then one day when he was seven the youngest of the grandchildren had a birthday party and he wasn't invited. He went out to the garage and put his arm against the doorjamb and slammed the heavy swinging door against it. Both bones were fractured and his arm bent double. Then he ran into the house where the party was in progress and showed them his broken arm.

"I wanted them to make over me," he said. "When it healed up it left a tiny hole in my arm. I still have it." He balled his fist and a tiny dimple appeared in the muscles of his forearm. "I went about showing everybody the hole in my arm. I was very proud of it."

"I imagine you were very spoiled," I said.

"There wasn't any way for me to keep from being," he said. "My mother lived for me. She got me everything I wanted. I never saw my father until I was fifteen, then my mother went to live with him and I ran away. I joined up with a carnival that had a pitch out on Wilshire Boulevard, and went to Texas with it. At first I was a roustabout then I got a job doubling for a guy who was faking as a Spanish Duke. His name was Harry Smith. He got into trouble with Poochy's wife and had to scale. Poochy was the guy who owned the act. I got the part steady after that."

"Is that where the 'Duke Dido' business comes in?" I asked. "She was a queen, you know, a really beautiful princess."

He gave me a slow, strange smile. "Do you think so?"

"Your mother's name is Davis. Is that yours too?"

"No, my father was named Medina. Alonzo Medina."

"Was he Spanish?"

"I don't know what he was, other than a bastard." I was shocked by the hatred in his voice.

"So you fell in love with Poochy's beautiful blond wife and had to scale, too," I said.

He looked startled. "It does sound like a pulp story, doesn't it? But she really was beautiful. She had long silky golden hair, and cuddled like a cat. You would have liked her," he said, looking at me out of the corners of his eyes.

After a moment he said, "She ruined me for other women. She never got enough; she wanted buckets of it. I was just sixteen and she was the first woman I ever had. We showed in White City and then Elkhart. That was where Poochy caught us and I had to run away without any clothes. I wore tails and a top hat for my act and I had to run away in that."

"Where did you go?" I asked, amused.

"Chicago. I think Poochy liked me for himself. He saw me in Chicago once and wanted me to go to the hotel with him."

I hated him when he talked like that. It made me sick thinking of what he might have been to someone else.

"After that I hoboed South," he said. "I got caught for grand larceny and did a year on a Florida chain gang. That was tough. My mother sent me some money then, to come home on, but I went to Philadelphia instead and got a job as an entertainer in a honky-tonk. Oh, I had plenty of gall. I worked out a song act, playing my own accompaniment on a banjo uke, but it didn't take so I tried to work in a dance routine with it. I might have made it go, sooner or later, if I hadn't broken my kneecaps."

"How did you do that?" I asked.

"Oh, I was riding a freight, coming out of Pittsburgh, and got to fighting with a guy. We were in a boxcar and he wanted to make me and he knocked me off the train."

It made me sick to hear him confess such things. I tried to change the conversation. "And after that what did you do?"

"I began impersonating females in the cabarets. There was a big call for that and I did all right. I didn't need legs; I did my song-and-banjo act. The toughest thing was dodging the patrons. It seems as if every old fat bald-headed man in the joint wanted to make the female impersonator, as soon as he had a few. I know you will think this is funny, but I was always a little hysterical about girls. Not sexually; I told you how I felt toward them sexually. I wanted to keep them up, buy them diamonds and furs and stuff. All the trouble I was ever in came from me trying to get something for some woman or other."

I fished out a cigarette and he took it and I lit another one. He strung his uke about his neck. "That's about all of it, Jimmy," he said. "I joined the army and then deserted after three months. That was after I did my bit in Florida. When I got arrested here the army came and got me and made me serve six months for desertion, and then they turned me over to the reformatory and I served two years. I was out twelve days and now I'm doing ten." He gave me a look and suddenly began grinning. "All right, I'll break out the blues," he said. "We're just a couple of old sob sisters, aren't we?"

"You must have had it tough in all those joints," I said. "With your sensitive mouth and the way your eyes look sometimes."

"The year in Florida was the toughest," he said. "Those wolves down there would try to rape you right in front of the hacks. The hacks wouldn't give you any protection if you weren't from the South. I used to carry a big chiv and they knew I would use it. Even then some of them still tried. But in the reformatory it was different. I took everything and never gave anything. That was a fine way to do, wasn't it?"

My feelings for him after that were never steady and, from day to day, never the same. But he was in my blood by then. I wanted to erase his past and have him start from scratch with me. I didn't want to admit that he had ever existed before he met me.

One day he was shuffling through some old letters and dropped one. He reached for it but I had already stooped and reached it first. My gesture hadn't been intentional. I wasn't trying to see it. I glanced at the address, involuntarily. It had been addressed to Dido in the insane asylum. A moment had passed before I realized just what it meant. I was thoroughly shocked.

"When were you in the insane asylum?" I asked.

For an instant he looked as if he would deny it. Then he changed his mind and told me all about it. The last time he had been arrested he had pretended to be insane. "It wasn't hard to do," he said. "My crime had been so damn hysterical they thought I really was insane. They kept me down there under observation for six months and then sent me here."

"Were you insane?" I asked.

"I might have been," he said. "I had lost my perspective. They were catching me too fast."

"I know how that is," I said, thinking of the time I'd tried to kill myself. "I've lost mine too."

"If we hadn't made up again I'd be back there now," he said.

I felt very tender toward the Dido I knew. I was scared for him. I wanted to protect him and change him all over from that Dido whom I didn't know, the one whom I found as repellent as a snake. I could not bear to think of him in connection with anyone except his mother and myself. I must have thought him capable of doing anything, I was so scared for him. It must have been that I was afraid he would turn back into that other Dido, the one whom I hated so.

26

EVERYTHING touched me that spring. I was very emotional. I had never been so emotional. Everything was soft inside of me and at the slightest thing it would bubble out, like foam. A single note on Dido's uke touched me. A bar of melody. Thoughts of my mother. A bird flying in the window and flying out again. That touched me plenty. And clouds in the sky. Or a convict with a flop. And those golden spring twilights without any shadows, soft and diffused with a golden glow, tinting everything with vividness.

Death row was in the 12 block. On those afternoons when they took the condemned men across the yard to the death house we stood in the windows and watched them pass. That always touched me. I would wonder what they were thinking. Long into the night I would wonder. What could they be thinking? You couldn't tell from looking at them. Some walked with shoulders back, swaggering, contemptuous. I'd think of Dido and wonder how he would walk that bitter half mile; wonder if in the end his sneer, and high and mighty contempt for everyone, would fail him. Others walked erect and soberly, as if they were silently praying. Some slouched along, indifferently, with their hands in their pockets. The priest walked with some and they looked penitent, but who knows how they felt or what they thought? Most appeared perfectly natural from where we looked down on them. They talked and laughed with the guards much the same as any convict going anywhere.

But all the time I wondered what they were thinking. I'd never had a chance to ask anyone who made the stroll and didn't burn, although there were two of them in prison. Dido said he talked to one of them, named Gardner. He said that Gardner told him that he was thinking about fishing the day he made the stroll because it was a hell of a good day to fish.

Thoughts of death touched me constantly. I would lie in bed at night and think of those burnt-up convicts lying on the prison yard. I'd think of those men walking to the death house. I'd think of all those convicts dead and dying in the hospital, and those mattresses out beside the hospital steps on mornings. I'd think of myself dead and rotting in the oblivion of prison, never having been a goddamned thing in life but just a number on a board; having in the end lived and died for nothing and left nothing, and was nothing and never to be nothing but some goddamned worms in the sonofabitching ground.

I'd fill with a raw sense of protest against something which I could not identify or define. It was all wrong, I protested. There was more to any man than just a number on a board. There was something inside of a man you couldn't put in black-painted numerals in a fingerprint card and Bertillon measurements. There was warmth and romance and hot-blooded passion. There were yearnings and desires and charity, too. There was that unaccountable gladness in a perfect day.

On Easter Sunday Dido and I went to Mass, although we were Protestants and weren't supposed to go. But he wanted to go with me to watch the candles burning. I had told him how I was affected by burning candles.

"If anything ever makes me truly religious it'll be candles burning on an altar," I said.

"Why?" he asked curiously.

"Oh, I don't know, I've never thought about it," I said. "I guess because they're so soft and insistent and eternal, like a good woman's love." A moment later I caught his eyes on me.

Everything touched me that spring, but Dido touched me more than anything. Dido with his morbid, brilliant, unsteady mind and kaleidoscopic moods, his weaknesses and his broodings and his gayety; sparkling one moment and surly the next—one moment so close I could feel him beside me in my heart, and then next as remote and distant as the answer to a prayer. Whose anger inspired anguish and whose pitiful bravado was like a whistling in the dark and made me want to stand between him and everything. Poor little kid, I thought, too bad he wasn't a woman. He had a woman's fascinating temperament, with a man's anatomy.

Ever since I had discovered he had been in the asylum I had thought of him as a little crazy. I couldn't keep from thinking it. He was so unstable and theatrical that everything he did seemed posed. But in that place of abnormality of body and mind there was something about his love for me that seemed to transcend degeneracy and even attained, perhaps, a touch of sacredness. Because whatever else he might have felt, he never felt that his love for me was wrong. And if the gods he worshipped were heathen gods, I thought, who could tell him better? No one in there.

And he was so unpredictable, unlike all other convicts whom I had ever known; and so inconsistent. Every moment with him had something all its own. He would challenge the best poker player in the dormitory to some head-and-head stud, or want to fight the biggest, toughest guy. I thought always that he was a little crazy. Perhaps he was. When he would go out to the poker game with one dollar, after solemnly promising to lose that and quit, and then come back an hour later seventeen dollars in debt, which I would have to pay, I would think he was a little crazy. And at nights when he wanted to talk and would come down and stand beside my bunk until dawn. He was extremely, abnormally affectionate, but he was never monotonous. He always touched me.

The fresh green sprouts of grass touched me and the buds on the trees and the robins, when they came. We saw several robins in the yard. The convicts marching down the sidewalks which split the new green grass, and the rainbows after the showers, touched me. And the words which came back to me from somewhere in the past: "And God made hope to spring eternal from the human heart."

There was a newness in the spring which touched me, and an oldness in the prison which touched me. There were the walls and the horizon and, in the distance, the roof tops of the city; an etched skyscraper and the scattered church spires. There were people there beyond the walls whom I couldn't see who touched me; ardent young lovers and flowers beginning to bloom. And there was laughter all out there which I could not hear, which touched me.

The director assembled a yard crew and had them plant grass seed in the barren spots and transplant the flowers and landscape the prison yard. We took our gloves and balls out of winter storage and the softball fever had us again and Captain Tom had it worse than ever. We began going out to our practice diamond, behind the old wooden dormitory, to get our team in shape. We wanted to beat everyone that year.

I shifted the players around and tried them out for every position. I had to teach Dido everything but he learned very quickly. "I could learn to do anything for you, Jimmy," he said. We found another convict who could catch and I went to second base.

Dido played softball as he did everything else. He was very good when I was there to see him. He rapidly developed into all-star material. I bought some elastic braces for his knees, and every night we had the team masseur work on them.

Tom was elated and Dido was in solid. As long as he played ball he was Caesar's wife, he could do no wrong. I was pleased and proud of him and he knew it. He was very enthusiastic and played with all his heart. During the games he kept up so much noise out in center field he could be heard all over the diamond. He kept all of us on our toes.

"Do you like it?" I asked him once.

"I like to do everything you like to do, or even like for me to do," he said.

It was funny how sensitive I was to his playing. I could make a dozen errors and they wouldn't faze me because I was good and knew it. But if he made one I was sick with dread. As with all other things he did, he kept me continually apprehensive. I knew how unstable and hysterical he could become and every moment I looked for him to go haywire. I hated to see the pressure get on a game because I felt he couldn't take it.

And then I broke my arm. We were playing our rookies a practice game out in back that day. Mose was pitching for the rookies, so we could get some batting practice. Johnny Brothers said to Candy and me, "Let's knock old Mose out the box and make him mad."

Johnny Brothers got up and hit one over the death house. It was a ground-rule double. I followed and hit a sharp liner toward Polack Paul, who was playing second for the rookies. He opened his hands and the ball went through and hit him in the mouth. Rounding first, I saw that he couldn't find the handle to the ball so I kept on into second. Candy yelled, "Slide!" and I went down in a fade-away, bracing my fall with my left arm. It was the one that had been broken before. It snapped like a twig. I scrambled up and looked at it and said, "Goddamn son of a bitch," and then grabbed it with my right hand and started running around the end of the dormitory toward the hospital. Soldier Boy, who had been catching Mose, ran over and grabbed me under the arm to help me and Johnny Brothers yelled, "Wait a minute and I'll get the stretchers." Johnny Brothers had a fetish for carrying convicts to the hospital on stretchers.

I said, "Screw the stretchers, I can walk." I was still running.

Then Brothers ran up and grabbed me under the other arm, and Candy and Signifier and some of the others followed. Tom brought up the rear, puffing and blowing like an overloaded switch engine. When we came to the railing which surrounded the hospital lawn we jumped over it and ran across the grass, and jumped over the railing at the front and ran up the stairs into the hospital.

" 'Mergency!" Brothers yelled. "Make way, 'mergency!" He was ducking his head and grinning, as I always imagined he had done when he had cut that man he knifed thirty-six times with his chiv.

The guard ran out and said, "What's the matter here?"

And I said, "I broke my arm."

And he said, "What about it? Sit down over there, the doctor's eating lunch."

Tom came in then, looking like the beginning of a heart attack, and went on back to get the doctor. I was one of his star players, and the manager of his softball team, and he didn't give a damn if the doctor was in bed with the warden's wife.

Doctor Blaine, one of the visiting surgeons who was head of the medical college at the university and also of the city's biggest hospital, happened to come in at the time, with a couple of internes. "What's the matter here?" he asked.

And Tom said, "This man's got a broken arm."

"Let's see, boy," he said. Someone cut off the sleeve of my shirt and the doctor felt the break. "Come here," he said to the internes. "Simple fracture of the ulna. Feel it." They felt my arm. Then he grabbed me by the wrist and the elbow and pulled the sections of the bone apart and let them back into place. "Now feel it," he said to the internes. They felt it again and looked amazed. Jake Ingalls and the convict doctor, Tino, came up and Doctor Blaine instructed them, "Put it in splints."

They put it in simple wooden splints and then took me back to the X-ray room and fluoroscoped it. The break was set perfectly, so that only a tiny jagged line in the bone showed where it had been broken. Just below it I could see where the bone overlapped from where it had been broken before. None of it had hurt, neither when I broke it nor when he set it. Jake Ingalls said they'd keep me in the hospital for a couple of weeks, anyway. Then Tom and the gang left. Candy said he'd send me over whatever I needed. It wasn't until then I thought of Dido. I hadn't seen him at all.

That night when the runner brought over my pajamas, bathrobe, toothbrush and things, he had a six-page letter from Dido. I smiled, thinking that he must have been writing on it ever since I got hurt.

"Dear Jimmy," it began. "I wish it had been my arm instead of yours. I would break both my arms for you. Love you so. Wonder why somebody won't let me break my arm for you. I want to so badly. I want to do everything for you. Got to stand and see you hurt. I could hurt somebody for that. It's hard to say everything that I mean when you mean so much more to me than I'll ever be able to ever say." And then he went on and said six pages of it. It was a wonderfully passionate and crazy letter and it cheered me tremendously. It was odd how unimportant a broken arm could become in view of all that worship.

The hospital was interesting that time. Quite a few bigshot doctors from the outside were coming in and experimenting on the convicts, and there was talk of some weird operations they performed. The weirdest of which, it seemed to me, was the one they performed on the convict who had a pus sac on the brain, back of the eyes, and was going blind. They took him into the operating room and gave him a drink of whisky, the nurse said—who was a convict and naturally a liar—and then ran a hypodermic needle from the base of his skull clear through his brain to the inside of his forehead and drew out the pus.

"And when they got through running the needle through his brain he went out and played seven innings of ball," I said sarcastically.

"No, he had a little headache and went to bed," the nurse replied.

"Now, if you'll give me a drink of whisky I'll go to bed and you won't even have to bother about all the rest," I said.

The nurse grinned. "You could have it, you know." I knew.

I was going on my second week when I received a letter from my mother saying the governor had promised to commute my sentence to make me eligible for parole in September. I got so excited I started to leave the hospital right then and go over to the dormitory in my pajamas. The guard asked me where did I think I was going and I said, "Home. I'm going home in September."

He said, "You better get the hell— September?"

"That's right," I said. "I hit the jack pot this time."

"Congratulations, Monroe," he said.

I saw Tim, the hospital runner, coming from upstairs and I called him over. "Say, take this letter to the dormitory and show it to Dido, will you?" I said.

He hesitated. "I can't, Jimmy."

"Aw, go ahead," the guard said. "Tell 'em I sent you if anybody wants to know." After Tim left he turned to me, "That Dido's your buddy, ain't he?"

"That's right," I said.

In ten minutes Tim brought back the reply, "Congratulations, Jimmy, aces to you and all of them. I'm so glad for you."

Five days later when I got back to the dormitory they all had it. A few of them congratulated me, but most didn't. It was fine with Tom but he wasn't too happy about losing a star player. At least the season would be over by then. But what he wanted to know, first off, was when I would be able to play again. In a couple of weeks, I told him.

And then I saw Dido. "I'm so happy for you, Jimmy," he said. "I knew you'd make it; I've always known you'd make it."

I grinned and then said, solemnly, "You're the one who helped me do it, kid. If it hadn't been for you I'd have blown it sure as hell. You don't know what you give me."

"I'm so flattered and glad you think I am able to give you something," he said.

"You give me everything," I said.

"Hand in hand."

"Hand in hand," I repeated after him solemnly.

"And to the top."

"And to the top."

It was a solemn moment, and then we were laughing, embarrassedly, at ourselves.

We were very close. Signifier told me how Dido had reacted when I broke my arm. "Man, he tried to kill himself. Every time he'd hit a ball he'd slide halfway to first through all those cinders. He ran into the wall once like he didn't even see it, and another time he stumbled over those rocks out there in center field and fell flat on his face. Tom had to stop him from playing. He was like a man trying to commit suicide."

"Yeah."

"He's certainly gone about you. It wouldn't have done for you to have broken your neck," he said.

I had to laugh. After that I wanted to bunk beside Dido. I propositioned old man Foley, who slept beneath him, to swap bunks with me. I had to pay him a couple of dollars. Then I asked Tom to get me transferred down to his bunk.

"I'll have to have somebody help me dress, as long as I wear these splints," I told him. "Dido will help me but I bunk too far away, so it's pretty inconvenient. The guy who sleeps underneath him said he'd swap bunks with me and that'll make it easier for him to help with my clothes. Then after I take off the splints I'll have to have someone rub my arm with cocoa butter so the muscles will get strong again."

"Can the bull," Tom said. "I'll get you transferred."

He had us transferred that afternoon. Dido and I were so excited at being so close to each other at last that all that night we couldn't sleep. He leaned over the side of his bunk and we talked all night long in whispers and giggled like two kids, then looked about to see who was watching. A new moon came out and walked across our window and we made believe it was a magic carpet and rode it everywhere. It was very thrilling but the next day we had to catch up on our sleep and everybody wondered why.

Dido helped me with my clothes the next morning, telling me to move this way and that and bossing me around in general and getting a big kick out of it. He helped me put on my shoes and while he was lacing them, he looked up teasingly, and said, "How does it feel to have someone kneeling at your feet?" He was very pleased with himself.

"Embarrassing," I said.

That afternoon he began working on a song. He sent over to the band room and got some score sheets and then, from after supper until bedtime, he sat around plunking out the notes and writing down the score. It was a monotonous dirge and after two days of it my nerves were frazzled.

"What the hell is it, anyway?" I asked. "It sounds like the 'Song of The Volga Boatman.' "

"Did you ever hear the woolen mill in operation?" he asked.

And I said suddenly, "Damn right, that's what it is."

I could hear again the slow clanking melody of the mills in the deathly silence that day, a long time ago. It was up in the idle house and Sergeant Cody had just shot a convict to death, and in the silence which followed the echoing of the gunshots the mill below had continued to clank its slow and eternal song—so deliberately, so mockingly. And I could imagine those convicts as I had imagined them then, working at the looms, feeding the stinking, dusty wool, stopping neither for the years nor for death, and I said, "If you get all that in your song you've really got something."

"It's going to be a love song," he said.

I was unreasonably disappointed. It left me feeling queer because it was the first time he had disappointed me.

"I don't know, I guess there's a whole lot of people who have been disappointed," I said.

"You wanted it to be a dirge, didn't you?" he said.

"No, I like the love idea," I lied.

"I know you don't but I can't help it."

"I do, honestly. I think it's a wonderful melody for a love song."

"You're a very obvious liar, but you're sweet," he said. And then something about him underwent a change and he said, "I'm up to my throat in death, as it is."

I looked at him. "You sound despondent. What's the matter?"

"I'm scared," he confessed.

I laughed. "What the hell for?"

"Oh, its just a silly thought, and I'm not very gallant to think it."

"What is it?" I was perplexed.

"I don't want you to go away. I don't want you to go home. I tried very hard to want you to but I don't." His voice was choked.

"I know," I said. "I've known it all along."

"I know I'm very ungallant and low and despicable and all," he said. "But I just can't help it. I don't want it to ever come to an end."

"It won't come to an end," I said. "We'll always be pals."

He shook his head. "Not outside, Jimmy. The world won't accept me."

"If they accept me they've got to accept you," I argued. "You're half of me."

"Let's don't talk about it, please," he begged.

"But I mean it," I said. "Why shouldn't we talk about it?"

"Sure," he said, forcing a smile. "I know you mean it, darling. And we'll always be friends, won't we?"

"Always," I said.

27

NOTHING was real. In all the world there was nothing so unreal. It was all fantasy and frenzy and delirium. It was dread and apprehension, new and weird and shameful; with its peaks very high and its depths in slop; but above all, indescribably fascinating. I had never known anyone like Dido, and knowing him was unreality, pure and sheer.

The days passed through this grotesque unreality, wired together and meteoric, headed for September. But each day was filled to overflowing and could not hold it all. Always there was some left over that spilled into the day that followed, and the day that followed could not hold it all.

There was not enough time to hold it all. There never had been.

There was no time to think. Everything was a feeling, an action, an emotion. Mostly emotion, ninety per cent emotion and the rest action and feeling, with perhaps a fraction of one per cent rationalization. It was like a fantastic dream. No one can rationalize in a dream. But even in the dream there was the tiny, insistent warning of awakening. September was coming. Time was running out.

We planned against it, thought against it. Like two little kids planning the grown-up future, we talked of how we were always going to be together.

"The very first thing I'm going to do is get some dough and get you a pardon."

"You don't have to, Jimmy. If you'll just go and see my mother and write to me sometimes and always remember me, I'll get out. It won't be so long. I'll be a model convict and they'll give me a parole the first time I go up."

"But I mean it. I'll get a recommendation from your sentencing judge and prosecutor, and then I'll square the prosecuting witness so he won't protest. How much did you get, anyway?"

"It wasn't but twelve dollars, but—"

"Hell, a hundred will square him easily. After that it'll be a cinch if you'll just keep your head and don't go haywire and get into some trouble here."

His face would light up like a Christmas tree and he would say, "And then we'll be together again and nothing will ever be able to separate us."

For a moment we would believe it. Enthusiasm would race through both of us and we would feel that we had it beat at long last.

"You keep on writing your songs. I'll go out to California and stay with your mother. I'll work out an angle and get some dough and in about six months we'll both come back and get you out. It might take a little more time though."

"But you'll write every day, or at least once a week, won't you?"

"Of course I will."

"You won't forget me?"

"How could I? I'll be thinking of you every moment."

"And I'll be the bestest convict ever was. I won't go haywire and I'll keep my head and I'll read your letters and think of you and you'll be proud of me yet."

And then something would fall on the moment like a

heavy weight and blight the mood. Maybe a colored convict over in the cell block singing—"Night is fallin' an' Ah'm recallin' . . ." The solid facts would surge back upon us and overwhelm us. I was going out in September and he had five more years to do. And after that we couldn't even pretend any more.

He'd jump up, dopey-faced and reckless, and cry in a ravaged voice, "Oh, goddammit, it's no use! It's no goddamn use!" Then his voice would go dull and lifeless and he'd say, "I was doing time in a Florida chain gang and a freight came by. And screamed. And the hack grabbed his rifle and stood up in his saddle. I was thinking about my mother out in Los Angeles. About how she loved me. And for the moment I was there. And then I came back. And the sun was hotter than hell. And I had chains on my ankles. And I said to myself, if I ever do time again I'll be doing it in death row waiting for the chair. And here I am, doing another stretch in another prison, and some black bastard has just dropped his uncultured voice through a little tinsel dream. And I'm saying it all over again. The next time I do time I'll be doing it in death row waiting for the chair." His face would be ugly and dead white.

Then he would go out to the poker game and go into debt and I wouldn't have the heart to stop him. At such times I would wonder if he ever recalled what he had said that first night we knew each other—"That's a hell of a lot of loneliness. Is anything worth it?" That seemed like a long time ago. Everything had changed since then, it seemed.

But whatever we did, it was always there, hanging over our heads like a Damoclean sword, staining every moment with a blind, futile desperation, a dull, hurting hopelessness—as if it might be the last. We tried to cram everything into each day but it failed to hold it all; some of it always overflowed into the next. It was always there, even in the middle of a laugh.

Maybe he hoped that I would do all those impossible things I had promised so earnestly. But it was hope without faith. And I couldn't really make myself believe he'd do anything but go completely haywire after I left. I knew he needed me to hold him up. I was like his heartbeat; without me he was dead. And it was so completely heartbreaking that most of the time I couldn't feel as hurt as he, because I was going home. But the desperation was as much of me as of him. Beneath it everything was magnified all out of proportion and often into a grotesqueness where each minor incident assumed a significance all out of proportion to its importance, so that we were continually upset and almost every moment were doing or saying something that hurt unreasonably; creating a persistent need for explanations and assuagements and avowals of affection.

It was that way when the dormitory ball team played its first game since I had broken my arm. Dido had been wonderful about taking care of me. The splints had finally been removed from my arm but I'd been instructed to keep it bandaged. Tom kept me supplied with rolls of cotton and bandages and adhesive tape, and each day Dido changed the dressing. He was very nice and pleasant and my slightest wish was his command. It was pleasant to have a broken arm and receive so much attention. But when game time came he didn't want to play.

"It's just a silly game without you, Jimmy," he said.

"Hell, I won't always be there with you," I said. I could have bitten off my tongue, watching the hurt grow in his eyes. I had forgotten I couldn't say things like that any more.

"I'll play," he said dully. "But I won't be any good without you."

And he wasn't. The team lost. When the pressure got on the game he was horrible to watch. He went to pieces right before my eyes. That was something I never wanted to see again.

Afterward I said, unreasonably angry, "It seems to me as if you'd have enough pride to keep from making a spectacle of yourself like that. It was disgusting. I'd be ashamed to let anyone see me break into pieces like that."

"I haven't got any pride," he said. "And you should be the one to know it. If I did—" And that was all. There weren't any more words; just a dull, hurting silence.

All that night I could hear his low muffled sobs. I wanted so badly to comfort him, to get up and say, Don't cry, kid, I'm with you. I don't give a damn what you do, I'll always be with you. But I couldn't. I just couldn't, that was all.

When early morning came he leaned over the side of his bunk and said, "I didn't mean what I said, Jimmy. The next time I'll be very good and you'll be proud of me." I was so relieved I could have cried.

But some perverse impulse prompted me to say, "It isn't that, that isn't it, it's just that—it's how in the world can I ever feel sure about you when I'm not here if you're going to be like that?"

"I'll be different, I swear," he said.

The next time they played I stayed in the dormitory so I wouldn't have to see it if he went to pieces. It was worse. They lost again and this time everyone was bitter about it.

"He was so damned sickening I had to take him out," Candy said.

"Who?" I asked.

"You know who," he said. I knew who, all right. He didn't lie. I had only hoped that I was wrong.

"Boy, that kid's solid nuts," Signifier said. "He'd fall down every time he'd start for a ball and one time he just lost his head and picked up the ball and threw it over the wall. It looked like he did it on purpose. When Tom got after him he said he didn't give a damn and wanted to fight Tom. You know that was wrong."

"And the bases were loaded," Candy added.

Mose came up and said, "Dammit, you got tuh do somp'n. Ah ain' gonna pitch no mo', long as dat fellow's on the team." His duck-bill lips were stuck out a country mile.

And I had to take it without a word.

Brothers joined the group. "Man, they killed us," he said. "Fourteen to two. We ain't never been beat that bad." He started to say more but he looked at me and didn't.

I saw Tom coming down the aisle, shaking his head. I knew what was coming. I tried to head it off.

"We'll have to get someone else for center field," I said, turning to Brothers. "What about Japcat?"

"That Dido!" Tom said, shaking his head. "What's the matter with him?"

"He's all right," I said. "He's a little excitable at times, but he's all right."

Tom kept on shaking his head as if he wanted to say something else, then Rifle Ed said, "When you going to be ready to play again, Jimmy?"

"I'm going to play the next time the team plays," I said.

Tom's eyebrows lifted.

"That's next Thursday," Brothers said.

"That's when I'm going to play," I said.

Tom didn't know whether to look relieved or not.

"You better come on back," Polack Paul said. "Ain't nobody on the team any good without you there."

Dido had stopped by the hospital. I went down to our bunks and waited for him. We had a board we'd placed across the bottom-bunk frames for a seat. After awhile he came in and looked at me without speaking and sat down.

His trousers were torn at the knees and both of his knees and his left elbow had been freshly bandaged. I noticed that he wasn't wearing his knee braces but I was determined not to argue about it.

"Skinned yourself up a little, eh, kid?" I said.

I was standing over him, leaning with my good arm against the upper-bunk frame. He looked up at me and I noticed that his face was sweaty and his eyes were feverish.

"Go ahead and say it and get it over with," he said, and abruptly I went blind. It wasn't until I could see again that I knew I had hit him in the face. His lips were split and bleeding slightly.

I was instantly contrite. "Hit me," I said. "Come on and hit me." I wanted him to hit me.

He put a handkerchief to his lips. Above it his eyes were unreadable. "Why don't you come on and hit me?" I said. "I hit you."

He took the handkerchief away from his lips and they were slightly smiling. He licked the blood from them and said, "No."

It wasn't real. There wasn't anything about it that was real. And very soon it would be gone. We tried to put everything into each moment. We were very frantic and scared and desperate. Happiness was like rain drops on the desert sands.

Once I said, "I don't think I've been happy for one half an hour in all my life."

"Don't I give you something?" he asked.

"It isn't that, that isn't it—" I began. But there were no words for it.

And that was the way it was, desperate and unreal and magnified and intense and grotesque and frantic. But life went on in the prison the same as it always had.

The water was shut off again during those hot summer days. The *Prison Times* said the move was necessitated by our wasteful habits. But yet, on those waterless afternoons when our tongues were so dry they stuck to the roofs of our mouths, we could look out the window and watch the sprinklers running on the front lawn. Washing in the cells and dormitories was prohibited and the rule was rigidly enforced. But the prison commissary continued to take outside orders for underwear, socks, pajamas, and such articles of wearing apparel which could be washed in no other way.

The Fourth of July brought another boxing tournament and some special eats and too much heat.

One hot afternoon they brought in four desperadoes who had killed a sheriff. We watched the approach of the cortege from the windows. The first car was loaded with special deputies who seemed armed for war. The second car contained the prisoners. Then there were three more cars of armed deputies and two army vans of National Guardsmen with mounted machine guns.

"Goddamn, that looks like the Big Parade," someone said.

"It's the last parade, anyway."

"That's the way they do it when you're tough," I said.

"Tough!" Dido said. He was touched by it for some reason. "They're not tough. They're in the second car." And that was being tough, I thought.

The warden tightened the vigil about the institution and put on extra guards about the walls. Cars were not allowed to park along the street. Every precaution was taken to keep the four prisoners from being rescued. They even went to the trouble to build a new bullet-proof tower on the stockade across from death row. And one Sunday afternoon, while it was under construction, three convicts walked across the yard with a ladder and put it up against the wall and told the guard in the tower they were going to install a spotlight.

"Come ahead," the guard said, and they went up the ladder and slugged him and dropped over the wall. The first anyone heard about it was when a complete stranger came around to the front and tried to get to see somebody to inform. But the front guards stopped him at the sidewalk and wouldn't let him enter. Among the precautions which had been taken to hold the four desperadoes were instructions to the front guards to keep out all strangers. So the man had to go away and find a telephone and call in to tell about the three convicts he had seen dropping over the walls. But by that time the convicts were gone. However, they were caught a few days later.

They had gone about fifteen miles down the railroad tracks and holed-up in a jungle. From some place they had secured quite a bit of money, and three rifles and two pistols and hundreds of rounds of ammunition, and a case of liquor. When the posse swooped down on them they grabbed the liquor and ran. They were taken back and put in the hole. But they were so drunk it didn't matter. All night long they sang "Mother Machree" at the tops of their voices. The same old thing.

Time went on with its inexorable chain of events which

we watched and discussed with detached interest. Nothing could make me so angry as when Dido let some part of it affect him.

"What burns me up with you," I would say, "is that you let some cheap, lousy convict get you mixed up in some cheap lousy situation and you make a damn fool out of yourself; whereas neither the convict nor whatever in the hell you're trying to do has the least importance. The thing is you let little, insignificant things get you so mixed up that you lose your sense of proportion. I've seen you get so worked up trying to beat Johnny Brothers playing cooncan that you didn't give a damn about anything else in the world except just to beat him. When in the first place cooncan's a nigger's game and you never will be able to beat him, and in the second place where you lost fourteen dollars, you couldn't have won but a dollar if you had beat him all night, and in the third place it wasn't important and never will be important. I don't mind what you do, but don't let it get important. Don't let it touch you. There's nothing worth touching you." I didn't even realize the incongruity of me preaching that doctrine.

True to my word, when our team played again I wrapped my arm securely with adhesive tape and played shortstop. It had been five weeks since I had broken it and it didn't trouble me at all. Once I fell forward on it fielding a slow roller, but no damage was done. Another time I made such a spectacular running catch that Tom swallowed his cigar and when they had beat him on the back and got him to breathing again he said, "That Jimmy's a ball-playing son of a bitch. I sure hate to lose him." Dido played center field and was excellent. He and I scored the winning runs. But they didn't like him for it and he didn't give a damn.

But after that everything was swell between us and we were sitting on top of the world again, down there in our private corner. The dormitory was still there and the walls were still there and the convicts were still there, but we were unaware of them. On those hot summer days we'd lie side-by-side on my bunk and look out the window at the clouds in the sky, rolling by in great dirty flocks beneath the sun, and he would call them sheep. They did look something like sheep. Once we got a pair of smoked glasses and looked at them and everything was purple-tinted and fantastically beautiful. It was swell to be young and alive and have such a wonderful friendship, even if we were in prison. I had my mother send him a tenor guitar and the next time she visited me she asked about him. It made me feel swell.

His mother sent him some pajamas and underwear and a very lovely scrapbook. It was wonderful of her and it made us feel a great deal better. When two people have things of their own, without being dependent on the other, it always makes things better. It put him on a more equal footing and he didn't have to feel badly about accepting things from me. The pajamas were fine and I took one pair that I liked extremely well. He wanted me to take both pairs but I didn't like the other pair so well.

After that he carried himself erectly and there was a new confidence in his bearing and he looked very handsome. We didn't have anything in particular to put in the scrapbook, so he pasted in some old pictures of me my mother had sent me.

Once he came back from a poker game and told me that if Signifier was a friend of mine I'd better talk to him, because Signifier had just called him a curly-headed punk and he wouldn't take that from anybody. I got up and went out to the game and asked Signifier about it. He said he wasn't talking about Dido, he was just cursing his luck and had said something about a curly-headed punk, but he wasn't talking about anyone.

"It's like this, Signifier," I said. "Dido's my friend and I'm going to try like hell to keep him out of trouble, but if he ever gets into any trouble I'm on his side. Anybody who hurts Dido hurts me." I looked at everybody when I said it.

"If that's the way you feel, Jimmy, I don't blame you," Signifier said. "But you tell that kid I wasn't talking about him. I wouldn't say anything like that about him. He's all right with me."

But I knew that he was lying about Dido being all right with him because Dido wasn't all right with anyone in that dormitory any more. They were all down on him. It was just because they liked me that they treated him decently at all. I knew that and I tried to keep things smooth.

"You don't really need to gamble," I told Dido when I returned to my bunk. "You've got everything you need. Let's rest up for awhile."

"Whatever you say," he said.

One night we were talking in low, muted whispers when all of a sudden we became aware of the moon shining through the window. It seemed enormous and pale and distant and beautiful.

"Can you see the face in the moon?" I asked.

"Who, the man eating green cheese?"

And then I said, "When the moon shines through your window think of me, maybe I'll be looking at it, too."

When his voice came it was choked. "Don't say that, please don't say that."

"I didn't mean to hurt you, boy," I said. "Don't take it like that. We can't do anything about it. It was inevitable from the very start."

"I know," he said. "I know. I'm sorry." And then from a long way off his voice came, low and muffled, "Don't ever lean your whole weight on happiness, Jimmy, you fall too hard when it gives away."

"You have a saying for everything, haven't you?" I said.

"Just the words," he said. "Not the music."

We were silent and I was thoughtful. "Whenever I see a full moon after this I'll think of you," I said. "And I'll think of this dormitory. I'll see this goddamn dormitory and I'll see you in it, and that isn't the way it ought to be."

He was subdued and quiet after that and when I asked him why, he said, "You don't need me at all any more, do you?"

"Even if I didn't, you'd always be my friend, kid," I said.

The first of August I was called over to the classification bureau for an interview. "We have a request from the governor's office to have a little talk with you," the sociologist said. I knew that this was it. I realized then that all along I had been afraid that it wasn't so. But I wasn't afraid any longer. I knew then, beyond all doubt, that I was going home. I thought of all the things I would do and of how glad my mother would be. And then I thought, Dido will certainly miss me. I felt very scared for him. I couldn't imagine him making it without me.

But when I told him about it he seemed extremely happy. He told me a thousand things he wanted me to do as if I was going home that very moment. He hugged me and wanted to kiss me. Signifier and Candy stopped by to find out about it and he told them I had made it. He was so excited and happy that he made all of us excited and happy, too.

"Let's get some blue boys and celebrate," he said.

"Fine," I said. We got some blue boys and got jagged and went out and played some poker.

He got broke but when I offered him some of my chips he declined, saying he wanted to lie down for awhile. I was winning so I kept on playing. I said I would be down after awhile.

When I went back to our bunks I found him typing.

"What are you writing, your life's history?" I kidded.

He was violently startled. He wheeled and looked at me and his face flooded crimson. "What the hell!" I said. He snatched the sheet from the typewriter and started to tear it up. "Don't." I stopped him. "Let me see it."

He looked at me for a long time with his face all broken up in a thousand different expressions, then he said, "All right, Jimmy, I'll do anything for you."

I sat down on the bunk and began reading the typed pages, frowning slightly:

> I am twenty-four and know life. I wouldn't know life if I wasn't twenty-four, and I wouldn't be twenty-four if I didn't know life. I learned life and life and life until I knew it so well that even when they said, No charge to you, baby, I love it, I didn't feel romantic.
>
> But love makes a difference. It comes like the Assyrian gleaming in neither purple nor gold but holding fast and hard to the path until its victim is won.
>
> Is that the wisdom of twenty-four?
>
> No, this is it. When the change is made there comes a most demanding need, greater than the need for plasma, for freedom, for life, greater than the need for heaven.
>
> Don't you understand?
>
> I need a . . . without it . . .

My mind began skipping words. My eyes saw them but my mind would not record them. I wanted to stop reading but I couldn't.

> . . . drunk or sober . . . one way or another. . . .

When I came to the end my eyes kept darting back and forth across the page, trying to find something, I didn't know what. I was afraid to look up. When I looked up I would have to face it. I didn't want ever to face it. I didn't think I could face it.

"Jesus Christ," I said finally.

I looked down at him and looked quickly away. He was sitting on the board between the bunks, looking up at me. His eyes were like those of a dog that fears punishment.

I took a deep breath and said, "Jesus Christ, I thought

we'd gotten above that. Especially that." I had to swallow. "You said once you put me in the stars. Remember? And now this puts us in the gutter. Right back where we started—before where we started. Listen, this takes away everything we ever thought we had." I was silent for a moment. He didn't speak. I asked, "Is this all you ever wanted from me?"

"What else would I ever want?" he said.

Everything went then. We were just two convicts who didn't like each other any more, two convicts afraid of the other's power to hurt. There was a beaten, unsmiling dullness in Dido's face. The closeness we'd had for so long was now completely gone.

"Listen," I said. "Listen. If it was like that—if it was always like that, then I've wasted a hell of a lot of feelings."

He bowed his face between his hands. His shoulders sagged. His voice was muffled. "Tell me what you want, Jimmy? How would I know? I've never got anything for nothing in all my life."

"Anyway," I said. "Anyway—" I finally got it out. "Anyway, not you. I don't want you. You're no different from all the rest."

He stood up, white-faced and remote, and began a dull, bitter plea. "Haven't I tried to be what you wanted me to, Jimmy? Haven't I gone around here and kissed these bastards' behinds just because you wanted me to get along with them and treat them right, when I know they hate my guts? I've changed goddamn near everything about me, Jimmy, and just for you. I never did any of it for myself. I never cared a goddamn thing for myself or anyone except you."

"It isn't that, that isn't it, what I want you to do I want you to do not because of me but because you want to yourself. I want you to want to do these things. That's the only way you'll ever live to make it and get out and become somebody in the world. I want you to be somebody in this world, just as much as I want to be somebody myself in the world. You could be so damn easily. You've got everything it takes but the right attitude. It's all sex with you," I said. "And no kind of sex was ever worth the value you put on it, much less your kind."

For a moment he looked as if he was going to faint. Then his eyes became haunted and crazy and his face cracked like the white drum of a new banjo that's been overheated. "You don't think so," he said, pushing the words out between paper-stiff lips. "You don't think it's worth that much. I'll show you what it's worth to me." His head cocked to one side and his chin lifted and that sneer marred his lips again. "I'll show you," he said, looking down his nose at me. "I'll kill myself."

I believed him and I was suddenly afraid. There came to me a vague feeling that his destiny hung on my next words; that I had been endowed with the power of God. The power was mine and I could feel it. I wanted to say the right thing because I felt that on my words hung his life, but for the life of me I could only say what came to mind.

"That won't prove anything. Anybody can kill himself."

"Be seeing you, pal," he said, and walked away.

I felt choked. It was a feeling of an opportunity gone to have done something a little noble. It was as if I'd kicked a cripple who had asked for a dime, or slugged a blind man who had bumped into me.

Just before bedtime he came back and knelt beside my bunk and burrowed his face in my blanket. "I didn't have the nerve," he said, his voice coming muffled from the blanket. "I'd like to do something very low, that's all I am."

I reached down and lifted his face in my hand. His eyes were bruised and dirty as if someone had filled them full of sweepings. "Go to bed and sleep it off, kid," I said. "You'll feel differently in the morning."

When the lights went off and the dormitory silenced I could hear him sobbing up above. One hell of a celebration, I thought.

After that he was despondent and very desperate, although he tried to be very gay and not show it. He never referred to that night and he seemed very happy about my going home. But I could see how desperate and despondent he was underneath. It showed in his eyes, in the way he talked, in the way he wanted to take any rape-fiend chance in an effort to please me. I was afraid even to say, "That schmo sure gets on my nerves," because he might have asked me who and then gone out and cut his throat. At night he began staying awake and talking to me until dawn. It was as if he was afraid that sleep might rob him of some precious moment with me.

Nothing was real.

28

AFTER THAT it was like being washed away in a flood. Everything happened at once, it seemed. Things surged down on me in great waves and I was powerless before them. Everything was violent and chaotic and haywire. They happened suddenly and violently with no chance for defense against them nor preparation for them, and then they were gone. But their consequences remained. Their consequences were far-reaching and long-staying, and were like the treacherous backwash in which you drowned after fighting through the crest of the wave. The things swooped down on me and carried me away.

My feelings toward Dido couldn't get back to where they had been before. There was a vague lack of confidence, and the understanding between us was lost so that we were never quite in tune with the other's mood, never quite sympathetic with it. I felt a slight, dull revulsion; a vague dissatisfaction. Maybe it was just a letdown after all the high hopes and driving, tense excitement. And he could feel it. It put a tight-drawn recklessness in his actions, a strained desperation which seemed always about to explode.

There was an excitement, but it was different. It was strained and frantic and panicky. It was infirm and chaotic and stained with a dull monotone of hopelessness. And through it the incidents rushed in, surging pell-mell, sweeping us before them, and neither of us knew where they would take us. I tried to keep my head, but I felt a helplessness. It was as if I was beginning to go haywire myself.

We were still close, but only superficially. The separation was deep and dull and hidden. He didn't give me anything any more, but he was my responsibility. August burnt through, like a fuse on a stick of dynamite, and each day tightened us more and more against the explosion that seemed so imminent.

His mother wrote me a letter which I received on the

20th, and that loosened us a little. It postponed the explosion but did not dispel the feeling of it.

> Dear James:
>
> I am so glad to hear that you are to be released next month. I do wish you all the success and good luck in life which I know you so truly deserve. I trust that it will not be long until I see you.
>
> I just wrote my son and know he will be very glad to get my letter and the good lot of news that I wrote him. I will tell you as I do my other son, be of good courage and be good boys and the time will soon pass, then we will all be able to see each other face to face, and what a day that will be. You seem so much like my own son since having heard so much of you through Pepi. He surely thinks that the sun rises and sets in you, so to speak, and him thinking that way about you I know that you must be nice and I am going to adopt you as my second son. He sent me a snapshot of you which I was pleased to have. I wonder sometimes why he does not send me one of himself, maybe they don't allow him to have any made. I pray for you both, and I want you to pray for me. Be as good as you can, and be of good cheer.
>
> With prayers for your success,
>
> Mother Davis.

When I read that letter I felt like crying, I felt so sorry for her. "You have a wonderful mother, kid," I said to him. He didn't answer. He wasn't talking much those days.

But her letter helped us a lot. It brought us closer together again. It took some of the desperation out of him and I was pleased. I felt encouraged. He might make it after all, I thought.

Then the whispering campaign started. It must have been going on all along, but we were just beginning to feel it. Tom called me down and told me about it. "Listen, Jim," he said, not looking at me, "I'm not trying to run your business, but you and Dido have got to watch yourselves."

I got on my muscle. "Why? Why have we got to watch ourselves?"

"Listen, Jim, there's no need of all that," he said, spreading his hands, palms upward. "Three lieutenants have asked me about you two and a week ago the deputy called me into his office and showed me a whole drawerful of notes which fellows up here in the dormitory had written over there, about you and Dido. They said you did whatever you wanted to and I let you do it."

That shocked me. I should have known that they would be ratting on us, but I had never given it a thought. We had been so wrapped up in each other that we hadn't thought about the other convicts in the dormitory.

"I told the deputy that there wasn't anything between you two," Tom went on. "I explained how Dido had helped you a little when your arm was in splints, but that was just because I had asked him to. They discharged you from the hospital with the splints still on and somebody had to help you get your clothes on, I told him. What have they got against Dido, anyway?" he asked.

"I don't know, Tom," I said. "It could be about him losing those two ball games but I doubt if they'd carry it this far. It's just that they don't like him, really. He doesn't associate with them and doesn't have to ask them for anything. His mother sends him everything he wants and they don't like that. The truth is, Tom, we've just been getting along too good for them."

"That's what I told the deputy," he said. "You've always got a little money and he gets what he wants from home. Just because you guys are getting along nobody likes it. I told the deputy you were just getting along too good for these envious bastards up here. You know, Jim, I can't understand what makes people like that. I've seen a lot of people outside like that. They did me the same way when I was commissioner. They couldn't stand to see me make a little dough. They started crying for an investigation, people I'd been supporting, feeding. You'd be surprised if I told you who some of the fellows were who wrote notes about you and Dido."

"You'd better not tell me, Tom," I said.

"What I wanted to tell you," Tom went on, "is that Gout sent a transfer up here for Dido this morning. He was going to transfer him to 5-4." That was the girl-boy company.

I sucked air. I was so scared I was weak. My stomach went hollow and my knees knocked together. My mouth came open but I couldn't get the words out.

"I sent the transfer back and then went out to see the warden," Tom said. "I've done him a lot of favors and I asked him to do me a favor. I told him to let you and Dido stay in here and I'd be responsible. I told him that I would see to it that no more complaints reached him. He had almost as many notes about you as the deputy had."

"What did he say?" I gasped.

"He said he'd let you stay on one condition, that he didn't receive another complaint. But listen, Jim, you'd better cut it out. Or make it less obvious, anyway."

"There isn't anything to cut out, Tom," I said. "We're just good friends." His eyebrows went up. "I'm not trying to string you, Tom," I said. "Listen, can't a man have a friend in this joint? Is there any crime in having a friend?"

He spread his hands. "I don't write the rules, Jim. You know how it is, you're not a fool."

"What do they want me to do, quit talking to him?" I said. "I guess they don't even want me to look at him. I guess they want to tell me who I can talk to, I guess that's what they want to do." The more I talked the less afraid and the more angry I became. "I guess they want a guy to do like they want him to or else they're going to rat on him."

"Take it easy, Jim," Tom said. "Keep your head, boy."

The softball team was going along great then. We hadn't lost a game nor looked back since I had begun playing again. It looked as if we were headed for an intra-wall championship. We hadn't played the dining room yet but we were pointing for them and we figured we could beat them. Tom didn't want anything to happen before that game. I knew that was his first thought but he didn't come right out and say it.

"You don't have to stop talking to him," he said. "But don't do it at night. And don't hang around your bunks all day. Come on out like you used to do and gamble and mix with the other fellows. That will help. You're living off the games but you don't even play in them any more."

"Hell, they can have the games," I said.

"That wouldn't help," he said. "You got to get back to your old self. And tell Dido to stop playing his guitar while the colored fellows are having church on Wednesday nights. They're the ones who have been putting up the biggest howl. You know the chaplain gave them privilege to hold church once a week and they've been ratting to the chaplain ever since Dido's been in the dormitory. You come on out and mingle with the fellows again, Jim. They all like you but they think you've gone high hat. They think you don't want to know them any more because you're going home. They think you think you're too good to associate with them. You know how to handle them. Do it,

Jim, and you and Dido take it easy. The next time I won't be able to do a thing."

"Okay, Tom, I will," I said.

"Don't be a fool boy," he said. "You've made it now. Don't spoil it."

At first I didn't tell Dido. But he couldn't understand why all of a sudden I wanted to go out in the aisle and walk around and talk to the other convicts.

"What's the matter, Jimmy, don't you like to talk to me any more?" he asked.

Then I had to tell him about the whispering campaign. He was flamingly furious. "The chicken-livered bastards," he raved. "I wish I knew just one of them."

"That's why I didn't find out," I said.

"You needn't worry," he said. "I won't do anything to hurt you. But oh, if it wasn't that you were going home I'd show them!"

He tried to show them anyway, it seemed. After that he wanted to fight everybody. If a convict just so much as looked at him he'd challenge him to a fight. It kept me constantly apprehensive. I knew that if he ever got into a fight I'd be in it too. That was the only thing that really kept him out of serious trouble. But he went out of his way to show them how contemptuous of them he was.

But he was transferred after all. Not out of the dormitory but down front, right next to the guard-stand. After that we both quit speaking to everybody. We walked over convicts who got in our way and didn't look at them. We treated them like scum.

The whole dormitory was watching us and waiting for an opportunity to laugh. But we didn't give them any. Either I was up at his bunk or he was down at mine.

"Don't let them see how much it hurts you, kid," I said. "That'll take the joy out of it." We didn't and it did. We laughed at them and laughed at everything and kept up a front of gayety and treated it like a lark. At night I would go down and sit on his bunk and talk to him for hours while everybody in the dormitory watched.

And on Wednesday nights, when the colored convicts held church, we went down and sat on the end of the table and Dido played his guitar so loud the congregation couldn't hear themselves pray. And I was with him all the way. We wanted someone to say they didn't like it. They might have jumped Dido alone but they didn't really want to do anything to hurt me. And I didn't even appreciate it.

The whole dormitory was against us. There was an undercurrent of tension which seemed about to explode any moment. We went down to a game one day and got to squeezing the players in pots, and when the gamekeeper tried to stop us from saving I jumped up and snatched the blanket off the table and broke up the game. It was just the goodness of their hearts that kept those convicts off me that time.

The next day Tom stopped all of the gambling and that night Captain Charlie banned it, too. And then things grew tense for real. But Dido and I still went about defiantly, as if daring anyone to protest. Our insolence was towering. The funny part about it was that before the dormitory got down on him I had almost lost all feeling for Dido. But now I was all the way for him. I quit trying to preach to him and let him have his way. And his way was my way.

At nights, when the dormitory was asleep, Captain Charlie would pull his chair over to Dido's bunk and try to talk to him. The next day Dido would tell me what Captain Charlie had said. "He's trying to reform me. He thinks I'm too nice to be like I am. He told me that if I'd stop you from coming down here and give you up entirely he'd go to the front for me. He's a kind of nice old man and he likes you, Jimmy. He thinks you are really great, but he doesn't think we ought to be friends. He doesn't think we're good for each other."

And the next morning he said, "Captain Charlie said we're making it pretty tough for him. He said I'd have to stop coming down here to your bunk altogether."

"What did you tell him?"

"He's such a nice old man and he talked so pitifully I couldn't—I didn't have the heart to refuse him. After all, he asked me if I wouldn't, he didn't order me to. I hope you're not angry."

"Of course not," I said. "You did just right, kid. He is a swell old fellow. I'll come down to your bunk after this."

"But he doesn't want that, either."

"Hell, can't anybody say anything about that. It's right under the gun. What can be said about that?"

So we sat on his bunk down front by the guard-stand after that. We quieted down a little and gave Captain Charlie a break. But it didn't help. There was a solid wall of antagonism in the dormitory against us. Tom told me that the notes were getting worse than ever.

"But you needn't worry, Jim," he said. "You just keep on like you're doing, and stay out of trouble, and I'll see to it nothing happens to you before you go home."

"Thanks, Tom," I said.

Dido and I read to each other. That was the most of what we had left but we got more out of it than ever. Once we were reading a story in a magazine and came across a line about someone who "forever remained unnamed."

"That touches your imagination, doesn't it?" I said. "To live in this world and to be so insignificant as to forever remain unnamed?"

"That might be any convict," Dido said, and I said, "It might be me."

The protest started boiling up again and I said, "To hell with these goddamned convicts, come on down to my bunk."

Dido gave me an odd, searching look. "If you say so, Jimmy," he said.

We went down and lay side-by-side on my bunk and began reading another story. One by one the rats went up and reported us to Captain Charlie. I saw them but I didn't give a damn. After awhile Captain Charlie sent for me. He looked pitiful.

"Jim," he said. "I've know you for a long time. Remember when you were over in 5-6 dormitory? That was your first year. Remember how we used to talk at nights and how my wife used to make candy and send it in to you? Remember the time we caught the fellows with that April Fool's candy that had cotton and stones inside of it?" The old man touched me then. "I've always liked you, Jim, and I've always figured that you liked me, too," he said. "I knew even 'way back then that you were going to make it and get out and become a fine, upright man in the world some day. I never lost confidence in you, Jim."

"Thank you, Cap," I said. "I like you too. I want you to know that, Cap. I want you to know that I like you, no matter what happens."

"I do know it, Jim," he said. "I'm going to tell you something that I've never told anyone. Remember back when they moved you fellows out of 1-6 and put some of you on 3-6 and some of you in here?" I nodded. "Well, that night they caught you down on 2-6 in the poker game and I had to sort of, er, speak up for you—"

"I remember, Cap," I said. "You told a lie for me to get me out of a jam. I've never told you, Cap, but I appreciated that. I appreciated that very much, sir."

"Captain Lansing was the guard on the third floor then. You remember he caught you going back up the stairs? Well, he knew that I was lying to protect you and he reported me to the warden. Captain Lansing had the ear of the warden then, you know. They put me on the walls at night shortly after that. You didn't know it because you had been transferred into the cells over on 2-2 by then. But I stayed on the walls at night for almost a year." His voice got so heavy with tears he wouldn't look at me. "It's lonely on the walls, son. You don't know how lonely it can get up there at night on those walls. There were some little gray mice up there and I used to feed them scraps out of my lunch so they would come around for company. They were nice little mice."

He paused for a moment. I was choked.

"I was sixty-six last week," he said after a time. "I couldn't do another year on those walls. Listen, Jim, I don't want to have to report you and Dido because I like both of you. I've never seen you do anything. But don't have him down there at your bunk any more. Do that for me, will you, Jim? If you don't, these convicts are going to put me on the wall again."

I had never been as sorry for anyone as I was for him. I looked away to keep from having to look at the pleading in his eyes. And then I saw the convicts. While we had been talking they had congregated about us. They stood behind me in a semicircle, not close enough to be disrespectful to him, but just standing there, pressuring him, waiting like vultures. I doubted if they had heard what he had said to me. They just wanted to see what he was going to do with me. I turned around to face them, trying to show the contempt I had for them. Then I turned back to Captain Charlie.

"You're all right, Cap," I said in a low voice. "You're square and you're fair and you're honest. I'd like for you to know that I'd like to do that for you. I like you, Cap, I really like you, sir. But when these convicts think they can run my business, then I'm forced to refuse." Watching the hurt come to his face I said, "Listen, Cap, you got a blackjack. You take your blackjack and knock me in the head and send me over for insubordination."

"You know I can't do that, Jim," he said.

"Try, Cap, just try." I lowered my head across the desk. "Just take out your blackjack and close your eyes and swing."

"That's not the way, Jim," he said. "You know that's not the way."

"Then do what you have to do, Cap," I said. I turned and faced the mob of convicts. I wanted to kill them. I wanted to stand up on the table with a tommy gun and shoot them down like dogs. But I just walked blindly through them. If any one of them had said anything to me I would have tried to kill him. But they just got out of the way and let me through.

I didn't see Dido until he grabbed me by the arm. "I'd better not go back to your bunk any more, Jimmy," he said.

"Come on back and sit down, goddammit," I said. "I'm not taking orders from all the convicts in the world."

He didn't want to go but I grabbed him by the arm and forced him. But he wouldn't sit down. He stood at the end of the bunk nearest the aisle.

"I don't think I'd better sit down on your bunk," he said. "I'd better stand out here where they can see we're not doing anything."

"Not doing anything? What the hell have we ever done?" I raved. "You got to stand out in the aisle at eight-thirty when all the lights are on and everybody is moving all about all over the dormitory, so some lousy convicts can see you're not doing anything?"

"I think I'd better go," he said.

"No, I don't want you to go," I said.

A few minutes later Captain Charlie came down and asked Dido to come down to his desk. Captain Charlie wouldn't look at me. Dido hesitated and I said, "Go down and see what he wants. He's okay, it's these convicts."

He went down the aisle with Captain Charlie. Everyone stood about and watched them. I saw him standing down at the desk talking to Captain Charlie. Nothing seemed to be happening, so I undressed and put on my pajamas. It was almost bedtime, anyway. I sat on my bunk trying to quiet my nerves. I was angry and excited and frustrated. Just before the lights blinked Chump Charlie came down and said, "Dido needs you, Jimmy. Cap Charlie is writing him up."

I jumped up and slipped into my house shoes and bathrobe. Then I caught myself. I'm going home next month, in maybe less than thirty days, I thought. I'd be a fool. I stood there for some time, thinking about going home. I've been in prison a long time, I thought—a hell of a long time. I'd like to be free. My mother went to a lot of trouble to try to get me out, I thought. To hell with Dido.

Then I walked slowly down the aisle toward the guardstand. The convicts stopped whatever they were doing and turned to watch me. I felt as if I were walking a gauntlet.

When I got to the desk I asked, "Why are you reporting him, Cap, what has he done?"

Captain Charlie looked as if he might cry. "I've got to," he said. "I've got to do something."

"You've got to put a charge on the report card," I said. "What charge are you going to put on the report card?"

The lights blinked then but no one began preparing for bed. They were all out in the aisles watching us.

"I've got to charge him with sex perversion," Captain Charlie said.

"That's a goddamn lie," I said. "Did you ever see us doing anything like that?"

"No," he admitted, "but that's what everyone says it is."

"You're letting them run your job."

"I'm sorry, Jim," he said. "I have to do it, son."

"Okay," I said. "But if you write him up, write me up. He couldn't do it by himself."

Dido was looking at me queerly. I turned and walked away, thinking, I've always been a fool. I went back and stood by my bunk, smoking a cigarette. No one spoke to me. Captain Charlie came around and took count. The convicts stood beside their bunks but they still craned their necks to see what would happen. Dido was still standing down by the guard-stand. I stood there, watching him, feeling as if I was someone else.

When Captain Charlie had turned in his count he came down to me and said, "Put on your clothes, Monroe. I've got to take you to the hole."

I nodded. I put on my new shoes and my good Sunday trousers. I'll show these sons of bitches what I think of them, I thought. When I finished dressing I went down front. Captain Charlie was waiting. I looked at Dido. He smiled slightly. He looked unreal. His eyes looked dazed and slightly disbelieving, as if he had never seen me before. I tried to smile.

"Don't worry about it until it happens, kid," I said. "Then I'll take care of it." But it didn't go off right, my voice cracked.

We went downstairs, and through the gate, into the anteroom off the guards room where Captain Charlie turned us over to the gatekeeper to be held until the night captain came around to take us to the hole. The night captain was in the 10&11 cell block and we had to wait. We sat on the wide window ledge, side-by-side.

I turned and looked out of the window at the prison. The fountain in the goldfish pool, which had replaced the alligator pond, caught little slivers of light in the darkness. It looked ethereal and ghostly and unreal. Everything looked unreal.

"It looks like a little city, doesn't it?" I said. "It looks like a little, lost city."

"Jimmy," he said. His voice sounded choked. I turned to look at him. His eyes were pinned on me. They were rapt and awe-struck. "No one has ever taken up for me like this before," he said. His voice was queer and light and unreal, too. "Why did you do it, Jimmy? I didn't expect you to and I wouldn't have blamed you if you hadn't. You've got so much to lose, but they can't hurt me."

"I don't know why I did it," I said. "I guess because I wanted to."

"You don't know what you've done for me," he said in that queer weightless voice. "You've done the one thing necessary to make something out of me."

"Let's don't be dramatic," I said, trying to smile. "When I get to analyzing it I'll probably discover that I had a very lousy reason for doing it. Whenever I think I'm doing something noble I always remember—" I broke off and didn't finish it.

"It's like seeing something for the first time," he said, raptly.

The night captain came in to take us to the hole and the gatekeeper gave him our report cards. But Captain Charlie hadn't put any charge on my report card and the night captain had to go upstairs and have him write a charge down. Then he came down and took us to the hole. I was put in cell number one while Dido was put obliquely across the block in cell number twelve.

All that night he kept up a disjointed, one-sided conversation in that queer, light voice, trying to tell me what I had done for him. There were other convicts in the hole and they yelled for him to shut up. They cursed him but he didn't care. He was trying to tell me something which I couldn't altogether understand.

The next morning they took us out separately for trials. Dido went first. As soon as they brought him back and locked him up they took me out. I didn't get a chance to ask him any questions.

The deputy was holding court. I asked him what my charge was. He said sex perversion. "That's a joke," I said. "Send for the guard." I had forgotten that Captain Charlie was off duty by then.

"I don't need to send for the guard, I don't need to send

for the guard. It's on the card, and I believe you're guilty," he said.

I burnt up. "It doesn't make any difference what you believe," I said. "This is a court and only what is proved counts in here. The charge is a goddamned lie and anybody who says it is a goddamned liar. If the convicts who told you all those lies are going to run this institution then why don't you quit and let them run it?"

"Take him on back," he said to the hole guard. "Take him on back. Take him on back. I believe he's guilty."

"That's what you believe," I raved. "But before I take a rap for this I'm going to let everybody in the state know about it. I'm going to take it to the welfare director. I'm going to take it to the governor. Who in the hell—?"

"Take him out, take him out, take him out," he said.

The hole guard grabbed me by the arm and shoved me back toward the hole.

"That's all right. That's all right," I said. "You won't get away with it. A whole lot of people are going to hear about this."

The hole guard pushed me through the door, back into the anteroom where we changed into overalls before they put us in the hole. I struggled with him for a moment but the hole porter came out of the hole to help him and I quit. The big Greek convict named Kish had been the hole porter the last time I had been in the hole but he had gone to the brick yard and a colored convict called Jungle Joe had the job. Jungle Joe winked at me to take it easy so I let the guard march me on back to my cell.

I didn't call Dido until they had finished taking all the fellows out to court who were going out that morning and had locked up again. Then I asked him, "What was your charge?"

He hesitated for a moment, knowing that everyone in the hole was listening, then said, "S.P. Do you understand that?"

"That was mine, too," I said. "What did you tell him?"

"I told him if he believed that I didn't have anything to say." Then after a moment he asked, "What else could I have said?"

"I blew my top," I said. "I called everybody a liar and said before I took it lying down I'd take it to the governor's office. And I will, too." He didn't say anything to that. "I'll be damned if I let them get away with a frame-up like that," I kept on. "Even if I was guilty, Captain

Charlie never saw it. Which I wasn't," I added, after a moment.

"*We* sounds better," he said. "Do you mind, Jimmy?"

"I stand rebuked," I said.

"It wasn't a rebuke," he said. "It was a request."

Dido surprised me. He took his punishment like a thoroughbred. I came to understand more of what he had been trying to tell me. He was changed. I had never admired him so much. Only once during the whole time did he become the least bit hysterical and that could have easily happened to anyone. There was a convict next to him who was going crazy. He had horrible fights with ghosts in his cell. It was enough to get on anybody's nerves and Dido was susceptible to any form of insanity, anyway. Finally they took the poor fellow to the insane asylum. Otherwise it was very quiet.

Jungle Joe came around occasionally and swept and mopped the cells. The other convicts had warned us that he listened to the conversations and ratted to the deputy. But he was all right with me, he was my pal. They fed him from the guards' setup. I told him that if he looked out for us I'd give him five dollars for each day we were in there when I got out. He gave Dido and me his food for the whole time we were in there. We had ham and eggs and steaks and pie and excellent coffee. It wasn't bad at all. He gave us all the smoking we wanted and watched out for the guard while we smoked.

The number-one cell where they had put me was the emergency cell. Jungle Joe had a key for it but his key wouldn't unlock any of the other cells. At night, after the night captain had come through and taken count, he would let me out so I could go around and talk to Dido. Joe warned me that the other convicts in there would rat on us so I had to be careful. He could see in the dark, it seemed, for he would take me by the hand and lead me through the darkness around to Dido's cell. I would sit on the floor close to the bars and we would carry on a whispered conversation. Then after awhile Joe would lead me back to my cell and lock me in again.

Then, when everything was in order, Joe would bring a chair out from the anteroom where he slept, and visit with all of us. He would sit there and tell lies by the clock to keep us amused. That boy could really lie. I never heard him repeat himself.

The afternoon of the fifth day they let us out. The deputy was sitting at the desk in the courtroom when we passed through. "I hope you're satisfied, Monroe," he said. "I hope you're satisfied, I hope you're satisfied. You've lost your commutation." I didn't answer. I had expected it.

We sat in the waiting room for a few minutes. Then the runner came from the transfer office and took us up to separate cells on 5-4, the girl-boy company. I got a special letter the next day and wrote to my mother, asking her to come and see me as soon as possible.

My mother came over a couple of days later and I told her what had happened. I told her that the charge wasn't true. I asked her to go to the welfare director and explain it to him, and then write to the governor and ask him to have the charge investigated. She promised that she would, but she didn't have any hope of their doing anything. She was so sick about it she cried all during the visit.

I was sick myself. But one thing it had done for me. It had given me reality again. I could see the relationship between Dido and myself in its true perspective. And even though a lot of it had been foolish, and a lot of it hysterical, there had been some of it that had been truly fine. I didn't have a single regret, nor would I have changed one bit of it, because there had been those moments that were priceless. I felt grateful to Dido for those moments. But there weren't any more. I had had them all.

My mother hated Dido after that. She hated him forever and unrelentingly. She said some very nasty things about him, most of which had been told to her by people in the front office. She blamed him for everything. But I couldn't blame her for that, though. She didn't have any way of knowing that in the end—in the full, final decision—I had done it for myself. I had done it to be a man. And if I had lost freedom by doing it, I'd never had freedom, anyway, and it couldn't hurt me much. It wasn't as bad as I had thought it would be. It had never been entirely real to me, anyway. And all I had to do was not think about it and it couldn't hurt me. I had done a lot of time and I could do plenty more. But I couldn't be a man later. I couldn't wait. I had waited long enough as it was. I had to be it, then. For me, though. Just for me.

Now we had the name without the game. That was the toughest part of it. "We never had the game, but now we've got the name," I told the guard. "It's tough," he said. He didn't believe me.

I didn't mind it so much for myself. They couldn't hurt me, I told myself. They had already hurt me long ago, as much as they could ever hurt me. They never would be able to hurt me again as much as they had already hurt me, even if I lived a hundred-thousand years. Some day I was going out, I knew. It wouldn't be too long. But Dido had to stay there. And they would hurt him in every way they couldn't me. But he took it with his chin up. I knew how much they'd hurt him. But he never let the others see it and no one but me could tell.

It was a lousy company. Most of the men in it were either degenerates or stir-simple. They cursed and argued and fought all the time. Their conversation was polluted. You couldn't hear an un-profane sentence up there in a month of Sundays. It was the noisiest company in the entire institution. The guards didn't bother to keep them quiet. They just locked them up and went away. If you had never felt like an outcast before, you felt like one up there.

Dido was fine. He had quieted down and there was a new quality of serenity about him that was strange. He didn't let little things touch him any more. I was glad. I hoped he would stay like that. But only for his sake. I didn't need him any more. I had gone on by him. I think he understood, though. I sent him my typewriter and suggested that he try writing short stories or poetry to occupy his time. He sent me back a note:

> Dear Jimmy:
>
> Thanks for the loan of the typewriter. But you don't have to worry. I'm okay. I love you, Jim. You are swell people. I am very glad to have met you, Mr. —— what was the name? Are you O.K.? I'm at the peak. Thought I would be beaten—defeated is a better word—but I'm not. I want you to know, though, I tried to make it perfect in every way.
>
> Seriously though, you've given me more than you'll ever know. I'm doing quite swell. I mean on the inside. And I'll continue to be that way after you're gone. You'll be going some day soon. I feel it. But you needn't worry about me. I'll be swell.
>
> Understand now what you meant by a lot of things. About putting something into anything you hope to get something out of. Does that sound very confused? And about treating people as people and using good judgment. I've learned that, too. I'll be doing swell, you needn't ever worry.
>
> What are you doing? Just percolating? That's my mother's favorite word. Let's percolate!
>
> I may clean up and wash some clothes if I don't

feel lazy. Can't know until I feel myself whether I'm lazy or not. I love you again in the same letter. Wouldja wouldja? Remember?

What did you do with the apple seeds?

The apple seeds were candy. I wrapped them in a paper and passed them down the range to him.

His letter made me feel better about not needing him any more. Maybe he knew and maybe he didn't. I didn't know. But I couldn't tell him.

We would stick our mirrors in the bars and smile at each other through them. But most of our conversations were carried on by notes. Those convicts up there would take a conversation away from you and think nothing about it. We didn't want to get into any fights. It was the easiest thing in the world to get into a fight up there. The hard thing was keeping out of them. I didn't want to fight. I didn't have any love for convicts then and I was afraid I might kill someone if I got into a fight. But I used to carry a swinging six-inch dagger down the back of my shirt, just for protection. It made me feel better. Everyone up there had some kind of weapon or other. I didn't want to have to run into any of them barehanded. But if you had a chiv as big as any of theirs you didn't need to fight. All you had to do was flash it and you'd made another friend.

We played poker and blackjack on the range, with the aid of mirrors. The dealer would deal all the hands on the range in front of his cell. He would keep both hands stuck through the bars so that they were visible to the other players. Then he would deal off the cards, keeping the backs to himself and the faces toward the other players, so they could see through their mirrors what they had. Only the player who was receiving a card could keep his mirror in the bars. Then, when the cards had been dealt, all of the players would stick their mirrors in the bars and bet or turn down. It took more time than the regular way but it was played the same.

Twice a week we went down to the ball diamond the same as the other companies. We went to shows on Saturdays. Dido and I were together whenever we left the cells. We marched together and went everywhere together. Practically everyone in the company was coupled up with someone else. Only a few played it singly. It wasn't so much a punishment company as just segregation.

Later I learned that when Captain Tom had reported for work that morning and heard that we were in the hole he had had a heart attack and had to be taken home. When he was able to work again the first thing he did was go over to the deputy and try to get us out. But the deputy had refused to listen to him. He went to the warden too, they said, but the warden wouldn't interfere. I knew how Tom had felt, with that game coming up with the dining-room company. I had to laugh about it. Old Tom, he'd never change, I thought.

We had a softball team up on 5-4 but it was more or less a joke. There were a few very good players but the rest were very bad. Those fags wouldn't do anything but stand out there on the field with their hands on their hips and flirt with someone on the sidelines, while the balls rolled by them for extra base hits. They called them the "Bloomer Girls."

But after Dido and I were transferred up there the guard started making plans to reorganize the team. He wanted to make me the captain but I refused. I had enough enemies as it was, without making any more. We consented to play, however.

Our first game was with 3-4. We beat them easily. But the fellows in the company had bet against their team as usual. When we won they tried to welch and there was a big fight out on the diamond. The riot squad came out and took the entire company to court. They didn't put anyone in the hole but the deputy barred me from playing.

"I've already taken sixty days of your good-time, Monroe," he said. "You ought to have enough, you ought to have enough."

"I see," I said. "A man can't even play ball in this joint."

"That's enough," he said. "That's enough, that's enough, that's enough."

The deputy didn't like me and I didn't like him. That was the way it stood.

Our next game was with the cripple company and I played, anyway. Tom tried to have me put off the field. He told the guard who was umpiring the game that the deputy had forbidden me to play. The guard said he didn't have any orders about it and refused to take me out. Tom went and got the lieutenant in charge of the exercises and tried to have him stop the game. I told the lieutenant that the warden had given me permission to play. The lieutenant wouldn't have anything to do with it. The game started and I took my position at short. Tom left the field and went after the deputy. I had played five innings before the deputy arrived. The deputy took me out of the game and said he was taking another thirty days of my good-time. If Tom had waited he could have saved himself the trouble and me the thirty days. I was lousy. I didn't catch a ball. When they took me out the score was fifteen-to-nothing against us.

After the game Tom said, "No hard feelings, Jim. I just didn't figure my boys could beat you, that was all."

"That's all right, Tom," I said. "I know how you felt." Tom was all right. I understood him.

My mother came over again that month on a special visit. She told me that she had talked to the warden and that he had promised to investigate the charge against me. Two days later Gout called me over to the transfer office and said that the warden had had my charge investigated and felt that I was innocent. Gout said that my good-time had been restored to me and that the warden had directed him to transfer me into any company in the institution I wanted to go to, with the exception of the cripple company.

"What about Dido?" I asked.

"There weren't any directions concerning Dido," he said. "I haven't got anything to do with it. If you got any beef to make, make it to the warden. I didn't put you up there and I don't know anything about it. But I think you're a god-damned fool. Now where do you want to go?"

"I'll stay where I am," I said.

"That's best," he said. That suited him just fine because he didn't want to transfer me, anyway. "It's nice and quiet up there and you have a cell to yourself. You can do some studying."

"Sure," I said.

A week later, Okay Collins, the magazine man, told me that he had seen my name at the top of the transfer list for the farm. The guy in the next cell heard him and yelled it all over the block. "Say, man, old Monroe's going to the farm. Sure is a lucky stiff." Then they all had it. They talked about the fine fresh milk and the good fresh air I would get out there. From those cramped, stinking cells up on 5-4 the farm seemed like heaven.

It scared Dido. I could see it in his eyes. But he didn't break down. He tried in every way he could to show how happy he was for me. We didn't know when they would call me but we figured in a day or two, anyway. All that night and the next day we were preparing for it. We both were very excited. I gave him a lot of things I wanted him to have and he gave me a picture of his mother and some things he wanted me to have. He wanted me to take his scrapbook but I wouldn't take that. I knew his mother wanted him to keep it.

We worked out an elaborate plan whereby we would send letters back and forth to each other by the driver of the milk truck who came in once a day from the farm. We contacted the driver, through the paper boy, and he promised to deliver the letters for a dollar each. Dido said he would go over to the Bertillon department and have a picture made to send to me. I promised to send him some money each month. We tried to cover all contingencies.

All that day and night, clear up until bedtime, we were sending notes back and forth to each other. Finally the guys in the cells between us began to complain about having to pass so many notes. One of the surly bastards quit passing them altogether and let the last one I had sent lie on the range in front of his cell. After that we had to get the other fellows to throw them by his cell. I promised to give them a dollar each the next day.

That night after the lights blinked I packed my things in two pillowcases. But I couldn't sleep. After the guard had taken count I called down to Dido. "I can't sleep," I said.

"I can't either," he called back.

So we stuck our mirrors in the bars and smiled at each other and tried to talk by forming the words with our lips. We couldn't understand each other but we could see each other's faces and that was all that mattered. All that night we braced ourselves and when morning came we were ready.

But I wasn't called until ten days later. The paper boy told me that when Gout saw my name at the top of the transfer list he blew his top. He went to the deputy and got his support and they tried to get the warden to take my name off the list. But the parole board had okayed the transfer and the warden wouldn't change it. So Gout held up the entire shipment, on one pretext and another, until the warden ordered him to get the men out of there.

I was ordered to pack and be ready to leave right after breakfast the next morning. On the way to supper I stopped by Dido's cell. He was smiling, although his lips were trembling and his eyes looked as if he had been crying. I tried to smile, too, but my lips felt very stiff.

"I'll see you again tomorrow morning," I said, "but I just want to tell you now that I've loved you from the first."

"I've loved you, too," he said, "from the very first."

He leaned forward and I kissed him. It was the first and

only time I had ever kissed him. There was no passion in the kiss but it had a great tenderness. A couple of guys passing on the range at the moment made kissing sounds but we didn't care.

"Take it easy, kid," I said. "Just don't let anything get too important."

"To the stars, Jimmy," he said. His voice was choked.

We didn't send any notes that night. We had said everything there was to say.

After the lights went off, I lay awake, thinking about him. I hope he'll make it, I thought. It'll certainly be tough on him. He really loves me, I thought. He gave me a lot, too, I thought. But now I'm going on, I thought. I hoped I had given him something in passing. Finally I went to sleep.

Along in the early hours of the morning I was awakened by a commotion down the range. I was abruptly alert, chilled by a sudden fear.

"Dido!" I yelled. "Dido!"

"He's hurt, Jimmy," someone called.

I stuck my mirror in the bars so I could see. Two guards were dragging Dido from his cell. His head dangled queerly to one side. There was something wrong with his neck.

"Dido! Dido!" I screamed. I grabbed my coffee bucket and raked it on the bars. "Let me out of here!" I screamed. "Goddammit, let me out of here." I could hear the entire block coming awake. I grabbed my mirror and stuck it back into the bars. They were carrying Dido around the corner of the range. No one paid any attention to me. I watched until they had taken him from sight.

"Captain Baker!" I yelled. Captain Baker was our night guard. "Captain Baker! Let me out of here!"

Everybody in the whole block was talking at once. I heard someone ask, "What's the matter up there?"

"A guy hung himself."

The block suddenly silenced.

"Who?"

"A guy named Dido."

I began crying, all down inside. I could feel a strange hurt going down through my lungs and stomach and tearing me all loose inside. "Somebody please let me out," I begged.

"Is he dead?" I heard someone ask.

"They don't know. They're taking him to the hospital."

I couldn't stand up any longer. I sagged down on the floor by the bars and clung to the bars for support. It seemed like a long time afterward I heard somebody say, "Yeah, he was dead when they cut him down." It seemed as if I had known all along that he was dead.

"What was the matter with him?"

"His buddy's going out. He couldn't take it."

"Who's his buddy?"

"Monroe."

"Jimmy Monroe?"

"Yeah."

"Hey, Jimmy!" I didn't answer. I couldn't have answered. "Hey, Jimmy! You ain't hanging yourself too, are you?"

"Not him," I heard someone say. "He likes himself too much to do anything like that."

You son of a bitch, I thought. You dirty son of a bitch. I wanted to scream curses at him but I couldn't make my voice work.

After awhile the block quieted down. Just another convict had hanged himself. I was grateful for the silence. I knelt where I had dropped. I hadn't moved. When the guard took count again he stopped and started to say something to me, then he changed his mind. He came back every now and then to see how I was getting along but he didn't say anything. After a long time I had an impulse to pray for Dido. But I couldn't bring myself to put the prayer into words. If God couldn't forgive him on His own account nothing I could say would help. What hurt most was that I hadn't done anything to stop him. Deep down inside of me I must have wanted him to do it.

I knew, beyond all doubt, that he had done it for me. He had done it to give me a perfect ending. It was so much like him to do this one irrevocable thing to let me know for always that I was the only one. Along with the terrible hurt I could not help but feel a great gladness and exaltation. I knew that he would have wanted me to.

When the lights came on I got up and dressed. A lot of the fellows stopped by my cell on their way to breakfast and tried to cheer me up. I was able to answer them without crying and I found that I could move around all right. I was filled with strange, numbing emotions but otherwise I was the same as always. I didn't go to breakfast. For a moment I considered going down to his cell and sitting there while the others were out to breakfast, but I couldn't bring myself to do it. I had already told him goodby.

They came for me right after breakfast. I picked up my

two sacks of belongings and followed the runner down the range.

"Good-by, Jimmy. . . . So long, Jimmy. . . . Take it easy, Jimmy. . . ." the various fellows called as I passed their cells.

"So long, fellows," I said.

"Good luck, Jimmy."

"The same to you " I said.

When I passed Dido's cell I looked straight ahead. They took me down to the guards room. There were three other fellows already waiting. They kept us there until they had assembled all fifteen of the fellows who were to go. As I sat there I thought about Dido's mother. I would have to write to her the first thing and explain what had happened, I thought. She would get the official notice but there would be so much she wouldn't understand. It would really be a blow to her, I thought. Then I thought of how Dido would never pass through those gates again in life. I could feel myself beginning to cry again inside.

But when they took us through the outer gates and down the front sidewalk to the waiting truck, I quit thinking about Dido. It was a bright, clear morning. It felt strange to be outside. I could look down the street without having my view blocked by walls. It began feeling good to be outside the walls. It would feel better still when I got out to the farm, I thought. Just before climbing into the truck I turned and looked back at the prison. You big tough son of a bitch, you tried to kill me but I've got you beat now, I thought. Because the farm was the way to freedom.